The Lies She Told

Lynda Renham

About the Author

Lynda Renham's novels are popular, fast paced and with a strong theme. She lives in Oxford UK and when not writing Lynda can usually be found wasting her time on Facebook.

Lynda is author of the best-selling thriller novel *Remember Me.*

Lynda Renham

The right of Lynda Renham to be identified as the author of the work has been asserted by her in accordance with the Copyright, Designs and Patents Act 1988.

Apart from any use permitted under UK copyright law, this publication may only be reproduced, stored, or transmitted, in any form, or by any means, with prior permission in writing of the publishers or, in the case of reprographic production, in accordance with the terms of licences issued by the Copyright Licensing Agency.
All characters in this publication are fictitious and any resemblance to real persons, living or dead, is purely coincidental.

Copyright © Raucous Publishing 2021
www.raucouspublishing.co.uk

Chapter One
July 2019: Stonesend, Oxfordshire

The day started like any other. No one could have predicted the tragedy that would later end it. It was just another summer's day. There was no hint of danger in the air or the smell of evil. Life was as it always was. At precisely 8.45, Nat Gordon, the butcher, lifted his shop shutter revealing bloody lumps of meat and naked chickens hanging from hooks. Inside it smelt of blood and sawdust, but its cool, tiled interior offered a refuge from the heat, which later would become unbearable, the sun beating down on the residents of Stonesend with unrestrained brutality. Even now, at nine in the morning, the mugginess was oppressive. Next to the butchers, the village newsagent opened its doors, fans were switched on, and windows thrown open. Children, their tiny hands clasped by weary mothers, trotted towards the village primary school, lingering for a few moments outside the shop, where the smell of liquorice and chocolate was difficult to resist. The school overlooked the playing fields, and here the mums would sit, chat, and smoke for fifteen minutes after dropping off their offspring.

Beth Harper edged her car out onto the busy high street. The humidity pressed down on her with a vengeance, and she wished her car had air conditioning. She could feel her loose shirt clinging to her back. The heat wasn't helping her hangover in the least. She shouldn't have drunk so much at Geoff's retirement do last night, but it had felt good to let her hair down finally. It was the first night in months that she hadn't thought about Ben. Was he thinking of her now, today, on their wedding anniversary?

'Expect another sizzler,' warned the Radio 1 DJ. 'No end to the heatwave yet. How are you all coping out there? Let us know what you're doing to keep cool. Phone us on ....'

Beth switched off the radio. She wasn't coping, and the heat was adding to her feelings of depression. She stopped the car outside the newsagents, stepped past a group of youngsters who had ignored the sign, *'Two children at a time in the shop,'* and headed to the counter.

'Don't they teach you to read at school?' she asked, pointing to the sign.

'Yes, but they don't teach us maths,' said one of the kids cheekily.

She recognised him. It was Danny Carpenter.

'Enough of your cheek, Danny.' She smiled. 'I know your dad, remember.'

'They're no trouble,' said Ron, the owner.

'Don't encourage them.'

She placed a packet of Paracetamol and a bottle of water onto the counter.

'Feeling fragile, are we?' asked Ron.

'Geoff's leaving do last night,' she explained.

'Yes, we heard all you law-abiding citizens living it up. Almost called the cops, we did.' He winked good-humouredly.

'It's going to be another hot one,' she said, wiping the sweat from her forehead.

'Need some rain for my sweetpeas,' grumbled Ron.

She drove slowly past the school and the cars parked on double yellow lines and manoeuvred her car into the police station car park. She swung the Polo round expertly and then pushed her foot hard on the brake.

'Who the ...'

Some arsehole had parked in her space.

'Shit. I don't believe this,' she groaned.

Like she wasn't late enough. She parked behind the blue Clio and hurried into the station. The air inside was cooler, but not that much. Give her winter any day.

'Okay, which one of you wankers parked in my space?' she demanded.

There was a deafening silence as her work colleagues turned to look at her.

'What? Why are you all looking at me like that?'

'Good morning, Detective Sergeant Harper,' said a voice behind her.

She turned to her chief. Sweat trickled down her back. Why weren't the offices better air-conditioned?

'Sorry I'm late, Sir. Gridlock outside the school,' she lied.

Beth then noticed the dark-haired man standing beside the Super. He looked familiar, but she couldn't quite place him. He was looking at her intently.

'I think the wanker might be me,' he said.

Beth noted it wasn't said with any kind of humour. Much to her annoyance, she felt herself blush.

'Well, that's my parking space,' she said defensively, attempting to cover her embarrassment.

'You missed the introductions, DS Harper,' interrupted Chief Superintendent Lewis. 'This is DI Tom Miller. You'll be working together. He's Geoff's replacement.'

Beth could feel everyone's eyes on her. DI Miller held out his hand.

'I'm looking forward to working with you,' he said softly. 'I should warn you, I'm a stickler for punctuality.'

His dark brown sultry eyes met hers. Beth kept hers steady. Tom Miller, where had she heard that name before? Beth knew the face, knew the name. Then, she realised. Now she knew why he looked familiar. He was even more handsome than he had looked in the newspaper photos.

'You're joking, right?' she exclaimed.

There were murmurs around the room. Christ, did they have to do this in front of everyone?

The Chief Super's lips tightened, then he said, 'A word, detective sergeant.'

He indicated his office, and Beth followed him in. 'What's he doing here?' Beth demanded as soon as the door closed.

'Detective Sergeant Harper, I would request you keep your voice down.'

'You can't be serious. Doesn't he have a drink problem?'

'Don't you have a hangover?'

'I don't have one every day.'

'He's been transferred. He's a good copper.'

'Good coppers don't mess up.'

'Don't they?'

'Not as far as I'm concerned.'

'He was under a lot of pressure.'

'He left a crucial murder witness alone in a hotel room so he could get a drink. Anything could have happened to her.'

'We all know the story, Beth. He's been transferred to a quieter division.'

Beth shook her head in surprise.

'A quieter division? Are we babysitters now? I could do the job better.'

'You had a chance to apply for the position. You chose not to.'

'My marriage had just fallen apart. I thought I wouldn't be up to it. But if I'd known alcoholics were eligible, I might have thought twice ….'

Chief Superintendent Lewis banged his hand down on the table. Beth jumped.

'Enough,' he said. 'He doesn't drink now. Get over it, Beth. You've got to work with him.'

'Against my better judgement,' she said.

'We don't make judgements. We try to be considerate.'

'Why didn't you tell me?'

'Because I knew you'd react like this.'

'He's fragile, Brian. How the hell can he be in charge?'

'You're dismissed, DS Harper.'

'But …'

'There is nothing else to discuss.'

Beth sighed and left the office. Miller was nowhere to be seen.

'In Geoff's office,' said Matt, nodding his head towards the door. 'Didn't anyone tell you? I thought you would have been the first to know.'

Beth shook her head.

'I didn't apply for the position because I didn't think a broken person would be good for the job,' she said miserably. 'I don't believe this.'

'I know,' said Matt, tapping her gently on the arm.

Beth pulled off her shoulder bag and hung it over her chair before knocking on the DI's door.

'Come in,' he called.

She stepped into the room and closed the door behind her. It was strange seeing someone else behind Geoff's desk. All the familiar things she'd come to know over the years had gone. The timeless portrait of him and Tina, smiling with their two boys, had always been a comfort, a reminder that even her boss was human. There were no photos on the desk now.

'I want you to know that I would have voiced my objections had I known you were coming,' she said bluntly.

His steady gaze met hers.

'Thanks for telling me.'

'You should know I'm not happy,' she said.

'I'd never have guessed.'

He didn't get up from behind the desk.

'I'm never late,' she said defensively.

'I'm pleased to hear that. Is that all?'

'You're in my parking space,' she said and left the office.

'Being angry doesn't suit you,' said Matt, as she sat at her desk opposite him. She forced a smile; she wasn't in the mood for Matt's chatter. His energy wore her out. It seemed endless some days. He was young, and she felt ancient. He played for the village rugby team and challenged everyone to a game of squash except her. Everyone knew she only ran when chased and avoided exercise in the same way she avoided church. For all that, she managed to stay, as she would put it, 'in good nick.' She didn't look thirty-five. At least, she hoped she didn't. She certainly felt more like seventy-five these days.

'He's in my bloody parking space,' she said and then laughed when she realised how ridiculous it sounded.

'He's going to find Stonesend a lot quieter than London. He'll probably go out of his mind with boredom and move on before you know it,' said Matt.

'A quiet division was what they wanted for him, apparently.'

'Can't get quieter than here. Perhaps we should ask him to come out for a drink tonight? Make him feel welcome. Cut him a bit of slack, you know.'

'I'm having dinner with my sister. It's her birthday. Besides, don't you think inviting an ex-alcoholic for a drink is rubbing salt in the wound?'

'It could be worse, you know', smiled Matt.

'Could it?'

'It could have been a woman,' he grinned.

'Oh, sod off,' she said.

Chapter Two

2000, Leeds (19 years earlier)
Mae

In the beginning, we were happy. I don't know when things started to change. It was very gradual. We hardly noticed it happening. I suppose the signs were there, but we chose to ignore them. Things got worse after Blanche. Rob had become so self-obsessed by that time. Or perhaps he'd always been self-obsessed, and I hadn't seen it. You overlook a lot of things when you're in love. All he ever thought about was work, business trips, and the next rung up the ladder. I'd never been ambitious, so I suppose I didn't understand it. I trained as a nurse, passed my exams and settled down to my career. I had no ambition to work my way up the pay scale. Rob could never understand that.

I'd met Rob at 'Freddie's' jazz club. I'd gone with my friend Jane. We'd both been wearing far too much makeup. We'd been around the shops earlier and had our faces done at the makeup counter in Debenhams. I never usually wore much makeup, so I was conscious that we were plastered in the stuff. My eyes had been sore and itchy, and I'm sure Rob and his mate thought I had been fluttering my eyelashes at them as I had been blinking so much. Rob told me later that he thought I was the most gorgeous girl he had ever met.

I'd never been very good at keeping boyfriends on account of mum. She never liked any of them, but she disliked Rob the most. I think she could see that it was something more serious with him. I suppose I decided to marry Rob so I could get away from her. She had clung to me to the point where I felt suffocated, and her incessant drinking was embarrassing. I never knew when I brought my friends back if she would be drunk or sober. Dad had left years before, shortly after my seventh birthday. I never saw him after that and don't remember much about him. I do remember the shouting stopped once he'd gone and how a miraculous number of toys I'd always wanted suddenly appeared.

'Whatever Mae wants, Mae can have,' Mum would say, kissing me on the cheek and suffocating me within her soft fluffy jumper.

It had been lovely at the beginning. Whenever I asked for something, my mother would get it, and this time my father wouldn't be there to take it away. It wouldn't be spoilt by the shouting. It was a cosy, warm time, just Mum and me. As I grew older, I realised that she expected my total devotion in exchange. I started to feel suffocated and controlled. If I went out in the evening with my friends, she would complain. I would usually get home to find her drunk and demanding.

'Why do you leave me alone like this? I sacrificed everything for you.'

Rob suggested she could come and live with us. The idea had appalled me. I wanted to get away from her. I didn't want her putting her two penn'orths in when it came to our flat. I had my ideas on design, and I knew she wouldn't like them.

Rob and I got married on a hot day in July. Mum never came. She said the heat had brought on one of her migraines, and for the duration of our wedding day, she stayed in bed. Rob and I left the reception early and spent the evening with her. I hated her for it and still do.

Shortly after our marriage, Rob got promoted, and I changed hospitals, so my shifts were more manageable. I visited mum twice a week. She wasn't happy about that and expected much more, but I just didn't have the time, not with running a home and holding down a job. Her regular migraines became a drain on me. She'd phone me at work and ask me to get her food shop on the way home. Or, ask if I could pop round and rustle something up, as she wasn't well enough to cook.

'If you could just make me a bit of cereal,' she'd say. 'Only this is a bad one. Nothing seems to shift it.'

I did suggest that, perhaps, if she drank less, then maybe the headaches would ease.

We had her stay some weekends, but Rob and I always seemed to argue on those weekends. Mum would point out Rob's faults, which I hadn't noticed before, but which were glaringly apparent once she had. I could tell from her expression that she enjoyed our arguments, so I stopped inviting her. Rob's promotion meant he spent more time working in the evenings and our trips to the jazz club stopped.

'I've got a bit of work to do,' he'd say.

'If you ask me, he's only interested in work,' mum would grumble.

It was around this time that I started getting migraines too. Rob had been marvellous in the beginning. He'd bring me tea in bed and sit watching TV by my side. I couldn't have asked for a more caring and attentive husband. I thought in time, the headaches would get better, but they didn't. Mum frightened me by saying a brain tumour could cause them. I mentioned this to Rob, who had smiled indulgently.

'Don't end up like your mother,' he'd said. He'd smiled, but I'd heard the irritation in his voice.

But what if it was a brain tumour? I didn't want to take any chances. I tried every migraine tablet on the market, but nothing seemed to help. Rob was patient and caring, bringing me tea and hot water bottles. Sometimes he would come home early so he could prepare dinner. He wasn't travelling then. That was after Blanche. Everything changed after Blanche.

After one horrible attack, Rob agreed that a visit to the doctor might be a good idea.

'If only to put your mind at rest,' he'd said.

I think he just wanted them gone because they were an irritation to him. I'd felt patronised, just like he patronised my mother. I had crippling headaches. Most likely inherited, but Rob made me feel like it was my fault. As though I brought them on.

After several tests, the doctor told me a hormonal imbalance caused them and that having a baby would make all the difference. Rob wasn't keen on starting a family.

'We've only been married a year. It would be nice to get a house and travel a bit before we get tied down with a baby,' he'd said. 'You just need to calm down. You're too anxious.'

I didn't think I was anxious. And I was content with our flat. At least, I was then. I thought it would be enough. I wasn't in the least bothered about holidays. I had everything I'd ever wanted.

'Don't you want to see something of the world?' Rob had asked.

'Not especially,' I'd answered.

Rob had gone on about the mortgage, how I'd have to stop working. That his salary was good, but not that good, and he wasn't ready for a baby.

'Not quite yet.'

'Perhaps the headaches will go,' I'd said optimistically.

'If you relax, they probably will.'

But they didn't stop, and I started throwing up each time I got one. So much so that I must have thrown up the pill because I was pregnant a month later.

Chapter Three

July 2019, Stonesend

It had been the hottest day that year. The hottest July for twenty years, the weatherman had said. It had been humid and stuffy in the station. No amount of air-conditioning had helped. Beth had spent most of the day training constables. By five, her throat was dry and sore. Her head still ached, and she was exhausted from the constant heat. It was a relief to get outside, even though it was airless. She had just enough time to shower and change before meeting Sandy and Ray at The Bell. Being the only pub in the village, the place would undoubtedly be packed on a warm night like this. Everyone making the most of the lovely evening. She found herself wondering what Tom Miller would be doing. He had declined the pub invite.

'He's got something else on,' Matt had said.

Suzy, the administrator, told her he was renting the cottage next to the cemetery.

'Cheerful view,' Beth had commented.

'Makes you appreciate being alive, though,' Suzy had laughed. 'He's probably still unpacking.'

After her shower, Beth wrapped the silver charm bracelet she had bought Sandy and placed it into a gift bag along with a card. She then walked to The Bell. It was humid, and several times she had to wipe the sweat from her forehead. Sandy met her at the door.

'No tables outside, I'm afraid. Busy tonight. You alright sitting inside?'

'Sure. Here, happy birthday.'

She pushed the gift bag into Sandy's hand.

'Thanks,' said Sandy, kissing her on the cheek.

She was glowing. Her blonde streaked hair hung loosely around her shoulders. Not a bead of sweat in sight thought Beth enviously.

She hadn't been graced with Sandy's beauty or her elegance. She'd always been the tomboy sister, preferring the outdoors. Beth hated her thick curly brown hair and always wore it clipped up. Sandy was always telling her that highlights would suit her, but Beth couldn't stand the thought of sitting for hours in a hair salon. She glimpsed her reflection in the mirror behind the bar and saw that loose strands of hair had escaped the clip and were now stuck to her neck. She was surprised at how pale she was. I look like a bloody corpse, she thought.

'You okay?' asked Sandy, looking at her sister intently.

'Sure.'

'You look tired.'

'Don't fuss, Sandy.'

Sandy hugged her.

'It's just, well, I know it's a special day. How could I forget?'

She wished Sandy wouldn't be so motherly. Alice felt her chin quiver. For all her bravado, the truth was, she was on the brink of spilling everything. A warm hug, a kind word and she feared it would all surge from her lips like a tsunami. It would be such a relief. But it wasn't that simple, was it? Humiliation couldn't be lanced like a cyst.

'I'm fine, Sandy, honestly.'

She spotted the group from the station and waved.

'Alright, Beth?' Matt shouted.

'My Danny said you gave him a real ticking off,' Laughed Luke Carpenter.

'Lying little sod,' she grinned.

Matt smiled. He loved it when they were off duty, and he could call her Beth rather than Ma'am. She followed Sandy to the table where Ray was waiting, dressed smartly as always. As soon as they'd ordered, Ray said,

'Are the rumours true then?'

Beth's heart skipped a beat.

'What rumours?' she asked, sipping her wine.

'That Tom Miller is your new boss.'

Her body relaxed again, and she rolled her eyes.

'News travels fast around here.'

'You know what it's like,' smiled Sandy.

'A bit of a celeb, isn't he?' said Ray.

'Not one I admire,' said Beth sullenly.

'Jack just told us,' said Ray, nodding towards the landlord. 'He's renting Monk's cottage, next to the church, so Jack said.'

'Let's hope the graveyard spooks him out, and he leaves,' said Beth.

'Beth,' exclaimed Sandy. 'Where's your compassion?'

Lynda Renham

'I'm a professional, anyway, he parked in my space,' said Beth and wondered why that was such an issue for her.

'What's he like?' asked Sandy.

Beth shrugged.

'Okay. I haven't had much to do with him.'

Beth took a sip of wine and said, 'So how has your birthday been so far?'

She didn't want to talk about Tom Miller.

*

Alice Tobias whipped the dinner plates from the table and began filling the dishwasher.

'Are we having ice cream?' asked Faith.

Adam looked up from his comic.

'Can I have chocolate mint?'

'We ate all our dinner.' Chimed in Faith.

Alice glanced at the clock on the white kitchen wall, her eyes sliding past the messy kitchen counters. Shit, why was she always running late?

'If you're quick, you can have ice cream.'

As she opened the freezer door, her eyes alighted on the prawns. Damn, she'd meant to take them out. They'd never thaw in time now.

'Mum.'

'I'm getting it.'

How did other mothers cope? She only had two kids, for goodness' sake. Why could she never get herself organised? She grabbed the ice cream, slamming the carton onto the table and the packet of prawns into the sink.

'Only one scoop,' she said, turning back to the dishwasher.

They ought to clean their teeth after the ice cream. Alice's eyes went to the clock again. No, there wouldn't be time. She wondered if it would be okay to defrost prawns in the microwave. Perhaps she'd do them a jacket potato instead. Joe liked jacket potatoes. No, it was too hot to have the oven on for that amount of time. Maybe pizza. The kids' pizza hadn't been in the oven that long. If only it weren't so damn hot.

'Right,' she said, locking the back door. The kitchen felt stifling in an instant. She could leave it open. It's not like anyone was going to rob them in Stonesend.

'It does matter,' Joe was always telling her. 'Insurances won't pay out to unlocked houses.'

Adam frowned as the ice cream was put back in the freezer.

'I don't know why I have to go,' he complained.

'Because you can't stay in the house by yourself.'

'Daddy will be home soon,' he argued.

'Daddy is going to be late, and so are we if we don't get our skates on.'

'We'll be even later if we stop to put our skates on,' laughed Faith. The clock now said six. They should have left five minutes ago.

'I hate piano lessons anyway,' said Faith.

'No, you don't,' said Alice, slamming the front door closed and ushering them down the road towards Kate's cottage. 'You're always saying you love your lessons.'

Her hands were sticky in theirs. It was too hot to hold hands, too hot to hurry and too hot to argue. They reached Kate's quaint cottage with its white gate and rose lined pathway. Alice thrust the piano primer into Faith's hands and tugged the old-fashioned bell-pull that hung elegantly at the front door. She ought to try and make their cottage pretty. Clear away their wellingtons from the porch. If only she had the time.

'She's not here. Can we go now?' asked Adam, fidgeting.

'Don't be silly. Of course, she is. She's expecting us.'

She tugged at the bell-pull again and heard the clang reverberate through the cottage. Adam pulled away and poked his head through the letterbox.

'Hello, Mrs Marshall, it's us.'

Alice pulled him back.

'Adam, stop that. It's rude. She's probably in the garden. We'll go around the back.'

Faith rushed ahead and opened the back gate. Kate wasn't in the garden, and the back door was closed. Alice glanced down the side path that led off Kate's garden and to the back of the allotment. Perhaps she'd gone to pick some stuff for dinner, thought Alice. All the same, it seemed an odd time to do it.

'She can't have forgotten,' mumbled Alice, rapping on the door. She struggled to remember if Kate had changed the day.

'Damn it.'

'Mummy, don't swear,' reprimanded Faith.

'Sorry.'

Perhaps she'd gone to football with Dan and the boys.

But she wouldn't have forgotten Faith's lesson, surely

'Do you think she's fallen?' said Adam.

'What?'

'Miss Hartwell, at school, said that when someone doesn't open the door when you expect them to, or they live alone, you should check they haven't fallen over.'

'Right,' said Alice, who doubted Kate had fallen. She was only in her forties, after all.

'Look through the window,' suggested Faith.

'It's rude to do that.'

'But if she's on the floor,' argued Adam.

Alice sighed. She supposed it would do no harm to look, just in case. Cupping her hands in front of her face, Alice peered in through the window. At first, the only thing she could see was her reflection. Then, she spotted something on the floor by the table. She couldn't quite make out what it was, so she tilted her head to try and make sense of it.

'Can you see anything?' asked Adam impatiently.

'Not really. I ...'

Then, Alice realised what she was looking at. It was a foot. It seemed to lay at an odd angle, but once Alice realised what it was, the rest fell into place. If she moved slightly to the left, she could see an arm. She was about to tell Adam how sensible he was and that, in fact, Mrs Marshall had fallen when the sight of the blood-splattered wall stopped her. Thin stripes of red as bright as poppies glared from the white walls. Alice felt her stomach churn. She fought down the urge to scream and reeled back from the window.

'Mrs Marshall has had an accident,' she said shakily.

'Let me see,' said Faith excitedly, hurrying to the window.

'No,' Alice screamed.

The children reeled back in horror at the urgency in her voice. Alice felt tears on her cheeks. What the hell had happened in there? Her hands were trembling. She needed to get the children away. But what about Kate? She'd call an ambulance from inside. That way, the children wouldn't hear. She turned the back door handle, expecting it to be locked, but it opened easily.

'Stay here,' she ordered. 'Don't move. Do you understand?'

'Yes, Mummy,' said Faith obediently, taking Adam's hand.

Alice stepped nervously into the kitchen, closing the door firmly behind her. There was a strange smell, like dirty nappies. It had been some time since Alice had changed one, but the smell was instantly recognisable. With shaking hands, she tapped 999 into her phone. Her foot slid beneath her, and Alice grabbed the table to stop herself from falling. She looked down to see she had slipped on some milk. The spilt carton lay beside the white liquid.

'Emergency, what service do you require?'

Her throat was dry and she had to swallow several times before she could speak.

'It's my neighbour. There's been some kind of accident,' Alice said, conscious that she needed to speak clearly.

'What kind of accident?'

Alice stepped gingerly around the table. She didn't want to look, but she had to. Her breath caught in her throat.

'Oh, Jesus.' She swallowed the bile that rose up into her throat and clutched the phone tightly. Kate's face was almost unrecognisable. Her head lay in a pool of blood, her honey-blonde hair soaked in it. Her eyes were swollen, and bloody spit drooled from her lips.

'Oh my God, Kate? Please send help. Please hurry.'

'What's the address?'

'Erm ...Oh Jesus.'

Her mind went blank.

'It's okay. Take a deep breath.'

'It's 28, Churchfields in Stonesend.'

'That's great. Can you see if she's still breathing?'

Alice's legs wouldn't move. It was as if her feet were rooted to the spot. There was a faint moan from Kate and the sound seemed to galvanise Alice into action.

'Yes, she is. But there's blood everywhere. It looks like she's been hit around the head. Oh Jesus, please help us.' She knelt beside Kate and took her bloody hand in hers. It was cold. 'Please send someone quickly.'

'An ambulance is on its way. Don't move her.'

'She's really cold. Is it all right to cover her?'

'Yes. It would be good to keep her warm.'

Alice leapt up only to slip on Kate's blood. She let out a strangled sob and rushed upstairs, tearing the duvet from the immaculately made bed. Her blood-stained dress clung to her knees. It was warm and sticky.

'I'll be back,' she whispered, laying the duvet gently over Kate. Tears slid down her cheeks and landed on Kate's blood-soaked blouse. 'Hold on, Kate, hold on.'

She backed away slowly. She was panting heavily. It was as if someone had stolen the oxygen around her. The children, she needed to get back to the children. She tore her eyes away from Kate's battered body and pulled the back door open. She fell vomiting into the backyard.

'Mummy,' cried Adam. 'What's wrong?'

'You're bleeding, Mummy, you're bleeding,' cried Faith hysterically. Alice looked down at the blood on her dress.

'It's okay, mummy's alright. Mrs Marshall has had a bad accident. We have to go next door. You have to stay there for a while until the ambulance arrives.'

'But I don't want to,' bawled Adam.

Alice hugged them and led them to Kate's neighbour. Jean Robinson was weeding her garden and smiled as Alice approached. The smile slid from her face at Alice's expression.

'Whatever is the matter?' she asked.

Her eyes landed on Alice's dress.

'Oh my God.'

'It's Kate. I've had to call for an ambulance. Can the kids stay with you for a bit?'

'Kate? What's happened?'

Alice shook her head, and Jean's face turned white.

'Come on, I've got ice cream,' she said shakily, leading the children into the house. Alice hurried back to Kate's cottage and knelt beside her, where she stayed until the ambulance arrived minutes later.

Chapter Four

Beth was studying the dessert menu when her mobile rang.

'It's DI Miller. A woman has been badly attacked in the village. Where are you?'

For a second, Beth didn't understand what he was saying.

'What?' she questioned. 'I'm in the middle of dinner.'

'Meet me at 28 Churchfields.'

'But ...'

The line went dead.

28 Churchfields. That was Kate's place. What was he talking about, a woman had been attacked? People don't get attacked in Stonesend. They don't even get burgled.

'Got to go,' she said, getting up.

'What, now?' asked Sandy, surprised. 'But we haven't had dessert.'

'Everything alright?' asked Ray.

'I don't know,' said Beth

*

Churchfields was on the outskirts of the village. Wide-open country fields greeted Beth as she drew closer. The air was still and silent and it unnerved her. She rounded the bend to see a line of crows perched on a fence. It was as if everything was waiting, but waiting for what? She shuddered. It seemed like a dark omen and that soon chaos and despair would shatter the peaceful silence.

She hoped Miller didn't smell the wine on her breath. She'd only had one, and she was officially off duty, after all. Beth marvelled, as she often did, at the quaintness of the village. She'd lived there most of her life. She had thought, stupidly it now seemed, that she and Ben would live here for the rest of their lives too.

The fields were parched. The rain desperately needed. She passed well cared for gardens and quaint cottages. As she neared Churchfields, the peaceful tranquillity was shattered by police sirens, paramedics and yellow tape. Beth stopped the car. Her heart was hammering in her chest. She'd expected to see one squad car, but not all this. She jumped out of her car and hurried to the house. A uniformed officer recognising her stepped to one side.

'Ma'am.'

Alice nodded at him and walked nervously into the hall. She heard voices coming from the kitchen. Paramedics were making their way out with a stretcher.

'What happened?' she asked.

She looked down at the woman lying on the stretcher and gasped. She recognised her. It was Kate.

'Oh my God, Kate,' she cried, reaching out to her.

Kate's face was just about recognisable. The black and blue shattered skin stood out grotesquely against the white pillows.

'Harper,' called a voice from the kitchen.

The paramedic looked at her sympathetically and said, 'We need to get her to the hospital.'

She turned to see Tom Miller standing in the doorway.

'I know Kate,' she said, sweat and tears running down her face. 'We're friends. I sometimes babysit the boys so she and Dan can go out. Oh God, poor Dan ....'

'Pull yourself together,' he said sharply.

'What,' she gasped.

'You're on duty, D.S Harper.'

She opened her mouth, a sharp retort on her tongue and then quickly stopped herself. She glanced at the police constable on the door. She knew him. Bradley that was his name. He avoided her eyes.

She wiped at the tears with the back of her hand.

'Sir,' she said simply and moved to let the paramedics pass.

Tom Miller nodded towards the kitchen.

'She was attacked in here.'

Beth struggled to stop trembling. Kate Marshall's kitchen was a mess. Her blood was splattered all over the room. Beth felt nausea rise up in her stomach. Please, don't let me throw up. Don't let me give him that pleasure. These things didn't happen in Stonesend. London maybe, but not here.

'Sorry to call you from your dinner,' said Miller. He'd obviously hurried too. His short-sleeved shirt was hanging out of his worn jeans. It seemed surreal to be standing in the middle of a crime scene wearing her Zara black dress, heels and makeup.

'Not a problem.' She was annoyed that her voice shook.

'Victim is Kate Marshall. Several blows to the head and body. No sign of the weapon, but we're still searching. She was hit with something heavy, that's for sure.'

'I know who she is,' she said sharply.

'So, tell me about her.'

'Kate, she's a nice person. No enemies. She didn't deserve this. There's not much else to say.'

Beth looked around the kitchen. Kate's lovely shabby chic kitchen. Who the hell would want to hurt Kate? She was one of the gentlest people Beth knew.

'I don't understand,' she said. 'No one would want to hurt Kate.'

'Burglary that went wrong?' he questioned.

'We don't have burglaries.'

'Everywhere has burglaries.'

'Not here,' she argued. 'Anyway, burglars don't normally try to bludgeon you to death, do they?'

'Not as a rule. She's in a pretty bad way. It was a savage attack. She's lucky to be alive,' said Miller. 'At least twenty blows, I reckon. We've tried to call the husband, but he's not answering his phone. Alice Tobias said he is most likely out of a signal area. He takes the boys to play football every Friday. I've sent someone to find them.'

'I know. I know Dan takes them to football. I know them. What's Alice got to do with it?'

'Alice Tobias found the body.' He nodded to the garden.

Beth glanced at the woman sitting on the garden wall, hugging a mug of tea. Her hair was pulled up in a messy bun that most young women seemed to favour wearing these days. Alice looked up, saw Beth and her face crumpled.

'I'll talk to her,' said Beth.

Alice jumped up, the mug shaking in her hand. Brown liquid splashed onto her already blood-stained dress.

'Oh Beth, who would do this?' she asked, tears streaming down her face.

'I don't know. I'm sorry you had to find her.'

'She's going to be alright, isn't she?

Beth fought back tears.

'I don't know, Alice.'

'Does Dan know? Oh God, Beth, those boys.'

'Did you see anyone, Alice?'

'No, no one. The back door wasn't locked. I just walked in.'

They turned at the sound of shouting. Beth hurried into the house where Dan Marshall was confronting Tom Miller. His hair was damp with sweat. His two sons were crying at his side. Beth's heart went out to them, and she began to tremble again.

'What the fuck is going on?' he yelled, trying to push past Miller.

'I'm Detective Inspector Miller, it's best if ….'

'Where's my wife?' Dan asked angrily.

'Dan,' said Beth, placing a hand on his arm. 'Kate has been taken to hospital.'

'Is there someone who could have the children, Mr Marshall?' asked Miller.

'Why, what the hell's happened?'

'I'll take the boys, Dan.' said Alice, entering the hallway. 'You need to talk to the police.'

'Alice, what the hell's going on? Where's Kate?'

'Oh Dan,' she said and burst into tears. She turned to Beth appealingly.

'I can be interviewed later, can't I? I need to take the children.'

Beth nodded.

'I'll come and see you later this evening.'

Dan Marshall looked confused but he handed the children over to Alice.

'Go with Alice. Daddy will get you later.'

'Where's Mummy?' cried one.

Dan looked to Beth.

'Beth, what the fuck?'

'She had an accident,' she said softly. 'She's been taken to hospital.'

'What kind of accident?'

She took Dan's arm.

'Come with me.'

'What happened? Will someone tell me what the fuck happened here?'

When they were out of earshot of the children, Beth said. 'Someone attacked Kate in the kitchen. It was pretty brutal. It's best you don't go in there.'

He blinked several times.

'What are you talking about? No one would want to harm Kate. That's ridiculous.'

'Someone did. Alice found her; she was in a bad way, I'm afraid. I'm so sorry, Dan.'

'She's going to be okay, though, isn't she?'

'She's unconscious.'

He ran his fingers through his hair.

'Oh my God.'

'Dan...'

'Jesus, I don't understand. I need to get to the hospital,' he said urgently.

'I'll get a car to take you.'

He looked baffled.

'No one would want to hurt Kate. You know that.'

'I know.' She gently touched his arm.

'We'll find out who did this.'

'You promise.'

'I promise.'

Chapter Five

'How well do you know the husband?' asked Tom.
Beth stared at him.
'It wasn't Dan,' she said firmly.
'We have to eliminate him.'
She nodded. 'I know.'
'How well do you know him?' he asked again.
'We're friends, Ben and ...' she stopped. 'We go out to dinner together, sometimes. I babysit their kids. Kate and I go shopping. We're friends.'
Tom nodded.
'Where does the lane next to their garden lead to?'
'The back of the allotment. Whoever it was most likely escaped that way. You can walk through the allotment and come out to the side of Churchfields.'
'We'll need to check with everyone who owns an allotment.'
'I want to question Alice,' she said.
He took a final look around the kitchen before saying, 'Nowhere is that safe. People should lock their doors.'
'This is the country,' she said.
'Oh, of course. Criminals don't like the country, do they?' he said sarcastically.
'It's not like London,' she said.
'We'll need to search the house. Is there a hotel the family can stay in until we've finished?'
'I'll organise it,' said Beth.
There was a rumbling sound, and Beth raised her eyebrows.
'Was that your stomach?'
'You'd better question Mrs Tobias.'
'Have you eaten?'
He didn't reply. Beth turned to the door.
'There's a chippy up the road,' she said and left the cottage.
Miranda Sullivan saw her and hurried forward.
'Beth, can I have a word?'

Beth turned and frowned. Miranda's eyes sparkled with excitement.

'Is she going to make it?' she asked breathlessly.

'What?' said Beth, taken aback.

'Can you give us an exclusive? That was Kate Marshall, wasn't it? Was it domestic?'

Beth rolled her eyes.

'Bloody hell Miranda. I know not much happens around here but do you have to look so gleeful about it?'

'I'm just doing my job like you're doing yours. Give me a bit of insight. News is news, right?'

'I can't, not yet.'

Miranda glanced at Tom Miller, who was talking to a police officer outside the house.

'How's it working out with Miller?'

'No comment.'

God, thought Beth, I sound like one of those cops off the tele. Miranda, realising she wasn't getting anywhere with Beth, rushed over to Tom.

'Detective Inspector, I'm Miranda Sullivan, a reporter for the Oxford Chronicle. Can you tell me what happened here?'

Beth watched, interested to see how he handled Miranda. He said a few words to the police officer at the door before turning to her.

'There will be a statement first thing tomorrow.'

'Yes, but ...'

'That's it.'

He beckoned to Beth.

'Harper, let's go.'

Beth smiled at Miranda. 'There you have it,' she said.

*

Joe Tobias opened the door. He looked harassed. His shirt was hanging out of his shorts, and his black-rimmed glasses had slipped down the ridge of his nose. Beads of sweat covered his forehead. He pushed his glasses up and was about to speak when a child grabbed his leg.

'Daddy, can we watch another one now?'

'Okay, just a minute.'

He turned to Beth.

'We're in shock. Come in.'

'I need to question Alice.'

'Yes, she said you were coming. I can't believe it, Beth. What should we do?'

'Take all the right precautions. Lock up properly ….'

'It's too damn hot to close all the windows at night.'

'Best to be safe,' said Beth.

'How can this happen in Stonesend?' he said, bewildered.

He closed the door and walked along the hallway calling 'Alice, Beth is here.' Beth followed him past the bundle of wellingtons and baby stroller that sat in the hallway.

'Sorry about the muddle,' apologised Joe. 'You know what it's like.'

Alice waved from the kitchen.

'I've made some lemonade,' she said, pouring it into two glasses. 'Let's have it on the patio.'

The kitchen looked like a tornado had hit it.

'Lovely, thanks. It's still light at nine o'clock. Amazing,' said Beth, glancing around at the immaculate garden and thinking what a marked difference it was to Alice's kitchen.

'Joe's in charge of the garden,' smiled Alice.

'I never said a word.'

'How's Kate?' Alice asked, her face clouding over.

'Not good, I'm afraid. She's in ICU. She took quite a beating.'

Alice shuddered. The sound of screaming children came from the house.

'We've let them watch a movie,' explained Alice. 'I don't think any of them are going to sleep much tonight. Has Dan seen the kitchen?'

'We've arranged for him and the boys to stay at a hotel until things have been cleaned up. It's good of you to have the children tonight.'

'Dan wanted to stay with Kate. God, I hope she's going to be alright. Do you think she will be?'

'I hope so. Can you tell me what happened when you arrived at the house?'

'Faith had her piano lesson with Kate. She has one every Friday.'

'I know.'

'She didn't answer the door. I normally only ring once. The truth is we're always late, so she is usually waiting for us. So, we went around the back. I thought as the weather was so nice, she may have gone into the garden. But the back door was closed, and she didn't answer when I knocked. Adam said we should check to see that she hadn't fallen over.'

'Did you see anyone else?'

Alice thought for a moment.

'No, not that I remember, we were hurrying, you see. I'm always bloody late.'

Beth smiled

'And you didn't hear anything?'

'No, nothing. I know Dan takes the boys to football on a Friday, and I wondered if Kate had gone with them and forgot about the lesson.'

'The back door was unlocked?'

'Yes, I just walked in.'

Alice let out a small sob.

'I can't believe it. Poor Kate. Why would anyone do this? Kate was so ...' she shrugged. 'So harmless. This village is so safe. One of the reasons we came here. Good school, safe environment for the kids, no worries about muggings. Now, this, it's....'

'Has Kate mentioned anything odd happening lately?'

Alice shook her head.

'I don't know. We weren't close friends. I mean, I knew her, but I don't think she would have confided in me. You knew her better than I did.'

'I wasn't her confidant. Do you know who she might have confided in?'

'I guess Mae Lethbridge was the closest to her.'

Beth didn't know Mae Lethbridge that well. She knew of her, of course, but she was relatively new to the village. Beth had seen her around with her sick daughter and read about them in the local paper. They'd become something of a local celebrity, raising money for charity and giving charitable help themselves. The kid was sick with just about everything. Poor kid really had been cursed at birth.

'Where does she live?'

'Not far from Kate. Mill House in Churchfields. She's at the top of Churchfields lane.'

'So, you haven't heard any rumours about Kate. Could she have been having an affair?'

Alice's eyes widened.

'Kate? You know her, Beth. She really isn't the type.'

'I know, but we have to explore all avenues. It would be helpful if you let us do a DNA test, Alice. It's just for elimination. You touched quite a lot in the house.'

'Oh, yes, of course.'

'Thanks, Alice. That's it for now. We may need to speak to you again, but for the moment, that's it.'

Alice stood up.

'You'll catch who did this, won't you?'

'We'll do everything we can to catch them. Was Faith her only student on a Friday, or is there usually someone else before you?'

'No, just Faith. Kate doesn't normally give lessons on a Friday, but she made an exception for Faith as it was the only evening we could do. What with football and dancing and all the rest …' she trailed off. 'God, Beth, I went into the cottage without thinking. Whoever did it could have still been in there.'

Beth squeezed her arm.

'Fortunately, they weren't.'

Nothing made any sense. Kate Marshall came home from school on Friday afternoon after seeing her boys off with her husband. Sometime between then and six, someone came and attempted to batter her to death. But why?

'Who'd want to kill a piano teacher?' said Alice.

Beth shrugged. She knew people had secrets. Didn't Beth have her own? She'd never tell the truth about her and Ben. It had been too difficult to accept the reality herself.

'Who'd want to kill anyone?' she said.

Surely someone must have seen something.

*

Beth could have kicked herself for thinking there was even a chance that Ben would remember. She'd hoped for something, a little note, a phone call perhaps. The only post she'd received that day had been bills. She was stupid. Even if he had remembered, he wouldn't make a thing of it. She opened the fridge and pulled out a bottle of coke. She was about to pour some into a glass when her mobile rang. Her heart beat faster.

'Hello,' she said breathlessly.

It wasn't the voice she had hoped to hear. The disappointment was acute, and she had to fight back the tears.

'I've just phoned the hospital. No change' said Tom. 'Anything from Mrs Tobias?'

'Not really. She did suggest we talk to Mae Lethbridge. She lives at Churchfields and was a close friend of Kate's. She may know if Kate was worried about anything.'

'I'll pick you up tomorrow morning at nine. We'll visit Mae Lethbridge first.'

'I have my own car,' she said.

'Don't see the point in taking two. Besides, I don't want to fight over the parking space.'

'I've always parked there,' she said, pouring the coke into the glass.

'I'll see you in the morning,' he said and hung up.

'Arsehole,' she muttered and clicked off the phone.

She rummaged in the kitchen drawer for some paracetamol.

'You could have sent a bloody card,' she muttered. 'Just something to say the past five years meant something.'

She swallowed the pills with the coke and sprawled on the couch. How was this her life now? She wondered. Coming home to an empty house and usually eating a microwave meal for one before going to bed at nine? She tossed the flat coke into the sink and topped the glass up with wine. Lifting the glass in a toast, she murmured.

'Happy anniversary Ben, wherever you are.'

Chapter Six

Tom Miller's car was a mess. Stuffed into the side door pockets were discarded sandwich packets and an empty can of coke. The back seat was littered with boxes.

'Excuse the mess,' he said.

'Is this what you live on?' she asked, holding up a pizza box.

'It's food,' he said flatly. 'Kate Marshall got through the night. I phoned this morning.'

'I know. I phoned too.'

Beth had barely slept. She couldn't get Kate's battered face out of her mind.

'Someone must have heard something,' she said.

'People hear things but don't hear them,' said Tom.

Mae Lethbridge's house was at the end of a rose bordered driveway.

'You know about the daughter?' Beth asked as they pulled up outside.

'Vaguely. She's sick, isn't she? The mother does a lot for charity. That's about all I know.'

'They're quite the celebrities,' said Beth. 'The daughter has health issues. She was diagnosed with cancer a year ago. Has epilepsy and asthma on top of that, but they continue to help others. Quite an inspiration.'

Beth knocked on the door. A tabby cat strolled down the drive and sniffed around their legs.

'Can't stand cats,' moaned Tom. 'I'm always waiting for them to piss up my trousers.'

'That's dogs,' sighed Beth.

The door creaked open, and a heavily built woman with long thick curly hair leant down to pick up the cat. She smelt of musk. A familiar body shop perfume that Beth hadn't smelt in a long time.

'Mae Lethbridge?' she asked.

The woman nodded and said solemnly, 'Is it about Kate?'

'Yes, we're investigating the case. Can we come in for a few moments?'

Mae studied them suspiciously.

'Can I see your ID? Only after what's happened, I'm a bit nervous. It's just my daughter and me, you see.'

Beth raised her eyebrows. Mae Lethbridge certainly knew Beth and knew that she was a police officer. They'd seen each other in the village a few times.

'Certainly,' said Tom holding up his ID. Beth had to fumble in her pocket for hers. She seldom showed it and was embarrassed to see it had a bit of chewing gum stuck to it.

Mae opened the door wider and invited them into the dark, musty hallway. She led them along the passage. Beth glanced up at the stairlift that sat at the top of the staircase and then followed Mae through a door on the left. A strong smell of disinfectant, mingled with something cooking, reached Beth's nostrils.

'Vegetable casserole,' said Mae, seeing Beth wrinkle her nose.

The living room was brighter than the hall, boasting a large bay window. A wheelchair sat in the corner. Beth tried not to look at it and instead glanced at the jigsaw puzzle on the table.

'My daughter likes them,' said Mae, nodding at the jigsaw. 'She's having her nap. Do you want me to wake her?'

'No, that's fine,' said Tom.

They'd already agreed that they wouldn't need to talk to the daughter. The house was tidy. Books were neatly piled on the coffee table. The sofa cushions were crease-free, and Beth wondered if anyone ever sat on them.

'Would you like some tea?' Mae asked.

'No, thank you,' said Beth. The smell of disinfectant seemed more potent than ever. Mae looked tired. Beth noticed she flexed her neck several times.

'How is Kate?' she asked.

'She's in a critical condition, I'm afraid,' said Beth.

'I wanted to go and see her, but the hospital said she's not allowed visitors.'

'How well do you know Kate?' Tom asked.

Mae wrung her hands.

'Very well. We're good friends. Kate often helps me with my daughter. She's sick, you see.'

Beth nodded.

'She will pull round, won't she?' Mae asked, her forehead creasing in concern. 'Joe Tobias said she's unconscious. Is she going to die?'

'We don't know. If Kate does come round, we can't be sure she'll remember anything. She'd taken several blows to the head. That's why it's important for us to find out all we can about that afternoon.'

Mae sighed.

'I'm still in shock. It doesn't seem possible. Not here in Stonesend. We've never even had a burglary here.'

'Did Kate confide in you? Has she been concerned about anything?'

Mae wiped a tear from her eye.

'Nothing. She's been the same as usual. Stonesend is a quiet village. We all know each other and take care of each other. It's been a godsend for my daughter and me. I often leave the back door unlocked. We all do. Who'd have thought that someone ….'

She trailed off.

'So, she didn't seem worried?' repeated Beth.

Mae shook her head.

'If she was concerned about something, she didn't share it with me.'

'When was the last time you saw her?' asked Tom.

'Thursday night. I had a bad migraine, so she looked after Blanche. We didn't talk much as I went to bed.'

'Did she seem anxious or upset?'

'No, she seemed fine.'

'Has she discussed her marriage with you?' asked Beth.

Mae lifted her eyes.

'Her marriage?' she said, surprised, 'Dan and Kate have a great marriage. You're surely not thinking Dan had something to do with this. That's ridiculous. He thinks the world of Kate.'

'We have to pursue all avenues,' said Tom.

'Of course,' she said, forcing a smile.

'Where were you Friday afternoon between five and six,' asked Tom.

Mae's eyes widened in surprise.

'Me? I was at home with Blanche. We always eat at five. Blanche has to have her medications with food.'

'You didn't hear anything unusual?'

'I heard the sirens and everything, but I didn't know what was happening until Joe told me.'

'You heard nothing unusual before that?'

Mae shook her head.

'No, nothing at all.'

'Okay, thanks,' said Beth, walking to the door. 'If you remember anything, don't hesitate to call us.'

'Do you think she'll remember? It's frightening not knowing who it was.'

'It's very hard to say. Blows to the head often affect memory.'

The house was too hot. Beth realised that Mae Lethbridge had not one single window open. The air was stuffy and oppressive.

'Should we be afraid?' asked Mae anxiously.

'Obviously, continue to take the usual precautions,' Beth smiled. She didn't want to cause a panic. But while the attacker was out there, she felt uneasy. 'It's perhaps best not to leave your back door unlocked.'

'We're working hard to catch whoever did this,' said Tom, comfortingly.

As Beth walked down the drive, she heard Mae turn the lock in the front door.

Chapter Seven

2001: Leeds
Rob

I wasn't happy about the pregnancy. There was a sense of dishonesty about the whole thing. I wanted to believe Mae when she said it had been an accident, that the migraines had caused her to throw up so much that the pill hadn't worked. I knew how much she wanted a baby, but I felt deceived. To me, it seemed that whatever Mae wanted, Mae got. I tried to tell her that a baby would change our lives and that our future would be different. Mae didn't have any ambition. I tried to instil some into her. She was young and a good nurse. It would have been easy for her to work her way up. We could both have been earning good salaries, and in five years, we could have started our family. We would then have had so much more to offer a child.

'I can't get rid of it if that's what you're suggesting,' she'd said, holding back the tears.

'I'm not suggesting that,' I'd said, but I suppose I had been. Abortion wouldn't have been the end of the world. Women have them all the time, don't they? Mistakes happen, and this had been a mistake, hadn't it? At least so Mae said. We couldn't really afford a baby. It felt like the bottom had fallen out of my world. I'd just got a promotion. If I worked hard, there was a good possibility that I'd become a head engineer for Rotech. I'd travel the world, stay in the best hotels. Mae could come with me, sometimes. We'd have a whale of a time. Not if we had a kid in tow, though. That just wouldn't work.

Then Mae got sick. She was twenty weeks pregnant when the sickness started. We were up most of the night. The following day, she looked terrible.

'I think you should call the doctor,' Mae had said.

I was already late for work. I had an important meeting that morning. I couldn't miss it, so I offered to bring her mother over.

'Can't you stay with me? She'd pleaded. 'I'm frightened. What if I lose the baby?'

'That's why it will be good if your mum comes.'

'Please stay, Rob,' she'd begged.

'I have a meeting.'

She'd stared at me. Her look said it all. 'What you mean is, your meeting is more important than me.'

I suppose things went downhill from that moment. Mae felt that I had put work before family. I couldn't seem to make her understand that if I lost my job, the family would suffer.

'It's only one morning,' she'd pleaded.

I didn't mention the evenings I'd left work early when she'd had her migraines or the days I'd worked at home to be with her. She'd never understood the importance of my work. Everyone we knew seemed to be excited about the pregnancy. I'd started to feel in the minority.

'You'll be doing up the spare bedroom, then?' Colin had said the evening he and Jenny had come for dinner. We'd almost cancelled it as Mae had thought a migraine was looming. That had made me irritable. I'd thought the whole idea of having the baby was to stop the headaches, not to make them worse. I'd imagine Mae in bed with her migraines and no one to care for the baby. We sure as hell couldn't afford a nanny, not with just me working. We could just about afford the baby. There was no way I could keep taking time off, either.

'It'll be a shame to cancel,' I'd said. 'We haven't seen Colin and Jenny in ages.'

The truth was we hadn't seen anyone for ages. Not since the migraines started, and I was desperate for some socialising.

'I think I'll be alright,' she'd said. 'I'll drink plenty of water. I'm sure it will be alright if you don't mind helping with the dinner.'

She made it sound like I never helped with anything. Or maybe I'd become touchy. I felt like I helped more around the house than any man I knew.

'I've got tons of ideas for the nursery,' she'd told Jenny.

'We'd like a kid,' Colin had said. 'But I don't think we can afford it just yet.'

I never said neither could we. What would have been the point? Jenny wouldn't have understood how it had happened. She wasn't the type that would deceive her husband. I suppose that's when the resentment really started. I'd felt that fatherhood had been thrust upon me when I'd least wanted it or been expecting it. I had ambitions. I wanted to make something of myself before becoming a dad. I don't know if Mae never understood that or simply couldn't care. What Mae wanted, Mae got. Perhaps I'd been too harsh. I guess all women want babies, but it would have been nice if we'd had one when we both felt ready.

I got pissed that night and said things I shouldn't have. The drink had loosened my tongue. I don't think Mae ever forgave me.

'Here's to parenthood,' Colin had cheered, lifting his wine glass. His cheeks had been red, and his eyes bloodshot. We'd all drunk too much, apart from Mae, of course.

'Now, what does it mean again?' Colin had laughed. 'Oh yeah, broken sleep, dirty nappies, shirts covered in sick. Goodbye life.'

'Colin!' Jenny had exclaimed.

But he'd been damn right.

'Don't think this was my idea,' I'd slurred. 'I did all the right things to stop it.'

'Ooh, I say,' Jenny had laughed nervously. 'What you do in your bedroom is your own affair.'

'Rob!' Mae had said, looking hurt.

'What I meant was....' I'd begun, but it was too late.

If a look could have struck me dead, Mae's would have succeeded.

'We've all drunk too much,' Jenny said, trying to calm things. 'We really ought to get going Col, it's getting late.'

Tears had filled Mae's eyes, and I'd felt guilty and resentful at the same time.

'Excuse me, I have a migraine coming,' she'd said and left the room.

'Bloody hell, mate,' Colin had groaned. 'I think you're in the dog house. You know their hormones are more up the creek than normal when they're preggers?'

'Oh, do shut the fuck up, Colin,' Jenny had snarled. 'Men, honestly. You're such a waste of oxygen.'

Mae never forgave me. Whenever I couldn't take time off or wasn't sympathetic about the migraines, she'd always say, 'Well, I know you never wanted this baby.' I couldn't deny it. It was the truth. I'd become tired of the migraines, morning sickness and the house being a mess. It was everything I hadn't wanted. But I loved Mae. Or perhaps she'd become a habit I didn't want to give up. I suppose that's why it took me so long to leave.

Chapter Eight

2018: London
Tom

There were bent screws. Everyone knew that. It was, after all, a bastard job protecting some of the inmates. No one liked child killers. Even criminals had morals, and you didn't fuck with children. Christ, they'd all had kids, and all agreed that any fucker with a warped mind and a hard dick needed it chopping off. They were the scum of the earth, the sons of devils. Everything they touched in the nick was tarnished with their evil semen. It was enough to make the toughest of men vomit.

Lester Lynch knew the strength of feeling, but he wasn't bothered. When he entered the prison that Friday evening, it was with the confidence of someone who knew he was safe. Much to the screws disgust, he'd sauntered in as if he was entering the Ritz Hotel rather than a high-security prison. His father, Benny Lynch, had paid off enough screws to keep Lester safe for years. No one would dare touch him. They could look at him in disgust as much as they liked. Wankers, the lot of them.

'Everyone has their price,' Benny had told him. 'Everyone. We'll get an appeal.'

If they didn't have a price, they certainly had an Achilles heel, and it never took Benny very long to find out what it was. Benny Lynch wasn't a man to be messed with. The whole of the East End feared Lynch. No gangster had ever had as much respect in the underworld since the Krays and Lynch gloried in it.

The only thorn in his side had been Lester.

'What do you expect with a fucking name like that?' he'd yelled at his wife, Frances.

It was her that had wanted to name him Lester. It was all her bloody fault. His son. His own flesh and blood and mad in the head. You had to be mad in the head to want young boys. No normal person did that kind of stuff. Benny could sort out most things, but buggering and killing young kids. Christ, even he'd wanted to hang, draw and quarter him. But it was his son. A father does all he can to protect his son.

'I didn't do it, Dad. That bastard Miller has stitched me up.'

It was better to believe that. Easier. The so-called 'witnesses' were just out to get the Lynches; that's what it was. The Old Bill had been after them for years.

'I'll fix it,' he told Lester. 'Everyone has their price.'

And most did, but he hadn't bargained on Tom fucking Miller. Detective Inspector Miller, with his cosy detached house, gravel driveway and beautiful pregnant wife. Lynch had also heard on the grapevine that promotion was on the cards too. A charmed fucking life, that's what Tom Miller had. Detective Inspector Miller didn't have a price, but he had his Achilles Heel, and Benny knew just what Tom Miller's was.

Chapter Nine
2019: Stonesend

The news of Kate's attack spread through the village like a tornado. The villagers looked to Beth. She was one of them, after all. Their faith in her was unshakable.

The local locksmith was inundated with requests to fix new locks. Everyone prayed that Kate would regain consciousness and tell the police who had attacked her so that they could again sleep peacefully in their beds.

Tom Miller didn't have any worries about sleeping. The pill he took every night knocked him out. The sleep was dreamless. The nightmares were now gone. Sometimes a word, a piece of music, or a ringtone and the pain would hit him so hard that he found it hard to stay upright, but those times were happening less and less.

Kate Marshall's attack had given him focus. Someone in the village must know her attacker. Why would a stranger come to her house, beat her to a pulp and take nothing?

He glanced out of the window at the churchyard beyond. He found it calming and restful. He wondered if Kate Marshall had been a churchgoer. A vicar was always worth questioning. He'd have a word with Harper this morning. He rummaged in one of the many boxes that sat on the kitchen floor and pulled out a bowl. The cottage was too small to have boxes strewn everywhere. He'd ask around for a cleaner. Get the place shipshape.

He was about to pour milk onto his cereal when there was a tap at the door. He opened it to Beth Harper.

'I thought I'd drive today,' she said.

He saw her eyes wander behind him.

'You wanted to be nosy, you mean,' he said bluntly.

He opened the door wider.

'You'd better come in,' he said ungraciously.

'Worse than your car,' she observed.

He ignored her and carried his breakfast to a small table by the window.

'Cheerful view,' she said, grimacing at the sight of the churchyard.

'It's peaceful. I like it.'

She glanced curiously into the kitchen.

'Looking for the booze?' he asked.

Beth blushed. The ringing of her phone saved her from answering. It was Dan Marshall.

'You know I said nothing was missing? Well, I was wrong. I've just realised something,' he said excitedly. 'I've been in such a state that it hadn't dawned on me until now. Kate hung a picture. She must have done it that afternoon. Jack had painted it at school that day. I remember her taking it off him and saying she would frame it and have it on the kitchen wall for when he got home. The thing is, my hammer's gone.'

'You're certain about that?' Beth asked, feeling his excitement.

'Yeah. It's always in the shed. Jack and I were going to put a cabinet together to surprise Kate when she came home from the hospital. She's been on about it for ... anyway. The hammer has gone. It's nowhere.'

At last, they had a potential weapon. It wasn't much, but it was something.

'If the hammer was the weapon, then that means the attack wasn't pre-meditated,' said Tom.

'Which means Kate might have known her attacker?' said Beth.

'Someone from the village,' said Tom.

'I can't believe it was someone in the village,' disagreed Beth.

'You don't think you're a bit naïve,' he said, putting the cereal bowl in the sink.

'Aren't you eating that?' she asked.

'Let's go to the school,' he said, making for the door.

Beth took another last look around the kitchen and followed him out. Her eyes were pulled to the photo that sat on a table by the door. A smiling, relaxed Tom Miller stared back at her, his arm loosely draped around a blonde-haired woman. She was breathtakingly beautiful, just as they'd said in the papers. Tom saw her studying it but said nothing.

'I'm sorry,' she said, finally.

'Thanks,' he said briskly and closed the door behind them.

*

One of the teachers remembered saying goodbye to Kate that Friday afternoon.

'She said she had a piano lesson,' she recalled.

'She didn't happen to mention to you that she was going to meet someone?' Beth asked.

'No, but then she never talked about her private life.'

'Had she seemed different that day? Anxious, preoccupied?'

The teacher shook her head.

'She seemed the same as normal.'

'Had you noticed any difference in her the past few days?'

She shook her head again.

Kate's neighbour, Jean Adamson, had been working on her garden that afternoon but had seen nothing.

'I had the radio on, and I did pop inside to make tea,' she said apologetically. 'I didn't even see Alice arrive.'

'You didn't hear any shouts or screams?' asked Tom.

'No, I don't recall hearing anything, but I have the radio fairly loud. I'm a bit deaf, you see.'

And that was it. No one heard screams or saw a strange car outside the house. It was as though a maniac had appeared for a few minutes to attack Kate and then disappeared into thin air. It seemed no one had visited the allotment that afternoon.

'Too hot, most likely,' said Bill, who oversaw it. 'Even I didn't pop down, and not much keeps me away.'

Had there been a fight, and her assailant had grabbed the hammer? Beth arranged police cover at the hospital. Although things didn't look good, and the chances of Kate recovering were slim, she didn't want her attacker coming back to finish things off. The villagers were mourning for their peaceful village, and the attack seemed to take its toll on everyone.

'Arrange a thorough search of the area for the hammer. Bins, undergrowth. It must be somewhere. We need to look into the Marshall phone records. See who called them the days leading up to the attack. Get permission from the husband. Arrange house to house. Someone must have seen something,' said Tom.

Beth nodded.

'I'll question the vicar,' he said.

'The vicar?' she repeated.

'You'd be surprised what vicars know.'

Chapter Ten

2001: Leeds

Mae

It was a difficult pregnancy. I was convinced that I was going to lose my girl. We were told the sex of the baby at 16 weeks, and I was sure I could feel her move, even that early. She was going to be a lively little thing for sure. I was thrilled it was a girl. I hadn't much fancied a boy. I'd have loved it just the same, of course, but a girl is much better, so much choice when it comes to clothes.

Mum knitted bootees and a matinee jacket, but she wasn't the most fantastic knitter, and the sleeves didn't match, but I didn't like to say anything. Rob seemed to work even more during my pregnancy. He said it was because we needed the money. He emphasized *'needed the money'* as if I had no idea that money was tight. I'd stopped work early. I had to. The migraines got worse during this time. I suppose my hormones were all over the place. That's what Mum said anyway. She said Rob should be more understanding, more attentive. She came round a lot more. I found it a bit of a strain, but it was helpful, as I had to be careful because of my blood pressure. I took it myself, just to be sure, and it was often high.

'It's nothing to worry about,' Rob had said. 'You shouldn't keep taking it.'

'I won't know if it's raised if I don't take it,' I'd argued.

He'd just shrugged. I sometimes thought he would have been happy if I'd miscarried.

'It's better if I don't overdo things,' I'd told him. 'Mum said she doesn't mind doing the housework.'

Rob hadn't said anything. He'd just nodded.

'It wouldn't hurt him to come home early some days and help out,' Mum had grumbled. 'If you ask me, there's more to this working late than meets the eye.'

It was then that I'd started to get suspicious. Since Rob's promotion, Rob had worked even later. I knew he hadn't been happy about the baby, but I had hoped he would come round and we could both be happy and excited. Perhaps there was another reason he was working late. I'd pushed it out of my mind, told myself I was being ridiculous. Rob wouldn't do something like that. Other women's husbands might, but not mine. Mum didn't know what she was talking about.

'I wish he were happier about the baby,' I'd said.

'He will be once he sees her,' Mum had assured me.

Mum talked about selling her house to help us out, but she only ever talked about it. It did seem ridiculous her having a three-bedroom home all to herself.

'Five hundred pounds we paid for it,' she used to tell me proudly. 'It's worth five hundred thousand now. Can you believe it?'

Dad had given her the house. He'd preferred that to paying maintenance.

'It means he doesn't ever have to see us again,' she'd said, venom in her voice. 'That's the kind of man your father is.'

She could have sold it and bought herself a little flat and then helped Rob and me. She knew I wasn't well and that I was worried about looking after the baby.

'We can't afford a nanny,' I'd said.

'Why on earth would you need a nanny when you've got me?' she'd replied.

Except, more often than not, you're drunk, I thought.

It was one thing having her help around the flat but quite another having her look after my baby.

'It would be lovely if we had a house,' I'd said. 'I just don't think we'll ever be able to afford one now.'

'You'll be able to return to work once the baby is a bit older.'

I hadn't anticipated feeling so rough during the pregnancy. I was so happy it was a girl. I really didn't think I could go through it all again. We hardly ever saw our friends, and I knew Rob was resentful about that. He always was more sociable than me. I'd started to believe that he was resentful of the baby as well. I was very lonely and anxious. I didn't know what to expect during my pregnancy. It was all so unknown.

'I have to do the extra hours,' he'd said. 'We need the money for a deposit if you want us to get a house.'

I spent more time at mum's. Most of the time, we argued about her drinking or the negative things she would say about Rob. I don't know why I went. Loneliness, I suppose. That particular day we were going shopping for baby clothes.

'I'll buy them, seeing as you're always complaining that you have no money.'

'It's not complaining,' I'd argued. 'It's a fact.'

It was eleven in the morning, and she'd already been drinking. There was a half-empty bottle of brandy on the kitchen table and an opened bottle of painkillers.

'You haven't taken pills with that brandy, have you?' I'd asked anxiously.

'You shouldn't worry about it,' she'd snapped.

'Of course, I worry. It's not good for my blood pressure to get anxious, you know that.'

'You're always worrying about your health. You're obsessed if you ask me. No wonder Rob is always working. He can't stand it. He's such a weakling,' she'd scoffed.

'He does it so we can save for a house,' I'd said, feeling hurt. 'We don't want to rent all our lives.'

'That's what he says.'

She'd stumbled up the stairs. Why was she always putting doubts into my head? Rob would never have an affair. I was sure of that.

'I need my handbag,' she'd said.

'Don't bother,' I'd said tearfully. 'I really don't want to go shopping with you now. All you ever do is say hurtful things.'

'What did you say?' she'd called.

I'd pulled my coat on and let myself out of the house. I didn't hear her call out. I never heard her body as it tumbled down the stairs. I was six months pregnant when my drunken mother fell and broke her neck.

Chapter Eleven

2019: Stonesend

Kate

Bright lights made her head throb. She wished Dan would turn them off. She closed her eyes again. There was a strange beeping noise. It sounded like the dishwasher. Why was it on so late? She needed to turn over, but for some reason, she couldn't. It felt like her hands were tied. There was a strange smell in the room. She didn't like it. Kate snapped her eyes open, and pain shot through her head. The beeping was relentless. Surely the dishwasher didn't usually beep like that. Something was wrong. She couldn't move. What was stopping her from moving?

A face she didn't recognise towered over her. It was a woman. A stranger. Her features looked deformed. She was too close.

'Kate, how are you feeling?'

The woman knew her name. She tried to answer. Tried to ask the woman who she was. But she couldn't. It was as if someone had glued her tongue to the roof of her mouth.

'You're in the hospital, Kate. I'm one of the nurses taking care of you. You had a bad accident. Do you remember what happened?'

A bad accident. A car accident? When? Oh God, had the kids been with her? Dan, was Dan okay?

'The ...the ... children?'

It didn't sound like her. The voice was slurred, weak and breathless.

'Your children are fine. Your husband will be back soon. He went to get a coffee.'

Oh, thank God.

'Here.'

Something wet was wiped across her lips, and she licked them gratefully. Then a whisper of air blew across Kate's face, and a familiar smell wafted towards her. It was Dan's smell. Dan's face was close to hers now. More wetness on her cheeks. Was he crying?

'Oh Kate, thank God.'

'Dan,' her throat was sore. Her voice sounded raspy and harsh.

'It's okay, Kate, everything is going to be okay.'

'What happened?'

He didn't reply. Kate could hear his breathing, the strange beeping and somewhere in the distance, a phone ringing.

'Don't you remember?'

'Was I in an accident?'

She'd always driven so carefully.

'Someone attacked you, Kate. In the house. Do you remember?'

Her head felt like it would burst. Her eyes were burning, and all she wanted to do was sleep.

'I ...'

She closed her eyes, and then there was blessed darkness.

*

'She doesn't remember,' Dan said, looking at Beth. 'I don't know if that's a good or bad thing.'

Their knees almost touched under the narrow table. Beth wanted to console Dan but didn't know how. She had nothing positive to tell him. Beth saw the hurt welling up in his eyes and felt inadequate. She looked away from him to the spilt ketchup on the cafeteria table. Someone hadn't bothered wiping it off. Probably in a hurry to get back to their sick relative.

'Perhaps it's a good thing,' she said.

Dan nodded.

'I don't understand any of it,' he said.

Tom returned with three weak teas.

'The best they've got, I'm afraid,' he apologised.

Dan clenched his fists and then relaxed them.

'We thought Stonesend was the safest place ever. It just goes to show.'

'Nowhere is safe,' said Tom.

'Stonesend has always been safe,' Beth argued.

'If I find out who did this, I'll...' said Dan angrily.

'I didn't hear that, Dan,' said Beth softly. She was disappointed. She'd hoped Kate would remember, even though the doctor had said it was unlikely.

'The mind has a way of protecting the body,' he'd warned them. 'It may be sometime before she remembers anything, and even then, it may come in small fragments, if at all.'

He was insistent that Kate shouldn't be pressured.

'It's going to be a slow recovery as it is.' He'd said. 'I would ask you not to put her under any stress.'

'How long can she have the police protection?' Dan asked. 'If the attacker knows she's come round, he might ….'

He stopped and looked out of the window.

'We can continue while she's in the hospital, but I don't know if I'll be able to justify it once she leaves,' said Tom.

'What if they come back? Surely you can ….'

'It's not my decision, Dan. I wish it were.'

They really needed Kate to remember.

'I'm going to question her. Do you want to be present, Dan?' asked Beth.

'I trust you, Beth,' he said.

*

It was hard for Beth to look at Kate. For all her training and experience, she still wasn't used to seeing a broken person. Kate's once pretty face that Beth remembered had now been replaced with blue and black swollen eyes, cracked bleeding lips, and matted blonde hair that was hidden behind a mass of bandages. There were so many tubes attached to her that Beth was afraid to get too close.

'Hello Kate, how are you?' she said, pulling up a chair.

Kate licked her dry lips and closed her eyes for a moment before opening them again.

'It's me, Beth.'

Kate nodded. Beth carefully reached out for Kate's hand and held it gently in hers. Tears sprang to her eyes, and she had to swallow several times before she could speak.

'Dan said that you don't remember anything about the day when you were attacked.'

Kate sighed and shook her head. Tears rolled unbidden down her cheeks.

'Do you remember walking from the school to your house?'

Kate clutched the bedsheets and again shook her head.

'I remember …'

Beth leant forward. Kate swallowed and turned her head towards the water swabs on the bedside cabinet. Beth took one and held it gently to Kate's lips.

'Better?'

Kate nodded gratefully.

'I remember Dan collecting the boys, I think.'

'Nothing after that?'

'No, I'm sorry, Beth.'

Beth squeezed her hand.

'It's okay, Kate. Everything is going to be okay.'

Her voice broke, and she took a deep breath to compose herself.

'What matters is that that you get better.'

'I don't understand, Beth.'

'I know.'

Beth was disappointed. They still knew nothing more about what had happened after Kate had left the school that day. The weapon used still hadn't been found. Their only hope had been that Kate would remember something.

'Kate, has there been anything worrying you?'

Kate shook her head.

'Has anything happened at school?'

'Nothing unusual,' said Kate, her voice raspy.

'Have you had any strange phone calls, anything like that?'

'I'm sorry,' said Kate, shaking her head.

'Think carefully. Do you remember hanging a picture your son painted? He gave it to you that afternoon.'

Kate closed her eyes as if trying to remember.

'No, I don't,' she said tearfully.

'It's okay,' Beth said gently.

Beth had hit a brick wall. Only Kate could help them, and God knows when that would be.

'She might never remember,' Beth said as they got into the car.

'We need to find the weapon that was used,' said Tom.

Beth's phone bleeped with a message. She clicked into it.

'It's from Matt. Calls made to the Marshall's home the month before the murder,' she said.

She scrolled down the screen, and then her eyes widened.

'There were several from the vicar,' she said, surprised. 'Three calls in the week of the attack. Why would he phone a parishioner that often?'

'One way to find out,' said Tom. 'Any other odd calls?'

'No,' said Beth, scrolling down. 'Calls from the school, Mae Lethbridge, some of the villagers. Kate is on one of the school committees. Normal phone calls you'd expect. Doctors confirming an appointment. Nothing odd. No withheld numbers.'

'Right, let's have a word with the Reverend.'

Chapter Twelve

Tom stood in front of the pews and inhaled deeply. The smell of wood polish and incense, mixed with the musty odour of stone, crept into his nostrils. He looked ahead to the altar, where a man, aged around forty, was lighting candles. Slowly Tom stepped towards him, passing the high stained-glass windows and statues of religious figures.

'Good afternoon,' said the vicar, turning. 'Welcome to St Lawrence's.'

Tom pulled out his ID and held it up.

'I'd like a few words with you about Kate Marshall.'

The vicar's face clouded over, and he sighed. He was younger than Tom had at first thought. He couldn't have been more than thirty.

'Yes, of course, poor Kate. Dan must be beside himself. Shall we go into the rectory?' He asked, stepping toward Tom.

'Here is fine,' said Tom.

His voice was cold and Reverend Scott looked at him curiously before saying.

'Then please take a seat. I'm Reverend Anthony Scott. I'm visiting Kate later. How is she doing?'

'Not great. Are the Marshalls regular churchgoers?' asked Tom.

'Kate comes most Sundays. Dan isn't a regular worshipper. We see him at Christmas, children's carol service, you know the kind of thing.'

'Did Kate Marshall ever visit you to talk confidentially?'

Reverend Scott cocked his head to one side.

'You surely understand that I can't answer that question.'

'Why not?'

Tom tried to hide the hostility from his voice but failed miserably.

'Because if she had, and I told you, it would no longer be confidential, would it?'

Tom's cheek twitched.

'How well do you know Mrs Marshall?'

'As well as I know most people in the village. It's a small community.'

'Did she share anything with you that could be connected with her attack?'

Tom watched the vicar closely. His expression didn't change. There was a pause before Anthony said, 'No, she didn't.'

'But she told you something, didn't she? Why else did you need to phone the Marshall house three times last week?'

'What?' Anthony's face registered his shock. 'I don't have to discuss with the police why I phone my parishioners.'

'If you know anything that could lead us to her attacker, you really need to share it. Surely, God would want us to find them.'

The vicar stood up abruptly.

'I'm sure God will lead you in the right direction.'

'Were you aware of anyone in the village having an issue with Kate?'

'No, I wasn't aware of anything like that.'

'It won't help us if the investigation is hindered by a secret that the church isn't willing to reveal.'

Reverend Scott raised his eyebrows.

'I don't like the tone this conversation is taking. I'm starting to feel the church is on trial. I can see that you believe God has let you down at some point in your life. If you wish to come and visit me to discuss that, I'd be more than happy to do so. I have nothing more to say about Kate Marshall.'

'And if you suddenly remember something that might help this investigation. Feel free to visit me, and we can discuss *that*.' said Tom sharply.

'I trust this interview is now at an end?' said Reverend Scott stiffly.

'For the moment,' said Tom and strolled out of the church.

*

'Dinner?' said Beth, surprised.

'You do eat dinner?' said Chief Superintendent Lewis.

'On occasions, but you've never asked me to dinner before, Sir.'

'Well, I am now. We don't talk about work, and you don't have to call me Sir.'

'Who else is going to be there?' she asked suspiciously.

'DI Miller.'

Beth laughed.

'I knew there was an ulterior motive.'

'It's good social relations.'
'Is it? can I say no?'
'I prefer you didn't.'
'When?'

Chief Superintendent Lewis smiled. He knew Beth would come round.

'Next Friday?'

'I don't eat garlic,' she said and walked from the office.

Chapter Thirteen

2001: Leeds

Mae

We were in the middle of dinner when Liz, mum's neighbour, phoned.

'I think something has happened to Joan', she said. 'Only, her newspaper is stuck in the letterbox, and there's a package on the doorstep and a bottle of milk. Has she gone away?'

'No. I saw Mum yesterday. She's fine.'

Liz seemed unconvinced.

'I'm a bit worried,' she said. 'It's not like Joan to leave her milk out.'

'I'll pop round,' I assured her. 'I have a key.'

Rob looked concerned when I told him.

'That's not like Joan,' he said worriedly. 'Even if she went out, she would have taken the milk in. We ought to check on her.'

I didn't mention the argument I'd had with her the day before. There seemed little point. Rob seemed impatient to leave, so I cleared away the dishes but left them on the kitchen counter instead of stacking them in the dishwasher. Rob drove faster than usual to Mum's. The milk and package were still on the doorstep when we arrived. I opened the front door and was about to walk in when Rob hurried ahead of me.

'Stay there,' he ordered, but I'd already seen her lying at the foot of the stairs.

'Don't look,' Rob said, gently pushing me back. I saw her splayed legs and the black tie-up shoes she'd put on yesterday. Above them, I could just make out the hem of her tartan skirt.

'We need to call an ambulance,' said Rob.

I shuffled back a step or two until the fresh air hit my face. Rob called for the ambulance. He sounded breathless, as if he'd been running.

'Ambulance, right away.'

I could hear a distant voice at the other end of the telephone. Rob knelt beside Mum.

'No, she isn't,' he said, his voice breaking. Then he hung up and didn't speak at all. He led me back to the car. It was a relief to be out of the house.

'She's dead, Mae. I don't know how long she's been lying there.'

I exhaled slowly. I had to keep calm for my baby.

'I should have phoned earlier.'

'It's not your fault,' he said, hugging me. It felt nice to be in his arms. It seemed ages since we'd been this close.

'She must have fallen yesterday,' I said. 'She's wearing the same skirt and her shoes. She always wears her slippers if she's going to be in the house.'

Rob didn't reply. I suppose there was no need to.

*

'I should never have left her, not in the state she was in,' I said over and over.

'Then you would never ever have left,' Rob assured me. 'She was always in a state.'

It hadn't been my fault. Not really. It was bound to have happened sooner or later. She was unsteady on her feet. I was always telling her to stop drinking. She was a tragedy waiting to happen.

The funeral was awful. I felt so unwell that day.

People were so kind and extremely sympathetic. It was all too much for me.

'Such an awful time, especially with a baby on the way,' they said.

'For her to have lain there for twenty-four hours,' said Liz. It sounded like an accusation. The coroner's report said that from her injuries, she must have fallen at about the time I'd left her the previous day and may have been conscious for a short time but unable to move. She'd died from a broken neck. I didn't like to dwell on the fact that if I'd gone back, I might have saved her. It wasn't my fault. I'd had to think of my baby.

'Joan was so looking forward to being a grandmother,' said Liz.

Of course, I knew that wasn't true. I didn't tell her that Mum was, in fact, quite jealous of her future grandchild. Who would have believed me? I knew once Blanche was born, there would have been endless arguments. Mum would have felt shut out. The truth was I had been dreading it.

Mum didn't have many friends, so the funeral was a small affair. I asked several of her neighbours, and fortunately, no one mentioned Mum's drinking. I thought about contacting my father but changed my mind. I was stressed enough, and he hadn't cared about us. Not once had he got in touch with me. What would I say to him anyway?

I decided on cremation. I would scatter the ashes after Blanche was born.

Mum left us the house and a considerable cash sum. When I thought of how Rob and I struggled at the beginning of my pregnancy, it made me a bit cross. To think she could have helped us but didn't bother.

The coroner recorded death by misadventure. It said she must have lost her footing due to being intoxicated. There was a high level of alcohol in her blood combined with the pain medication, which meant she would have been very unsteady on her feet.

At first, I wanted to sell mum's house and buy something new, but Rob talked me out of it.

'With you halfway through the pregnancy and your blood pressure what it is. I don't think moving house is a good idea.'

I was worried about seeing the stairs every day and the memory of mum's body lying at the bottom of them. Rob suggested changing the stair carpet and decorating the hallway.

'It will look completely different once that's done.'

In time, I said, I would put the house into joint names. I never did. Things did look different after the decoration, and I felt much happier moving in. I was worried my pregnancy would suffer, but everything was fine apart from my raised blood pressure. I rested as much as possible. I hoped that now the financial pressure was off, that Rob would spend more time at home, but he didn't. He still had evening meetings. We argued about it a lot. I'd spend my days reading pregnancy books, watching lots of daytime television, and talking to my daughter.

'We're going to be fine, Blanche,' I would tell her. 'You and me, we're going to be just fine.'

I've always loved the name Blanche ever since I first heard it. We went to see a production of 'A Streetcar named Desire', and I decided then, if I ever had a daughter, that's what I would call her. On my good days, I would get the box room ready for Blanche to have as a nursery. With Mum's money, we were able to buy a new cot. Rob came to help choose it. That had been a nice day. Rob had some holiday, so he took the day off. We had lunch in a small pub not far from home. Rob had been relaxed.

'At least we don't have to worry about saving,' he'd said, ordering himself another beer.

The fish and chips we'd ordered had made me feel sick, but I didn't say anything. I hadn't wanted to spoil the relaxed atmosphere. Rob always got irritable if I mentioned that I felt off colour.

'You don't have to work so many hours now,' I'd said, thinking I was helpful.

'I can't start slacking just because we have a bit of money behind us,' he'd snapped.

'No, I know. I didn't mean that.'

I never mentioned it again. I didn't want Rob and I to fight. We had a house, a baby on the way and money in the bank. We should have been happy. Things should have got better, but somehow, they just got worse. Then Blanche arrived, and things were never the same again.

Chapter Fourteen

2019: Stonesend

She'd changed three times, but nothing seemed right. She didn't seem right. The woman staring back at her from the wardrobe mirror wasn't someone she recognised. It was a stranger. An underweight thirty-something train wreck. What were those dark rings under her eyes? She didn't remember seeing those yesterday. Christ, she was going downhill faster than a car with no brakes.

'Bugger,' she cursed, pulling off the woollen dress. It was too bloody warm to wear that.

Now her armpits were smelly. Why couldn't they have a thunderstorm? How much longer was this damn heatwave going to go on for? She finally decided on a linen blouse and leggings and wondered what Tom Miller would be wearing. She had no idea what they were going to talk about. It was going to be the longest evening of her life.

After grabbing a bottle of wine from the fridge, she closed the back door and locked it. She'd taken to shooting the top bolt across too. She still found it hard to accept that Kate had been attacked in her own kitchen on a bright summer's afternoon. Who would be so bold?

'Probably the Gypos,' Ray had said, who tended to blame everything on the gypsies, ever since they had parked themselves on the grass verge around the corner from Sandy and Ray's house.

'I can't see why they'd want to attack someone in the village,' Beth had replied.

All the same, she'd questioned them, but poaching seemed the only crime she could pin on them.

'It's frightening,' Sandy had said, wringing her hands. 'To think someone attacked her in broad daylight.'

'Things like that don't happen around here,' Ray had said as if it were somehow Beth's fault for allowing it to happen.

For a second, she considered phoning the Chief and saying her car wouldn't start, but she knew she couldn't lie. She'd just have to grin and bear it. She didn't go into town often. Ben did. He liked the wine bars and the theatres. She didn't want to bump into him. He wouldn't be alone, and she couldn't bear the embarrassment and that awful feeling she had when she saw them together, as though she was insignificant, inferior, a mistake. She drove through Oxford and towards Jericho, ignoring the small French restaurant she and Ben used to go to. She'd never been to the Chief's house before, and it surprised her. It was smaller than she'd imagined and terraced. For some reason, she'd thought he and Dina had a detached house.

Dina opened the door and smiled warmly. She was wearing a long evening dress, and around her neck hung a string of pearls.

'I hope I'm not late,' Beth said, knowing full well that she was.

'Lovely to see you,' Dina said, kissing her on the cheek. She smelt of roses. Beth wished she could turn around and go back. She was so underdressed.

'Ah, you've arrived,' boomed Chief Brian Lewis. 'Come in.'

Beth stepped self-consciously into the hallway and followed Brian along it to a stylishly decorated lounge. The walls were adorned with smiling photographs of their two sons in university garb. Standing by the fireplace, with a glass of orange juice in his hand, and looking as uncomfortable as Beth felt, was Tom Miller.

'Hello,' he said.

Beth was relieved to see he was casually dressed.

'What can I offer you to drink?' Brian asked. 'We have red wine, white wine, orange juice, beer ….'

'I'll have a beer,' she said, feeling slightly uncomfortable to be talking alcohol in front of Miller.

'Dinner will be ready soon,' smiled Dina. 'We'll eat outside under the gazebo. No garlic, Beth.'

'Great.'

Brian handed her a bottle of beer.

'Glass if you want it?'

'No, this is great.'

'I'll just check on the chicken. Brian, give me a hand,' said Dina.

Christ, they're not leaving us alone, are they? Panicked Beth. She looked at Tom Miller and saw her panic reflected in his dark blue eyes.

The door closed, and Miller said, 'I'm not enjoying this either.'

'At least you'll get a decent dinner,' she remarked.

'We could try and get along, just for this evening,' he said, raising his eyebrows.

'I could have applied for your job. I didn't because I'd had a few problems in my personal life. I didn't want my emotions to get in the way of my decisions. Do you know what I mean?'

'My emotions won't affect my decisions,' he said firmly.

'I hope not.'

'I'm sorry about your personal problems.'

'I don't need your sympathy.'

'Ditto,' he shot back.

She took a long gulp of the beer and wished Brian would come back.

'You don't like garlic?' questioned Tom.

'No, I don't,' she said, walking towards the photos on the wall. 'Don't you find evenings like this difficult, with everyone drinking?' she asked, turning to face him.

'No, I don't.'

The door opened, and Brian came in. Beth sighed with relief.

'How are you two getting on?' he asked, a cheeky grin on his face.

'Oh, swimmingly,' said Beth sarcastically.

Chapter Fifteen
August 2019: Stonesend

Kate

Her stomach fluttered as the car rounded the bend and the village came into sight. She usually got a warm glow whenever they entered the village. A feeling of safety and peace would envelop her. Funny to think that now. It was where she'd felt at home. So at home. She loved it here. She was very happy in her job at the village school. She adored their little country cottage. It wasn't huge, but it was quaint. It was something she and Dan had dreamt about.

'A cottage in the country,' they used to say. 'That's what we'll have one day.'

'Goats and chickens,' Dan had laughed.

They never did get the goats or chickens. They had two boys instead. They had never imagined that they would actually get the cottage in the country. Then Dan's grandmother died, leaving them enough money for a deposit.

It had taken them five years to get it into shape. It had been a labour of love. Now it was perfect. Their dream home and Kate's dream garden. It was where she'd always felt safe, and it was an ideal place to raise children. Suddenly, her dream home had turned into one of nightmares, and she was scared of how she would feel when she saw it again. Would the sight of it jolt her memory? Or would that only happen when she entered the kitchen? Kate tensed slightly. She needed the painkillers. It had been four hours since the last ones, and the pain in her head was returning. Her hands shook. They never stopped. The doctor said they would. It was all a matter of time. They said she'd made a good recovery, but her ears still buzzed, as if there was a hive of bees in them. It made her feel sick. She had continual brain fog, and her eyes were sore and watery. Dan turned the car into Churchfields, and Kate took a deep breath.

'People have sent cards,' said Dan. 'You've had lots of flowers too.'

She knew his cheery voice was for her benefit. He's trying to take the edge off, she thought. He knows I'm nervous. Afraid of entering my own home.

'Mae has made a chicken casserole for our dinner. The village has been amazing.'

'That's kind,' she said.

She hadn't thought about dinner. She couldn't think about anything except who had tried to kill her. *To kill her*. It sounded ridiculous. Why would anyone want to kill her? She didn't have any enemies. People who get murdered have violent partners or shady secrets. Or someone with a grudge against them. Total strangers don't just walk into your home and bludgeon you to death. She sometimes wondered if the police had got it all wrong, but someone had come into their house, and whoever that person had been, he or she had tried to kill her. Kate shivered.

'Are you cold?' Dan asked.

'I'm fine,' she said, forcing a smile. There was the cottage. It looked innocent enough. Beth had asked her if everything was alright between her and Dan. If she hadn't felt so awful, she would have laughed. Dan attacking her? It was ludicrous.

He stopped the car, and she turned to him.

'They asked if we argued much,' she said.

He frowned.

'They always suspect the husband, apparently,' she smiled. She wanted to reassure him.

Dan, who wouldn't kill a spider. Everyone she knew was kind. She couldn't think of anyone who would want to hurt her or her family.

'I guess that makes sense,' he smiled.

She squeezed his hand.

'Ready?' he asked.

She nodded. She wasn't ready, not really. If she could have driven back to the hospital, she would have done. She felt safe there. She looked at their little cottage and waited for the memories to flood her brain, but nothing happened. The front door opened and the boys stood there with Dan's mother, Polly. She was crying. Not in front of the children, Kate thought. Don't upset them.

Dan helped her to the door and Polly hugged her.

'We're so glad you're home.'

The boys stared at her.

'Don't I get a hug?' she said, smiling weakly.

They then leapt towards her, and Dan panicking, said, 'Careful boys.'

'It's fine,' she said.

Jack looked curiously at the bandages on her head.

'Does it hurt a lot, Mum?' he asked.

'Not too much,' she lied.

Ryan clutched her hand and said simply. 'I love you. We'll help you get better.' Kate fought back the tears. She didn't want them to see her crying. Dan led her to the living room, but she shook her head.

'I want to go into the kitchen. Let's make some tea.'

Polly gave Dan a concerned look.

'I have to go in there sometime,' Kate said. Polly nodded, and together they walked to the kitchen. Kate didn't know what to expect. It looked exactly as it always had.

'It smells of bleach,' she said.

'I think that's what they used to clean the walls,' said Dan.

'Oh,' said Kate.

She stood in the doorway and waited as though a re-enactment of that afternoon would suddenly materialise in front of her eyes, but, of course, it didn't. There was nothing.

'Don't force it,' Doctor Adamson had said. 'Let it come when it's ready. Don't stress yourself. Accept the fact that maybe it will never resurface. It may even be for the best.'

She wanted to remember, and yet she didn't. She wanted to remember because she needed to know. She needed to know who her enemy was. She didn't want to remember because she didn't want to relive the horror of that afternoon and learn who her enemy was.

'I'll make tea.'

The chicken casserole sat on the kitchen counter. So thoughtful of Mae. On the windowsill were Get Well cards.

'Such a caring village,' said Polly, clicking on the kettle.

Vases of flowers were lined up on the kitchen dresser.

'How lovely,' Kate said.

'Sophie brought them round,' said Dan.

For a second, she looked blank. She couldn't remember who Sophie was.

'Sophie Johnson,' Dan reminded her.

Of course. Sophie. She and Sophie were on the school's parents' committee. She looked up at the picture on the wall. The one that she had hung the afternoon of the attack. It didn't look at all familiar. As hard as she tried, she just couldn't remember Adam giving it to her. She must have gone out to the shed to get the hammer. Dan saw her looking.

'It's a good drawing, isn't it?'

'It's my best,' said Adam.

'It's perfect,' she said.

A chair was missing. Kate looked around and was about to ask Dan where it was when he said. 'It got broken ….'

'Oh,' she said.

The boys were nagging for chocolate. 'You promised,' they said in unison. Kate sat down at the table. Her legs were beginning to tremble. Tiredness overwhelmed her.

'Mum made us a cake,' said Dan.

'I think I might lie down,' Kate said.

They all looked mortified. Surely, they hadn't expected her to come home and continue as if nothing had happened. She supposed that would make things easy for them. They could all forget it had ever happened. But how could she ever forget? Someone had tried to murder her. Someone she probably knew.

'I'll bring your tea up,' said Dan.

She took the painkillers from her bag.

'I'll help you upstairs,' said Dan, his face a mask of worry.

'Can you fix a bolt to the bedroom door?'

He gawped at her.

'A bolt?'

It had never occurred to them to put locks on the bedroom doors. They lived in Stonesend, where it was safe. But it wasn't safe, was it? Not anymore.

Chapter Sixteen

'It's been suggested from up high that we do a Crimewatch reconstruction of Kate Marshall's attack,' said Brian.

Dina sighed.

'I thought you weren't going to talk shop,' she said.

'Just this one thing,' he said apologetically.

Beth took the dish of oven-roasted vegetables from Dina and placed a heaped spoonful onto her plate.

'It will spotlight the village,' she said. 'I'm not sure they will like that.'

'If it means we catch the attacker, then surely it's worth it,' argued Tom.

'You don't understand villagers and village life,' she said irritably. 'It's not like London.'

'So you keep reminding me.'

Brian passed Beth another beer. It was her third.

'I don't think I should have another,' she said.

'Tom will give you a lift home. You can collect your car tomorrow,' said Brian, popping the top from the bottle.

'Well ...' she began.

'Won't you, Tom?' Dina asked.

'Of course,' smiled Tom.

'Have you made any headway with the case?' Brian asked.

Beth shook her head.

'No, not even the weapon used during the assault has been found.'

'There was a fair amount of DNA on Kate's clothes. But she'd been at the school that day, as well as with her own kids. We found matches with that of her husband and Alice Tobias, who found her. There was saliva on the dress, but we have no matches for that,' said Tom.

'Her kids?' questioned Brian.

'I took samples,' said Beth. 'They didn't match the saliva. It could have been any one of the kids at the school.'

'The reconstruction could jolt someone's memory. So it's your next logical step.'

'I agree,' said Tom. 'It's worth a shot.'

Men sticking together thought Beth.

'Seems I'm outnumbered. I would prefer not to be the spokesperson, though.'

She didn't want Ben seeing what she had become. She never wanted him to know how badly she had taken the breakup. Tom looked uncomfortable, and it occurred to Beth that he didn't want to be the spokesperson either.

'I think under the circumstances, it would be better if it were you, Beth. We don't want the focus to move away from the crime,' said Brian.

'Oh, I see,' she said, putting her fork down. 'You don't want DI Miller to have the limelight, but it doesn't matter about me.'

'It might detract from the crime,' said Tom.

'With all due respect, Sir, this is your job.'

'You don't have to call me sir, not tonight,' said Tom.

'You're the DI, and you should be the spokesman.'

'I'd prefer it was you, Beth,' said Brian. 'I don't want to pull rank, but ….'

'Bloody hell,' she said, taking a long swig of the beer. 'But you will, right?'

'Okay, enough shop talk,' broke in Dina. 'Eat up, so we can enjoy pudding.'

*

'Thanks for coming,' called Dina.'

Beth waved from the car.

'Thank God that's over,' she muttered. She noticed the boxes and rubbish had been cleared from Tom's car. He saw her looking and said, 'I had a clean-up,'

She was conscious of his leg close to hers and moved slightly.

'Can I ask why you don't want to be the spokesperson for Crimewatch?' he asked.

She bowed her head as she felt the tears well up. Bugger, she should have drunk less.

'I don't want my husband to see what our marriage break-up has done to me,' she said flatly.

'I'm sorry,' he said quietly, starting the engine.

'Well, at least he's not dead. It must be much worse for you.'

The minute the words were out of her mouth, she regretted them. She heard him take a deep breath.

'It gets easier,' he said, finally.

'I'm sorry,' she said. 'I can't imagine your pain.'

They reached her cottage at the edge of the village, and as she opened the door, he said, 'You'll be a good spokesperson. You know the people here. They trust you.'

'Sure,' she said. 'They trust me, now.'

She stepped from the car.

'I'll see you into the house,' he said.

'No need,' she said quickly.

She climbed from the car, gave a small wave and walked up the driveway. He didn't start the engine again until he knew she was safely inside. Beth watched him from the window, and when his car was out of sight, she pulled the curtains and locked the front door. She shouldn't have mentioned his wife. It had been insensitive.

'One beer too many,' she reprimanded herself.

She was now wide awake. Her mind was buzzing with Brian's Crimewatch suggestion. How would Kate feel about it? They couldn't go ahead if Kate wasn't happy. Their peaceful village would be splashed across people's television screens. Beth wasn't sure she wanted the village or herself to be the centre of attention. Supposing they never found the attacker? She didn't want to be the copper everyone remembered. The copper that had failed to find a brutal attacker. Beth would talk to Kate tomorrow and see how she felt about it. Right now, her head was thumping unbearably. She thought of the tranquillisers in the bathroom cabinet. No. They were for the days when she really couldn't cope. Taking them meant she had failed. A good cop is a strong cop, not one who falls to pieces when her husband dumps her for … She shook her head, causing it to thump even more. She didn't bother pulling back the duvet. It was too hot anyway. The windows stayed closed. Follow your own advice, she told herself before falling into a deep, dreamless sleep.

Chapter Seventeen

2001: Leeds

Mae

It had been the early hours of a Sunday morning when the first contraction started. I'd woken with a start and clenched my fists as a wave of pain attacked me. Rob had been snoring beside me. I'd turned on my side and waited, hoping the pain would go. Some time passed, and just as I'd decided it had been nothing and had been about to relax again, the next contraction came. I'd shaken Rob gently. He hated being woken suddenly.

'I think the baby is coming,' I said. 'I'm having labour pains.'

He rubbed his eyes sleepily.

'Are you sure?' he muttered.

He probably thought I'd imagined it.

'Yes,' I said, trying to keep my voice calm. I didn't want him to think I was overreacting. I carefully manoeuvred myself, so I was sitting on the edge of the bed. Rob leant across to check the time on the bedside clock.

'How often are they coming?' he asked.

'I've had two.'

He flopped back onto the pillows.

'It could be hours,' he said. Rob was most likely right, but I insisted on being taken to the hospital anyway. If I was going to be hours in labour, I wanted to be in the right place. Eight hours later and I was still having contractions. The pain was unbearable. I was exhausted and convinced something was wrong with the baby. When Rob asked, 'Should it take this long?' I became even more worried.

'I don't think so,' I said, anxiously clutching my stomach as though to protect my unborn daughter. Several hours later and the doctor examined me again, his face concerned.

'We're going to have to perform a C section,' he said.

I'd read about caesareans, and I didn't want one.

'Do we have to?' I panted as another contraction took my breath away. 'It's dangerous for the baby, isn't it?'

'Your baby is in the breech position. The sooner we get her out, the better.'

I had to agree. What else could I have done? I abandoned my baby and put her life in their hands. I felt so guilty. I had let her down before she'd even been born. I should have been there to see her into the world. She needed my arms and not some strange nurse's. It wasn't at all what I'd planned. Rob held my hand as they took me down to the theatre.

'It's going to be okay, Mae,' he said.

I started to cry. I felt a sharp jab in my arm, and then I fell asleep. I was out of control.

Chapter Eighteen

Rob

Our daughter was born on a Monday morning. Twenty-four hours after Mae had started her contractions. Monday's child is full of grace. I knew immediately that was the name for our daughter. She was beautiful. No, she was beyond beautiful. As soon as I held her in my arms, I knew she was special. She was the most beautiful baby I had ever seen. Mae had been knackered and very upset about the caesarean. She couldn't stop going on about it. We had this beautiful baby, but she somehow felt the wonderful moment had been ruined by it. I thought she was making too much of it and should really have been enjoying the incredible moment of bringing a new life into the world. I had held my adorable daughter in my arms while Mae cried.

'What if there are complications from the caesarean?' she hiccupped.

Tears had rained down her face. It seemed an extreme reaction, and I'd put it down to a change in hormones. I told her that many women have caesareans, but that didn't help, and she just cried more.

'I wanted to give her a natural birth. You read all kinds of horrible things about caesarean births,' she cried.

I took her hand and said reassuringly, 'But she's perfect. So let's enjoy her.'

Mae snatched her hand away and said angrily, 'You never wanted her, remember? So I suppose you don't care if she's been damaged.'

The words stunned me. I'd never denied the pregnancy had been a shock. I hadn't been ready for a baby, but no way would I not have cared if she'd been damaged.

'That's a ridiculous thing to say, Mae. Of course, I care about her.'

She cried even more then, grabbing my hand and begging me to forgive her.

'I'm sorry, Rob. I just wanted everything to be perfect.'

'It is,' I told her.

She wiped her eyes and then said, 'We'll call her Blanche.'

I stared at her. What kind of name was that?'

'I thought we could name her Grace. Considering she was born on a Monday.'

Mae's eyes hardened.

'Mum's middle name was Grace,' she said.

'Even better,' I said.

'We can't name her Grace; it will remind me of Mum.'

I thought that was a good thing, a nice way to remember her mother, but Mae was adamant. It didn't seem fitting for my daughter. It was too harsh. She was a sweet, pretty baby and the name Grace was serene and calm.

'How about Grace Blanche,' I suggested knowing full well it sounded odd.

'Surely it's my right to name her after the awful pregnancy I've been through?'

So, I'd been manipulated again. If I had continued, she would undoubtedly have said how disinterested I had been and how alone she had felt throughout the pregnancy and that I had no right to choose our daughter's name. Maybe I should have been more attentive. I had tried.

'If that's what you want,' I sighed. 'It's an unusual name, that's all. You don't want her being bullied at school.'

But Mae wasn't listening. Instead, she put her arms out, and I handed the baby to her.

'Hopefully, she'll be okay,' she said. 'She seems fine.'

'Of course, she'll be okay.'

There must have been irritation in my voice because tears welled up in her eyes again.

'Don't worry,' I added gently.

It had felt strange, thinking of myself as a father. I'd felt unprepared and far too young. But I suppose there was never a good time, and it was done. I had to get on with it. If only we'd called her Grace.

Chapter Nineteen

August 2019: Stonesend

Kate

Bolting the bedroom door felt odd to Kate, and Dan couldn't get used to it and would often forget. He'd get up in the night, still half asleep, have a pee and leave the bolt off. It annoyed and unnerved Kate, even though she knew the front and back doors were securely locked. It took her ages to fall asleep. She considered taking the sleeping pills they had prescribed for her at the hospital, but she was frightened to take anything that might stop her memory from returning. So, she'd lie there in the silence that was more deafening than any noise and try to remember that afternoon. She used to love the peace and quiet of the village: no traffic sounds or half pissed young people rolling home after a night out. Life had been dramatically different since they'd left the city ten years ago. They'd felt secure in the knowledge that the crime rate in the country was low. But now ... If only she could remember.

Think, think.

Dan, collecting the boys in his football gear.

'Ready, lads,' he'd said. 'Ready to thrash the other side?'

She remembered thinking how handsome he was, from the depth of his eyes to the gentle expressions of his voice. She loved the way his voice quickened when he sparkled with a new idea. The problem was, he said pretty much the same thing to the boys every week, and he always wore his football gear. She could be remembering any Friday. She didn't remember the painting or waving them goodbye. Everything after that was blank until she woke up in the hospital. Sometimes, when she tried really hard, she could sense something hovering on the edge of her brain, almost within reach, but not quite. She'd forced herself to retrace her steps that day, concentrating hard on the walk home from school.

Had she met someone and stopped for a chat? Had she argued with someone? It was so unlikely as she never argued with anyone. She would have had Faith for a piano lesson that afternoon because she came every Friday. She would have prepared for that. It had been hot that day. She would have come home and most certainly taken a shower and then opened the back door. The police keep telling her it had to have been someone she knew. She must have let them in, but supposing she'd left the door open? They could have just walked in. It could have been anyone, she told them. She would have checked the piano books for Faith and then ... and then ... Some nights, her head throbbed unbearably from trying to remember. Alice, poor Alice, had found her sprawled on the kitchen floor. There had been blood everywhere. A terrible thing for her to see. Kate hadn't spoken to her since it happened. Once Kate wrote down the names of all the people she knew. Perhaps she'd upset someone without realising it, but she couldn't think of anyone who would want to hurt her. Everyone had been so kind since it happened. Mae popped round most days and often made meals for them. It had to have been a stranger. No one she or Dan knew would want to harm her.

During the day, she kept all the doors locked. It was stifling in the cottage, but she was too afraid to open them. It would be the school summer holidays in a week. Kate had hoped to return to work. Something to keep her mind off things. Beth phoned her every day. She'd start off polite, asking her how she was and then she'd ask if Kate had remembered anything. She so much wanted to tell her, yes, but she was starting to believe her memory would never come back.

The villagers had been devastated. The place where they had all felt so safe didn't feel such a haven anymore. Michael, the Church Warden, had taken to locking the church doors. He would never have considered that in the past. The locksmith had fitted new locks to people's back and front doors, and even when the weather was hot, Kate had taken to opening the fanlight windows only. It was a summer they'd never forget. Kate overheard Dan telling his mother what he would do to the bastard if he ever found out who he was. She now struggled to recall the weeks before the attack, but they were hazy too. Had she disagreed with someone? Disagreed enough, to the point that they would want to kill her?

Eventually, she would tire herself with her endless thoughts and drift into a dreamless sleep. Dreams had strangely stopped. If only this had been a dream. She'd give anything for that.

*

'They're suggesting a Crimewatch reconstruction,' said Beth. 'How do you feel about that?'

'Will we have to go on television?' asked Dan. 'I don't think that's a good idea. I don't want the boys upset all over again.'

'It'll be a reconstruction, using actors,' Beth assured them.

'It might jog someone's memory,' said Tom.

Kate bit her lip.

'I don't know,' she said doubtfully.

'It's up to you,' said Beth gently. 'You don't have to do anything you're not comfortable with.'

'It will put the village on the map, won't it?' said Dan.

'We don't have to use your real names,' Tom assured them. 'The idea is to jolt people's memory of that afternoon.'

Kate looked at Dan.

'I suppose it wouldn't hurt. If it leads to something ….'

'It's your decision Kate,' he said.

'What would you do?' she asked Beth.

Beth shifted in her seat.

'I'll be honest, I'm not keen on being spotlighted either, but we need to find the attacker. We should try everything.'

Kate nodded.

'Okay. Let's do it.'

'Tell us everything you can remember from that day so we can be as accurate as possible.' Tom said.

Kate was tired of repeating herself. The more she told her story, the less it felt like hers and more like someone else's. She supposed the police hoped if she recounted it enough times, something would jog her memory. Sometimes, she felt that she didn't want to remember. Sometimes, she felt that whatever happened that day was too horrible to face, and she didn't want to live with that memory.

Chapter Twenty

2005: Leeds

Rob

I suppose it was inevitable that Mae and Blanche would form a close bond. They were together all the time, whereas I was rarely at home. I started to feel shut out. I suppose it was my fault. I was at work too much. I jumped at every opportunity for overtime. Each time, I thought, 'no, it wouldn't be fair on Mae.' But my next thought would always be to hell with that. Did she think of my life when she stopped taking the pill?' I was convinced the pregnancy had been deliberate. Convinced that Mae hadn't thrown up the contraceptive pill at all and that she had deliberately not taken it. I started using condoms after that. Mae wasn't happy about it. She didn't say as much, but I could tell. I wasn't getting caught out a second time. I was riding a wave at work. Things were going really well. I'd had two pay rises in one year and a bonus. I wasn't candid with Mae about my salary or the bonuses. I was pissed that she hadn't put the house in joint names as she'd promised. I broached the subject once, and she'd just shrugged.

'I'll do it,' she'd said, but she never did.

I knew she had no intention of putting me on the deeds.

So, why should I have been honest when she hadn't been? She and Blanche had a special relationship that never included me. So, I never rushed home after work. There seemed little point. I took to visiting a wine bar that was close to the office. Mae had already got into the habit of eating dinner without me. Blanche was always in bed when I got home. I'd go up and read her a story while Mae got my dinner ready. Those were the only times I saw Blanche during the week. We had a relationship, but it wasn't a close one. After dinner, Mae would put the dishwasher on and then watch television while I worked in my study upstairs. She nearly always went to bed before me and would be asleep when I joined her. I knew she faked it sometimes, but I was too weary to care. Life had changed so much since Blanche was born. I suppose I hadn't been a great father, but I don't think Mae had helped much with that. She never trusted me when Blanche was a baby. I was never allowed to change her nappy in case I got it wrong. Whenever I held her, Mae would sit watching, her body tense and anxious as if afraid I would drop her. Eventually, I stopped trying to help and felt more trapped than ever. I was just the person who brought home the bacon. At least that's how it felt. I still loved Mae, but it was getting harder and harder to be close to her.

Blanche was five when the strain really began to show. Blanche started throwing up. Every time she ate something, she'd be sick.

'Perhaps you're overfeeding her,' I'd suggested.

It was a Saturday morning, and Blanche had thrown up again. Mae had cleaned Blanche up, and then they'd sat together reading a book. I had been shut out again.

'She's got a fever,' Mae had said worriedly. 'I think we should call the doctor.'

I'd felt Blanche's head. It had felt cool to me.

'She's not that hot,' I'd said, trying to keep some perspective. 'She's just getting over the vomiting, that's all.'

'It's more than that,' Mae had said anxiously, feeling Blanche's forehead.

'Children get temperatures,' I'd said. 'It's nothing to worry about.'

Mae's lips had tightened in that way I had come to know so well.

'For Christ's sake,' she'd snapped. 'Can't you take anything seriously?'

I'd walked out of the room. I was tired of being got it. Mae would later say that she hadn't been getting at me. It was just me feeling guilty and that I should have stayed and supported her, but I was tired of the vomiting, the anxiety and the crying. So I went for a walk and ended up at the wine bar. I only had one beer, but Mae said later that it was embarrassing that the alcohol could be smelt on my breath. By the time I got back, there was an ambulance outside the house. Blanche had had a fit shortly after I'd left. Where was I when she most needed me, Mae had demanded. Then she'd smelt the beer on my breath and had given me a cold look of disgust.

'That's so irresponsible,' she'd said. I'd watched the ambulance drive away. I could have followed, but I chose not to. Blanche stayed in the hospital for twenty-four hours. Mae sat with her. I went to the wine bar and got drunk. After all, what was the point of us both being at the hospital? I'd only be made to feel guilty, and I couldn't stand that.

It was that night that I met Jo.

Chapter Twenty-One

August 2019: Stonesend

Beth looked down at her hands. They were shaking. She hadn't expected the whole village to be out.

'It's good,' Tom said. 'The more memories, the better.'

The actress playing Kate looked uncannily like her that for a moment Beth thought it was her.

'You okay?' Tom asked.

'Of course,' Beth said defensively.

The actress, whose name was Lorraine, waited for her direction at the school doors. The actor playing Dan stubbed out his cigarette and stood waiting with two small boys. They looked far too young to be actors.

'Quiet everyone, we're about to shoot the scene.'

The chatter died down and everyone watched expectantly. Beth clenched her fists.

'Action,' called the director.

It was surreal watching a Kate lookalike take a painting from one of the boys and then walk to the Marshalls house with half the village following her.

'Is that okay?' she asked the director. 'People following her?'

'They'll be out of shot,' he smiled.

'I don't remember Jack giving me that picture,' said Kate, who was standing beside her.

'Don't worry,' said Beth, squeezing her hand.

Jack, the landlord, waved from the doors of the pub. He'd offered to put together a lunch for after the filming. Beth found herself wondering if the attacker was there. She watched everyone closely for something, anything, that would lead them to the person who had entered Kate's cottage that afternoon,

The re-enactment at Kate's house was very tense, and Beth noted that Alice was not around to watch the scene. Beth was tenser than a stretched elastic band. She tried some deep breathing techniques, but they didn't help. She thought of the tranquillizers in her bag and fought the desire to take one. Finally, it was her turn to face the camera. In the end, it was easier than she'd imagined.

'If anyone remembers anything, we'd ask them to contact the police. Even the smallest thing could help us. This is a quiet, peaceful village, and crime is extremely low here. This attack took place late afternoon, early evening, and we believe someone must have seen something. We urge people to come forward and help us find the person responsible for this horrific attack. You can contact us anonymously. Please help us find the person responsible. Thank you.'

'Are you concerned the attacker could strike again?' asked the interviewer.

Beth looked over to where Tom was standing. He shook his head.

'No, we think this was an isolated incident.'

She hated herself for wondering how she looked. This wasn't about her, for Christ's sake. She'd done her best to cover the circles under her eyes, but she was bloody useless with make-up, always had been.

Then, it was over. All they had to do now was wait for the phone calls. The cameras were packed away, the street swept, hands were shaken, and then everyone made their way to the pub.

'Well done,' Tom said, approaching her. 'You did well.'

'Don't ever do that to me again,' she hissed. 'If you want a Crimewatch reconstruction, next time you do it. I only did this for Kate.'

'Well done,' said Chief Superintendent Lewis, joining them.

'Oh, for God's sake,' she grumbled and went into the pub.

'Alright, Beth?' called Jack 'Well ...'

'Don't you bloody say *well done*,' she said crossly.

'What are you having, Beth?' said Dan. 'It's on me.'

'I could do with a whisky, but I'm on duty, so it's a diet coke.'

'I'll drop your food order round later,' called Nat 'On the house this time. I'll throw in an extra pork chop too.'

Tom nodded to a table, and Beth followed him and the chief.

'Do you often get given things on the house?' Tom asked.

Beth looked at him in surprise.

'What?'

'Could be misconstrued.'

'Are you joking?'

'Seen as a bribe.'

'This is a village community. It's how people show their gratitude. It's only a drink and a couple of pork chops.'

'Don't accept anymore.'

She rolled her eyes.

'Sir?' she said, looking at the chief.

'Tom's right, Beth.'

'It's two bloody pork chops,' she said. 'I'd expect Sirloin steak if it was a bribe and a double whisky, not a bloody diet coke.'

'Puts you in a difficult position,' explained Tom.

'Jesus,' she cursed and then grimaced as Reverend Scott walked past them. He approached Kate and chatted to her and Dan.

'He's hiding something,' said Tom suspiciously.

'What, Anthony?' said Beth surprised.

'He knows more than he's letting on.'

Beth followed Tom's eyes to Anthony, who was in deep conversation with Kate.

'No,' she said disbelievingly.

Tom narrowed his eyes.

'How well do you know him?'

'As well as anyone in the village.'

'I think Kate confided in him. When I asked, he clammed up.'

'You don't think he's the attacker, do you?' she asked, surprised.

He sighed.

'No, but those phone calls indicate she shared something with him. It could be connected.'

Kate saw Beth looking at them and stood up. She and Dan walked to the door.

'Thanks, Beth. I hope it helps,' she said, hugging her.

'I'm sure it will,' said Beth. 'Aren't you staying for lunch?'

'Mae has asked us for lunch. She didn't want to bring Blanche to the reconstruction. Mae thought it would set off Blanche's anxiety.'

'Thank you for agreeing to this,' said Tom. 'Did it trigger anything?'

'I'm afraid it didn't,' said Dan.

Tom eyes flickered to Dan and then to Kate.

'Well, if you do remember anything, Kate, don't hesitate to contact either DS Harper or me.'

'Let's hope it has helped.'

'I'm sure it has,' smiled Beth, while deep down feeling sure it hadn't.

Chapter Twenty-Two

2005: Leeds

Mae

Doctor Adams said Blanche had allergies, and that was why she kept throwing up. The scan had shown no reason for the fit.

'She starts school soon,' I told him. 'What if she has a fit there?'

'She's had all the tests,' he said. 'I don't see why she should have any more fits. It was most likely due to the temperature. It's not unusual for a child of her age.'

I wasn't convinced and took her to see another doctor who gave us medication should it ever happen again.

'A mild form of epilepsy,' Doctor Morris said.

'There were complications at her birth,' I told him.

'Most likely the cause,' he said.

He seemed far more interested in Blanche's symptoms, so I stopped seeing Doctor Adams and changed to Doctor Morris.

'Eliminate things from her diet one by one.' He advised. 'Allergies could be causing it too. It's the only way. That way, you may discover what she is allergic to.'

It was hard work. First, I cut out eggs, but still, Blanche was sick. Then I took milk out of her diet. This went on for weeks until we discovered that Blanche had a wheat allergy. Shortly after taking wheat out of her diet, Blanche stopped being sick. But just weeks later, she broke out in a horrible rash, and we had to start all over again. I changed the washing powder, and it stopped. Just as I thought we had everything beaten, Blanche had a severe asthma attack. I couldn't get hold of Rob and went into a massive panic and in desperation phoned Liz, who was marvellous. She rushed us to A&E. I called Rob and left a message. As soon as he read it, he hurried to join us. Blanche was stable by then. He looked at her disbelievingly.

'She seems fine,' he said, looking at me accusingly.

'She is now,' I said. 'Thanks to Liz.'

Which, when translated, meant, *With no thanks to you*.

'Just a coughing fit probably,' he scoffed. 'You overreact.'

I could have slapped him. I wondered if he'd been with his girlfriend when I phoned. It had been lunchtime. Perhaps they'd been having a cosy meal together. I'd known about her for some time. Rob had been working late more often. Sometimes at night, he'd creep out of bed when he thought I was asleep and sneak into the bathroom, where I'd hear him talking on his mobile. One night as Rob lay snoring next to me, it bleeped. The screen had lit up, so I could clearly read the notification, *Sweet dreams xx*.

That was the night the gin started. We'd always had a small amount of alcohol in the house for when people came over. I thought a small glass of gin and tonic would help me sleep. I never imagined it would become a habit. As things became more and more strained between us, the more difficult I found it was to sleep. It wasn't like I drank during the day. I didn't consider I had a problem.

In the morning, I mentioned to Rob that his phone had woken me.

'Sorry about that,' he'd said, the lies rolling quickly off his tongue. 'It was my boss, Neil. He wanted me to bring some papers in with me this morning.'

He'd lied. I'd seen it in his eyes.

When Liz had suggested that Blanche and I might like to attend church with her, I quickly said yes.

'You'll get a lot of support there,' she'd said.

The Reverend Michael put us in touch with so many good people. I finally had friends that cared and understood. Everyone told me how well I was doing with Blanche. No one said I was overreacting. I felt supported and appreciated. Doctor Morris, one of the congregants, asked if I would talk at a local support group that his wife ran. So, I did, and they paid me £50. I enjoyed it. Blanche came with me, and we talked about how we coped with her allergies. I didn't expect to get paid for it, so it was a pleasant surprise. They also gave us a large basket of fruit. After that, I looked online for more groups where I could speak about our experiences. I did a talk for the WI on asthma. Again, they paid me £50 and gave Blanche a book voucher. Rob never commented on my talks or even asked how they went. Too taken up with his girlfriend, I suppose. It had been on my mind to put his name on the house's deeds, but I then decided not to. Supposing he left us for this woman? He'd want me to sell the house so he could get his share. I'd never be able to buy something decent for Blanche and me, and I was determined that we would

The Lies She Told

never live in a flat. If Rob thought he was going to share half of my inheritance with his slutty girlfriend, then he could think again. We somehow got into a routine. Blanche started school, but because of her health problems, she only went twice a week. I homeschooled her the rest of the time. They were the best times when Blanche and I were together. I stopped telling Rob about her health issues. He wasn't really interested. I took responsibility for medicating her. In the beginning, I felt resentful, but as time passed, I found I didn't care if Rob came home late. Then Doctor Morris told me about the vacancy at his clinic for a health assistant. He knew of my nursing training and asked if I would be interested. He was flexible, he said, and I could work the hours around the time Blanche went to school. It was perfect. A chance for me to put my nursing skills into practice again and to earn my own money. I accepted the job, and that day I moved my stuff out of our bedroom and into the spare room next to Blanche's. When Rob came home that evening, I was reading in bed. I shall never forget that night. I saw a different Rob to the man I had married. A frightening monster of a man.

Chapter Twenty-Three

August 2019: Stonesend

Kate

Mae suggested they go to the park. Kate was uncertain. The only time she had left the house since the attack had been for the Crimewatch reconstruction.

'It's a nice day,' Mae had said. 'Not too hot. It will do you good to get some fresh air.'

Kate had finally agreed. She couldn't shut herself away in the house every time Dan went to work.

'It will do you good,' Dan had said when she'd phoned him.

She knew that she needed to get out. She was grateful it was the school holidays. She wasn't ready to return to school yet. The noise and chatter would set off her headaches. But she needed to get her confidence back.

'After the summer break,' the head had said, 'We don't expect you before then.'

'Give yourself time.' Dan had said.

The headaches, when they came, were debilitating. The bad ones only came occasionally, but the constant ache had become part of her life, as had swallowing painkillers. It was part of her routine. She now had a whole new norm.

'We can have a picnic,' Mae had suggested.

Kate felt vulnerable when alone. Strange to think that not long ago, she would have preferred to have been alone. She'd never been a great socialiser. Dan had always been better at that than her. She used to like her own company. Now being on her own frightened her. She'd been alone when it had happened. If someone else had been home with her, would it not have happened? Would she have been saved? She often used to walk in their beautiful village. She'd always felt completely safe. Now she felt nervous and edgy.

It was warm in the sun, and they found a nice sheltered area so Blanche could enjoy it too without being in direct sunlight. Some of her medications reacted against the sun causing unsightly pigmentation. Kate thought Blanche looked tired. Her eyes were red, and her skin sallow. The cancer treatment was taking its toll, Mae said. Blanche looked worse than ever. Kate noticed a blue tinge around one of her eyes.

'What did you do to your eye?' Kate asked.

'I think she must have rubbed it,' said Mae, stroking Blanche's arm. 'The medication seems to make her bruise easy.'

'What do the doctors say?' Kate asked.

'It's the side effect of treatment. There's not much they can do,' said Mae, hugging Blanche. 'Did the reconstruction help? Has anyone come forward?'

'I don't think so. Beth hasn't mentioned anything?'

'Don't think about it,' said Mae, trying to reassure her. 'Did I tell you about our fabulous donation for Blanche's birthday?' she said, her face lighting up. 'I'm sure I did tell you.'

'That's wonderful. You most likely did. I expect I forgot.'

She'd forgotten so many things. Her memory had been severely affected. It wasn't just the attack that she couldn't recall.

She forgot simple things, like her mobile number and Dan's work number. She used to know them off by heart. Sometimes she would even forget to cook dinner. How could she possibly be expected to remember the person that attacked her?

'We've been offered a free holiday to Disneyland,' said Mae excitedly.

'Oh, Blanche,' Kate said, genuinely happy for her. 'That's wonderful.'

Blanche smiled. Her lips were dry and cracked.

'Yes, I'm very excited.'

Kate couldn't help thinking that Blanche was a bit old for Disneyland, but many adults enjoyed it again.

'When are you going?' she asked, thinking that with them gone, it would be one less person to see.

'Just before Christmas. Can you imagine? It will be magical that time of year,' said Mae. 'Blanche will love it.'

Blanche was looking longingly at Kate's bar of chocolate, and Kate felt a stab of guilt. She'd forgotten all about Blanche's allergies. She was usually very good at remembering those and would never bring anything to tempt her. She tucked the chocolate back into her bag and said, 'I much prefer your homemade vegan chocolate.'

Blanche looked at her disbelievingly. 'I know you don't', the look said, 'but thanks for being so nice.'

Kate suddenly felt sad for both of them. There was a good chance she, Kate, would get better, at least that's what the doctors said. Blanche would never get better. If anything, she would only get worse. She faced a lifetime of suffering and self-denial. Kate knew Mae blamed herself.

'It was the caesarean,' she'd told Kate. 'There were complications when Blanche went into the breech position. They left her that way for too long. If they'd turned her, she wouldn't have had epilepsy.'

Mae had moved to the village two years after Kate and Dan when Blanche had been eleven. The two women had immediately become good friends. Jack was then two, and Kate was expecting Ryan. She'd been hoping the second one would be a girl. She and Dan had agreed they would have two children. It was what they could comfortably afford, and it meant they would want for nothing. Kate saw Blanche as the daughter she'd never have. Some of the villagers were uncomfortable with Blanche. Kate could sense that when she and Jack went to church with them. Sickness makes people uncomfortable. Blanche had always been brave. Mae was a wonderful mother, and Kate helped her with the homeschooling of Blanche. If Mae had one of her debilitating headaches, Kate would take Blanche home to have dinner with them. That was always a challenge for Kate, as Blanche had so many allergies that she could only give her boiled carrots and potato. Then she would feel terribly guilty at not cooking something nicer, but she didn't want Blanche to have an asthma attack or a fit.

Dan wasn't religious at all. Kate wasn't, not really, but she found the services calming, and it was a way to socialise. Mae was a devoted Christian and never missed church. Reverend Scott took them under his wing, and several charities were set up to help Blanche. Mae told Kate that she had given talks about life with a sick child. Kate told Reverend Scott, and he arranged for Mae to give a talk in the village hall. The following week it was featured in the local paper, and lots of people feeling sympathy for Blanche sent letters and soft toys. Mae was interviewed for a woman's magazine, and she and Blanche were offered a food basket every month from one of the big supermarkets. Suddenly, Stonesend had a celebrity in their village, and everyone felt like they were involved in helping Blanche.

Six months ago, Mae had broken down at Ryan's birthday party and announced that Blanche had leukaemia. Everyone had been shocked. How could this happen? Hadn't Blanche suffered enough? It

The Lies She Told

was so unfair. Kate had felt sorry for them both, but beneath her empathy, there was simmering anger. Anger that Mae should choose Ryan's day to break the news. It was as if she and Blanche had to be the centre of attention. As though Mae couldn't bear anyone else being in the limelight. She'd then felt guilty. Both her children were healthy. She shouldn't begrudge Mae the opportunity to unburden herself.

'I just don't feel we're getting the right treatment,' Mae had said. She'd been devastated and even missed church one Sunday because she was too distressed to attend.

'It's so hard,' she'd said.

'It shouldn't be this difficult,' Kate had said.

'There's a specialist, but we could never afford it,' Mae had confided.

Kate had mentioned Blanche's father then for the first time. She knew from some of the things Mae had let slip that he had been absent for most of Blanche's life.

'Would Blanche's father help, financially, I mean?'

Mae's lips had tightened.

'I'd never ask him for anything,' she'd said, her tone hardening. 'Blanche and I have survived this far without him, and we'll continue to do so. Besides, he doesn't have anything to offer us.'

The Parish Council had a meeting, and it was decided that they would hold a fete, and the proceeds from the fete would go towards Blanche's treatment. On Blanche's good days, she helped make the posters. The money raised was enough that Blanche could be seen by the private specialist. Her treatment changed, and she went into remission. Kate and Dan had a little party in their garden to celebrate. When Kate thought about the party now, it was just a vague memory, just like all her memories. Every memory was a struggle, hazy at first and then slowly emerging through the fog. Except for that day. The day of the attack. That day she couldn't seem to get through the mist at all.

Kate sat next to Blanche and they shared the vegan chocolate. Mae opened her large rucksack and produced Blanche's medications. Blanche took them without complaint and then asked Kate if she'd ever been to Disneyland. Kate shook her head. She took the painkillers from her bag and swallowed two.

'No, I've never been. You'll have to take lots of photos.'

'Are you still getting the headaches?' asked Mae, concerned.

'Pretty much every day. Some days it's severe, but most days, I can cope. It's my memory that's the worst.'

'What does the doctor say?' asked Mae.

'He doesn't think the memory will return. He's seen cases like this. A flood of adrenaline stops the brain's ability to store memories. He thinks it's a blessing in disguise. It's a struggle trying to remember anything,' she said and realised she was complaining. Her suffering was nothing compared to Blanche's.

'That's horrible,' said Blanche, reaching across her wheelchair to take Kate's hand. It almost brought Kate to tears that this lovely girl, suffering so much, was thinking of Kate's pain. She was so empathetic. She has an extraordinary insight for her age, thought Kate.

'I wish you could come to Disneyland with us,' Blanche said wistfully.

'It's a family ticket from a charity. I am sure you could come if we said you were Blanche's carer,' added Mae.

Kate smiled. 'A break would do me good.'

Dan had suggested a holiday.

'Mum and Dad could have the kids. We could go, just the two of us.'

She'd said she would think about it. She'd started feeling insecure in the village that she knew really well. She couldn't imagine how she would be in a strange place, even if Dan were with her. She'd miss the kids and worry about them. She'd become increasingly anxious since the attack.

'It will get better,' Dan had assured her.

He didn't know that, not for sure. Kate needed to remember. She knew that. She needed to remember so the person who did this would never do it to someone else.

'You could,' said Mae. 'It would be lovely to have you with us.'

Kate sighed.

'I'd love to, but I just don't think I'm confident enough.'

Blanche handed her more chocolate before indulging herself. Mae shook her head and gently removed the container from Blanche's hands.

'You shouldn't have too much, Blanche,' she said quietly.

Kate looked around. The park was busy now, with people enjoying the sunshine during their lunch break. It could have been any one of these people that had come into her home. She could cope with the thought that a stranger had attacked her. It was incomprehensible to her that it could have been someone she knew.

'A burglar would have taken something,' Beth had said, using her words carefully. 'Your handbag was on the chair.'

They'd questioned her friends, work colleagues and even the parents of the children she taught. DI Miller had queried if a parent had had an issue with her. But surely no problem was that big that would warrant a parent trying to murder a teacher.

'Perhaps it was a case of mistaken identity,' Kate had said.

Kate had been clinging to this idea of late. It made the most sense to her. Perhaps the murderer had got the wrong house, and it most likely hadn't been her they had wanted at all.

'It's possible,' Beth had agreed.

But Kate somehow felt Beth didn't really believe that.

'Do you want to head back?' Mae asked.

'No, I'm fine, really,' she said.

Mae laid her hand on Kate's.

'It will get better, Kate, I'm sure it will. Perhaps you should stop trying to remember. It's most likely stressing you.'

'Yes, you're probably right.'

Perhaps the headaches would get better in time but would the anxiety ever leave her? If it had been a mistaken identity case, who had they really wanted, and why had there been no further attacks? Had it been her they'd wanted after all? Kate shivered at the thought. The air seemed to turn cold suddenly.

'Maybe we should get back,' she said.

Chapter Twenty-Four

Kath Martin was having a cigarette break outside the Coop when Beth left the station and headed towards the store.

'Alright, Beth?' she said, blowing smoke out of the corner of her mouth.

'I've been sent to buy doughnuts,' Beth smiled.

'We've got plenty of them,' said Kath.

She waited until Beth had entered the store and then crushed the half-smoked cigarette under her foot before hurrying to the police station.

'Hello there Kath, everything alright?' asked Owen Smith, the on-duty desk sergeant. Kath had known Owen since he was a kid. He'd gone to school with her Darren.

'I'd like to speak with the person in charge of the Kate Marshall case,' she said.

'Is it something I can help with?'

'No.'

She looked anxiously at her watch.

'I don't have long. Is he here?'

'Just a tick,' said Owen, picking up the phone.

'Someone to see you, Sir. Mrs Katherine Martin. It's about the Kate Marshall attack.'

Kath waited impatiently.

'Yes, sir,' said Owen.

He replaced the receiver.

'He's on his way.'

Kath looked nervously at the doors. She didn't want Beth to see her here.

'Katherine Martin?'

Kath jumped at the sound of her name.

'Would you like to come through,' Tom said.

Kath appraised the good-looking man in front of her.

'It's confidential, isn't it? What I tell you?'

'Of course,' smiled Tom.

She followed him through a door and into an air-conditioned room.

Tom motioned to a chair, but Kath shook her head. She had no intention of staying long.

'You have some information regarding the attack on Kate Marshall?' he said without preamble.

Kath bit her lip nervously.

'It came to me after I saw the reconstruction,' she said.

'What came to you?'

'I was out walking my dog that evening. I suppose it was about five when we set off. I usually walk through the village, along Churchfields and sometimes over the field. I saw him hanging around Churchfields. Not at Kate's place. At the end of the road. He was sort of pacing up and down. I don't think he saw me. I didn't speak to him. I was surprised to see him, to be honest.'

'Surprised to see who?' asked Tom, fighting down his impatience.

'He won't know it was me that told you, will he? Only I don't want to get anyone into trouble.'

'It's your duty to help with our enquiries. I assure you he won't know who informed us. Who was it you saw Katherine?'

Kath bit her lip. It was her duty, and if he had nothing to do with it, then it would be okay. He'd be able to say why he was there.

'Ben Harper,' she said.

Kath saw the name register immediately with the detective.

'Beth Harper's husband,' she confirmed.

Tom pulled a notebook from his pocket.

'Sit down, Katherine. Would you like a cup of tea or coffee?' he offered.

'I have to get back,' she said urgently. 'I'm on my break.'

'I won't keep you too long. Are you sure you saw Ben Harper?'

She nodded emphatically.

'Oh yes. I remember being surprised because I hadn't seen him in months, not since they broke up.'

'You're quite certain it was him?'

'Oh yes.'

'And he was in Churchfields?'

'I remember wondering why he was there. Beth lives two roads up. It's not far from Churchfields, I suppose. It's just I remember he walked up and down the road and looked worried; you know?'

'Did you speak to him?'

'No, I don't think he saw me.'

'This was about quarter past five, you said?'

'Somewhere around there.'

'Did you see him on the way back?'

'No.'

'What time do you think you walked back along Churchfields?'

She frowned.

'I can't be sure. Just before six, I imagine.'

'You didn't see Alice Tobias?'

'Not that I remember.'

She stood up.

'I really have to get back to work.'

'Of course.'

He opened the door for her. Kath stopped abruptly at the sight of Beth. In her hand were two bags of doughnuts.

'Everything alright, Kath?' Beth asked, looking concerned.

'Oh yeah. I just had a question.' She struggled not to meet Beth's eyes and hurried past her.

'See ya,' she said.

Beth looked at Tom questioningly.

'What was all that about?'

He nodded to the doughnuts.

'You'd better give those out before we have a riot on our hands.'

She offered one of the bags to him.

'Jam or custard?' she smiled.

He grimaced.

'I can't eat that junk.'

Beth sighed.

'Right, more for us then.'

'A word when you've done that.'

Beth looked at him curiously before saying, 'Sure.'

Chapter Twenty-Five

Kate

Kate pushed Blanche's wheelchair as they walked home. It made her feel secure, having that bit of support.

Mae wanted to pop into the supermarket, so Blanche and Kate waited outside.

'I won't be long,' she promised.

'We'll be fine, won't we?' Kate said, glancing down at Blanche. Blanche's head was covered in a bobbly hat that Kate had knitted. That way, no one could see the hair she had lost. Being with Blanche put everything into perspective for Kate. Things could have been so much worse, she told herself. She could have been brain-damaged and in a wheelchair just like Blanche. Or even on life-support. She shuddered at the thought. She'd recovered. Headaches and memory loss were something she could live with.

'I like you in that hat,' said Kate.

'I like yours too,' smiled Blanche.

Both of us wearing hats to cover what we don't want others to see, thought Kate sadly.

'Can I come to your house later?' asked Blanche.

'Of course.'

Blanche rubbed at her eyes.

'Are you okay, Blanche?' Kate asked.

Blanche turned her head to look at her.

'Yes, thank you, Kate. Are you okay?'

Her selflessness brought tears to Kate's eyes. She smiled and stroked Blanche's head and then quickly pulled away. Blanche didn't like being treated as the victim, Kate reminded herself. Then, suddenly, there was a glimpse of a memory. It took her totally by surprise. It was as if someone had flashed a photograph in front of her and then snatched it away again. She heard someone say, 'Aw, Kate.' And then slightly louder 'Kate!' Anxious, fearful. Who? Who said it? She tried to grasp the memory, to grab the photograph and bring it back into focus. That snapshot of a moment, where did it go?

'Hello,' said a shy voice.

Kate pulled her attention back to the present to see Alice Tobias standing in front of her. Kate hadn't been aware of her approaching. Alice looked uncomfortable. It was only the second time Kate had seen her since the attack. The first had been from a distance during the reconstruction.

'Hi, how are you?' Kate said casually.

Alice would always be a reminder of that day. It was something neither of them would ever forget. Alice looked at Blanche as she spoke,

'I've meant to pop round.'

'Don't worry.'

Alice fiddled with her hair.

'I've had a bit of post-traumatic stress,' she explained.

Kate touched her arm.

'I'm so sorry. It must have been dreadful for you.'

'Worse for you, Kate,' blurted Blanche.

'Oh, I …' stuttered Alice.

'I understand,' Kate said. 'Truly I do.'

'Well …' Alice faltered.

'Is Faith coming for her piano lesson on Friday?'

It would be her first lesson since it happened.

'If that's okay,' said Alice uncertainly. 'If you're sure it won't be too much.'

'Of course. We all need to get back to normal.'

'Yes, absolutely.'

She seemed to relax a bit.

'Are you feeling better?' she asked as if Kate was just recovering from a cold.

'I'm getting there. The doctors say it will take a while. I still don't remember anything.'

'I'm always bloody late. Maybe if we'd been on time …' Alice trailed off.

Thankfully Mae joined them then and saved Kate from answering. Her arms were loaded with shopping bags.

'I only went in for one thing,' she laughed.

Alice smiled and said, 'See you on Friday then, Kate.'

Kate nodded, and they watched her hurry away.

'We're in the local paper,' said Mae, handing it to Blanche. 'It's about our holiday to Disneyland. I got one for you, Kate.'

Kate tucked the newspaper into her handbag to read later.

'How was Alice?' asked Mae.

'Fine,' said Kate. 'I guess I'm a bad memory for her.'

'It wasn't your fault.'

Blanche shivered, and Mae pulled a blanket from the back of the wheelchair and threw it over her legs.

'It's getting a bit chilly,' Mae said.

Kate's heart went out to her. It must be so difficult coping with Blanche all on her own. She couldn't have done it. She found the boys hard work, and they were fit and able. At least she had Dan. Mae rarely talked about her ex.

'He would drink,' she once said. 'He was jealous of Blanche. Always had been.'

After that, from the odd occasion that she did mention him, Kate got the impression that he had hit Mae. She and Dan had offered their support wherever they could. Kate thought Mae was a wonderful mother, patient and selfless.

She knew the offer to go with them to Disneyland was self-motivated. Mae, no doubt, hoped she would get a break. But Kate wasn't as selfless, and she was afraid. That was why it was so important to her to remember. She needed to know who she was scared of.

Chapter Twenty-Six

'You wanted a word?' said Beth. Something in Miller's expression made her nervous.

'Two doughnuts over,' she said lightly. 'I hope you're not going to make me eat both.'

His expression didn't change.

'Christ, it's only a sodding doughnut,' she said. 'It won't kill you.'

'We've had some feedback on the reconstruction,' he said.

Beth sat down and put the plate of doughnuts on the table.

'Great. What is it?'

Tom flexed his shoulders and said, 'Did you see your ex on Friday evening?'

Beth reeled back. Of all the things she had imagined he would say, she hadn't been expecting that. She looked at him, puzzlement etched across her face.

'What?'

'Did your ex visit you on the night of the attack?'

She frowned.

'No, he didn't. I went out. It was my sister's birthday, so we went to the pub for a meal. What's this about? What's Ben got to do with anything?'

'Someone saw him in Churchfields between five and six on Friday evening.'

'What?' She shook her head in disbelief. 'No, they must have seen someone else. It wasn't Ben. He lives in Swindon.'

Tom was silent. Beth stared at him wide-eyed.

'Christ, you think my ex attacked Kate? Why would he? We were friends, I told you.'

'If he didn't visit you that night, what other reason would he have for being in Stonesend that evening?'

Beth scraped her chair back and stood up.

'I don't know. I'm not his keeper. Perhaps he was visiting someone in the village. He has friends here.'

'We have to follow it up, Beth.'

'Who saw him?'

'They asked me not to say.'

'It was Kath, wasn't it? She's a gossip. Everyone knows that.'

'Would you prefer not to be there when I question him?' he asked gently.

'What, in case my emotions get in the way of the job?' she said crossly.

'I never said that.'

'But that's what you meant. No, I want to be there.'

She couldn't believe that Ben had been in Churchfields on the night of Kate's attack. It couldn't have been him. Kath must surely have been mistaken.

'Do you have his address?'

She shook her head.

'We're separated. I only know he lives in Swindon.'

'I'll get the address, and we'll leave at four this afternoon.'

'Right,' said Beth. 'I'll finish my paperwork.'

She left his office, the doughnuts still uneaten on his desk. Tom sat down heavily and combed his fingers through his hair and wondered what the hell the connection could be between Kate and Ben Harper. He pulled himself up out of the chair and walked out into the busy main office. The clatter of keyboards and ringing phones greeted him. No one looked up.

'Just popping out,' he said to Beth as he passed. 'You forgot these,' he added, dropping the doughnuts onto her desk.

'Thanks,' she said.

He wanted to say something, words that would comfort her. But he didn't know what they were, so he left without saying anything.

Chapter Twenty-Seven

Kate was in the garden when the doorbell rang. She heard the faint tinkle, and her body froze. She wasn't expecting anyone and her heart began to hammer in her chest. She pulled off her gardening gloves and went into the cottage, locking the back door behind her. Through the front door peephole, she saw it was Detective Inspector Miller.

'Just a moment,' she said, unlocking the door and shooting the bolts back.

'We have a few extra locks,' she apologised when she finally opened the door.

'It's just a quick word,' he smiled.

'I'm probably neurotic,' she explained. 'But the days I'm on my own, I get nervous. The kids break up soon, so … Sorry I'm waffling.'

He smiled again.

'Come into the kitchen,' she said, leading the way. 'Would you like a cup of tea?'

'No thanks. I just have a couple of questions. How well do you know Ben Harper?' he said, coming straight to the point.

'Ben?' she said, looking surprised. 'Well, we knew him very well. He was married to Beth.'

He nodded.

'Yes, I suppose you know that,' she smiled.

'When did you last see him?'

She chewed her lip thoughtfully.

'Gosh, I can't remember exactly. It was just before they broke up. That's been almost six months. I think it was the last Sunday lunch we had together.'

'You haven't seen him since?'

She shook her head.

'No, why are you asking?'

'Routine. Was there any bad feeling between you after they broke up?'

Kate shrugged.

'It wasn't really our business, but I felt for Beth. She really went through it. Has something happened to Ben?' she asked anxiously.

'Ben Harper was seen in Churchfields the evening you were attacked. I wondered if he visited you.'

'Ben was in Stonesend?' she said, surprised. 'No, I didn't see him. He probably came to visit Beth.'

Tom sniffed the air.

'Something smells good,' he said, changing the subject.

'I made an apple pie.'

'I love apple pie,' he smiled. 'Before I go, we had a look at your phone records. We were looking for hang-ups, something odd. I noticed the vicar phoned you several times. He's quite discreet about it.'

He watched her face closely. Saw the redness rise in her cheeks.

'I ... I don't remember those calls,' she said, but the slight tremble in her voice and the way she averted her eyes told Tom she did remember them.

'Okay, thanks. I'll leave you in peace.'

He left Kate Marshall and headed back to the station. What was Kate hiding? He'd get Beth to talk to her, woman to woman. That usually worked.

He wasn't sure it was a good idea for Beth to accompany him to Swindon. He hoped she would keep it together. He found himself curious about what Ben Harper looked like and even more interested in knowing why he was in Stonesend on that Friday afternoon.

*

Beth was quiet for the entire journey. When Tom told her Ben had been in Churchfields that Friday afternoon, she had racked her brains as to why.

Tom turned the car into a busy street and drove to the end, where ahead of them sat a block of flats. He stopped the car and nodded at the building.

'This is it?' she said, surprised.

Beth stared at the large high rise. For some reason, she thought they lived in a house. It wasn't even in a nice area. Ben wouldn't have chosen this.

'No 36,' said Tom.

'You've been looking into him,' she said. 'He doesn't have a record, you know.'

'I know.'

She looked back at the building.

'Ben hates flats,' she said, glancing over at the boys playing football outside the entrance.

Of course, the cottage in Stonesend had been hers. Left to her by her grandmother. They hadn't battled over that. He'd taken the better car. She'd just presumed he'd buy a house with the inheritance from his mother.

She licked her dry lips.

'Before we go in, there's something I want to tell you,' she said.

Tom stopped, his hand on the door handle.

'I know he left you for someone else.'

She shook her head.

'God, is nothing sacred in the village? Who told you?'

'The chief, the night we had dinner there. He told me before you arrived.'

'What I'm going to tell you, he doesn't know, and I'd prefer it stayed that way. It's personal. I'd be grateful if you didn't tell anyone else,' she added.

She didn't want to share this. Not with someone she barely knew, but what choice did she have?

'I won't.' he said, turning to face her.

'It's just if they're both home, I don't want your surprise to show.'

Tom raised his eyebrows.

'Sounds ominous.'

Just say it, she told herself. Get it over with.

'Ben didn't leave me for another woman like everyone thinks. He left me for a man.'

Tom fought back his surprise.

'I'm sorry.'

Beth bit her lip to control her tears.

'It was a shock,' she said, nodding. 'He'd hidden it really well. I had no idea. His mother had just died, and it freed him, he said. He had planned to live a lie for years to protect her. He knew it would have killed her if she'd found out. She wouldn't have understood. He told me straight after the funeral.'

She didn't know why she was sharing so much with Tom but saying it to someone else filled her with relief. Her body felt as though it had just been released from chains.

She remembered that day like it was yesterday. Ben had been distracted during the funeral service, and she'd put it down to the shock. Laura had collapsed two weeks earlier with a massive coronary. She'd died immediately, and Ben had been devastated. The night of the funeral, they'd ordered pizza. Neither of them had been able to eat anything at the wake. It was over their Americano that he'd told her he loved someone else. He'd been prepared to live a lie for as long as his mother was alive. It seemed Beth had always been on borrowed time. He loved her, he'd said, but differently. He could now 'unshackle', he'd said. It was the word 'unshackle' that had tipped her over, as though being with her had been like living in prison. She'd screamed abuse at him, called him names. Cried and then vomited over their new couch before throwing a glass at him.

'You used me,' she'd sobbed. 'How long have you been fucking deceiving me.'

He'd winced. He hated swearing, so she hadn't stopped until he had walked out of the door.

'I didn't see it like that, Beth,' he'd said quietly. Always the calm, reasonable one. She was the one who ranted and raved. The quieter he was, the angrier she got.

'So, how did you fucking rationalise it?'

'I love you, Beth. I always have. Just not in the same way I love Mark.'

'Get out,' she'd screamed. 'I never want to see you again. How could you do this to us? You're nothing but a piece of shit.'

He'd left immediately, returning a few days later for his things. That quick, that easy. That easy for her life to be over.

'It must have been a terrible blow for you,' said Tom, breaking into her thoughts.

She dabbed at her eyes.

'I loved him, but I knew that I could never give him the love that he needed. I felt inadequate.' she said simply.

'Are you sure you want to see him? I can go in alone.'

'No, I have to do this. Nobody in the village knows. They presumed, you see, that it was another woman. That pity was enough. You just don't know how people will react.'

'Does Kate Marshall know?' he asked.

'No, no one knows, not even my sister.'

'Let's go.' He said, climbing from the car. The kids kicking their football stopped to look at them.

'This is private property,' said Beth, pointing to the sign on the grass. 'Haven't you learnt to read yet?'

'Is that right, love,' said the boy. 'What business is it of yours?'

Beth was grateful for them. It took away her nerves and refuelled her anger.

'Police business,' she said, flashing her ID. 'Find somewhere else. If you're still here when I come back, sonny Jim, you and I will have to have a chat with your parents. Won't that be cosy?'

The lads pulled a face and walked off. Tom pushed the buzzer and Beth found herself hoping that no one was at home, but there was a click and then a voice she recognised. It made her heart beat faster.

'Hello?'

'Ben Harper?' asked Tom.

'Yes, who is this?'

'I'm Detective Inspector Miller. I'm here with Detective Sergeant Harper. We'd like to ask you a few questions about an incident in Stonesend on Friday, July 20th.'

There were several seconds of silence, and Tom glanced at Beth before leaning closer to the intercom.

'Mr Harper?'

The door clicked and Tom pushed it open. The foyer smelt fresh and flowery. Someone had just hoovered the carpet. They stepped into the lift, and Beth took several deep breaths. The door opened onto the third floor and Beth's heart started to race.

'You okay?' Tom asked.

She nodded. Tom rang the doorbell, and a few seconds later, Ben opened the door. Her first thought was, 'He's gained weight' His cheeks seemed chubbier than she remembered, and his hair was shorter too, almost cropped. He wore a short-sleeved white shirt over jeans. Beth's breath caught in her throat, and for a moment, she couldn't speak.

'Beth,' he asked. 'Is everything alright?'

Beth just stared at him.

'Can we come in, Mr Harper?' asked Tom.

His voice seemed to tear through the very air between them.

'Yes, of course.'

They stepped into the hallway.

'Are you okay?' Ben asked, leaning so close that she could smell his familiar aftershave. A hundred memories shot through her brain.

'Yes, I'm fine,' she said.

'Who is it?' called a voice.

'Come into the living room,' said Ben, leading them along the hallway.

Mark stood in the doorway, his hair wet and tousled as if he'd just stepped out of the shower. He narrowed his eyes at the sight of Beth.

'What's going on?' he asked.

'We just need to ask Ben a few questions. Nothing to worry about.'

Beth looked around the living room. 'I thought you'd buy a house,' she heard herself say.

'We are,' said Mark. 'It's not gone through yet. We're renting this in the meantime.'

'It's cheap,' said Ben. He turned to Mark.

'How about a cup of tea? Mark. Would you mind?'

Mark's cheek twitched. He looked about to say something, changed his mind and went into the kitchen.

'Is it about the attack? I saw it on the news. I've been wondering who it was,' said Ben.

'It was Kate,' said Beth.

He rubbed his hand across his forehead.

'Jesus, poor Kate. How is she?'

'Can you tell us where you were on July 20th between five and six that afternoon?' Tom asked.

Ben looked away and creased his forehead thoughtfully.

'To be honest, I can't remember.'

Beth knew that wasn't true. Ben never forgot anything.

'Someone reported seeing you in Stonesend that evening. In Churchfields, to be precise. Do you want to tell us what you were doing there the evening Kate Marshall was attacked?'

Chapter Twenty-Eight

2005: Leeds

Mae

Rob had come home late that night. Blanche had finally fallen asleep. We'd waited a while for Rob to go and read to her, but it got too late, and in the end, I tucked her in, promising Rob would come up as soon as he got home.

I was in bed when I heard his key turn in the lock. I'd been reading. The clock said 10:30. No one worked that late, not even Rob. It was sometime before he came upstairs. I heard our bedroom door open. Then silence for a time, and then he'd barged into the spare room.

He stopped in the doorway and glared at me.

'What's going on?'

'Do you know what the time is, Rob? Blanche was waiting for you to read to her.'

'Why are you sleeping in here?'

'I think it's for the best.'

'Best for whom?' he asked, with a sarcastic laugh.

'You've been drinking ... again.' I said, closing my book. He looked at the floor. I could smell the alcohol on his breath.

'Yeah, I'm sorry. I should have messaged. There's been a bit of a crisis at work and ....'

'Oh, don't give me that crap,' I retorted, throwing the book to the floor.

His head snapped up.

'I'm serious, Mae, things aren't looking good. I've been in a long meeting trying to work out how we can save the company.'

'You've been in a long meeting with your slutty girlfriend, is what you mean,' I shot back.

'Keep your voice down, or you'll wake Blanche.'

'Huh, like you care about your daughter,' I said, climbing from the bed. 'You stink of booze.'

'I went with the guys for a pint after. We were all stressed.'

'You don't think I'm stressed?'

He sighed.

'You wanted a child.'

I glared at him.

'And we all know you didn't.'

I waltzed past him and went downstairs. I didn't want Blanche to hear us arguing. It would stress her, and that wouldn't help her asthma. Rob followed me and pulled a bottle of wine from the fridge.

'You lied about that,' he said evenly. 'Just like you lied about the money.'

'What money?' I asked, trying to keep my voice steady. There was no way he could have known about the money.

'The money your mother left you. It wasn't ten thousand, was it? More like fifty thousand. I went through your drawer and ….'

'You had no right,' I shouted. 'How dare you go through my private things.'

'You lied to me. I saw the solicitor's letter. You put ten thousand of that money into our account. You've kept the rest.'

'It was my inheritance.'

I wasn't going to let him make me feel guilty. It was my money, and I needed that security for Blanche and me. I'd thought it all through. Supposing Rob left us for that woman? He might try to get whatever money mum had left. I decided it was safer not to leave it in my bank account. Rob might one day see a bank statement or work out my password for online banking. So, I'd drawn it out slowly and hidden it away. It was to be our security stash, Blanche's and mine.

'We're married. We're supposed to share everything.'

'You think I'm going to let you have my inheritance so you can spend it on your girlfriend and booze. Anyway, I've invested it.'

'You've driven me to drink,' he said accusingly. 'You've done nothing but shut me out.'

I couldn't believe what I was hearing. Tears welled up in my eyes.

'That's so unfair,' I argued. 'Ever since Blanche was born, you've been distant.'

He scoffed and refilled his glass.

'What bollocks, Mae. I was never allowed to get close. I've never been part of your little world. It's as though you can only love one person at a time.'

I turned from him then and walked from the kitchen.

'You're the one having an affair,' I said. 'I'm going back to bed.'

'We haven't finished talking,' he said harshly.

I ignored him and turned to the stairs.

'You're not sleeping in the spare room, Mae. That's the final fucking straw.'

He grabbed my arm to stop me. I slapped at his hand and again made for the stairs, but he grabbed me by the hair, yanking me back.

'You're sleeping in our bed,' he hissed. 'I'm sick of this. Fucking sick of it.'

I stumbled several times as he dragged me upstairs. I tried not to cry out. I didn't want to frighten Blanche.

'Rob, please. This isn't right.'

'You sleeping in the spare room isn't right,' he said, pushing me into the bedroom and closing the door.

'I'll sleep where I bloody like.'

'You'll sleep where I tell you to sleep,' he said, his face contorting in anger.

Maybe I shouldn't have antagonised him after he'd been drinking. Perhaps it had been partly my fault. I shouldn't have made for the door. I was worried about Blanche. Concerned she may have heard us rowing. It would have upset her. I pushed past Rob and yanked the bedroom door open. I never made it across the threshold before he grabbed at my arm and dragged me back.

'It's enough,' he yelled, throwing me onto the bed.

I saw red then. How dare he tell *me* what enough was. I lashed out with my foot and kicked him in the groin. His face crumpled in pain, and I shot up from the bed. I saw his expression quickly change, and that's when I saw a different Rob. He lifted his hand and slapped it hard against my face sending me back onto the bed. I had to fight back my scream of shock. My face stung, and for a moment, my head swam. I saw him leaning over me and shielded my face.

'God Mae, I'm so sorry,' he whispered. 'Jesus, why do you work me up like this?'

I shied away from him, not understanding how this was suddenly my fault.

'I'm sorry, Mae. I wouldn't hurt you; you know that. I was at the end of my tether, what with work and ….'

'You have to stop seeing her,' I said. 'I'll have to leave if you don't.'

He reached out to me, and I reluctantly let him take me into his arms.

'I promise. I'll finish it. You and Blanche are all that matter.'

I wanted to laugh. He had no idea what Blanche and I went through. I had no intention of telling him either. At least not until he had proved himself.

'I'm so sorry,' he said again.

I laid a hand on my smarting cheek. He looked crestfallen. I decided then to ask God to forgive him.

'It will never happen again,' he said.

Stupidly, I believed him.

Chapter Twenty-Nine
August 2019: Swindon

The flat is so tiny, thought Beth. It's so shabby compared to our cottage. She could hear Mark clattering in the kitchen. That should be her. What was so remarkable about this life he had with Mark? Why hadn't she been enough? If only they'd had a baby. He wouldn't have left her then. He wouldn't have left a child. Not a helpless child. She'd always been too immersed in her work to think about babies, and he'd not seemed in any hurry for a child. Of course, she now knew why.

He looked embarrassed. He avoided her eyes when he said.

'I went to Stonesend to see Beth. Nothing suspicious about it.'

'What?' said Beth, surprised.

'Churchfields is some way from Beth's road,' said Tom. 'Why were you there?'

Ben sighed.

'I lost my nerve. I got to the village and then wondered if I was making a mistake. I didn't want to park near the cottage. So, I parked in Churchfields and then walked a bit. I was trying to get up the courage.'

'Why did you come to see me?' asked Beth quietly.

He met her eyes.

'It was our anniversary. Five years. I hadn't forgotten.'

Don't cry, Beth thought. Don't you dare bloody cry. Mark stood in the doorway with a tea tray.

'I can corroborate his story,' he said, putting the tea tray onto the coffee table.

'I got to the cottage, and Beth wasn't home. I remembered then that it was Sandy's birthday and that they'd probably gone out to celebrate.'

'I'd like to take a DNA swab. Just for elimination. It's voluntary,' said Tom, standing up.

'Of course.'

'You can have it done at Swindon station. I'll arrange it.'

Beth stood up and turned to the door.

'What about your tea?' asked Mark.

'Not for me, thanks. We need to get back to the station.'

Tea with Ben and his partner wasn't something she could do quite yet.

'Thanks, anyway,' said Tom and followed Beth out of the flat. The kids had gone, and Beth was disappointed. She'd hoped to take her anger out on them.

'Do you think he's telling the truth?' Tom asked.

'I'm the last person to ask. He lied to me for five years, and I didn't have a clue.'

'I'll drop you at the church,' he said. 'See what you can get out of the vicar.'

She climbed into the car and slammed the door. She wanted to go home. To immerse herself in a hot bath and relive Ben's words. 'I went to Stonesend to see Beth.' 'It was our anniversary. Five years. I hadn't forgotten.' He hadn't forgotten. That's what she'll remember. He hadn't forgotten.

*

Reverend Scott didn't seem surprised to see Beth.

'Beth. How are you?' he smiled.

Beth had thought about turning to religion when Ben had left. She'd wanted to know why. Why it had happened to her, but she couldn't face it. She couldn't face telling the Vicar that Ben had left her for a man. Besides, she didn't believe in God. It would have been hypocritical.

'I'm on police business, I'm afraid,' she apologised.

'How can I help?'

'Shall we go into the church?' she suggested. 'It'll be cool in there.'

Beth somehow felt the need to be somewhere calm and serene. Seeing Ben had distressed her more than she had thought it would.

'We've come to a dead-end with the investigation to find Kate's attacker. The Crimewatch reconstruction hasn't produced anything new.'

'I'm sorry to hear that, but I don't know how I can help.'

'I appreciate that you are told things in confidence, but I'm worried Kate's attacker is someone she knows ... Someone we know.

If she shared anything with you that would help us find this person, you must tell us.'

'I promise you I would not keep to myself something that would put Kate in danger.'

Beth met his eyes.

'I hope not, Reverend. If you decide the phone calls you shared might be relevant to the investigation, please call me.'

'You do understand my position, Beth?'

'I'm trying to.'

She stood up and looked around the church.

'It's peaceful here,' she said.

'You should come more often.'

She smiled.

'It would be for all the wrong reasons.'

'If it helps you.'

She smiled.

'Are you going to the party?' he asked.

'Party?'

'Blanche Lethbridge. It's her eighteenth.'

'Eighteen,' she exclaimed. 'Really? I thought she was much younger.'

'Yes, poor child.'

Beth opened the heavy church doors.

'I hope it goes well.'

Whatever Kate had shared with the vicar, Beth felt sure it had nothing to do with the attack. They'd achieved nothing. The attacker was still out there, and nobody knew when he'd strike again.

*

'Beth,' smiled Kate. 'I've just put the kettle on.'

'I'll pass. It's just a few questions.'

'More?' said Kate with a sigh, walking into the kitchen.

'I'm sorry to bring this up, but until we can eliminate them, I do need to ask you about the phone calls you shared with the vicar ….'

Kate's face darkened.

'It was personal,' she interrupted.

'Kate,' Beth said softly. 'It could have a bearing on your attack ….'

'It doesn't,' said Kate sharply.

'I promise if you tell me, it will stay confidential unless I think it could be connected to your attack.'

'For God's sake Beth,' said Kate, banging the teacups onto the counter. 'Just drop it. It's not connected.'

Beth stepped back.

'Okay, Kate. We won't ask anymore.'

Kate sat at the kitchen table and put her head in her hands.

'God, I'm sorry, Beth. I'm a bit on edge. It's nothing to do with the attack. If you want to know, I had an abortion. I couldn't tell Dan. I just know he'd have wanted to go ahead with it. I had to tell someone. I couldn't have another child. I'm forty-four. I couldn't face another pregnancy. Anthony was very supportive. I had terrible guilt for weeks afterwards. I had to let it out.'

Beth winced.

'God, I'm sorry, Kate. I shouldn't have pushed.'

'I had to tell someone. Anthony has helped me.'

Beth felt like kicking herself.

'It's not my business, Kate. I'm so sorry I badgered you.'

Kate nodded sadly.

'I know. You're only doing your job.'

Beth turned to the door.

'Don't feel guilty, Kate. It's your body.'

She closed the front door quietly behind her and cursed.

'Damn it.'

Chapter Thirty

Kate

Kate thought a lot about going to Disneyland with Mae and Blanche. It would be during the Christmas holidays so she wouldn't have to worry about work.

'What about the boys?' she'd asked Dan.

'Mum would be happy to help out for a few days, I'm sure,' he'd said.

She'd sensed he was apprehensive about her going but didn't want to be the one that stopped her.

'I'll give it some thought,' she'd said. 'I don't want to raise Mae's hopes unless I'm sure.'

She could always get a last-minute deal.

It was Blanche's birthday, and they'd bought her a tablet. She'd often looked on enviously when Jack played on his. Dan thought it was an expense, but Kate wanted to get it. After all, she'd told him, you're only eighteen once. She decided to tell Mae about her decision to go with them to Disneyland when she saw her later.

'Are you sure she's eighteen?' Dan had asked when they'd looked at birthday cards.

'Yes, that's why she's had such a fabulous holiday offer.'

'She doesn't seem eighteen,' he'd said, glancing through the cards. 'I always think of her as much younger.'

'Mentally, I suppose she is younger,' Kate had said, thoughtfully.

Mae was having a few of the villagers round to celebrate. Kate had offered to make a cake. The boys had gone ice-skating with Dan, so she was alone. She put the radio on for company but still found herself jumping at the slightest sound. Twice she checked that the front door was locked and continually glanced at the back door, even though she had shot two bolts across. It was hard to concentrate on the recipe. She found herself wondering if she'd been pottering about when the attacker came? Had the back door been open? Had she turned with a smile of recognition? If the radio had been on, what had she been listening to? Why hadn't she thought of that before? She stopped stirring the chocolate mixture and hastily wiped her hands on a tea towel before unlocking the door leading to the garage. She peered nervously into the darkness and fumbled shakily for the light switch. Nothing was threatening in there, just old paint tins and Dan's paraphernalia. In one corner was a pile of papers and magazines that they kept there for lighting the fire. Somewhere amongst them would be the Radio Times for that week in July. It took her a while to find it, but eventually, she came across it. She would have arrived home at about 4:30. That would have given her an hour and a half before Faith arrived. On Radio 4, at 4:30 that afternoon, there had been a play titled, 'Mummy's Secret'.

She took the magazine into the kitchen and locked the door that led to the garage. As she greased the cake tin, she tried to remember the play. She would have been preparing for Faith, so she wouldn't have listened closely to it. She plugged in her computer and played the podcast. Perhaps, hearing it again would jolt some memory of it, and maybe then, other memories would follow. There was always a chance.

Dan and the boys returned, and they got ready for Blanche's birthday party. Any hope Kate had of her memory returning while listening to the play were dashed. Perhaps she'd never listened to it at all.

'Let's go, or we'll be late,' said Dan.

Bright, colourful bunting hung outside Mae's cottage. Across the front door was a large banner that read 'Happy 18th'. There were already a few other villagers there when they arrived. Sophie Johnson hugged her and gushed about the cake.

'Gosh, look at that,' she said. 'Well done you.'

Kate forced a smile. Well done, Kate, she thought. Well done on baking a cake after almost being bludgeoned to death. She knew Sophie hadn't meant it like that, but that was how it felt. Blanche's face lit up on seeing Kate. She was wearing a pink chiffon dress and a flowery scarf around her head.

'Happy birthday,' Kate said, handing her the prettily wrapped gift and card. 'You're looking beautiful today.'

'Thank you for the cake. It looks delicious.'

'Nothing untoward in it,' Kate smiled.

The boys had already made a beeline for the buffet table.

'Don't act like you're starved,' said Dan.

Alice laughed.

'Mine almost ravaged it. You'd think we never fed the monsters.'

There was a lot of noise. People chattering and children's high-pitched laughter. Kate's head started to throb, and she felt in her bag for the painkillers.

'You okay?' asked Dan.

'Yes, I'm fine,' she smiled. 'Just a slight headache.'

The boys were tucking into pork pies and ham sandwiches. Mae had certainly gone to town on the food. Kate helped herself to salmon quiche and salad. She felt sorry for Blanche, not being able to eat half of the goodies on the table. She didn't seem to mind, however, and was enjoying the attention. No one mentioned the attack, and Kate was grateful for that. She'd been dreading the party for that one reason. The boys played happily with Alice's kids, and the men grabbed some beers and retreated to Mae's living room. Around six, Blanche cut the cake, and everyone sang Happy Birthday. Kate helped Mae make tea, and shortly after, people started to head off until there was just Kate, Dan, Sophie and Grant Johnson, and the vicar. It was so quiet in the village that everyone heard the loud booming of music from an approaching car and then the screech as it braked sharply outside. Mae glanced out of the window, and then her hands began to shake.

'It's Rob,' she said in disbelief.

Kate joined her at the window and watched as the car door was slung open and a man stumbled out. A giant pink box was clutched in his hand. A woman hurried out of the car from the driver's side and ran around to him, gesticulating madly. He shook her off angrily and stumbled down the drive.

'Oh my God,' muttered Mae.

Blanche had turned white and looked about to cry. The doorbell rang once, then twice and then continuously.

'Open the fucking door, Mae,' he yelled.

Reverend Scott winced.

'Who is he?' asked Dan.

'It's my ex,' said Mae. 'Blanche's dad. He's obviously been drinking.'

Blanche cowered in her wheelchair. Kate went to her and took her hand.

'It's alright, Blanche.'

The doorbell rang again.

'Do you want me to answer it?' asked Dan.

'Do you mind?' said Mae, clearly embarrassed. Kate could hear the couple arguing outside.

'I'll come with you,' she said.

Dan opened the door. Mae's ex-husband glared at them. Kate was surprised at how good looking he was. He had that film star kind of look. His eyes were a bright blue and now sparkled with anger. Kate stepped back nervously.

'Where's Mae?' he slurred.

Kate sensed he was struggling to control his anger.

'What are you doing here?' said Mae from behind Dan. 'How did you find out where we lived?'

'It's her eighteenth birthday. I'm entitled to see my daughter on her special birthday.'

He peered around Dan.

'Blanche, it's your dad. Happy birthday, babe.'

Kate turned to see Blanche sitting white-faced and shaking in her wheelchair.

'Dad?' she mouthed.

Reverend Scott edged forward and smiled.

'Can I be of any help?'

Rob Lethbridge scowled at the dog collar around the vicar's neck and said caustically.

'I don't need your fucking help.'

Sophie gasped.

'I'm so sorry,' said Mae tearfully.

'Perhaps I should go,' said Reverend Scott' Thanks for a lovely party.'

He looked at Rob as he passed.

'God bless you,' he said.

Rob spat on the ground. Reverend Scott stepped back in surprise.

'Rob, please go,' Mae pleaded.

'I want to give Blanche her present,' he said, pushing past her. 'Where are you, babe?'

Dan reached out to stop him, but he shoved Dan to one side and headed straight towards Blanche. He stopped abruptly on seeing her.

'What the hell is she doing in a wheelchair?' he said, shock etched on his face.

'Rob, please,' begged Mae.

'I bought you something,' he said, kneeling down to Blanche. Blanche stared at him in shocked awe.

'Happy birthday,' he said, pushing the gift onto her lap. His voice was now soft and gentle. Blanche opened her mouth, but no words came out.

'Shall we go for a walk?' he asked, straightening up. 'Just you and me?'

He stepped behind the wheelchair, and Mae leapt forward.

'Don't touch it,' she said, reaching out to stop him.

'It's just a walk, for Christ's sake. Get out of our way.'

'No,' Mae screamed.

The kids were staring open-mouthed. We ought to get them home, Kate thought.

Mae grabbed Rob's arm. He turned angrily, lashing out at her. Sophie screamed as the back of his hand slammed into Mae's face, sending her sprawling to the floor. Dan and Grant hurried forward and wrestled him from the wheelchair where Blanche was crying hysterically.

'It's time for you to go,' said Dan.

Rob fought against them, but finally, they had him outside. The dark-haired woman he arrived with was waiting tearfully by the gate.

'I'm so sorry,' she said. 'I tried to stop him.'

'Take him home,' said Grant. 'If he doesn't go, we'll have to call the police.'

Rob was gesturing towards the house.

'That bitch. I'll get my own back, Mae. You bloody owe me.'

'Go home, mate. We don't want trouble, and neither do you,' said Dan.

'You don't know anything about this,' yelled Rob.

The dark-haired woman spoke earnestly to him, and he finally climbed into the car. Mae was consoling Blanche. Her cheek was red, and the beginnings of a bruise were starting to show.

'Oh Mae, are you okay?' Kate asked, hugging her.

'The children are upset,' said Sophie. 'They're in the garden.'

'We should get them home,' said Dan.

Kate nodded.

'Will you be okay, Mae?' she asked. 'Do you want me to pop back?'

Mae was stroking Blanche's hair.

'You see,' she said to Blanche. 'You see what he's like. I told you.'

Blanche nodded miserably.

'He's never put us first,' said Mae.

She turned to Kate.

'We'll be fine. Thank you, Kate. We know where you are.'

'I'll come back and help you clear up.'

Mae didn't look round. Her arms were wrapped around Blanche, and they were both crying.

Chapter Thirty-One

2005: Leeds

Rob

The drink didn't agree with me. It brought out the worst in me. I should have realised that and stopped, but somehow, I couldn't. It had been gradual at first. I found it helped numb the pain. I'd never really been a big drinker. A couple of pints with the lads used to be my limit. I'd never drink when Mae and I were going out. I'd always be the one driving. Then Mae learnt to drive. I'd only have a couple of glasses of wine if we had dinner with friends. Then Mae got pregnant. I struggled with that. It had helped to have a whisky while I worked in the evenings. It had made me feel powerful, in control.

It became a habit to go to the pub after work with the guys from the office. I'd stay a bit longer and maybe have a couple more. I was finding it more and more difficult to go home. Either Mae would be lying on the couch with a migraine. Or her blood pressure would have shot up so her mum would be there cooking dinner. I'd started to feel like a stranger in my own home. I'd been worried about the baby coming too.

When Blanche finally came, I felt more shut out than ever. Money wasn't such an issue now that we had Jean's house and a bit of cash. Then there had been Jo. That had been stupid. I realise that now. I just couldn't cope with a sick kid. I'd keep thinking about how it would affect us. Holidays would be difficult with her allergies. We'd have to take tons of medications with us. It was all too complicated. Then Mae told me that tests had shown Blanche to be mentally challenged.

'Doctor Morris said the caesarean had damaged her brain. It isn't maturing as it should. That and epilepsy.'

I had no idea that Blanche had epilepsy. I'd always thought it had been a high temperature that had caused the fits.

'I did tell you,' Mae said, exasperation in her voice.

'What does that mean, *mentally challenged*?' I asked.

'Retarded, that's what it means, Rob. I told you the birth was all wrong.'

'Don't use that word,' I said, shocked.

The more I decided what a bad husband and father I was, the more I drank. I should have gone to the hospital appointments with Mae, but I just couldn't face them. After a while, she stopped telling me about them.

I decided to stop drinking. It was getting out of control. I needed to focus on my family. I was prepared to end it with Jo. Mae and I could get our sex life back. There hadn't been much of that with Mae, not since Blanche. Mae said her periods were all over the place, and when they weren't, she was too dry to have sex. We did it occasionally, but I was tense, afraid I might hurt her. As time went on, I started to feel differently towards her and then I discovered the lies.

I hadn't deliberately gone through her bedroom drawer. I'd been looking for my CV. Things weren't looking good at Rotech, and I'd messed up an important contract. I'd been distracted with Jo, and several mornings I'd had some major hangovers. I forgot things. The bastards said I was losing my touch. The company wasn't doing well, and I could see the end was coming. I knew Mae's ten thousand inheritance wouldn't last us forever. I needed to look for a new job. I'd felt sure my CV had been in my desk drawer. I'd searched my bedside cabinet drawer and then Mae's, just in case. I found the letter, the one from her mother's solicitor, confirming her inheritance of the house and £50,000 that had been in Jean's bank account. I'd felt sick to my stomach. How could she have lied to me like that? I'd been struggling, and all the time, she'd been fucking rolling in it.

I hadn't deserved that. We could have done a lot with fifty grand. We could have gone on a decent holiday and paid for someone to help with Blanche. I'd been furious. If that wasn't enough, I later learnt that the company was in dire straits. It became clear who they planned to get rid of.

'We don't want to make people redundant,' they'd said. 'But we have little choice.'

One month's salary, that was their severance pay, the tight bastards. What else was there for me to do except get drunk? I'd already had a fair few when Jo met me. We'd gone onto a club, and of course, I'd had more. I lost track of time. Jo got irritable when later I couldn't get it up and told me 'to bugger off home.'

'Home to the bitch,' I'd muttered.

Only to find her sleeping in the fucking spare room. That was it. That was the final humiliation. The way she'd spoken to me like I was her second mentally challenged child. I hated her at that moment.

I couldn't have my wife sleeping in another room. It was humiliating enough to live in *her* house. She had no intention of putting my name on the deeds or sharing her inheritance, and now she thought she could move out of the bedroom? No fucking way. I was in bloody charge, and it was about time she knew it. So, I showed her. I felt terrible afterwards, but God knows she deserved it.

I promised I wouldn't see Jo again, but what were promises in this marriage? They meant nothing.

Chapter Thirty-Two

August 2019: Stonesend

'For God's sake, don't say how tired she looks.'

Sandy opened the oven door and stepped back as waves of steam rose up into her face.

'What do you mean?' she asked, turning over the sizzling chicken.

'It's just you always say that whenever you see her.'

That's because she does look tired, thought Sandy.

'That's her,' he said at the sound of the doorbell.

Sandy wiped her greasy hands on a tea towel and went to the front door. Beth looked more tired than usual, and Sandy bit her lip. Sandy vowed that she would try hard not to mention it. By the time they reached dessert, however, she could hold back no longer.

'Is the new DI overworking you?' she asked.

Ray couldn't very well glare at her. She didn't exactly say how tired Beth was looking.

'No, not really.'

'Is he working out?' asked Ray, handing her a jug of custard.

'We all had dinner at Brian Lewis' house,' said Beth.

'Blimey,' exclaimed Ray. 'You were honoured.'

'Group bonding,' sighed Beth. 'I don't think it worked.'

'I was reading about the Lester Lynch case. It must have really messed with his head. I wonder who he saw for his post-traumatic stress,' said Sandy.

'It was grief as well as PTS,' said Ray, leaning back in his chair. It was the beginnings of the kind of conversation he liked.

'You're not at work now, you know,' laughed Beth.

'Ah, but that's where you're wrong. Once a doctor, always a doctor,' grinned Ray.

'Has he mentioned it?' asked Sandy.

Beth stood and helped clear the table.

'Is that why you invited me? To talk about Tom Miller?'

'Of course not. You've looked so tired lately and ....'

Ray smiled.

'Sandy worries,' he said.

'You know I could prescribe something to help you sleep,' said Sandy gently.

'I've still got the Valium. I don't want anything else. I just need time.'

'Leave her alone, Sandy,' admonished Ray.

'It's okay,' Beth smiled.

She didn't mind them asking after her welfare. It made her feel cared for, important. When Ben had first left, she'd felt worthless and inadequate. Sandy had been there for her every step of the way, and yet, still Beth couldn't share her secret.

'I mentioned his wife the other day,' she said, feeling the need to share something. 'I didn't mean to. I drank too much at Brian's. He has a photo of her on display at the cottage. Christ, can you imagine what he went through?'

'I hope he got the right therapy. What bastards,' said Sandy angrily.

Beth sighed.

'I think sending him here was a mistake. What if he fucks up here too? It will affect everyone.'

She followed Sandy into the kitchen while Ray went upstairs to check on their daughter.

'I saw Ben today,' Beth said quietly.

Sandy turned from the sink, her eyes wide.

'You did, why?'

'Don't get any ideas. It was police business. Ben was seen in Stonesend the night Kate was attacked.'

'What the hell ...' Sandy gasped.

'He came to see me. Remember, it was our anniversary?'

I could tell her, thought Beth. I could tell her right now about Mark. God knows, Sandy would know how to counsel her. Or know the right person. But the words just wouldn't come. They wanted to. They were clawing at her tongue, begging to be freed, but her lips wouldn't release them. It wasn't the time. She swallowed them down with a glass of water.

'Jesus, is he a suspect?'

Beth shook her head.

'He agreed to give a DNA sample. It will eliminate him, I'm sure. It was just odd seeing him. He looked different.'

'It's been a while since you've seen him.'

Strangely, instead of making things worse, seeing Ben again had made her realise just how much she had been romanticising their relationship. He wasn't the Ben she had lived with, not any more. He was Mark's Ben, now, and it somehow released her. She would always love him, but it was over. Seeing him again had cemented that reality.

Sandy lowered her eyes.

'Did you see her?'

Beth blushed. She hated lying to her sister.

'No,' she said.

Tell her, screamed a voice in her head. Do it now.

'Sandy, it wasn't ….'

Ray came in then, and she stopped abruptly.

'It wasn't what?' asked Sandy, stacking the dishwasher.

Beth laughed.

'Do you know, it's gone right out of my head.'

The words were pushed down again, and she thought they would choke her. It didn't seem right that she had shared her secret with Tom Miller but wasn't able to share it with her sister. Why did she feel so ashamed? She'd done nothing wrong. Ben had fallen in love with someone else, that's all. It shouldn't matter if it were a man or a woman. But it did matter. It mattered because she could never give him the love he needed.

Chapter Thirty-Three

Kate

The visit from Rob had the whole village talking. Mae had immediately applied to have a restraining order on him.

'I never want him near Blanche again,' she'd said.

The incident had shaken Kate, and she and Dan had disagreed about it that night.

'He seemed beside himself, somehow,' Dan said.

They'd finally got the boys settled and were getting ready for bed. Kate couldn't stop thinking about Mae's bruised cheek.

'I can't believe he came to see Blanche in that drunken state,' she said.

'You get too involved with them,' said Dan. 'He seemed desperate to me.'

'Desperate in what way?'

'To see his daughter.'

'He's an abuser,' Kate said, climbing in beside Dan.

He frowned.

'Did Mae tell you that?'

She nodded and huddled closer to him.

'He shouldn't have hit her.'

'No, I agree, but there are always two sides to every story.'

'We're so lucky,' she said, feeling suddenly grateful.

'Don't you forget it?' he smiled.

Kate went to see Mae the following day. Blanche seemed to have recovered and was immersed in her gifts.

'Thank you so much for the tablet. It means everything to me.'

'It's amazing what she can do on it,' said Mae. 'She's a real whizz-kid.'

Kate could tell that Mae was edgy.

'I've been on the phone to a solicitor. I'm taking a restraining order against him. I won't press charges unless he argues about it.'

'Oh Mae, I'm so sorry.'

She seemed about to cry, but she'd then nodded towards Blanche and pulled herself together.

'Come in the kitchen,' she said.

Kate followed her, leaving Blanche to look at her new DVDs.

'I don't know how he found out where we were,' she said shakily, filling the kettle. 'I've been dreading this.'

'Surely he won't bother you again once he gets the restraining order?'

'I hope not.'

Kate sat at the kitchen table.

'Perhaps he just wanted to see Blanche on her 18th birthday.'

Mae's eyes flashed angrily.

'I would happily have let him see her if he'd been different. I can't risk Blanche being hurt, not in her condition. It's enough he beat the pulp out of me, without ….'

'I know,' Kate butted in. 'I didn't mean ….'

'He's never cared about her. He only cares about himself.'

'Just think about your Disney trip,' Kate said, trying to lighten the atmosphere.

'Yes,' she smiled. 'Have you decided?'

'Not yet,' Kate lied, but she had. She wanted to go, but something in her couldn't quite commit to it. She still had reservations about being alone. She felt safe when Dan was around. What if the person who had attacked her sees it as the perfect opportunity to try again? This time she'd be with Mae and Blanche. What if he hurt one of them? She didn't know why she felt sure it was a man. It wasn't as if she could remember.

'Did he hurt you badly?' She asked.

Mae placed two mugs of tea onto the table.

'Enough,' she said, not meeting her eyes. 'I always told people I'd fallen over.'

'Oh Mae,' Kate said, her heart breaking for her friend. 'How did you get away from him in the end?'

'I took all my courage in both hands, and Blanche and I left one morning after he'd gone to work. I put the house on the market without telling him. It was my house. My mum had left it to me. I needed to sell it to buy a home for Blanche and me.'

'So, you came to Stonesend?'

'It seemed a lovely place and a long way from Leeds, where we were living. I never thought Rob would bother coming all this way, even if he did find us.'

Kate tried to think what Dan would do. She imagined he would travel to the ends of the earth for one of the boy's birthdays, but she didn't say that to Mae.

Chapter Thirty-Four

'Not one lead,' said Tom with a heavy sigh. 'I don't understand it.'

Beth unwrapped a Cornish pasty.

'Do you want some?' she asked.

He grimaced.

'Don't you ever stop eating?' he asked.

'It's my dinner. Some of us do eat dinner, you know.'

'It smells disgusting.'

Beth shook her head in exasperation.

'I happen to be enjoying it, so if you could keep your opinions on Cornish pasties to yourself.'

'Did we do a background check on the vicar? He might have a record.'

'He's a vicar. I think you're scraping the barrel now. Besides, why would he want to hurt anybody? I questioned Kate about the phone calls. We can dismiss them. Trust me, they have nothing to do with the attack.'

'What were they about?'

'I promised Kate I wouldn't say.'

'You're sure it has nothing to do with her attack?'

'Yes, a hundred per cent sure.'

Tom loosened his tie and walked over to the kettle. Beth looked over at her boss. She had to admit he was an attractive man. He paced across the room in even strides, his feet gently pounding on the floor. He pulled a mug from the cupboard and dropped a teabag into it.

'Would you like a cuppa, Beth?' she said sarcastically. 'Yes, thanks, I wouldn't mind.'

'Oh,' he said absently, taking another mug from the cupboard. 'What about the sick kid? We haven't questioned her.'

Beth wiped her hands on a piece of kitchen towel.

'She was having dinner, remember?'

'She still may have seen something,' he said, handing her the tea.

Beth yawned.

'Okay, I'll question her tomorrow.'

Tom glanced at the clock.

'Let's do it now.'

Beth sighed.

'Can I finish my dinner?'

'Is that what you live on?' he asked, nodding at the Cornish pasty.

'Look who's talking. You're not exactly on a health kick, are you?'

She stood up and dusted crumbs from her trousers.

Tom headed for the door.

'Blimey,' she complained, quickly grabbing her bag and the box of custard tarts she'd bought for dessert. 'Hold on.'

*

'She's probably in bed,' said Beth, looking up at the bedroom window.

'No,' said Tom, climbing from the car. 'It's not that late.'

'And of course, you'd know,' muttered Beth, following him. Sounds of the television reached their ears. At the ring of the doorbell, the canned laughter from a comedy show stopped. A voice called from behind the door.

'Who is it?

'It's DS Harper and DI Miller. We'd like a chat if it's okay.'

Mae Lethbridge was in her dressing gown.

'I was just about to take a bath,' she explained.

'We won't keep you long,' said Tom.

'Is there something wrong?' she asked, looking worried. Beth thought she could smell alcohol on Mae's breath.

'We'd like to speak to Blanche,' said Beth, moving forward. It was then she saw the bruise on Mae's cheek.

At the sound of her daughter's name, Mae stepped to one side, blocking the doorway.

'Blanche? Why?' she asked, a note of suspicion in her voice. 'What's this about?'

'The attack on Kate Marshall. We're questioning everyone,' explained Tom.

Her eyes betrayed her fear.

'We won't upset her,' Beth said kindly.

Mae bit her lip.

'It's just, she's rather fragile. Stress is bad for her.'

'I have no intention of stressing her,' said Tom. Beth noticed Mae's hands were shaking. Something was wrong.

'Is everything alright, Mrs Lethbridge?'

'It was her birthday yesterday, and unfortunately, my ex came and caused a scene. It upset her.'

'Is that how you got the bruise?' asked Beth gently.

'You'd better come in.'

'Did your ex-husband hit you?' Beth asked when the door had closed behind them.

'He was upset,' she said. 'He'd been drinking.'

'You can press charges, Mrs Lethbridge,' said Tom gently.

She shook her head emphatically.

'No, I don't want to antagonise him. I've applied for a restraining order.'

She stood by the closed living room door and took a deep breath.

'I'll just explain to Blanche while you're here if that's alright?'

'Of course,' said Tom.

She closed the door behind her, and Tom looked at Beth and raised his eyebrows. Moments later, Mae led them into the living room, where a pretty girl sat on the couch. Beth thought how underweight she was. Her shoulders fell forward in a way that would be more befitting a grandmother. Her eyes met Beth's, and then she turned away. I'd never have thought her to be eighteen, thought Beth. She moved closer and nodded to the couch.

'Is it okay if I sit next to you?' she asked.

Blanche nodded. She was nervous and repeatedly scratched at her arm.

'Did you have a nice birthday?' Beth asked.

Blanche nodded again.

'It was a special one, wasn't it?'

'Yes, I was eighteen.'

She had a gentle way of speaking.

'Lots of presents then?' smiled Tom.

Blanche relaxed slightly, and the frown disappeared from her forehead.

'Yes,' she smiled.

Blanche said she didn't remember seeing anything the night of Kate's attack. They'd had dinner on trays so she could finish watching a documentary about her favourite singer, Lady Gaga. She thinks that was about five-thirty, but she couldn't be sure.

'What time did that programme start?' asked Tom.

'It was on catch up,' said Mae. 'I'd recorded it.'

'You didn't hear a car or anyone shouting?' asked Beth.

Blanche shook her head.

'I had it a bit loud,' she said apologetically.

She looked weary, so Beth stood up.

'We won't tire you.'

'Thanks for your time,' said Tom.

Once outside, Tom looked back at the house and said,

'Poor kid.'

Chapter Thirty-Five
2005: Leeds

Rob

I never mentioned the money again. There seemed little point. It just caused bad feeling between us. It grated on me every day, though. I was slogging my guts out while somewhere there were forty thousand pounds. Exactly where I had no idea. To make matters worse, Mae was giving a hell of a lot to the church. She spent more time there than she did at home.

'It gives me strength,' she said when I questioned her. 'You should come. You may find it will help.'

Blanche was sicker than ever. If that was God helping us, then I wanted fuck all to do with it. I found being around Blanche depressing, and then I'd have pangs of guilt for feeling that way about my own daughter. To drown out the guilt, I'd drink, even though I knew it had a bad effect on me. Each week there appeared to be new medication for Blanche, and then we all started eating special food.

'It's better for Blanche if we all eat the same thing. I don't want her to feel different,' Mae would say.

I'd had several jobs since Rotech, but none of them satisfied me as much as Rotech had, but they paid the bills. It rankled me that Mae never offered to help out. Then Blanche stopped going to school. It was too dangerous for her allergies, Mae said. It seemed one day the school had been careless and given Blanche the wrong dinner, and she'd broken out in hives. I hated the meals Mae cooked. They were too bland. Several times a week, I'd stop off at the pub on the way home and have dinner there, and of course, a couple of pints. I'd promised Mae I wouldn't drink, but she had church, so surely I was entitled to something too. I'd already decided I was an awful father. I just had no idea how to deal with a sick kid. I'd just wanted a normal family. Maybe Mae had been right. We should never have allowed the caesarean. I'm ashamed to say I was embarrassed too. I hated Mae giving those little talks on life with a sick child. I despised the people that felt sorry for us and offered Blanche all kinds of gifts. I never wanted to be the father of a sick kid. When Mae said that she and Blanche wanted to do something for other kids like Blanche and that a national paper would sponsor them, I lost it.

'For Christ's sake, Mae. Everyone will know our business if we're in the papers.'

I didn't want people at work seeing Blanche. I'd given the impression that we lived a normal life, that we had a normal daughter like everyone else. The last thing I wanted them to know was that my kid was mentally challenged, whatever the fuck that meant.

Mae went ahead with it anyway. Nothing I ever said made any difference. Blanche received all kinds of gifts, from a laptop to a new bed. Every time I thought of buying her something, someone else would get there before me. I began to feel redundant. Church meetings started to take place at our house because it made it easier for Mae to attend. I had offered to stay with Blanche, but Mae said she could never be sure I would be home on time. The church stuff did my head in, especially when the vicar told me God had chosen Blanche because she could do so much for everyone else. He'd chosen the wrong time to say that to me. I'd had a few beers, not many. I wanted to come home to some peace and quiet, but there they all were, planning another fundraiser.

Mae had put on a front when I'd walked through the door. She always knew when I'd been drinking.

'Oh, Rob,' she said. 'You're in time to hear our news.'

'What's that? Television next time is it?'

There was silence. Mae had laughed.

'I wish,' she said. 'No, Blanche has been offered a trip to America to see a specialist there. A lovely donor has offered to pay for everything.'

'What kind of specialist?' I asked, reaching into the fridge for a bottle of wine.

Mae's eyes hardened, but she kept the smile on her face.

The vicar, whose name I could never remember, asked, 'How are you, Bob?'

He didn't even know my fucking name.

'It's Rob, and I'm tired,' I said, hoping they'd take the hint and leave.

'Haven't seen you in church for a while?'

'That's because I haven't been there.'

'Rob's very busy at work,' Mae said, trying to gloss things over.

'Surely, they don't have you working on a Sunday?' he asked, surprised.

'I play badminton,' I smiled. 'I'm sure God wouldn't begrudge me a bit of exercise.'

He smiled, but the smile didn't reach his eyes.

'It's wonderful what Blanche is doing for others, isn't it? God chose her, I'm sure. He knew what good works she would do.'

I downed half a glass of wine. I probably should have waited until they'd left.

'So, we have God to thank for our sick daughter, do we?' I said caustically. 'That's good to know.'

'Rob, I don't think ...' Mae began.

'No, you don't,' I snapped before downing the rest of the wine.

The woman who played the organ at their services gasped. I tried to remember her name but couldn't. They were Mae's friends, not mine. Our old friends had all disappeared since we had Blanche.

'Where is my daughter, anyway?' I asked.

'She's watching television in her room,' Mae replied.

The vicar made for the door. Good riddance, I wanted to say but kept my mouth shut. I helped myself to the cake on the table and wolfed it down with the rest of the wine. Mae had been livid when she'd returned from seeing them out. I could see her eyes blazing.

'You made a fool of yourself,' she said, lifting the cake dish from the table.

'I don't give a shit what they think of me.'

'They've done a lot for us.' She crashed plates into the dishwasher.

'They just want your donations,' I snarled. 'How much have they had of your inheritance?'

She ignored me and continued wiping crumbs from the table.

'Where are you keeping all that money, or is there nothing left?' I asked, grabbing her arm.

The moment I grabbed her arm, I should have realised. I was out of control. It felt like I was drowning in my own misery. I had a crappy job, not much money, a wife who kept things back from me and a sick child I couldn't care for. I felt a failure, a useless specimen of a man. I was sexually frustrated. Mae and I barely made love, and I needed an outlet, a release.

'Don't start, Rob,' she said in a tone that you would use for a child.

I tried to turn her to face me. I must have been too rough, for her blouse ripped in my hand. I saw the swell of her breasts, my breasts. She belonged to me. I was overcome with passion. Perhaps she did fight. Maybe I did force her. I was desperate. I loved her and needed to be comforted. I never meant to hurt her.

Chapter Thirty-Six
August 2019: Stonesend

'Do you fancy a drink?' asked Tom casually as they got into the car.

Beth's eyes widened.

'A drink with you?' she said, surprised.

He shrugged.

'Well, if it's that distasteful ….'

'I'm shocked that you're so bold about it.'

'Oh, for God's sake Harper. I'm not going to drink bloody alcohol, am I? If I wanted a sneaky drink, do you really think I'd ask you along as a witness?'

Beth winced. What an idiot she was sometimes.

'Only if you promise to have some food.'

'As long as it's not a Cornish pasty, then okay.'

The pub was quiet, and Beth was relieved, but she had no doubt the news that she and Miller had been to the pub together would soon be around the village.

'Any developments?' Jack asked.

'You'll be the first to know,' said Tom. 'In the meantime, can we have a diet coke and …' he turned to Beth.

'Seeing as I was officially off duty an hour ago, I'll have a red wine.'

Tom dug into his pocket for his wallet.

'On the house, after all, all that you're doing to find Kate's attacker …' began Jack.

'We're paid to get the bad guys,' said Tom firmly. 'We can't accept freebies, I'm afraid.'

'But …'

'How much?'

Jack looked to Beth, who simply shrugged.

'Don't look at me. I'm not even allowed to accept a pork chop.'

'He's a stickler for the rules,' mumbled Jack.

'All police officers are a stickler for the rules,' said Tom, without looking at Beth.

He took their drinks to a table.

'What's up with him,' said Jack.

'He does it all proper. Give us some menus, will you?'

She slid a menu across the table to Tom.

'They don't mean any harm, you know.' She watched him while he studied the menu. She noticed several grey hairs and wondered if they were recent. The police force aged one before one's time. The newspapers had reported him as forty-something. Beth couldn't remember what the something was. She knew London cops saw things that sickened them. Many transferred to the country where the crime rate was low because they couldn't stand the strain. Tom Miller, she knew, wasn't one of those. She'd followed the Lester Lynch case, like everyone else. Miller was the first to find the boys bodies. Two of the cops with him had left the site to vomit outside. Miller had wrapped the dead boys in blankets and carried them out, one by one, from the basement of a dilapidated house. Someone in the crowd outside had videoed it on their phone. A short ten-second piece, but the sight of police officers crying had torn at every heartstring in the country. The cop in charge, Tom Miller, had become a hero overnight while, at the same time, becoming London's underworld's biggest enemy. When Lester Lynch was sentenced, his father, gangland boss Benny Lynch, had vowed to take revenge.

'Tom Miller stitched up my son,' he told reporters outside the court. 'No one stitches up the Lynches.'

He'd turned his face onto the cameras then, his face ugly with rage,

'Do you hear that? Tom Miller? Nobody.'

'What's the pie like?' Tom asked, looking up and seeing her studying him.

'Bit like a Cornish pasty,' she said. 'Meat on the inside, pastry on the outside.'

'That tells me a lot.'

'I'm having the fish and chips,' she said.

Beth watched as he strolled confidently to the bar to place their order and felt her heart flutter. There was no doubt that he was appealing. She remembered the photo she'd seen at the cottage. His wife had been beautiful. The type of woman you would expect a good-looking man like Tom Miller to marry. He returned with another coke and red wine.

'Supposing Mae Lethbridge's ex came to visit the Friday that Kate was attacked. What if he was drunk and got the wrong house?' he asked.

'The wrong house, the wrong woman. He had to have been very drunk. Kate doesn't look a bit like Mae Lethbridge.'

Tom sighed.

'Not one bloody lead,' he said. 'We must be missing something.'

'The only thing I'm missing is sleep,' yawned Beth.

'It's overrated.'

Overrated or not. Beth decided that as soon as she got home, she would crawl into bed.

'Ben's DNA didn't match anything found at Kate Marshall's, by the way. The report came back earlier this evening.'

Beth felt some of the tension leave her body. She was saved from commenting by Jack coming over with their food order.

'Any sauces?' he asked. 'They're free. All part of the service and not a bribe, before you ask.'

'In that case, I'll have some mustard,' said Tom.

Beth smiled and tucked into her fish and chips.

Chapter Thirty-Seven

September 2019: Stonesend

He jerked awake from the nightmare. For a moment, he was disorientated. Then he remembered where he was. He sat up and listened. Had he heard a crash, a scream? But all was silent. The clock said four. He closed his eyes and saw the room again, just as it had been in his dream, Just as it had been that morning. Lorna had been sitting on the stool in front of the dressing table. Sunlight had filtered in through the closed blinds. Dust particles had floated around her, and for a moment, she had looked like an angel.

'What's the time?' he'd asked.

'Nearly eight,' she'd said, turning to smile at him.

'Come back to bed,' he'd said.

She'd blown a kiss.

'I'll be late if I do.'

He'd watched as she'd pulled a comb through her thick blonde hair.

'See you tonight,' she'd said, leaning over him. Her soft floral perfume filling his nostrils.

Her tender lips had touched his, and he'd pulled her down onto the bed.

'Love you,' she'd whispered.

'Love you too.'

She'd left him then. Left him forever. There had been so much he hadn't told her. So much they had left to share.

'*A tragic accident.*' '*We're so sorry.* '*Nothing could be done.*'

She'd lost control of the car, they'd said. She had been driving very fast, said one witness. Went through a red light. Tom knew that Lorna would never drive through a red. Hit the lorry with such force that the car had spun around numerous times. Lorna had died instantly, along with their unborn baby.

He'd lost his senses. He'd screamed. Tried to deny it. Had expected her to walk through the door as usual. They'd made a mistake. It wasn't Lorna.

A few days after the accident, his boss, Larry Fajerman, broke the news.

'The brakes had been tampered with. It wasn't an accident, Tom.'

Tom felt it should have been him, but that would have been too easy. Benny Lynch wanted him to hurt. The card came on the day of the funeral.

'You took my child, and I took yours. We're now even.'

It wasn't signed, but Tom knew it had come from Benny.

He sat up abruptly.

'We're not fucking even,' he said through gritted teeth.

He was wide awake now. He threw back the sheets and reached out for the file on Kate Marshall. Nearly six weeks had passed since her attack, and they were no nearer to finding the culprit than they had been at the beginning. He and Beth had chased up the odd lead, but as always, they had led nowhere.

He wandered into the kitchen and made a coffee. As he reached up for the coffee jar, his hand crept towards the unopened bottle of whisky. He stroked it and then pulled his hand away.

'You're too good for that,' said a voice in his head. 'Don't mess up, not now.'

He was losing his touch. In the past, he'd have found Kate Marshall's attacker in half the time.

'Christ,' he muttered, throwing the folder onto the kitchen table. If only Kate would remember. The more time went on, the more unlikely it seemed that she would.

Things were slowly returning to normal in the village. The only hope now was an update on Crimewatch. Tom hoped it might refresh someone's memory, but he wasn't overconfident.

He groaned at the invitation that sat propped up on top of the fridge. He'd nearly forgotten about the Lethbridge charity do. He'd have to go, or he'd be in the dog house.

'It's for a good cause,' Beth had badgered him. 'Everyone is going. You'll be conspicuous by your absence.'

He'd put in an appearance, but that was all he'd do. Give a tenner or something and go home.

*

In the end, Kate didn't go to Disneyland. Blanche was too ill. She had started having fits again, and Mae was anxious something would happen when they were there, so she cancelled the trip.

'It's still a little way off,' Kate said. 'Maybe she will be better by then.'

But Mae felt sure she wouldn't be. The charity gave Blanche and Mae the airfare so that they could go anytime they wanted. Mae blamed Rob. She said the whole business had upset Blanche more than she'd realised.

'It's alright for some,' Dan had quipped. 'No one's going to give us money.'

'Dan,' Kate had said surprised. 'Surely, you wouldn't want one of the boys to be sick like Blanche.'

'No, of course not. It's the biblical stuff that gets on my nerves. God's will that they shouldn't go, and God guiding the charity to give them the airfare so Blanche could go when she's better. The charity gave the money, not God.'

'It comforts her. I wish I had a stronger faith.'

'For goodness' sake, Kate.'

'It would help me cope with my panic attacks if I thought there was a divine reason for them.'

'Aw Kate,' he'd said, pulling her closer. 'I didn't mean to upset you.'

There it was again, a quick snapshot. Someone speaking. 'Aw, Kate.' Hang onto it. Whose voice? Don't let it go. But, just like before, the memory faded, and Kate could never seem to pull it back. She could have cried with frustration.

A few days before the charity event, Mae developed a migraine, so Kate offered to have Blanche for the day. Blanche was pale and quiet but keen to help in the kitchen.

'How are you feeling?' Kate asked.

'I'm better, thank you.'

'We can make cakes if you'd like?' Kate suggested.

They made the cakes according to Mae's special recipe and then made a batch of chocolate muffins for Dan and the boys. Blanche had become surprisingly energetic. Dan had taken the boys ice skating, so it was just Blanche and Kate that afternoon.

'Have you ever ice skated?' Kate asked.

Blanche's face clouded over.

'No, not ever.'

'It's pretty scary,' Kate laughed.

'I'm so sorry about the attack,' Blanche said suddenly, tears filling her eyes.

'It's okay, Blanche,' Kate said, hugging her.

It was only later when she was clearing away and packing the cakes into a tin, that she realised she was one chocolate muffin short. She'd been careful not to mix the cakes up. She knew Blanche couldn't eat chocolate with her allergies. Had she taken one? Kate worried for days, expecting Mae to tell her that Blanche had been very unwell. But when she next saw them, Blanche was fine.

Chapter Thirty-Eight

'Is that what you're wearing?' Beth asked.

Tom looked at his suit.

'What's wrong with it?'

'It's too formal. That's what's wrong with it.'

He glanced at Beth in her jeans and blouse and said, 'You scrub up well.'

'Blimey,' she said, embarrassed. 'Is that a compliment?'

'It's the closest I'll get.'

He disappeared upstairs, and Beth took the opportunity to take a closer look at the photograph on the table. Lorna Miller's beautiful face smiled back at her. Tom Miller looked relaxed, his face free from lines. She remembered Sandy's words. 'I hope he got the right therapy. What bastards.'

The investigation into Lorna Miller's death had gone on for months. Finally, Benny Lynch was arrested on a charge of murder. Everyone had been sickened when six months later he'd got off due to lack of evidence.

'I've been vindicated,' he said outside the court. 'DI Tom Miller has framed both my son and me. This is police corruption at its worst. We will be appealing Lester's conviction.'

Lester's appeal was thrown out. No one could forget those three children.

'It should have been me.'

She turned to Tom, who was standing behind her. He'd changed into a pair of jeans.

'I'm so sorry,' she said.

He looked at the photograph.

'You didn't do it,' he said simply.

He opened the front door.

'Shall we go?'

*

Tom stood at the bar and casually glanced around the pub. He watched how people interacted with Kate Marshall. He just needed a tiny crumb of evidence. Something he could get his hooks into. It was like looking for a needle in a haystack.

'Enjoying yourself?' Beth asked.

'I'm riveted by it all.'

'You're too bloody cynical,' said Beth. 'Have you bought a ticket for the tombola?'

Tom sighed.

'No, I haven't.'

He dug into his jeans pocket and pulled out his wallet.

'You could buy some homemade scones?' she suggested.

'Did you make them?' he asked, widening his eyes.

'Why do you say it like that?' she demanded.

'Like what?' he asked innocently.

'You know, looking surprised that I could make scones.'

'Can you?'

'No, but ...'

A loud rapping on one of the tables made them turn. The chatter and laughter slowly died away.

'Blanche is going to sing a song,' said Jack, clearing people back so Blanche could be seen.

The pub was silent, and Blanche began to sing something that she and her mother had written. Beth winced at its corniness but watched and listened in wide-eyed wonder along with everyone else. Blanche's voice was croaky and out of tune, but everyone clapped and cheered when she had finished.

'Bravo,' yelled Jack. He was about to say more when Mae took the microphone from him.

'Thank you so much to all of you who have come this evening. It means the world to Blanche and me.'

Beth glanced at Blanche. She looked tired and sad. It was clearly too much for her, and Beth wondered why her mother put her through it.

'It's been a difficult year,' continued Mae. 'We're so grateful for the continued financial support we have received. We're so lucky to have such wonderful and supportive friends ....'

She broke off suddenly, and Kate hurried to her side.

'Most of all,' she finished tearfully, 'I'm so lucky, Blanche, to be your mum.'

There wasn't a dry eye in the house, except perhaps for Blanche's. She was looking at her mother, Tom thought, not with love and gratitude but with sympathy. He thought that odd, considering everyone else was looking at Blanche with sympathy. He finished his coke, pushed a twenty-pound note into the charity box and waved to Beth.

'You're not leaving already?'

'I'll see you in the morning.'

She watched him walk through the doors without a backward glance.

'Unfriendly bugger,' she muttered and wandered back to the bar.

'Let's have some of those sausage rolls,' she said to Jack.

'On the house?' he laughed.

'Why not,' she smiled.

Chapter Thirty-Nine

2005: Leeds

Mae

I'd never stood in front of so many people before. I was nervous but fully prepared. Doctor Morris said the turnout had far exceeded his expectations. Blanche had written a poem, especially for the evening. I had asked Rob to come. I thought he would be proud to hear Blanche's poem.

'Is it all about sickness?' he asked.

'It's about our battle, yes,' I said.

'Battle?'

I thought he'd smirked.

'I've got work to do this evening,' he said.

I knew that wasn't true. The new job didn't have the pressures of Rotech. What he meant was, he'd prefer to stay home and get drunk. I'd done my best not to antagonise him in those days, but It felt like everything I said or did, made him angry. I sometimes thought he would have been happier if Blanche had never been born. He'd been mad about the money. Maybe I should have shared it with him, but I had wanted to give Blanche the best of everything, and Rob would have wanted to spend it on other things, like holidays and meals out. Everyone at church said what a wonderful mother I was. They rarely mentioned Rob. Once I'd told them that Rob wasn't a church person, they'd stopped asking after him. They were family to us. On the days I worked at the surgery, one of the church community would care for Blanche. I never wanted Rob to know how much Blanche and I earned from our talks. That was our security, Blanche's and mine. I found different hiding places for our money. I was a good caring mother. Surely, I deserved to be rewarded.

Rob loved me. I felt sure of that. It was just the drink that had a bad effect on him. He'd worry about work. I never understood why he was so unhappy. We had a nice house and a lovely daughter and

People at church who cared about us. If only he'd come home earlier, then he would see Blanche more. He didn't like the meals I cooked. That was why he came home late. He ate out instead. I couldn't understand his selfishness. Surely, he hadn't expected me to cook separate meals for Blanche? He has this odd idea that he and I should have a date night every so often. How ridiculous. We'd been married for eleven years. I wished so much that he would come to church with us. I was sure he'd gain so much from it.

I'd listened to Blanche recite her poem, and tears had filled my eyes. Then it had been my turn.

'I'm truly blessed to be your mum,' I began.

I saw people wiping their eyes as I told them how my lovely daughter's life had been ruined by a caesarean birth her mother never wanted. Blanche had sat beside me, and we'd held hands. We had been joined by this terrible tragedy that had befallen us, and people cared. Doctor Morris had watched us with approving eyes. We were special. If only Rob had been able to see that and be part of it. They presented us with a beautiful bouquet and a cheque for £500 to go towards Blanche's treatment.

'For your wonderful charity,' said the woman who handed over the cheque. I should have got the charity properly registered. I kept meaning to. It's just there was always so much else to do.

'You're such an inspiration, both of you,' Leah Morris said.

John Morris and his wife had been marvellous. I don't know what we would have done without them.

'Blanche is looking well, isn't she?' said Leah.

'Do you think?'

'Oh yes.'

'I'm rather worried about the back pain she has started having. I hope it isn't anything.'

Her face had clouded over.

'Oh no. Have you mentioned it to John?'

'I will.'

He had always been so understanding, unlike Blanche's previous GP.

'I don't know how you cope,' she said, hugging me.

It had been such a wonderful evening. I so wished Rob had been there with us. I'd told everyone he had an important contract to finish.

I couldn't very well say he despised the church, and the last place he wanted to spend an evening was in a stuffy church hall.

'He must be so proud of you both,' people said.

We left later than I'd planned, and Blanche seemed tired. I decided to get her back x-rayed the next day to be on the safe side. Rob was home when we got back and seemed happy to see us.

'How did it go?' he asked.

'Everyone liked my poem,' Blanche told him,

'That's terrific, babe,' he smiled.

At least he wasn't drunk. He'd had some wine, the bottle was on the kitchen table, but it was still half full.

My daughter, that was how I thought of her, not our daughter had developed into a beautiful girl. Her almond-shaped brown eyes shone with happiness at her father's interest.

'I'm glad it went well,' he said, looking at me.

At that moment, I believed we could be a family again. I couldn't have been more wrong.

Chapter Forty

September 2019: Stonesend

It had turned chilly. Sophie wished she'd worn a jumper. Cold licked at her face and crept under her clothes, spreading across her skin like the lacy tide on a chilly winter beach. She couldn't believe how quickly the weather had turned. Again, she checked the messages on her phone. There was still no reply. Several times she stopped and looked behind her, feeling sure she had heard footsteps, but of course, there was no one there. She let out a relieved sigh when she saw lights on inside Mae's house, and her car was sitting on the driveway. It was all right, after all. She'd let her imagination run wild. Nothing terrible had happened. Mae didn't have to answer every message. All the same, she was glad she had come. She'd brought an early print of the village magazine for Mae to see. It had her piece about the charity evening in it.

'Just thought I'd drop this in,' she'd say. But, of course, she needn't mention the unanswered calls and messages.

Any minute the door would open, and everything would be as it always was. But it didn't open, not even after Sophie had pushed the bell three times. The knot in her stomach tightened. It would be an overreaction to phone the police. All the same …

'Mae,' she called through the letterbox. 'It's Sophie.'

The 999 call was logged at 7.30 on a chilly September evening.

'Emergency, what service do you require?'

Sophie wasn't sure. Now that she was actually through to someone, she began to worry that perhaps she was being stupid. Letting her imagination get the better of her. But, after what had happened to Kate.'

'It's my neighbour. She's not answering her phone or replying to any of her messages. It's not like her. I'm at her house, and her car is in the driveway. I'm concerned about her. She has a sick daughter, you see. I've rung the doorbell several times, but she's not answering.'

The Lies She Told

It all sounded so ridiculous when she said it out loud. But it was unusual for Mae not to respond to WhatsApp messages.

'Are you calling from your own phone?'

'Yes, I am.'

'Who am I talking to?'

Why didn't they just get on with it?

'Sophie, Sophie Johnson. I'm a neighbour. The thing is, she hasn't been answering her phone all day. I should have come earlier, but I thought maybe she was out of signal or ….'

She was waffling. Keep calm.

'Can you see through the window?'

'No, the curtains are closed, so I can't see in. Her car is here, so she must be home.'

'What is the address of the house?'

'Millhouse, Churchfields, that's in Stonesend. It's a small village.'

A quiet, friendly community, that's how the agent had described it to them all those years ago. 'Not many villages like this nowadays,' he'd smiled. The house details had shown a picturesque, quintessential English village. They'd fallen in love with it immediately.

'Perfect,' Grant had enthused. 'Not too far from London but far enough to escape the hubbub.'

It was off the beaten track, but everyone liked it that way. It was easy to get to the shops, and the local school was excellent. Lainey had flourished there. It had been the best decision they'd made. At least that's what Sophie had thought, until seven weeks ago.

'I will get a police officer out to you. Is it possible your neighbour has gone away?'

'No, she was due at our craft morning today but didn't come, and she always does.'

'A police officer is on his way to you.'

Sophie thanked her and hung up. From the pub, she could hear music playing. She'd forgotten it was a live music night. She always did. Every Monday, she determined that she and Grant would go, but they had both forgotten all about it by Friday. She ought to WhatsApp Grant, tell him what's going on. He'll no doubt think she has overreacted. Perhaps she has. In her stomach, though, was a horrible sinking feeling. It had been there ever since Kate and that terrible day when their quiet, quintessential English village had become the centre of a police investigation. Please God, she prayed, don't let it have happened again.

Chapter Forty-One

Sergeant Matt Wilkins paid for his sausage and chips and headed back to the patrol car to eat them. He only got as far as unwrapping the paper. The aroma of vinegared chips reached his nostrils. He grabbed one to satisfy his craving and then answered a call on his radio.

He recognised the name of the road. It was the street where Kate Marshall lived. A surge of adrenalin shot through Matt's body.

'On my way,' he said.

He hadn't expected to be the dispatch officer going to Churchfields seven weeks after the Marshall attack. It was most likely nothing, but all the same, the story was strangely similar. Neighbour not answering her door and no reason why she shouldn't. Not responding to phone messages. A car parked in the driveway.

It would be stupid to call for backup before he'd even arrived, but it was indeed sensible to tell someone at the station that this weird call had been made. Just to be sure, just to cover himself.

'I'll pass it on,' said Patsy on the switchboard.

The pub was lively. Outside, a blackboard advertised live folk music. Matt would have gone if he hadn't had been on the late shift. He approached the house, and a woman, Matt gauged to be in her thirties, hurried towards the patrol car. He recognised her but didn't know her personally.

'Oh, thank goodness,' she said breathlessly.

He smiled at her.

'Sophie?'

'Yes, thanks so much for coming.'

'I'm Sergeant Wilkins. So, you can't get your friend to answer the door?' he asked, climbing from the car.

The woman looked anxious. Her cheek was twitching, and she spoke very fast.

'I've been ringing the bell, but she's not answering. The curtains are closed so you can't see inside. The back gate is bolted. It's probably nothing but ....'

They were both thinking the same thing. Was it a repeat of the Marshall attack?

'You did the right thing,' he assured her.

'She hasn't been answering the phone all day. I should have come round earlier, but ….'

'Who lives at the house?'

'Mae Lethbridge. The thing is, she has a daughter who has lots of health problems. She's had cancer treatment. I don't understand why Mae isn't opening the door. We had the village craft morning today, and they didn't turn up. They always do. At first, I thought maybe Blanche had been taken to hospital, so I phoned Mae, but she never answered. There must be something wrong. I keep messaging her, and she hasn't even read them. It's not like her. She usually answers right away.'

Sophie was aware she was talking too quickly. Matt looked up at the house and then strode towards the front door. He rang the doorbell just as Sophie had done. He then peered in through the window.

'What about her husband. Have you contacted him?'

'Mae doesn't have a husband. It's just her and Blanche, her daughter.'

Sophie couldn't understand why he wasn't doing more. Although she wasn't sure what else he could do aside from breaking the door down, and she supposed that was premature under the circumstances.

'It's just … well, one of my neighbours, Kate Marshall …' she trailed off when she saw the expression on the officer's face.

'Yes, I understand your concern,' he said. 'Does anyone else have a key to the house?'

'No, I don't think so.'

He leant down to the letterbox and shouted.

'Mae, I'm Sergeant Wilkins, can you hear me? Is anyone at home?'

Sophie bit her nails as they waited.

'Anyone in the house, please make yourself known,' Matt called again.

'Can you call her mobile again?' he asked.

Sophie pulled her phone from her bag called Mae again, while Matt pushed his ear close to the open letterbox and listened. He could hear a faint ringtone. Then it stopped.

'Can you try again?'

Sophie hit the number again. She was feeling frustrated. Why didn't he do something?

Again, Matt heard the ringtone. 'Her phone is in the house,' he said.

Sophie's heart thumped in her chest. Matt calmly called for backup after announcing he was going in.

Chapter Forty-Two

September 2019: Belmarsh Prison, London

Sid Dawson was a good hater. He hated his job. He hated the weather, and most of all, Sid hated child killers. Especially the dirty, warped bastards who messed with the little ones first.

'Saw their cocks off and let the buggers bleed to death,' was Sid's punishment for Paedophiles.

It broke his heart when a kid got murdered and broke his heart, even more, when he saw their killers protected in the nick.

Lester Lynch was filth as far as he was concerned. He treated the place like the fucking Savoy and dished out his orders as if he were royalty. It sickened Sid that the warped bastard had photographs of kids pasted around his cell.

On this particular evening, Sid was in a worse mood than usual. His piles were playing up. He hated late shifts. His wife had nagged him continuously over dinner about how he kept promising to take her to Ikea but never did. Then he couldn't get the car to start, and Barb had admitted to perhaps leaving the lights on the night before after she got back from the bingo.

'Jesus,' he'd cursed.

He'd had to get a taxi into work. It had been too late to catch the train. He was fed up before he even started his shift. Then he'd seen the birthday balloons outside Lester's cell.

'It's the pervert's birthday,' said one of the inmates. 'You gonna have some of the cake?'

'You gonna move on?' asked Sid.

He walked towards the cell and nodded at the warden who stood outside.

'Bit of a celebration, is it?' he asked.

Mick forced a smile.

'You could say that.'

'Alright, Mick?' asked Sid, looking at him closely.

Mick shook his head. Sid thought he looked a bit grey.

'Not feeling a hundred per cent,' said Mick, wiping the sweat from his forehead.

'You going down with something?'

'He can go down on me if he likes,' laughed Lester from inside his cell.

'Shut your fucking, filthy mouth, or I'll shut it for you,' said Sid, through gritted teeth.

Sid turned to Mick.

'Perhaps you should go home.'

'He'll miss the cake,' chimed in Lynch.

Sid balled his fists and wished he could smash them into the fucker's face. Mick clenched his stomach and grimaced in pain.

'Jesus, you look rough,' commented Sid. 'Get home before you pebble dash the walls. I'll cover here.'

'I don't know,' Mick said uncertainly. 'You don't usually watch here.'

'I'll just stick around while you report in sick and they send someone. How's that?'

Mick nodded. 'Thanks, Sid.'

Sid waited until Mick was out of sight before turning to Lynch.

'So,' he said, smiling at Lynch. 'You've got me for a bit, birthday boy, so you'd better fucking behave.'

Lynch gave a cocky grin.

'That's nice. You'll have to pop in and have a bit of cake with me. I can show you me boys,' he said, pointing to the pictures.

Sid wanted to rip all the photos off the wall and ram them down the little prick's throat.

'Not every screw in here has been bought,' he said menacingly and walked away.

'You got a grandson, ain't ya?' called Lynch.

Sid stopped abruptly.

'What did you say?' he said harshly.

Lynch laughed.

'I thought so. Good guess, huh? Pretty, is he? Don't suppose you have a photo of him that I could put in my boy's gallery?'

'You fucking piece of shit,' snarled Sid, taking a few paces towards him.

'Fucking piece of shit,' sang some of the inmates. 'Fucking piece of horseshit.'

'You lot shut it,' yelled Sid.

'Go on, lay one on me. I dare you,' taunted Lynch.

Sid now shook with anger and took two more steps towards Lester, who was beckoning him to come closer. Finally, Sid reached the doors of the cell.

'Come in,' said Lester. 'I won't bite.'

Lynch's eyes sparkled with excitement when Sid unlocked the cell. Sid's eyes met Lynch's for a few seconds. He saw they were icy cold and glittering. Then, clenching his fists, Sid walked away.

'Come and tell me all about your little boy,' smirked Lester. 'I bet he's got skin as smooth as silk and ….'

'Shut your filthy mouth,' snarled Sid.

He didn't want to picture his little Charlie through this scum's eyes.

'Fucking piece of shit,' cried the inmates.

Lynch stepped back in anticipation. Sid just nodded and then turned to walk away.

'You can't leave my cell unlocked,' cried Lester, feeling a wave of anger.

Sid passed the cells, his hands clenched tightly in his pockets. If he was ten years younger and …

'Babies they were. Wee little bairns didn't stand a fucking chance. Give me just thirty minutes with him, and I'll teach the bastard a lesson,' said Fergus Monroe. 'It could have been your little grandson. There but for the grace of God.'

Sid stared at him. His cheek twitched.

'Their poor parents. Having to live with what that scum did.'

Monroe nodded toward Lynch.

Sid glanced around, and secure in the knowledge that no one could see, he quickly unlocked Monroe's cell.

'You're not supposed to leave my cell unlocked,' Lynch cried. Sid ignored his calls and carried on walking.

'Come back, you bastard,' screamed Lynch, but Sid barely heard him above the chorus of voices singing, 'Fucking piece of shit.'

Chapter Forty-Three

2007: Leeds

Rob

I never expected to see Jo again. I heard that after we'd broken up, she'd gone back home to Brighton. It was a hell of a way from Leeds. I'd thought about her so often that when I actually saw her, I thought I must be imagining it. I'd been waiting my turn in the sandwich bar just around the corner from the office. She'd been in front of me the whole time, and I hadn't even noticed. It was only when she turned to leave that I realised it was her. Our eyes had met. Hers had shown more than surprise. Pleasure, perhaps. I couldn't imagine what mine showed. Desire? Need? I know I was happy to see her. Then guilt had punched me in the stomach when I remembered how I'd ended it. I'd sent a text. The coward's way out. I'd slipped out of the queue. I hadn't wanted her to walk out of the door and out of my life again. I never thought it through. I'd seen her, and I wanted her.

'Jo,' I tried to sound nonchalant, but my voice betrayed me.

'Rob, how are you?' her voice had trembled.

'I've been better,' I said and realised it sounded self-pitying. We were blocking the door. I took her arm and led her outside.

'It's good to see you.'

She moved away, so my hand slid from her arm. 'I thought you were in Brighton.'

She looked wonderful. Her eyes shone, and her cheeks had that rosy glow.

'I was,' she replied. 'There was nothing there. No work. At least nothing challenging.'

I learned she had been working quite close to my office. She'd been there almost a year, and I'd never once seen her.

'How are things?' she asked, avoiding my eyes.

'Not great. Worse than before.'

'I'm sorry.'

She glanced at her watch.

'I'm running late.'

She turned to leave, and I panicked.

'Can I see you again? Please?'

She looked around as though she thought people were eavesdropping.

'Aren't you trying to make things work with your wife?'

I sighed.

'They're not working,' I said.

She bit her lip before saying, 'Meet me at The Crown. Eight o'clock?'

I'm sure I beamed with pleasure.

'Great.'

I wanted to kiss her goodbye but held myself back. I'd been given a second chance and I wasn't going to do anything to blow it. Of course, I thought of Mae. I always did. It wasn't really in my nature to be unfaithful, but a man gets desperate, and a desperate man will do anything. I know now it was a stupid way to think, but I'd started to believe that Blanche was bad luck. Call them the imaginings of a desperate man, but it had seemed to me that everything had gone wrong the moment I'd planted that seed in Mae's womb. Blanche had come between us right from the very beginning. Blanche had taken Mae away from me. It was Blanche who received all of Mae's love. It would be Blanche who would benefit from Mae's inheritance too. I think Mae often forgot that she wouldn't have Blanche if it hadn't been for me. Some days I hated them both, and others, I loved them more than life itself.

Chapter Forty-Four

September 2019: Stonesend

Beth was heading for the door when Stella's message came through.

'Sgt Wilkins asked me to pass on his call out. A woman called the police. She can't get her neighbour to open the door.'

Beth looked at Tom.

'There's no reason to think it is a repeat of the Kate Marshall case,' he said.

'You're very positive,' said Beth.

'There could be any number of reasons why she's not opening the door.'

He grabbed his wallet and phone.

'All the same, we should check it out. Get them to phone through the details.'

Beth thought of her cosy, warm bed and sighed. They reached the car just as the radio crackled. 'Sergeant Wilkins requesting back up at Mill house in Churchfields.'

'Mill House?' repeated Beth. 'That's the Lethbridge place.'

The fact that Matt was requesting backup took them both by surprise.

'We're on our way,' Beth said into the radio. 'Patch me through to him.'

'Too much of a coincidence,' she said, her hands tensing in her lap. Had Kate's attacker struck again? Her radio crackled and then Matt's voice came through.

'Woman's name is Mrs Mae Lethbridge,' he said. 'Lives with her daughter. Mobile phone is ringing inside the house. I've called through the letterbox, but no response. The back gate is locked. I'm going to climb over and see if I can get in by the back door.'

Beth's hands were still clenched. What if he'd done it again? What if this time he had succeeded? She could hear Matt breathing as he walked round to the back gate.

'Mrs Lethbridge, are you there?' he called.

Beth strained her ears but heard nothing.

'I'm climbing over,' said Matt.

'Don't take risks,' Tom said firmly. 'Wait for backup.'

Beth listened intently. She could hear Matt's heavy breathing as he climbed the gate.

'The back door's been forced. I'm going in.'

'I repeat, wait for backup,' urged Tom.

Beth realised she'd been holding her breath and exhaled heavily. There was a creaking sound as a door opened.

'Mae Lethbridge, it's Sergeant Wilkins from the police,' called Matt. Beth heard the tremble in his voice.

Beth waited to hear Mae Lethbridge's voice, but there was only silence.

'Hello, is there anyone here?' called Matt.

'We're almost there,' said Beth. Tom rounded the bend, and Mae's house came into view. Sophie Johnson stood outside looking up at the house. Tom stopped the car, and Beth hurried from it.

'We're here, Sergeant Wilkins,' Tom said into the radio before following her. Beth struggled to control her breathing. Something had happened at Mae Lethbridge's house, and Beth felt sure it was something terrible. It had taken him seven weeks to strike again. How long would she have before the next time?

Chapter Forty-Five

2005: Leeds

Mae

'Scoliosis, what's that?' Rob asked, frowning.
'It means her spine is curved. She needs a brace to help straighten it.'
He looked at me as though I had gone mad.
'You mean like teeth braces?'
Blanche was in bed. I still hadn't had time to explain the brace to her. She was not going to like it. It was alright for Rob; he didn't have to deal with these problems. He'd been keen enough for the caesarean, though, hadn't he? I opened the cupboard under the stairs and removed the box that held the brace and showed it to him.
'She's got to wear that all the time?' he said, shocked.
'At night. I told you, she should have had a natural birth.'
'I can't believe the caesarean is the cause of all this.'
I shoved the brace back into the box.
'If her spine doesn't straighten, she won't be able to walk properly.'
'This is ridiculous,' he snapped, striding into the kitchen. 'I'm going to see Doctor Morris. I don't want her wearing that bloody thing.'
I followed him into the kitchen. He was pouring wine into a glass.
'Don't drink, Rob. It's not the answer.'
He turned on me, his face contorted with anger.
'Sometimes, I think you like her being sick.'
I reeled back.
'That's a terrible thing to say. Everyone says what a wonderful mother I am, except you, of course. I don't hear people saying what a marvellous father you are.'
'When have I had a chance to be any kind of father? There's never been room for me.'
'That's nonsense,' I said crossly.

'You mean the people at church, don't you? Those fucking do-gooders. Be honest, Mae, if Blanche were a healthy kid, you wouldn't be getting anywhere near the attention you're getting. Or the money come to that. Does Vicar whatsisname know you pocket all that so-called charity money?'

I gasped.

'I do not pocket it. I'm just keeping it safe until I get round to setting up a charity account.'

He laughed.

'Yeah, right. Well, you don't need my money, do you?'

My eyes filled with tears. How could Rob say such terrible things to me? I was the one person who loved Blanche more than life itself. I did everything to make her life better.

'You're cruel,' I said.

'I think you're talking about the wrong person here, Mae.'

I turned and hurried from the kitchen. I didn't want him to see my tears. Tomorrow I'll go to see Michael, the vicar, and his wife, Lisa. They would understand. I'll ask them to pray for Blanche on Sunday.

'You've changed,' he yelled from the kitchen.

'I became a mother,' I yelled back.

'Yes, and just in case you've forgotten, I also became a father.'

The front door slammed. He'd left again. He was doing that a lot lately. It was an excellent excuse to see *her*. I knew all about it. He sometimes smelled of her perfume. In a way, I was glad. I had tried to make things work, but it had been futile. We had lost everything we once had. Blanche had come between us. It wasn't true what people said, that children brought you closer together. Rob and I couldn't have been further apart. I knew that one day he would leave, and I almost looked forward to it. I was a Christian woman, and as such, I would stay with my husband. No one would be able to say that I'd been in the wrong. I took the brace from the box and studied it. Blanche and I would cope. We would get all the support we needed from church and, who knows, maybe someone would offer Blanche a lovely holiday. She needed that. I placed the brace back in the box and sat at the kitchen table with my computer. Blanche and I had a talk in a week, and I needed to prepare. The bottle of wine still sat on the table, and I poured myself a glass. Blanche and I would be absolutely fine when Rob left. I had enough money. Maybe Blanche and I could move to the country. We could start afresh, just the two of us. I'd never have to worry about bumping into Rob and his fancy piece. Yes, that's what we'd do.

Chapter Forty-Six

September 2019: Stonesend

Adrenalin flooded through Beth's body. The walk down Mae Lethbridge's front path seemed to take forever. She recognised the woman standing by the front door.

'We'll need you to stand at the gate,' said Tom, ushering her back.

'It's alright, Soph,' Beth said gently. 'It's for your protection.'

Sophie wrung her hands anxiously.

'Has something happened to Mae?' she asked tearfully. 'Are they okay?'

'We're going to find out,' said Tom.

The side gate opened as they reached it. Matt nodded and pointed to the back door.

'I called out, but no response. I then came out to wait for backup.'

'Sensible move, sergeant,' said Tom.

Beth glanced down at her hands and saw they were shaking. Her heart was beating so fast she was having difficulty breathing. She licked her lips to relieve their dryness.

'Ready?' Tom asked.

He's not even sweating, thought Beth. His hands are as steady as a rock. Minutes later, they were in Mae's kitchen. It was tidy. Much to Beth's relief there were no blood-splattered walls. Tom moved slowly through the kitchen and opened the door into the hallway. They crept along until they were standing at the bottom of the stairs. Beth looked up.

'The stairlift chair is at the top,' she said.

'Mrs Lethbridge,' Tom called.

He gestured to the living room, and Beth grasped the door handle.

'Mrs Lethbridge, are you home?'

She opened the door slowly, preparing for the worst.

'Careful,' warned Tom.

'This is a village,' she hissed.

'Oh yeah, crime-free,' he muttered.

She peered around the door of the living room. The curtains were drawn and the lights on.

'It's DS Beth Harper, Mrs Lethbridge. Are you okay? We've been ringing the doorbell?'

Beth walked cautiously into the room. It was empty.

'Check the other rooms,' said Tom.

Beth noted Blanche's wheelchair in the corner. They can't have gone out, she thought. Blanche couldn't go anywhere unless she were in her wheelchair. Beth had read a piece that the local paper had done on them. Blanche was very sick. Mae had done a lot to raise awareness of the difficulties facing parents with a severely ill child. They were good people, so who the hell would want to harm them?

'Seventeen years old, but with the mental age of a twelve-year-old due to brain damage at birth.' The article had read. 'Blanche Lethbridge was a caesarean baby. Her mother, Mae Lethbridge, has always claimed that the hospital where Blanche was born had taken too long in making the decision to perform the caesarean.'

Beth had barely been able to read the piece without tears blurring her vision. Blanche had coped after suffering from Muscular Dystrophy, asthma, and severe epilepsy. Finally, to have the added burden of cancer. It seemed so cruel.

'The diagnosis of Leukaemia was a real blow to us. For Blanche to lose her lovely long curly hair was heart-breaking,' Mae had said.

The house seemed deathly quiet now. Something was very wrong, and Beth knew it was just a matter of time before they discovered what it was. Matt opened the door to the dining room and called out. There was no response. Everything in the dining room looked normal.

Tom turned to Matt.

'Check the garden and the shed if there is one.'

Matt nodded and turned back to the kitchen. Beth and Tom cautiously made their way upstairs. The house smelt sickeningly of antiseptic and floral disinfectant.

'It smells like a hospital,' commented Tom.

'It doesn't make sense that they're not in the house. Blanche needs her wheelchair to go out. That's in the living room.'

'And the stairlift is upstairs,' he said, nodding towards it.

The stairs creaked as they climbed them. As they neared the top, the smell changed, and Tom's stomach contracted. He knew that smell. The first door on the landing was ajar. Tom pushed it gently and it swung open, revealing a spotlessly clean bathroom. A creak on the stairs made them turn, their shoulders tensed.

'It's their cat,' said Beth, exhaling heavily. The cat scratched at the door in front of them. Beth hesitated for a second. Her throat was so dry that she could barely speak.

'Mae,' she called. 'It's Beth Harper. Is everything alright?'

There was no response. Beth had desperately hoped for one.

'We're coming in,' said Tom, his voice clear and firm. Even before he opened the door, Beth knew that everything was not alright.

Chapter Forty-Seven

2005: Leeds

Rob

As the years passed, I got used to being the outsider in Blanche's life. I tried to be part of everything she and her mother did, but it just didn't work. I hated the church and its hypocrisy. I hated that everything revolved around Blanche's health. I went to see Doctor Morris after Mae told me about the body brace. I couldn't bear the thought of Blanche wearing that ugly thing. Surely there was something else they could do? I'd shied away from the illnesses. It unnerved me. I didn't even want to see the damn brace.

Doctor Morris had treated me like an imbecile.

'Mae said you might come and see me,' he said. 'She explained that you had some difficulty coping with Blanche's frailties.'

'How can she be so sick all the time?' I asked and heard the accusing tone in my voice. 'Why can't you help her?'

He smiled at me condescendingly

'We have done everything in our power to help Blanche,' he said calmly. 'Caesarean births sometimes …

'That's a load of baloney,' I interrupted. 'Loads of babies are born that way, and they don't have all these health problems.'

'Blanche is not a strong child ….'

'I think you believe too much of what my wife tells you.'

'Excuse me?' His lips tightened. I'd hit a raw nerve.

'Mae panics when Blanche gets slightly hot and ….'

'Mae is a good mother, caring and attentive.'

Meaning I wasn't, I suppose.

'You think you know my wife better than I do?'

'That's not what I said. Mae is an excellent nurse. I think she monitors Blanche's health very well. I can understand how difficult it must be to live with a sick child. It can be very stressful and ….'

'I'm not stressed, at least not about Blanche.'

He laid a hand on my arm, and I flinched.

'Mae has mentioned you've had some difficulties ....'

Mae had talked about our relationship without telling me? I turned to the door.

'She had no right,' I said angrily.

'Some children are sickly,' he said casually. 'It's just the way it is.'

'Why does she have to wear that body brace?'

'You will need to speak to the hospital specialist regarding that, I'm afraid. I don't know anything about the body brace.'

I opened the door and left. I went to Jo's straight after work and stayed the night. I'd never stayed overnight before. I'd always messaged Mae when I was going to be late, but I didn't bother this time. I felt hurt and angry at her betrayal. I'd been thrown out like a piece of garbage. I felt used. My salary was still being paid into our joint account, yet Mae never shared a penny of her money. I felt I deserved Jo. I needed to feel important to someone. It never occurred to me that Mae might worry where I was.

'You should message her,' Jo said. 'She might be worried. Tell her the truth. Tell her you're with me. Get it out in the open.'

'I will tell her tomorrow,' I said.

She snuggled closer, and we sat there for some time, feeling the warmth of each other.

'Will you leave her?' she asked.

I stroked her hair. It always felt silky to the touch.

'Yes,' I said.

There was no reason for me to stay. Mae had Blanche, and that seemed to be all she needed. I needed comfort too. I knew I'd never get that at home. I loved Mae, but I just couldn't live with her anymore.

Chapter Forty-Eight
September 2019: Stonesend

Tom cautiously turned the knob of the bedroom door. Who knew what lay the other side? His hand shook as he remembered the last time he'd kicked open a door. He'd never forget that moment. It was etched on his mind forever. He remembered the chill that had run through him and the sound of Dennis's heavy breathing.

'I don't like this,' Dennis had whispered from behind him.

They hadn't wanted to see beyond the door. They already knew the horror that lay behind it. The smell had hit their nostrils the minute they had smashed down the front door. The relief Tom had felt at having finally found them was mixed with the horror and reality of having to see them. The smell of dry rot had mingled with the scent of death. Tom had taken a deep breath and kicked in the door. Dennis had shone his torch, its light flickering with the trembling of his hand. The beam had landed on a bundle in the corner.

'Jesus, God almighty,' Dennis had groaned and rushed, retching, up the basement steps.

Colin had followed Tom, but the smell and sight of the three young boys lying prostrate on the floor had been too much for him too.

Tom had shouted for blankets. Slowly and methodically, he had wrapped one boy at a time in a blanket, covering their faces. He knew by the time they got the boys out, there would be a crowd waiting. He recognised each child. God knows he'd studied their photos enough. They'd become family to him.

'It's over,' he'd whispered. 'It's finally over.'

One by one, he'd brought the children out from the cold basement while grown men wept on the pavement.

He'd wanted to burn the house down. Burn the house and Lester Lynch with it.

'Tom,' said Beth, breaking into his thoughts.

He pulled his mind back to the present.

'Stand back,' he ordered.

He kicked the door. It swung open, slamming against the bedroom wall.

'Mae,' he called loudly.

The room was in darkness. Beth knew that beyond was something terrible. The feeling of impending doom that Beth had felt from the moment Stella's message came through was now about to become a reality, and she wasn't sure she could face it. Ten years in the police force and she'd never seen anything that would give her nightmares, that was, until now.

'Mae, it's Beth Harper. We're coming in.' Beth knew that Mae would not answer. Tiny shafts of light sneaked in through a gap in the curtains. She could hear Tom breathing heavily.

'Mae, it's Beth Harper. I'm going to turn on the light.' Beth's hand fumbled along the wall for the switch, found it and the room was immediately hit by a flood of light. At that moment, Beth felt her stomach contract. Her body grew cold, and she began to shiver as if someone had just opened a window. The white sheets on Mae's bed were crumpled beneath her and covered dark red with her blood. Beth's eyes travelled to the body. Mae's eyes stared wildly at them, registering the horror she'd been subjected to. Blood had splattered onto the curtains and the cream quilted headboard. It looked as though Mae had been attacked as she slept. God, thought Beth, she must have woken to see her attacker. The fear must have been unreal. Nausea overwhelmed her, and she swayed slightly. Tom grasped her arm.

'You okay? Do you need some air?'

She shook her head.

'No, I'm okay.'

They turned at the sound of pounding footsteps on the stairs.

'Anything?' Matt questioned, entering the room. 'Nothing in the garden and ….'

He stopped at the sight of the massacre in front of him.

'Jesus Christ,' he gasped.

He'd been nervous when they'd entered the house, but he sure as hell hadn't expected this.

'Where's the daughter?' asked Matt.

'Search again.' Ordered Tom. 'She has to be somewhere. She needs a wheelchair so she can't be far away.'

'Right,' said Matt, shakily.

'Are we looking for a body?' asked Beth.

Tom frowned.

'I hope not, but I'm not ruling it out.'

Who'd kill a helpless kid?

'Don't touch anything,' Tom said. 'I'll contact the pathologist.'

Beth cautiously approached the body and saw that Mae was wearing a nightgown. It had a teddy bear motif on it. Somehow it made the whole thing so much worse. Beside the bed were a packet of pills and a bottle of gin. Beth glanced at the medication label through misty eyes. She roughly wiped at her cheeks. Keep it together, she told herself firmly. She noted the blood on Mae's nightie was dark in colour, as was the blood on the bedsheets. Not fresh blood thought Beth. She must have been killed early this morning or late last night. Which meant that if Blanche wasn't in the house, she'd been missing for several hours.

Had Kate been right all along? Had it been a case of mistaken identity? Had the killer wanted Mae Lethbridge? Had he or she perhaps got the wrong house, or were they dealing with a serial killer? In which case, he or she could strike again and at any time. She could hear Matt calling out to Blanche, the sound of doors opening. Tom on the phone calling forensics.

At the side of the bed was an opened suitcase. Beth cocked her head and moved closer to it, careful not to disturb anything. Why would Mae have pulled out a suitcase? Were they planning on going somewhere? She then saw the suitcase was battered. A padlock on the case had been forced. The case was empty. Had the murderer come for the contents?

'The next bedroom,' said Tom, breaking into her thoughts. Beth followed, praying they wouldn't find another body. Tom turned the knob, but the door wouldn't open. He pushed his body against it and tried again.

'It's locked,' he said.

Below them came the slamming of doors, a shout and the loud whine of sirens. The Stonesend community thrown into turmoil again. Was he watching and laughing at them? Catch me if you can.

'You bastard. We will find you. So help me, God,' she muttered.

'We need to force it,' Tom said. 'This is DI Miller. We're coming in.'

Beth stood back while Tom forced the lock. The door finally swung open, and the smell hit her immediately. She couldn't quite define it. It was familiar, though. That sterile smell you get in hospitals. The smell of sickness. The room was in darkness. A blackout curtain hung at the window. She swung the torch around and found a light switch. Then she heard it. A whimper? Or was it the cry of a cat?

'Who's here?' she said, clicking on the light.

She let out a small gasp.

'Blanche?' she questioned. 'Blanche Lethbridge?'

Chapter Forty-Nine
2005 Leeds

Mae

I was frantic. Usually, Rob messaged me to say he was going to be late. I'd been used to that. When I didn't get a message, I just presumed he was coming home for dinner. Blanche and I had dinner at seven like we always did, and I left Rob's in the microwave to heat up when he got home. By eight, I started to get worried and rechecked my phone. Blanche had gone to bed, and I watched an episode of a thriller series I'd been following. By eight forty-five, I began to get an anxious fluttering in my stomach. Rob always messaged.

I knew he was most likely with her, but all the same, he always let me know if he was going to be late home. Finally, against my better judgement, I texted him, but the message wasn't received. Either he'd turned his phone off, or he had no signal. I checked it several times, but it still hadn't been read. By nine, I was frantic and had convinced myself he had been in a car accident. Maybe he was unconscious, and no one knew who he was. I told myself how silly that was. He would have his driving licence on him. They would trace me from that. All the same, I decided to phone the hospitals and was relieved to hear that no road accidents had come in that evening. I'd then gone from frantic to angry. It was cruel and unnecessary to deliberately make me worry.

I considered phoning him but changed my mind. Instead, I went to bed and had my usual nightcap, but even the gin didn't help me sleep. Had Rob left me? Was the marriage finally over? His clothes were still in the wardrobe. Was he planning to come and get them the next day? Had she given him an ultimatum? Leave your wife or else?

Mother always said he would leave me in the end. 'He's not the reliable type,' she used to say. 'He's always had an eye for the ladies.'

I never believed her. I felt sure she had only said those things so she could have more of me to herself. I'd grow angry just remembering all the things she used to say and when I thought of all that money she'd had, hoarding it the whole time while Rob and I had struggled. Maybe if she had given it to us earlier, we might have survived. It had been her fault. It had served her right what had happened. I tried not to think about it, knowing it would only disturb me more. I tried to sleep. If Rob had left me, then Blanche and I would move. It wouldn't take long to sell the house. I wouldn't have to give Rob anything, or would I? If he took me to court, I'd have to. Best he didn't know about it. We could move and he'd need never know where we'd gone. He should never have abandoned us. Leaving me alone, frantic with worry, while he was no doubt fucking the brains out of his new love. For the first time in our marriage, I found I actually hated Rob.

It was the early hours before I finally fell asleep. I'd kept checking my phone, but Rob hadn't read them. Sometime the following day, Rob came home and took some of his clothes.

'You could have messaged me,' I said.

'I'm moving out,' he said flatly.

That was it. No arguments, no shouting. I think we'd both had enough. I didn't mention selling the house, and he didn't mention his mistress.

'I'm sorry,' was all he said before he walked down the stairs and out of my life.

The next day I put the house on the market. The agent couldn't understand why I didn't want a board outside.

'Gets you more viewings,' he said.

'I'd rather not.'

I just had to hope that Rob wouldn't check properties online. There was no reason why he should. A week later, he phoned to ask if he could collect the rest of his things. I asked him to do it when Blanche and I were at church.

'What do you want me to tell her?' I asked.

'That we couldn't be happy together. I'd like to visit her once a week,' he said. 'I don't think that's unreasonable.'

I'd wanted to laugh. Rob had been unreasonable throughout our marriage. I rather think mum had been right about that. I often think about mum. It had been her fault everything had gone wrong. My marriage hadn't stood a chance while she was around, but I never imagined it would fall apart after she'd gone. I really believed that Blanche would complete us as a family, and I couldn't bear the thought of mum interfering with that. It had all been a waste of time.

Rob had gone anyway. Still, I had Blanche. She was all mine. I knew Mum would have put a stop to that. She said as much the day of the accident. She shouldn't have been so cruel. I'd tried to shut out what had happened that day, that awful day, but after Rob went, it all came rushing back. Some nights I would wake up in a cold sweat and feel sure that she was there, standing at the bottom of the bed, laughing at me.

'I told you so,' she'd laugh.

I haven't told the truth about that day. Not to anyone. How could I? It was my little secret, a secret hidden behind closed doors. I would have lost Blanche if anyone had found out.

I'd followed Mum upstairs that day, shouting, 'Don't worry, I don't want to go out with you.'

'What did you say?' she'd called.

I'd followed her into the bedroom.

'Forget ...' I'd stopped in the doorway, stunned at what was in front of me. Mum had been leaning over a box that sat on the bed. It was stuffed full of fifty-pound notes.

'What's that?' I'd asked.

'It's mine. You don't imagine I'd leave it in the bank where the taxman can get it, do you?'

Something had switched in my brain. Anger had surged within me. My body had tingled from top to bottom, and Blanche, sensing something, had kicked fiercely, as though she too felt the injustice.

'Where did it come from?'

'Hard work and your nanna left me a bit.'

She had all that money and the house, and she'd watched us struggle.

'When the baby comes, I'll help out. It will be the three of us. He won't stay much longer,' she'd said, trying to appease me.

The words 'the three of us' had made me shudder. She wasn't going to have my baby. I couldn't let the drunken bitch have Blanche.

'He's got a roaming eye, that one. He won't stay with you once the baby comes. You'll need me then. I'll most likely have to move in. Men can't stand not being the centre of attention. Look at your dad. He couldn't bear it when you came along. Hated that I gave you all my attention.'

'Rob won't leave me,' I'd said confidently. 'He loves me.'

'I'm the only one that loves you,' she'd said, swaying towards me.

'If you loved me, then you'd sell this house and buy a smaller one.' I'd snapped. I never use to snap. It was the hormones.

'Why should I help you? You'll abandon me then. Let me move in with you, Mae,' she'd pleaded. 'I'll help then, I promise.'

She'd clung to me, her drunken breath wafting in my face.

'Stop it. You'll upset the baby.'

'Don't be stupid.'

I'd pulled away and walked from the room, but she'd followed me.

'Stop telling me I'm stupid,' I'd yelled.

'Mae, wait.'

'You have all that money and you won't help us?'

'Mae, let's go shopping. We can talk about it over lunch. You can't afford a nanny, so ….'

'You're not moving in,' I'd shouted. 'You'll break us up.'

'He's going to go, anyway,' she'd persisted.

'No, he isn't. Rob and I are happy.'

'Mae,' she'd pleaded, pulling at my arm.

I'd twisted away from her, and when she'd gone to reach for me again, something in me snapped, and the next thing I knew, I'd pushed her. I did the right thing. She should have helped us like good mothers do. I had to leave her. I suppose I should have phoned for an ambulance, but supposing she had told them I pushed her? I couldn't go back. I couldn't take that chance. I thought I heard her call my name. I was about to become a mother. Blanche needed me. If I had told Rob the truth, he would have been horrified and left me. Mother should have put me first. That's what good mothers do. I would always put Blanche first. I'm a good mother. Everyone says so, don't they?

Chapter Fifty

September 2019: Stonesend

Tom carried Blanche downstairs to where the paramedics were waiting. Beth looked slowly around the room, her eyes taking everything in. She walked to the window and opened the curtains and blind.

The room was devoid of beauty. Its walls, painted in a simple cream, gave the room a bit of softness. There was no decoration at all, save for the limp curtains that hung at the side of the blackout blind. Beth sniffed at the undertone of bleach in the air. If Blanche had ever wanted to escape her illnesses, it would have been impossible in this room. Beside the bed was a body brace, and Beth shivered at the sight of it. The thought of Blanche's slim body squeezed into it made her feel uncomfortable. There was nothing in the room to indicate it was a young girl's bedroom. No posters on the wall. No music player. There wasn't a single teenage magazine to be seen. What girl of Blanche's age didn't read a fashion magazine? A radio sat on the bedside table, crammed between bottles of water and hand sanitiser wipes. Against the wall was an oxygen pump and mask. In the other corner was a sink. Alongside it, a tall glass cabinet that Beth could see was full of medication, thermometers, surgical gloves, and inhalers. On another shelf beside it were syringes and more medication.

'This isn't a bedroom,' she muttered. 'It's a hospital room.'

'Forensics asked if they could come in here,' said Matt from behind her.

Beth jumped at the sound of his voice.

'Yes, I should speak to the paramedics about Blanche's illness.'

'Pretty sick kid,' Matt commented, looking around.

Beth nodded.

'This will really set her back.'

'Poor kid.'

A head popped around the door. Beth recognised Don Faire, head of forensics.

'Don Faire from Oxford. Can I have a word?' he asked.

'What's up?'

'Thought you might like to know that the MO is similar to that of the Kate Marshall attack. I'm guessing here, but it could have been the same weapon.'

'When will you be sure?'

'In a few hours, I imagine. The victim took blows to the head and body. There was clearly a struggle. I'll let you have a full report later today. The estimated time of death would have been sometime last night. We'll come in here next and then work in the garden and the front. Just need to set up the lights.'

'Thanks, Don.'

'Good luck,' he said, tapping her on the shoulder.

Tom came back into the room.

'How is Blanche?' she asked.

'In shock. She must have heard the whole thing.'

'God, how terrible.'

'Any idea what was in the suitcase?' He asked, changing the subject.

'From first glance,' said Don. 'I would say it was money. There is staining at the bottom of the case. The type you would expect from notes. There's a particular odour too which confirms it, but as I said, I can let you have more later.'

'So, it could have been a burglary gone wrong?' said Matt.

'Too coincidental,' said Beth. 'Practically next door to Kate. Possibly the same weapon. This wasn't a burglary.'

'But the money?' questioned Matt.

'Added bonus?' suggested Beth.

'How did they know there was money in the suitcase?' asked Matt.

'Good question,' said Tom. 'Hopefully, the daughter will be able to tell us more.'

Beth took one last look around the bedroom and said,

'It's all yours, Don.'

*

The sound of sirens cut through the night. Sophie watched the police cars as they screeched to a halt. Two ambulances followed. Her heart had been racing ever since the first police car had arrived. She just knew that something terrible had happened. Surely not again. It can't have. Things like that just didn't happen in Stonesend. She couldn't help thinking about Blanche. Poor, helpless Blanche. Please don't let anyone have hurt her. A policeman cordoned off the front of the house. Sophie approached him.

'Excuse me, can you please tell me if my neighbour is alright. I called the police.'

'Just a moment,' he said and disappeared into the house.

Her mobile rang, and she pulled it from her pocket. It was Grant. She felt comforted just seeing his name on the screen.

'Oh, Grant, there are police everywhere. I think something awful must have happened at Mae's.'

'Do you want me to come, only Lainey ...'

'No, I'll come home.'

She turned to walk down the street when she saw Beth come out of the house.

'Sophie, are you okay?' she asked, approaching her.

'I thought I'd go home. Oh, Beth, has something terrible happened?'

'Can I ask you a few questions before you go? We can sit in the car.'

'Oh, yes, okay.'

She should message Grant; tell him she'd been delayed. He might worry.

'I'll just message Grant. He's expecting me home.'

'Of course.'

She sent Grant a quick text and then climbed into the police car.

'What time did you first try to get hold of Mae?'

'It was after the craft morning when Mae didn't arrive. She'd said she was coming. She always did. I messaged her afterwards and asked if Blanche was okay. I thought that might have been why she never turned up.'

'Did you try her last night?'

'No, there was no reason to. I tried her again later this afternoon. I thought maybe she had been at the hospital with Blanche and had no signal earlier.'

She looked into Beth's eyes.

'Something awful has happened, hasn't it? I should have come sooner, shouldn't I?'

'No, no. You must not blame yourself.'

Sophie reached into her handbag for a tissue.

'Mae's dead,' said Beth.

Sophie gasped. Her head whirled. Mae dead? Her hands began to shake.

'Blanche?' she asked tearfully.

'She's in shock, but she's alright.'

Sophie shook her head in denial.

'Oh my God, Beth.'

'When you came to the house, did you see anyone lingering outside or anyone leaving the house?'

'No, no one. What happened? Was it the same as Kate?

'It's too soon to say.'

Sophie wiped her eyes with a tissue.

'Was it an accident?'

'I'm sorry. I can't really discuss it.'

'It's so frightening. First Kate and now ….'

'Let me get someone to drive you home,' said Beth.

'No, I can walk. It's not far.'

She needed the fresh air.

*

The blue lights of the ambulance danced on the village green. The sirens had been heard above the folk singing in the pub. Jack peered out of the window.

'What's happening, Jack?' someone asked.

'Can't see that well,' said Jack.

Someone hurried to the doors and looked out.

'Police everywhere. It looks like they're at Mae's house.'

More people hurried out to look. Joe Tobias called his wife from the pub.

'Police at Mae's house,' he told her.

'Oh God,' Alice cried. 'You don't think he's struck again?'

*

Sophie had to pass the pub on her way home. She saw people huddled together and approached them.

'Do you know what's happening, Soph?' asked Joe.

'It's Mae …'

'What's happened?' asked Jack.

Sophie's face crumpled, and tears fell unbidden down her cheeks.

'She's dead.'

There was a collective gasp.

'Oh God,' said Laura, the barmaid. 'Not again.'

'What about Blanche?' asked Joe.

'She's alright. In shock.'

A wave of fear swept through the group. The unspoken question on everyone's lips was 'who would be next.' Laura rushed inside to tell the band to stop playing.

Miranda Sullivan looked up from her wine.

'What's happened?' she asked.

Laura looked at her suspiciously. The last thing they needed was for Stonesend to hit the newspapers again.

'An accident,' said Laura.

Miranda knew they wouldn't stop the music unless it were something serious. She'd been a reporter long enough to be able to sniff out an exclusive.

'Must be serious if you're cutting the live music,' said Miranda, standing up.

'Don't go printing a story before you know the facts,' said Jack, blocking the doorway.

Miranda smiled.

'Come on, Jack, we all have our jobs to do.'

'Wasn't it enough you bombarded the Marshalls?' said Laura crossly.

'Getting a story out helps the investigation,' argued Miranda.

'There's a sick girl involved here. Wait until there is some kind of statement,' said Laura.

'Is it Blanche Lethbridge?' she asked.

Jack cursed, and Laura could have kicked herself.

'Sorry,' she mumbled. 'Me and my big mouth.'

Miranda stepped past them. God knows things were boring enough on the local rag, so she wasn't going to let an exclusive pass her by. She'd never get out of this God-forsaken place and onto a decent paper if she kept holding back.

*

Kate

Kate woke to the scream of sirens. At first, she thought she'd been dreaming, but then she saw the blue flashing lights bouncing off the ceiling. They'd been watching a movie in bed and she must have dozed. The TV was now off, and Dan was standing at the bedroom window. She climbed from the bed and joined him. Her legs felt wobbly beneath her. The stirrings of a panic attack hovered close. Something had happened. Her head seemed to throb more than ever.

'What's happening?' she asked, while not wanting to hear his reply.

He grabbed his jumper from the bed. 'I don't know. There are police cars outside Mae's.'

'Oh no, I hope it's not Blanche.'

Kate pulled her jumper over her nightie and scrambled into a pair of jeans, wobbling slightly as she did so.

'Are you okay?' Dan asked, concerned.

'I've not long woken up.'

She looked at the clock on the bedside cabinet. It was nearly ten.

'Sorry I dosed,' she said, feeling a stab of guilt.

'No worries, you must have been tired.'

He opened the bedroom door.

'Might be best if you stay with the boys,' he said.

'But …'

He turned a concerned face to her.

'We don't know what's happened. Make sure you lock the door after me. I'll check the back door.'

'Oh God,' she mumbled when she realised what he was thinking.

If something had happened to Mae or Blanche, then there was nothing stopping that person from coming after her again. What if they were already in the house? No, of course, they weren't. Not with police cars right outside.

'Dan, you don't think ….'

'That's a lot of police for a sick child. I think it's more than that. I'll check everywhere before I go,' he said reassuringly.

He always could read her mind. Kate sat with her hands clenched in her lap while Dan searched the house. She heard him speaking to Jack and the sound of his TV. She sighed with relief. Moments later, Dan returned.

'Everything's okay. Jack's watching TV, and Ryan is asleep. Lock the front door after me.'

Kate followed him downstairs.

'Message me,' she said.

He nodded. She locked the door behind him and sat at the kitchen table, her phone held tightly in her hand and her eyes glued to the back door.

Chapter Fifty-One

Dan could see several people standing outside Mae's cottage, which had been cordoned off with blue and white tape. The street was lined with police cars. He saw Jack and headed towards him.

'Dan, maybe you shouldn't,' Jack advised, holding out a hand to stop him.

'What's happened?' Dan asked.

'Mae's dead,' Jack said flatly. 'Sophie called the police when she couldn't get hold of her. We don't know what's happened.'

'Dead?' echoed Dan. 'God, what's happening?'

'There's Blanche,' said Jack, nodding towards a stretcher.

Two paramedics were helping Blanche out. There was a wild, harried appearance about her. Her wide blue eyes stared back at Dan. She'd been crying, and her whole body trembled. Dan made to go to her, but a policewoman stopped him.

'I know her. My wife is good friends with her mother,' Dan protested.

At that moment, Miranda rushed forward and began taking photos with her mobile phone.

'For Christ's sake,' yelled Dan. 'What the hell do you think you're doing?'

'It's terrible, isn't it? Do you think it's connected to the attack on Kate?' Miranda asked.

'Stop taking photos,' he barked.

'Twice in seven weeks,' she said. 'It's frightening, isn't it? Don't you think the public should know about this?'

He spotted Beth in the doorway and called out to her. Beth lifted her hand in acknowledgement and hurried towards them. Before Miranda could speak, Beth had snatched the phone out of her hand.

'You can collect this from the station tomorrow once we've deleted the photos. You have no right, Miranda. This is a crime scene. You'll get a statement in due course.'

'This is horrific,' said Miranda calmly. 'You need to let the press warn the public.'

Beth didn't reply but beckoned to an officer to move Miranda on.

'What's wrong with her?' Dan nodded to Blanche.

'She's in shock,' said Beth. 'Can you wait a second?'

Dan waited while Beth hurried over to the paramedics. Memories of that afternoon when he'd come home to find the same police cars outside his own home returned to him. A paramedic closed the ambulance door, and Dan watched it drive away. He thought his heart would break.

'Dan, do you have the contact details for Blanche's father?' Beth asked.

He shook his head.

'I can ask Kate, but I don't think she has, either.'

'No worries. We'll get them.'

'What happened?'

'I can't say anything at the moment,' Beth said bluntly.

'Do you think it was the same person who attacked Kate?'

'Let's just say it's a coincidence.'

'This is a fucking nightmare,' he groaned.

'Would Kate know what medication Blanche was on?'

He shook his head.

'I don't think so, but I can ask.'

'Thanks, I'd appreciate that. You didn't see anything unusual last night, did you?'

'Last night?' he said, surprised.

'That's when we believed it happened,' confirmed Beth.

He creased his forehead in concentration.

'Not that I can remember?'

'Let us know if you do.'

'I should let Kate know. This is fucking scary. I hope you get the bastard.'

*

Kate stared in stunned disbelief. It couldn't be true, but Dan's crestfallen face told her it was.

'No, it can't be true.'

'It's like a bad dream,' agreed Dan.

It couldn't be possible. Hadn't Kate only seen Mae a few days ago? They had talked about a shopping trip to Oxford. Kate had been hesitant, but Mae had reassured her, and she'd started looking forward to it.

'It can't be her. They've made a mistake.'

'There's no mistake,' Dan said softly.

'Blanche?' she asked, while not wanting to hear his reply.

'They've taken her to hospital. She's in shock, but okay.'

Mae couldn't be dead. It was impossible. Who would want to kill Mae? What the hell was happening?

'I need to be with Blanche,' she said, jumping up.

'They've taken her to hospital, Kate. There's nothing you can do.'

Kate paced the floor in helpless despair. How would Blanche ever cope without Mae?

'Oh God, Dan. Was it the same person? Do you think they mistook me for Mae?'

'Kate, calm down. I'll get you a Valium. Where are they?'

But she couldn't remember. Her damn stupid memory.

'I can't bloody remember.'

'I'll check your handbag.'

'I don't need them.'

'The doctor said you should take them if you have a panic attack,' Dan said, tipping the contents of her handbag onto the floor.

'I'm not having a panic attack.'

He handed her the bottle, and she took a tablet reluctantly.

'Do you think it was me they wanted?' She asked.

Dan ran his hand through his hair and was about to answer when Jack called out.

'Dad, why are there police at Blanche's house?'

'Oh God,' Kate groaned. 'How do we tell them?'

'We have to tell them,' said Dan.

'Tell us what?' asked Jack, appearing in the doorway.

Beth pulled him into her arms.

'Darling, something has happened to Aunty Mae.'

'She's not my Aunty, Mum. I keep telling you that. An aunty has to be your sister or Dad's sister.'

Beth smiled. 'I know, darling.'

'What's happened to her?'

Kate looked pleadingly at Dan.

'Mae has died,' he said.

Jack's little face turned white, and Kate pulled him to her.

'It's okay, Jack.'

'What happened?' he asked shakily.

'We don't know yet,' Kate said quickly, giving Dan a warning look.

'There's nothing we can do,' said Dan. 'You should go back to bed. We'll find out in the morning.'

'Is Blanche alright?' he asked worriedly.

'Yes, she's okay.' Dan leant down to pick him up, but Jack pulled away.

'I'm not a baby. Was it the same person who hit mum?'

'We don't know,' said Kate gently. 'Go to bed now. You can read for longer.'

Once Jack had gone, Kate sat on the sofa and waited for the effects of the Valium to kick in. She just couldn't accept that Mae was dead. Why would anyone do this? Everyone loved Mae. Except ... The memory of Blanche's birthday party came back to her and the ugly, angry face of Mae's ex-husband. He was bitter and violent. Supposing he had ...

'We should tell the police about Rob Lethbridge,' she said as Dan walked back into the room.

'Tell them what?'

'How he attacked Mae at Blanche's birthday party.'

'He didn't actually attack her, Kate. He was a bit drunk and in a state.'

She glared at him.

'He may have killed her, Dan.'

'You can't say things like that, Kate.'

She dropped her head into her hands.

'Oh God, what's happening, Dan?'

His arm, warm and comforting, pulled her to him.

'I don't know, but I now feel sure that what happened to you was a case of mistaken identity.'

'I'm scared,' she whimpered.

'We can fit a burglar alarm and extra locks on the windows.'

The Valium had started to work, and her body released some of its tension.

'Poor Blanche, what will happen to her?'

Dan didn't answer. Maybe he was thinking the same thing as Kate. Should they offer to have her come and live with them?

Chapter Fifty-Two

2005: Leeds

Mae

An old couple wanting to downsize bought the house. The house had been the last link with my mother, and I was pleased to see the back of it. Maybe she would finally stop haunting me.

I began looking at properties as far afield as I could. Rob would come by on a Saturday to see Blanche. I insisted he saw her at the house and that he didn't take her anywhere near his floozy. Some Saturdays, I lied and told him that Blanche was unwell so Blanche and I could look at houses. Eventually, every Saturday became every other Saturday.

I didn't tell anyone we were selling. Not even those at church. I didn't want anyone to dissuade me. I still hadn't set up the charity properly, and money was still coming in from church donations. I had all the envelopes in a shoebox. I hadn't even had time to count the money.

I got a bit worried when the vicar asked me if I could produce the accounts for the charity so they could show them at the Parish council meeting. I made an excuse and said Blanche hadn't been so good and would they mind waiting a few months.

We travelled to Oxfordshire to view some properties. I was getting pretty desperate. I had no idea what had happened to the money that we'd been given over the years. I hadn't kept receipts or records. I never imagined anyone would ask. The money had been for us. I don't know why they had to know what we'd spent it on. It was getting complicated, and the only way out of it that I could see was to move.

The village of Stonesend was perfect. It was quiet and peaceful. Exactly what Blanche and I needed, and the cottage was within our price range and would even leave us with money over. It had a lovely garden, and the people were so friendly and waved while we were there that I felt we had finally come home.

'Idyllic isn't it.' the estate agent had said.

'It's perfect,' I'd replied. 'Is anyone else interested?'

'You're the third to view today,' he'd said.

'Can we make an offer?' I'd asked eagerly.

So, we did. I offered the total asking price as I didn't want to lose it. Rob would never find us in Oxfordshire. He would come to see Blanche one Saturday, and we wouldn't be here. I didn't feel bad about it. Rob had never been interested in Blanche. He'd walked out and abandoned us. There was no reason why we couldn't do the same. We would leave him. Then it would be just Blanche and me, starting all over again, surrounded by apple blossom, green fields, and tranquillity.

Two days later, the owners accepted our offer. I'd been panicking. I'd expected to hear right away and had convinced myself that someone else had got in before us. I was ecstatic. It was all I could do not to tell everyone. I would miss church terribly, but Stonesend had a lovely old church, and I knew Blanche, and I would make friends in no time. I did think of changing my name so that Rob could never find us, but that all seemed a bit complicated, so in the end, I left it as it was.

I was disappointed in Blanche, when two days before we were due to move, she asked if we had to.

'What about Dad?' she asked.

'Dad can visit us.'

'It's a long way,' she whined, and it annoyed me.

'If he loves us enough, he will come.'

She'd sulked for the rest of the day. I'd told her a hundred times that Rob wasn't interested in us anymore. That he had a new life now and that life didn't include us. Much later, I had to tell her the truth, that her father had never wanted her. If Rob had really wanted to see Blanche, it wouldn't have been that hard for him to find us. He just couldn't be bothered. It was painful for Blanche and me, but it is always better to face the truth.

The day we moved into Stonesend had been wonderful. The sun had shone, and it had been so quiet and peaceful that all we heard were the birds singing. It had never been like that in Leeds. Villagers had come by asking if we needed anything. Everyone had been friendly and welcoming. I'd known immediately that we had come to the right place. Our closest neighbour, Kate, had popped in with a mug of tea and a glass of orange juice.

'I thought you may not have unpacked any crockery yet,' she'd smiled.

I didn't like to say that Blanche couldn't drink bottled orange because of her allergies. I didn't want Kate to think we were ungrateful.

'When will your husband be joining you?' another neighbour, named Alice, asked.

'I'm divorced,' I said bluntly. 'It's just Blanche and me.'

This news must have gotten around the village because people took us under their wing. Within a short time, we felt part of the community. Rob never made contact, and Blanche stopped asking about him. I no longer had to fear Rob coming home drunk. When I was invited to talk about the life Blanche and I led, I decided then and there to set up a proper charity. This time I would keep receipts and records of all the money that came in. We'd finally come home.

Chapter Fifty-Three

September 2019: Belmarsh prison

Lester knew it was all over the minute Monroe played the music. In a way, he felt it was a fitting end. If he had to die to music, then he would have chosen Marin Marais.

The papers had made a lot of it. The fact that he'd played the composer when he'd taken his pleasures.

'It was the music,' he told the police. 'It affects me.'

He'd kept all the cuttings. 'Paedophile with taste' ran one headline. He'd liked that. In his warped mind, he saw it as something of a tribute.

He tried to block the cell door, but it was pointless. He looked at the remains of the birthday cake. He hadn't finished it or the champagne his father had brought in. Stupid fuckers, he thought. No appreciation for the finer things in life. It'll be him that will make the front page, not them.

'Like the tune, birthday boy,' someone shouted from across the corridor. But Lester only had eyes for Fergus Monroe, who was striding towards his cell. Monroe had had it in for Lester from day one. His eyes now sparkled with excitement. Lester saw something flash in his left hand. Listen to the music, he told himself, feel it. But fear overwhelmed him, and he scrambled back as far into the cell as he could.

'Help me, someone fucking help me,' he yelled.

'Champagne?' said Monroe, clearly impressed. 'I'll have me some of that.'

Lester watched as Monroe threw back the last of the champagne. It dribbled from his mouth and ran down the front of his top.

'Having a nice birthday?' asked Monroe, licking his lips. 'I got a little present for you.'

'Fucking piece of shit,' echoed the voices around them. The music seemed even louder. Why didn't one of the screws tell Monroe to turn it down? Everyone knew what that fucking piece of music meant.

'Get away from me,' Lester screamed as Monroe moved closer.

'Don't you want my present?' grinned Monroe.

'Help, help!' Lester screamed, kicking out.

The next thing he knew, he was thrown against the wall and his hands pulled behind his back. The sound of a zip being undone caused his body to freeze. He tried to open his mouth to scream again, but Monroe had clamped a hand over it. He was strong, powerful. Any other time Lester would have enjoyed it, but now he was terrified.

'Here's your present, birthday boy. Let's give you a taste of what those little kids felt, shall we? Just so as you don't forget.'

He almost sighed with relief. He was going to rape him, that's all. He could get through that.

It was rough. His head thumped against the wall, and it seemed to go on forever. The screws would come soon. They'd been paid enough. Where the hell were the fuckers?

'You're not moaning enough,' Monroe hissed into his ear. 'Perhaps I'm not big enough for you.'

Then, he rammed something so huge inside Lester that he felt sure he was being ripped apart. He screamed and would have slumped to the ground had Monroe not been holding him up. The pain was unbearable, and the music seemed louder than ever. His ears buzzed. He couldn't see clearly anymore. He felt a sharp pain in his side and struggled to breathe. He tasted something metallic in his mouth and swallowed, but his mouth just filled up again. There was pain everywhere. He heard shouting. Were they coming to help him at last? The music now seemed to fade in and out. He was looking at someone's shoes. He must be on the floor.

He saw the boy then. He stood smiling at him. Lester tried to remember his name. He'd been the prettiest, though. He remembered that. He'd liked him. Why couldn't he remember his name? Pity there would be no more. He reached out to him just as the final and fatal thrust went through his heart. The last words he heard were 'Rot in hell, you perverted fucker.'

Chapter Fifty-Four

September 2019: Stonesend

Blanche was under sedation.

'She's in a severe state of shock,' the doctor told Beth. 'You won't be able to question her until the morning, I'm afraid.'

'We'll contact her next of kin.' said Tom.

Back at the station, Tom briefed the team. Beth had difficulty concentrating. She couldn't stop thinking of Mae's blood-soaked body and her wide, frightened eyes.

'This is what we know so far,' said Tom. 'Sometime Thursday evening, or possibly early Friday morning, we'll know more when the pathologist has finished, someone broke into Mae Lethbridge's home via the back door. The daughter who was in the house too was locked in her bedroom.'

'She must have heard everything,' said Beth. 'Can you imagine hearing your mother murdered? My God.'

'The key was on the mother's bedside table.' said Tom. 'We need a thorough search of the premises. We're looking for the murder weapon. As soon as we can, we will interview the daughter and the ex-husband. Meanwhile, question all the neighbours'. Someone must have seen something. Anything out of the ordinary, we follow up. In the meantime, I want a media blackout. We haven't contacted her ex-husband yet.'

Beth gave a slight cough.

'Miranda Salisbury was taking pictures outside the house this evening,' she said.

'What the hell?' exploded Tom.

'I confiscated her phone,' she said, holding it up.

'Matt, get her to come into the station tomorrow. Okay, that's it.'

He took the phone and strode into his office.

'Thanks, Harper, well done,' she said, sarcastically to his back.

'Pretty horrific stuff isn't it?' said Matt, coming to her side.

'I can't stop thinking about her. It must have been terrifying,' agreed Beth.

'Let's hope the daughter has information,' said Matt.

'Harper?' called Tom.

'You're being summoned,' smiled Matt. Beth pulled herself out of her chair and went into Tom's office. '

'Who is this Miranda woman?'

'Local reporter trying to get a name for herself. Hankers after the big time. She wants a job on a national.'

'Great. That's all we need.'

'You know that this will make the nationals. It's a murder. They will probably make a thing of you being the investigating officer.'

He shrugged.

'I just don't want it turning into a circus and hindering the investigation.'

He looked at her closely.

'Is this your first murder?' he asked.

She gave a small laugh.

'You've seen this village? What do you think?'

'I think you did well. It was a massacre.'

She thought of the tiny bodies he'd removed from Lynch's basement and said, 'You've seen worse.'

'It doesn't make it any easier.'

Matt knocked at the door and then popped his head around.

'We've got Rob Lethbridge's address. A place in Leeds. Here's his phone number.'

He waved a piece of paper in front of them. Beth glanced at the clock on the wall. It was late. In her experience, people didn't answer the phone at this time of night.

'Call the local nick. They can pay a visit first thing,' said Tom. 'And go home, Matt. It's late.'

The door closed, and Tom reached into one of the desk drawers.

'Here,' he said, handing her a miniature bottle of whisky. 'For times such as these. I think you need it.'

Beth looked at the bottle disapprovingly.

'I won't be joining you,' he assured her.

She nodded.

'I won't say no.'

The whisky hit the back of her throat, and then the warmth moved through her body.

'This is a good one,' she noted.

'Oh yeah,' he smiled.

'Thanks,' she said gratefully. His eyes met hers, and he quickly looked away.

'Any hunches on who did it?' he asked.

She shook her head.

'What have forensics come up with?'

'Not much yet, but they think the weapon used was similar to the one used on Kate Marshall. Injuries are identical, aside from the fact that Mae Lethbridge's were much worse. Some hair fragments were found on the body. It could well be the victims, but they're checking the DNA. The front door was locked and bolted. The back door locked but forced. The suitcase in the bedroom had been forced open. Mae kept that locked too. It seems likely that whoever murdered her knew there was something worth having in that suitcase. Forensics think it was money.'

'Why would you keep money in the house? It's a bit risky, isn't it?'

'Maybe she didn't want anyone to know how much money she had.'

Beth shrugged.

'It's a bit outdated to keep money at home. Why not the bank or Post Office?'

'People still do it. My gran has got tons stashed away.'

Beth chewed her lip thoughtfully.

'Kate Marshall was a good friend of hers. I'll question her tomorrow.'

She finished her whisky and handed Tom the glass.

'Thanks for that. I'd better write up my report.'

'Yep,' he said, taking the glass from her in such a way that his hand stroked hers. She tried to hide her shiver, but she knew he'd seen it.

'Get some sleep,' he said. 'Busy day tomorrow.'

Chapter Fifty-Five

September 2019: Belmarsh prison

Sid Dawson had only taken a few drags of his second cigarette when he heard the commotion.

It was quick. He knew it would be. That filthy piece of scum had finally got what he deserved. A few days in hospital would bring him down to size.

He stubbed out his cigarette and made his way back inside, where Sirens blasted throughout the building. It was mayhem. Guards were yelling and running into each other. Cell doors slammed shut. The inmates, high on adrenalin, were kicking at their cell doors.

Monroe gave a slight nod in Sid's direction. Sid ignored it and hurried to Lynch's cell, where guards were surrounding it. It was barely six feet by four, and Sid had to push his way in. The thick grey walls were stained with Lester Lynch's blood. His body lay on the floor like a ghoulish mannequin. It looked as if a special effects team had worked overtime for some Friday the thirteenth movie set, but that smell ... That smell could only come from slaughtered animals. In this case, the animal was human, and his corpse still warm, the blood thickening but not yet dried on his waxy skin.

'Jesus Christ,' Sid gasped. He hadn't expected Monroe to kill the filthy little prick. He thought he'd put the frighteners on him, give him a kicking.

'They've killed the fucker,' said warden Kevin Smith, his body shaking. 'Knifed the son of a bitch, God knows how many times.'

'Someone must have heard something,' said Sid, feeling sick. 'Why didn't they stop it?'

'No one hurried,' said Mac, another guard. 'You know how everyone felt about him.'

'All the same,' said Sid, shaking with shock. He never imagined it would go this far.

'How did they get in?' he asked, reaching for the set of keys that always hung on the belt loop of his trousers.

Kevin felt for his keys and sighed with relief when his shaking hands felt the metal of the keyring. He'd only been on the job for six months. He couldn't afford to get into trouble.

'Fuck knows,' said Mac. 'Wouldn't put it past one of those bastards to lift a key. You can't turn your bloody back for two seconds.'

Sid glanced over at the cell opposite. Fergus Monroe was beckoning to him. He looked back at Lynch's body and then walked across to the cell.

'I fixed that piece of scum, didn't I?' said Monroe, with a toothless grin.

'Are you confessing, Monroe?'

'Are you?' mocked Fergus.

Sid narrowed his eyes.

'Don't worry, dude. We're all grateful. Spoilt our appetite did that fucker. Four hundred fags should do it, and everyone will keep their mouths shut about the cell door being left open.'

'I don't know what you're talking about,' said Sid, discreetly locking the cell door.

'As I said, we're grateful. Four hundred fags and Lynch will be forgotten in no time.'

Sid knew the cons didn't want to get on the wrong side of Monroe. They wouldn't open their mouths, but four hundred cigarettes were nothing, and it was extra security.

Sid nodded. In the mayhem, no one saw the exchange between the two men. Sid moved away slowly and joined the throng of prison wardens.

Lester Lynch's body was escorted from the prison under an armed guard. All the wardens knew that the other prisoners had it in for Lester Lynch. It was a tragedy waiting to happen. He was a child killer, after all. There had been trouble ever since Lynch was banged up. No one admitted to unlocking the cell. It could have been any one of the wardens. It was even suggested that one of the prisoners had picked the lock. Sid knew there would be an enquiry. There always was, but nothing ever came of them. Who gave a shit about a dirty fucker like Lester Lynch? He'd be forgotten in no time. Sid wouldn't lose any sleep over him.

*

Benny Lynch knew somebody was to blame and, in his warp that somebody was the copper who put his son away. someone, was Tom Miller.

Chapter Fifty-Six

September 2019: Stonesend

Beth switched on the radio as she prepared for bed. The whisky had calmed her, and the memory of Mae's bloodied body had dimmed slightly. Her eyes went to the back door, and she double-checked the lock. Who on earth could have it in for Kate and Mae? It was becoming more certain in Beth's mind that Kate's attack had been a case of mistaken identity, which meant the killer had been interested in Mae and whatever had been in that suitcase. She turned to go into the bathroom when her ears caught the name Lester Lynch. She turned up the radio and sat at the kitchen table to listen.

'Back to the big story of this evening. Police say no one has been arrested for the attack on paedophile Lester Lynch, who was found dead in his cell early this evening. Lynch, aged 32, was sentenced to life imprisonment. His body was taken to The Royal Free Hospital. The families of Lynch's victims said they would not condemn the murder. "He was trash. I hope they flush his ashes down the loo," said Sadie Jones, the mother of Dylan Jones, whose body was found in the basement of a dilapidated house in Stratford. 'Whoever killed him has our blessing.' We're now going over to Dudley Phillips at Belmarsh Prison for more information on the killing.'

Beth turned off the radio and pulled on her jeans before grabbing her car keys and leaving the cottage.

*

Miranda topped up her glass with prosecco and relaxed to watch the late news. Well, well, she thought. Lester Lynch dead, and the copper who put him away is none other than their local bobby, Tom Miller. Talk about topical. The Prosecco had fired her imagination. She grabbed the landline phone and cursed Beth Harper for confiscating her mobile. It rang for a while, but finally, her editor answered.

'Bryn, it's Miranda.'

'Yeah, Miranda, what now?' he said in a husky voice that came from too much smoking. 'I was just going to bed.'

'Have you seen the news?'

'Of course, I've seen the news. I'm not blind.'

'What about a feature on Tom Miller? Good looking copper loses wife, comes to the country to recuperate and faces more murder. Connect to the recent stabbing of Lester Lynch ….'

'Police haven't confirmed what happened at the Lethbridge's was murder.'

'Oh, come on, Ed, they haven't denied it either. It's only a matter of time. I saw the daughter being taken out of the house. She was in a terrible state of shock. I could have the story ready for the morning.'

She could almost hear him mulling it over.

'Get all the facts right. I don't want fucking Miller suing us. If it's any good, we'll run it next week.'

Miranda had to stop herself from leaping into the air. At last, her chance to impress the big boys in London had finally come.

*

It was gone midnight, but Tom's lights were on. Beth shivered as she made her way to the front door. The full moon gave the cemetery an eerie glow. Weird shadows danced on the tombstones, and it seemed like the dead were having a party. She rang the doorbell and waited nervously. It seemed forever before Tom unlocked the door.

'Harper,' he said, surprised.

'I was driving by and ….'

He raised his eyebrows.

'At this time?'

'Okay,' she said, shivering. 'I saw the news and thought you might like to talk.'

'Talk about what?'

'Were you born ungrateful? Can I come in before I get hyperthermia?'

'You're unlikely to get hyperthermia in September.'

He opened the door and she stepped inside. The television was on.

'He had it coming,' she said, nodding at the TV.

'They gave him the easy way out,' he said bitterly. 'Do you want something to drink?'

'Thanks.'

She followed him into the kitchen.

'Did you have therapy after it happened?'

'Therapy?' he repeated, taking a box of teabags from the cupboard.

'My sister, Sandy, is a therapist. Her husband's a psychiatrist ….'

'You think I need a psychiatrist? Earl Grey or normal?'

'Earl Grey and no, I don't. It's just my sister asked if you had therapy and ….'

The kettle whistled, and Beth sighed.

'I appreciate you and your sister's concern. I had enough therapy. But therapy doesn't bring back the dead, does it? Those boys lost their future. No parent should bury a child. I shouldn't have buried my wife and ….'

He broke off and turned to the mugs of tea. Beth wanted to put a comforting arm around his shoulders but didn't. Instead, she took the mug and walked into the living room.

'Life's so fucked up, right?' she said.

'It's people that are fucked up,' he said.

He switched channels, and together, they watched News 24 in silence. Beth finished the last of her tea and stood up.

'It was an inside job,' she said. 'Someone set him up.'

Tom nodded.

'He was a sadistic bastard. I hope it wasn't quick.'

She laid a hand on his arm and, just as quickly, pulled it away.

'I should go,' she said.

He nodded and followed her to the door.

'Thanks for coming,' he said.

'Sure,' she smiled. She stood uncertainly, unsure whether to hug him or not. He looked uncomfortable. Beth nodded to the cemetery.

'That looks eerie, don't you think?'

'The dead can't hurt you,' he said, and she knew they were both still thinking of Lester Lynch.

'See you in the morning,' she said.

Chapter Fifty-Seven

Kate

Kate glanced at the clock. It was four a.m. She'd lain awake for hours, listening to every sound and going over in her head the times she and Mae had spent together. Could her attack have been connected to Mae's, and if so, in what way? She kept seeing Rob Lethbridge's face at Blanche's birthday party. Could he have killed Mae? Had he tried before and got the wrong house and mistaken Kate for Mae? He didn't show any recognition at the party. She tossed and turned so much that she woke Dan.

'Sorry. I'll get up,' she said. 'A hot drink might help.'

He mumbled something and then went back to sleep.

Kate sat at the kitchen table with a mug of hot milk and thought about Blanche. What must she be going through right now? Was she awake and mourning her mother? Would Rob take her home with him? Kate got up and paced the floor. Why couldn't she remember what had happened that afternoon? It was just a few minutes. How could they have been wiped from her memory? She debated whether to take a Valium and decided against it. The pills made her brain foggy.

She went into the living room and looked out of the window. Everything was quiet now. The police had gone, but the police cordon was still there in front of Mae's house. Any hope she'd had that it had all been a bad dream was quickly dashed. She sat on the couch and cried.

She must have fallen asleep because the next thing she knew, Dan was waking her up.

'I made you a coffee. Beth just phoned. She's coming by in an hour. She wants to ask us a few questions about Mae.'

For a few seconds, Kate had forgotten about Mae and the murder. It hit her again like a sledgehammer, and she started to cry.

'Alice phoned and asked if you needed anything.'

'Oh, Dan.'

He put his arm around her.

'Alice has taken the kids to school. I didn't think you'd want me to wake you.'

'Thanks, Dan, that's good of Alice. She must be in shock too.'

'The whole village is. I'm going to take the day off.'

The news that Dan was going to be home calmed her.

'We must go and see Blanche. What will happen to her?'

'We should ask Beth. I don't think she can just come and live here with us. I know that's what you're thinking, Kate. But it won't be that easy. She has a father, remember.'

Kate nodded.

'I know.'

Beth was on time. She told Dan ten o'clock, and on the dot, the doorbell rang.

'How are you, Kate?' she asked.

'I'm okay. Shocked about Mae obviously, and anxious about it. I just can't believe it.'

'We're wondering, as no doubt you are, whether your attack was a case of mistaken identity. I know I phone you every week and ask if you've recalled anything. I have to ask again. Did anything trigger your memory when you heard about Mae?' Beth asked.

'No, I hoped it would, but nothing. I can't remember anything, Beth. I really can't.'

'I'm really sorry, Kate. I know Mae was a good friend.'

'What about Blanche?' she asked, fighting back her tears. It was all Kate could think about. She knew Mae would have wanted her to look out for Blanche.

'She's under sedation. We're contacting her father.'

Kate's face betrayed her. Beth asked.

'Is there something you'd like to tell me about Rob Lethbridge?'

Kate looked to Dan, who nodded.

'Mae said he used to hit her. She didn't want him knowing where she lived. He never showed any interest in Blanche, apparently. He turned up here. It was at Blanche's eighteenth birthday party.'

'He seemed pretty desperate,' added Dan. 'I got the impression he hadn't seen his daughter for some time.'

'Mae told us he caused a bit of a scene,' said Beth.

'He was drunk,' Kate said. 'Acting completely irrational. He tried to take Blanche out for a walk, but Mae got defensive, and Rob hit her.'

'I don't think it was intentional,' said Dan.

Kate ignored him and said, 'He shouldn't have hit her.'

'Did Rob act normally with you?' asked Beth.

'You think it may have been him that attacked me?' Kate asked.

'We have to explore all avenues,' Beth explained

'He barely spoke to me.'

'Had Mae seemed worried about anything?' Beth asked, fidgeting on the couch. It felt odd to her to be questioning her friends about a murder.

'No, she seemed the same as normal until Rob came. She was agitated after that and took out a restraining order.'

'Do you know anything about a suitcase that Mae kept money in?'

Dan and Kate looked at each other.

'No.'

'We think Mae was afraid of something. Blanche had been locked in her room as if Mae was trying to protect her from someone. Did she ever mention doing that to you?'

Kate shook her head.

'God, sorry. I feel so useless. She was very protective of Blanche,'

'Did either of you hear anything on Thursday evening? Arguing, shouting anything unusual?'

'I don't recall,' said Dan. 'The thing is, you hear stuff but don't register it.'

Kate chewed her lip nervously.

'I saw Jack go into Mae's about sixish,' she said. 'But Jack wouldn't hurt a fly.

'Jack, the landlord?' asked Beth, surprised. 'Did you see him leave?'

'No, I didn't.'

'Were he and Mae friends?'

'Everyone knows everyone here,' said Dan. 'You know that. She'd just held a fundraiser at the pub. It was most likely to do with that.'

Beth stood up. She'd been in Kate's house many times but never on official business, and it felt weird.

'I think this might be the trigger that will jolt your memory. Phone me anytime. If anything comes back to you, no matter how small, give me a ring.'

'Will you let us know about Blanche?' Dan asked.

'Of course.'

She hugged them both and left. Kate realised Beth was relying on her to remember.

Chapter Fifty-Eight

'Any luck with the Marshalls?' Matt asked as Beth walked back into the station.

'No, they didn't see anything.'

'Odd, don't you think?' Matt said, biting into a doughnut.

'What is?' asked Beth, clicking on the kettle.

'Everything happening since he arrived.' He nodded in the direction of Tom's office.

Luke Carpenter's ears pricked up.

'Yeah, you know what, I thought that when I saw the newspapers this morning. Nasty piece of work that Lynch family.'

Beth lifted her head.

'That's bollocks,' she said.

'Is it?' Matt asked. 'The village was nice and peaceful. A few petty thefts, maybe the odd break-in. Let's face it, we don't know we're born here. Then he comes from London after a nasty run-in with a well-known gangland boss, and suddenly there's a vicious attack and now a murder. A bit coincidental if you ask me.'

'What if that Benny Lynch is out to get him?' Luke said.

'What's wrong with you two? Did someone steal your brains in the night?' scoffed Beth.

'Killed his wife, didn't they?' said Matt. 'Now Lynch is dead. Who's to say they won't come after Miller next. None of us is safe.'

'Keep your voice down, Matt,' Beth said, glancing at Tom's office.

Much to Beth's relief, Matt's phone rang at that moment. He listened intently, and then his face lit up with excitement.

'Great stuff,' he said and hung up. He looked at Beth. 'They've found the hammer. It was in Lethbridge's garden. Forensics has confirmed it has Mae Lethbridge's blood on it. They're checking other fibres to see if they belong to Kate Marshall. If they do, then we know we're looking for the same person.'

The door to Tom's office opened.

'We've found the murder weapon, sir. The hammer was in Mae's garden.'

Tom nodded.

'Great, a step forward. Harper, get your coat.'

'Where are we going?'

'To visit Blanche.'

'Full of charm, isn't he,' said Matt.

Beth clicked off the kettle and followed Tom out of the office. On the way to the hospital, she thought about the murder weapon. If the hammer found was Dan's, it meant that the person who had attacked Kate had also murdered Mae. What could the connection be? Had it been Mae they'd wanted all along? The radio blasted out a song from the eighties, and Beth turned it off. She needed quiet to think. Oxford town was heaving. This is where you'd expect a murder, she thought, not in a tiny village off the beaten track. This hadn't been a burglary gone wrong, any more than Kate's had been. Beth hoped that Blanche held some of the answers. Tom drove the car into a space marked 'staff only', and they walked into the hospital. The clinical white walls and smell of sickness didn't bother Beth. She bypassed the lift and took the stairs to the second floor, where the wards were.

'I need the exercise,' she said.

'You should have joined me on my run this morning.'

'I only run when being chased.'

A nurse greeted them.

'We have her in a private room,' she said. 'I'll page Doctor Werner and let him know you are here.'

'Thanks, can we go in and see her?' Tom asked. The nurse smiled kindly, but her words were firm.

'If you would wait until Doctor Werner arrives.'

'No problem,' said Beth.

She helped herself to a cup of water, and Tom paced the corridor until the doctor arrived.

'Detectives, sorry to keep you waiting,' he said in broken English.

'How is she?' Beth asked without preamble.

'She's still sedated. We had quite a hysterical outburst in the middle of the night when she asked for her mother. We had to tell her what had happened, and then it must have come flooding back, for she became quite distressed. We had to sedate her. I would suggest you come back this evening. As you know, she has health issues which we are still looking into. Any news on her father?'

'Not yet,' said Beth.

'I need to question her urgently,' Tom said firmly.

'Of course, and I hope by this evening you will be able to, but I have to put my patient's welfare first. You understand?'

Tom knew better than to push it any further.

'Of course,' he said.

Blanche was the best witness to the murder that they had. Tom didn't like too many hours going by before interviewing the prime witness.

'We'll come back at six.'

'I'll contact you if it's possible to see her before.'

Frustrated, they made their way back to the station. It felt to Beth that with every step they took forward, they took two back. The killer was always one step ahead of them.

'Good news,' Matt said when they arrived. 'We've traced Rob Lethbridge. He's only in bloody Oxford.'

'You're kidding?'

'He's staying at Bladon Chains caravan site.' he said. 'It's a pop-up site on the grounds of Blenheim Palace. He left his home in Leeds Wednesday night. He's taking a week's holiday. Told a work colleague he was visiting his daughter.'

'So, he may have been in Oxfordshire at the time of the murder?'

'Let's go,' said Tom, turning back to the door.

'Where to?' asked Beth.

'Bladon Chains caravan site.'

'Can't I have a cup of tea first?' she moaned.

'No time.'

Beth rolled her eyes.

'Harper, are you coming?' he called.

'Better hurry,' laughed Matt. 'He may be the one. You don't want Miller taking all the glory.'

Beth didn't think it was going to be as easy as that. If Rob Lethbridge had been the killer, then surely, he wouldn't have told his bosses he was going to Oxfordshire to see his daughter. Or was that all part of his cleverness? She was curious to meet Rob Lethbridge.

Miranda walked through the doors as they approached, and Beth's heart sank.

'Shit,' she muttered.

'Where's my phone,' Miranda demanded. 'You told me to come here.'

'You can collect the phone from reception. I had to remove the photos you took at the crime scene,' said Beth.

Miranda tossed back her neat bob and, ignoring Beth, turned a warm smile onto Tom.

'Look, I'm just a girl trying to make a living.'

My God thought Beth, she's only coming onto him.

'The officer on the reception desk will be able to help you,' he said dismissively.

'Now hold on,' said Miranda, following them. 'You had no right to take my phone. I'm a member of the public and have every right to take photos ….'

'You're a member of the Press and have no right to compromise a crime scene or hinder us in our investigations. We still have a family to contact, and the last thing they need is to read about it in the paper before hearing from us,' snapped Tom.

'It's in the public's interest,' she argued.

'You'll get your story when we're ready and not before,' Tom said, walking away.

'Do you have anything to say about the death of Lester Lynch?' she called.

Tom stopped. Beth shot her a dirty look.

'No comment,' said Tom sharply before getting into his car.

'I wonder how the people of Stonesend feel about a drunk handling this case,' she said, turning to Beth.

Beth shook her head.

'You'd better not repeat that statement publicly.'

Melanie blushed.

'It's not slander. Anyone can read the Lynch story on the internet. It's all there. What happened afterwards. How everyone coped or didn't….'

'Don't step on people's toes, Miranda,' Beth said and climbed into the car beside Tom. She knew this would happen that Miller would be the focus of this investigation. The chief had it all wrong. What if other people in the village thought like Matt? That if Tom Miller had never come to Stonesend, then maybe the attacks would never have happened.

Chapter Fifty-Nine

Beth had been to Blenheim Palace once. Ben had booked tickets for a concert there. She had only seen the grounds and had thought them spectacular.

'Can't be cheap,' she commented as they drove into the caravan park.

Most of the caravans were a decent size and Felicity wondered if Rob owned his or had rented it. The reception area smelt of cigar smoke. The long-haired, bearded man who sat behind the desk looked bored. Tom flashed his ID at him.

'We're looking for Rob Lethbridge. He's staying on the site. We need to know what caravan he is in.'

The man looked at them suspiciously.

'Why, what's he done?'

'Hopefully nothing,' said Beth. 'You are?'

'Staying out of trouble,' he smiled. 'Chris Wild. Wild by name, not by nature.'

'Got a G. S. O. H. I see,' said Beth.

'Keeping things light. Only it's not good for business having the police parade around. Know what I mean?'

'I do,' agreed Tom. 'I wouldn't think you get much business this time of year.'

'Things are going on all year-round. People like to have a break.'

'Well, the quicker we find him, and have a chat, then the quicker we leave,' smiled Tom.

The man sighed and clicked into his laptop.

'Rob Lethbridge, you say.'

'That's right.'

'We've got a Robert Lethbridge staying in 52. You'll find it in Block D. He's paid-up.'

'Well, that's good,' smiled Beth. Tom was already out of the door and heading for Block D.

Most of the caravans were empty. It didn't take him long to find No 52. It was a small caravan. Big enough for one. Beside it was a grey Polo that had seen better days. Beth joined him and glanced at the bald tyre.

Tom knocked on the caravan door and waited. After a few moments, it opened, and they came face to face with Rob Lethbridge. He wasn't what Beth had been expecting. Mae hadn't been the prettiest women in town, and Beth hadn't expected her ex-husband to be anything special either, but he was, in fact, quite stunning. He had the kind of looks that Beth had only ever seen on television. He smiled at her, and his eyes twinkled warmly.

'Robert Lethbridge?' she asked.

'Who's asking?'

She showed him her ID.

'I've got a bald tyre, I know,' he said. 'I'm taking it to the garage this afternoon.'

'It's not about the tyre.' Tom said.

Rob Lethbridge's expression changed.

'What is it about then?'

'We have some bad news, I'm afraid,' said Beth. 'Can we step inside?'

'What kind of bad news?'

'If we could come inside,' repeated Beth.

'Yeah, sure,' he said, stepping back. 'Christ, it isn't Blanche, is it?'

The inside was tidy and clean. Beth was surprised. She expected it to be a bit of a dump.

'It's about Mae Lethbridge,' said Tom gently

'What about her?'

'She's dead, I'm afraid,' said Beth.

She watched his expression. For a second, it didn't change, and then he shook his head in confusion.

'You what? What are you talking about?'

'She was murdered on Thursday night. A neighbour called the police on Friday evening after being unable to reach her.'

His mouth opened and closed several times before he stepped back and sat on the small bed that Beth could see had been neatly made.

'Murdered? Someone murdered Mae? Are you sure you've got the right person?'

'I'm afraid so.'

'My daughter? What's happened to Blanche?' He jumped up and then fell back onto the bed. He seems genuine, thought Beth. Either that, or he's a good actor.

'She's in a state of shock. She's under sedation at the hospital.'

'My God, I need to go and see her.'

'We need to ask you a few questions,' said Tom.

'How did she die?' Rob asked.

'We believe she was beaten with a hammer,' said Tom.

'Jesus,' he moaned, putting his hands to his face.

'Do you mind if I ask you where you were Thursday evening?'

Rob Lethbridge looked up.

'I was here.'

'You didn't visit Mae?'

'Am I a suspect?'

'We just need to eliminate you.'

He bowed his head.

'To be honest, I need a fair bit of courage to visit Mae. It never goes well, you see. I got here Wednesday night late. I thought I'd visit them at the weekend.'

'What was your relationship like?' Beth asked.

Rob gave a sardonic grin.

'I wouldn't have called it a relationship. That's how strained it was. Look, I really ought to see my daughter.'

'When did you last see her?' asked Tom.

'On my daughter's birthday. The visit didn't go well. I expect you've already heard about that. Mae walked out on me several years ago and took Blanche with her. I had no idea where they went ….'

'But you found them,' interrupted Beth.

'I hired a private investigator. I wanted to see my daughter on her eighteenth birthday. It was an expense I couldn't really afford.'

'Did you often hit your wife, Mr Lethbridge?'

He gave a cynical laugh.

'I thought you said I wasn't a suspect?'

'It's just routine questioning,' said Tom.

'We had our ups and downs. She wasn't an easy person to live with ….'

'So, you hit her?' said Beth.

'I never said that. Maybe once. I wasn't proud of it.'

'Why are you here now?' Beth asked.

'I wanted to see my daughter. She's sicker than I thought. Mae took out a restraining order against me. I wanted to talk about it with her.'

'Did you know that Mae kept a suitcase full of money?'

He gave an ugly laugh.

'That doesn't surprise me. She was always hiding money.'

'Do you know how much she hid?'

'Most certainly forty thousand.'

Beth's eyes widened.

'How much?'

'That's a lot of money,' said Tom.

'It was inherited from her mother. I imagine she had more on top of that. She made a lot of money from her little talks. I don't think she ever declared it. It was supposed to have been charity money. The only thing about charity that Mae knew was that charity began at home.'

There was an undertone of bitterness in his voice.

'Why didn't she put it in the bank?' Beth asked.

'Don't ask me. The Taxman, most likely.'

'Could anyone else have known about that money?' asked Tom.

'I couldn't tell you. I have no idea who Mae mixed with. Can I go and see my daughter, now?'

'Is there anyone who can confirm you were here Thursday evening?'

'Nope,' said Rob, grabbing his jacket and scarf. 'I can't prove it. What hospital is my daughter in?'

'The John Radcliffe,' said Beth.

She stepped from the caravan and Tom followed. At his car, Rob stopped.

'Are you sure about Mae? You couldn't have made a mistake?'

'I'm sorry,' said Beth.

He rubbed at his eyes and then climbed into his car. Tom watched him drive away before saying, 'Do you believe him?'

'I don't know. He knew Mae hid the money. He's very upfront about it, though. But he doesn't have an alibi. Let's see what forensics turn up on the hammer and what Blanche has to say.'

*

'There are multiple DNA samples on the hammer,' said Don Faire, placing the hammer onto the table.

Faire pointed to the covered body. Beth took a deep breath and followed him to the table where it lay. Faire pulled back the sheets to reveal Mae's battered face. Beth only half looked.

'As you can see, the head and face took most of the beating.'

'I'm not looking, Don,' said Beth.

'Not got a strong stomach?'

'Just carry on,' Beth turned her head and took a deep breath.

'We found traces of nitrazepam in her blood.'

'What's that?' asked Beth.

'A sleeping drug. We also found traces of alcohol.'

Beth remembered the tablets on Mae's bedside table.

'The weapon used was the hammer. It has the victim's blood on it. The cause of death was bleeding in the brain, internal haemorrhaging. At a guess, I would say the fifth blow killed her. Also, there were hair fibres on the hammer. Several belonged to the victim, but there were others which we've matched to Kate Marshall. So, it's fairly evident that the same weapon was used in both cases.'

'You said multiple DNA samples?' said Beth.

'Yeah.'

Beth bit her tongue. She knew better than to hurry Don Faire. She'd heard he liked to deliver his news slowly and with the maximum impact.

'There was some blood that didn't match Kate's or the Lethbridge woman on the hammer. Some of them may well be Kate Marshall's husband. It was his hammer. Need to check against his prints.'

'Okay,' said Tom, patiently

'Something else that was interesting.'

Beth and Tom waited. Don pulled a packet of polo mints from his pocket and offered them around before popping two into his mouth.

'We found a small trace of blood at the bottom of the suitcase. A minute amount, but it doesn't belong to the victim. Again, it matched what was on the hammer.'

'Could belong to the murderer then?' said Beth, trying to hide her excitement.

'Anything is possible,' said Don.

So bloody unhelpful thought Beth.

'Thanks, Don. Let us know if you come up with anything else, and in the meantime, we'll get DNA samples from the neighbour and Mae's ex-husband,' said Tom.

'Let's hope you get him this time.' said Don.

'This time?' queried Beth.

'Second time around.'

'Right,' said Beth, smarting at his words. She was getting too sensitive these days. She needed to harden up.

'Oh yes. The suitcase definitely contained money. Very recently too. Chances are there will be blood on that too.'

'Thanks,' said Beth.

'Can someone fix the bloody heating too?' Don remarked, making for the door. 'The place is sodding freezing.'

'That's out of our remit,' shot back Tom.

'Must be within someone's,' said Don as he closed the door behind him.

'It's a bloody morgue,' said Beth.

'He's got cold blood in him. That's the problem,' smiled Tom.

Beth hurried from the room, relieved to get fresh air into her lungs. How Don Faire could eat those mints, she'd never know.

Chapter Sixty

Leeds: 2005

Rob

I'd had an affair. That was wrong, and I'd always admit that. But walking out, taking everything, taking my daughter without a single word of warning. That's downright cruel, not to mention humiliating. I never imagined Mae was capable of such deceit. The worst part was the neighbours watching from behind their curtains. I stood on the doorstep like a fool and then peeked through the windows. My body slumped when I saw that the furniture had gone. I stood there, dazed, and that's when Liz came, holding a bottle of brandy.

'I've still got my spare key,' she said, opening the front door.

I walked through the house, my steps echoing around me, looking to see what crumbs Mae had left me, hoping to find a note which would explain everything.

'I had a feeling you didn't know,' said Liz, opening the brandy. It's a cruel thing she's done.'

She handed me the bottle. I took a swig.

'I was supposed to be seeing my daughter. We'd arranged it.' The brandy hit my throat, and I coughed.

Liz looked around the empty lounge.

'She's cleared you out, hasn't she?'

I didn't want her to see how close I was to breaking down. I simply nodded. I knew if I tried to speak, my voice would have broken with the emotion. Liz was right. Mae had left nothing.

'Deceiving little bitch,' she said. 'I never liked her. She sold the house, you know.'

'Sold it?' I said, finding my voice.

I thought she'd just moved out. Done a runner. I never imagined she was that callous.

'Call me nosy, but one day I popped in, and she had viewers here. She tried to pretend she was selling some furniture on

Gumtree. I phoned around the agents to see if it was on the market. I thought you knew. I thought you were all going. I was a bit upset that she'd never said anything or you. But then, today, when I saw the removal men and no sign of you, I thought, something's not right here.'

'It was her house,' I heard myself say. 'Do you know who the agents are?'

'Chancellors. You should phone them. Not that you can do much now.'

'Like I said, it was her house.'

You're married,' Liz said, frowning. 'You have a right to half the house, don't you?'

I had a right to my daughter too, but how the hell do I find them? They could have gone anywhere, even abroad.

Liz took the brandy from my hand and lifted it to her lips. It must have loosened her tongue, for she said,

'She killed her mother, you know,'

The words took my breath away for a moment.

'Don't be ridiculous,' I said.

'You think it's ridiculous. I knew Joan for years. She's always liked a tipple. She could hold her drink. She didn't fall down those stairs. Mae always got what she wanted, and she wanted her mother's money. They were going shopping, Joan told me. But I saw Mae leaving the house no sooner had she arrived. Something happened.'

I took back the brandy.

'You need to be careful what you say,' I said.

'She's a sly one,' she insisted, walking to the door.

'Get yourself a private detective,' she advised. 'Don't let her take your child.'

'I'll phone around,' I said. 'See if anyone knows anything.'

Liz left the brandy, and I drank half of it while digesting her words.

'She killed her mother, you know.'

My body turned cold at the realisation that what Liz said might be true.

The brandy gave me the courage I needed and I phoned the vicar.

'Gone?' he said. 'To Canada?'

It felt like someone had punched me in the stomach.

'Canada?' I repeated.

'We had a fundraiser. Mae was going to take her to Canada, where the specialist was that was going to treat her cancer. We raised the money for the airfare and the treatment. I thought you'd be going too.'

I was dumbfounded. Blanche had cancer? Why hadn't Mae told me? I spent the next few days trying to trace them. I took time off work and phoned everyone I knew. Doctor Morris said he knew nothing about Blanche having cancer.

'I can phone the specialists at the hospital and see if they know about Blanche's condition,' he offered.

I tried to track down the Canadian cancer specialist. I spent a fortune on telephone calls, but no one had heard of Blanche Lethbridge. Not one hospital was treating her. Doctor Morris phoned and said there was no record of Blanche ever being treated for cancer in Leeds.

'I don't understand,' he said, sounding confused.

With every passing hour, my love for Mae began to chip away until there was no love left. She'd taken everything from me. She was punishing me because I hadn't been able to handle Blanche being ill. I hated her for that. Jo said I should try and find them.

'She took your daughter. You can't just leave things at that.'

But I didn't have the resources to keep looking. Private detectives were expensive, and I had little money. I'd been clinging to my job by the skin of my teeth. I'd also been worried about what I might do if I saw Mae again. I'd become consumed with anger and hate towards her. I felt it was best not to look for them. Not yet, anyway. I decided that when the time was right, I would get my daughter back. I'd do whatever I could to have her in my life again.

Chapter Sixty-One

September 2019: Stonesend

Jack Winters was welcoming.

'What can I get you?' he asked.

'Just a diet coke for me,' said Beth.

'Same here,' said Tom.

Jack got the drinks and said, 'I suppose you're here to question me. Let's take the drinks to a table, shall we?'

'I won't beat about the bush,' Tom said. 'We know you visited Mae Lethbridge on Thursday evening. The night of her murder.'

'I'm not denying it,' he said, placing the glasses in front of them. 'I'll tell you now. We argued.'

'What about?' asked Tom.

Jack wiped the table with a damp cloth.

'I let her have that fundraiser here. I laid on the food. It was a big fundraiser. People like to support Blanche, as you know. We made £1,500. I went around with the cheque. Mae wanted me to make it out to her. I wouldn't. I wanted to make it out to the charity she runs, but she got really mad with me.'

'Mad, why?' asked Beth.

'Accused me of not trusting her. Well, quite honestly, I didn't. She wouldn't give me the bank details of the charity. We've raised a fair bit for Blanche in the past and just given it to Mae. I figured £1,500 should be accounted for, you know. People like to know where their money's gone.'

'So, you didn't give her the cheque.'

'No, I didn't. I wasn't going to hand over £1,500 for her to pocket. She yelled all sorts at me. I'd never seen her like that. I told her I thought she was a charlatan. The next day I heard she'd died.'

'What time did you leave her house?'

'I don't know, around 7:30 at a guess.'

The Lies She Told

'It would help if you did a DNA test. We can't force you, but it will help to eliminate you from the suspects,' Tom said, standing up.

'Sure. I didn't like her, but I wouldn't have killed her.'

'Did you see anyone hanging around outside the house when you left?'

'Not that I noticed.'

Tom pulled a wallet from his pocket.

'What's the damage?'

'On the house,' smiled Jack.

'I'm surprised you make a living,' said Tom, handing him a ten-pound note.

'Is there anyone else in the village that felt angry towards her?' asked Beth.

Jack shrugged.

'I don't know. People are scared right now. That's all I know. I hope you're close to catching whoever did this.'

'We'll get whoever it was,' said Tom determinedly.

*

'He's not the killer,' said Beth when they were outside the pub. 'He's not the murdering kind.'

'I'm sure someone said that about Harold Shipman.'

Beth wondered if Rob Lethbridge was the murdering kind. As if reading her thoughts, Tom asked.

'What's your take on Rob Lethbridge? I get a frustrated father finally relieved to be spending time with his sick daughter. He couldn't do that before, not if accounts given by Kate and Dan Marshall are anything to go by.'

'Is it something you would kill your ex-wife for?' asked Beth. 'If he got caught, he wouldn't see his daughter ever again.'

'You've got a point. But sometimes, emotions override common sense. There may have been a lot more going on. It seems there was something of a financial issue. Who knows? Perhaps she kept money back from him as well as his daughter.'

'He may have been a lousy father. She may have taken Blanche to protect her.'

'Which makes him a prime suspect, either way, doesn't it?'

Beth looked thoughtful.

'He seemed pretty confident. He hasn't even attempted to get himself an alibi. Kate Marshall didn't get goosebumps when she saw him. But who else would want to kill Mae? Who would want to attack Kate unless it was a case of mistaken identity, in which case it couldn't have been Rob as he clearly knew where Mae and her daughter lived?' she said.

'I don't know. The connection between Kate and Mae confuses me. Yet we know it was the same murder weapon,' said Tom, thoughtfully.

'But why leave it in the garden. He kept it after Kate's attack. Why get rid of it now?'

'Perhaps he has no intention of striking again,' said Tom hopefully.

'Seems careless to leave the murder weapon where it can be found when he was so careful the first time.'

Tom nodded.

'Maybe that's just it. He's becoming careless.'

'Something doesn't add up,' she said but had no idea what.

Chapter Sixty-Two

Rob arrived at the hospital. He hated them, always had. He hated the smell. He hated the wards with their bustling nurses and rows of sick men and women lying in beds. He couldn't abandon Blanche. He was all she had left in the world, but he had no idea how to deal with an eighteen-year-old disabled daughter. He'd never known how to deal with her.

He got lost in the corridors. They all looked the same and seemed to lead everywhere except to the wards. Eventually, he found Williams Ward. A gentle-faced nurse approached him at the entrance.

'I'm Blanche Lethbridge's father,' he said.

'Her room is the second on the right,' the nurse said kindly. 'You may find her a bit sleepy. We still have her on a low dose sedative.'

He nodded his thanks and went nervously to Blanche's room. He stood outside it for what seemed an eternity before knocking and going in. Blanche was in bed. Her eyes widened at the sight of him, and he thought she teared up, but she quickly wiped her eyes with the back of her hand. Her face was pale and drawn, and she looked so helpless lying there. He felt uncomfortable. He barely knew this young woman. It was like visiting a stranger.

'Hi,' he said nervously. 'How's it going?'

A stupid thing to say, he thought, angry with himself. It's going terrible. She'd just lost her mother. The only person that ever mattered to her.

'I'm not sure,' she said, her voice breaking. Her hands fiddled with the bedsheets.

'Oh baby,' he said, hurrying to her side.

His arms wrapped themselves easily around her thin body. Had she always been this thin? He wondered. Her head fell easily onto his shoulder, and her body shook against his.

'It's okay, Blanche, it's all going to be okay.'

'Mum,' she whimpered. 'Mum's dead.'

His breath caught in his throat for a moment, and words wouldn't come. He stroked her arm.

'I'm here now.'

He held her hand tightly in his.

'Mum said you never wanted me,' she said, but there was nothing accusing in her tone. All the same, the words cut through him.

'I always wanted you,' he said.

He had no idea how they would move forward. He hadn't had any time to think about the future. He wouldn't be able to take Blanche back to Leeds, not with a murder investigation ongoing. He had no idea how he would care for her.

'Are they giving you all your medication?'

He didn't even know what the medication was.

'I think so. Mum always took care of that.'

She looked closely at him.

'She said you never came to see us because you didn't love us enough.'

How could she? How could she lie like that to their own daughter?

'I didn't know where you were. I tried to find you at the beginning. Perhaps I didn't try hard enough. I'm sorry.'

'It's alright,' she said softly.

'Are they taking good care of you here?'

'Yes.'

The question that had been on his lips the moment he had walked through the door now escaped.

'Do you know who it was?'

He held his breath. He wanted to look into her eyes, but he couldn't bear to see the pain there. She shook her head and began to cry.

'She called for me.'

He squeezed her hand.

'We'll get through this.'

'Yes,' she said.

Rob realised this was the closest he had ever been to his daughter. He never imagined it would take the death of her mother to bring it about. He'd move into Mill house. He was sure Blanche would like Jo. They would make Blanche better. They could be a proper family this time.

*

Beth wasn't surprised to see Rob at his daughter's bedside. She was surprised, however, to see them holding hands.

'The doctor said it was okay to ask Blanche some questions,' she explained.

'Surely it can wait?' said Rob, standing up.

'I'm afraid not. The more time goes by, the harder it will be to find Mae's killer,' said Tom firmly.

'I'm all right to answer questions,' said Blanche. 'I want to.'

Her voice was soft but clear. Beth noted she was quite underweight. She looked tired and weary and Beth felt bad questioning her.

'We promise not to tire you,' she said.

'It's the drug they gave me,' explained Blanche. 'It makes me sleepy all the time.'

Rob stepped back so Beth could get nearer to the bed.

'I'd prefer to stay,' he said.

'Of course,' said Tom.

'Blanche, we are so very sorry for the loss of your mother. It must be terrible for you,' said Beth kindly.

Blanche licked her lips and nodded.

'Can you tell us what happened that night?' Tom asked gently.

Blanche took a deep breath.

'I don't want to remember it,' she said tearfully.

'I understand,' said Beth gently. 'But it's the only way if we're to find the person who did it.'

Blanche nodded and stared ahead as she spoke.

*

Blanche Lethbridge: Witness statement.
I went to bed as usual and was asleep by nine-thirty. I was woken by the screams.

I heard everything. It was terrible, horrific, and I was frightened to move. I didn't want whoever it was to hear me. My room was cold, but I could feel the sweat running down my body. I heard my mum scream. I hunched up my legs and wrapped my arms around my body. At one point, the screams were so blood-curdling that I had to block my ears, but still, I could hear them. I thought it would never end. My heart raced so fast, the sound of it thrashing horribly in my ears. I heard her call out.

'Help, help me, Blanche.'

But I was helpless. Just like I'd always been. I rocked back and forth, praying for it to stop. Then it did. I didn't hear her voice anymore. Suddenly everything was silent. I didn't allow myself to think about what was happening. I didn't move in case the person was close. Supposing they heard me breathing? What if they were outside the door? I wrapped a blanket around my shoulders and lay curled up with my heart hammering. My muscles were tense and sore. I squeezed my eyes shut and tried to push the memory of the screams from my mind and wished my dad were here to help us. I must have fallen asleep. When I awoke, it was morning and Mum didn't come and open the door. I waited and waited and prayed she would come.

All day, I lay there, waiting for help. Mum always locked me in so I couldn't get out. Finally, the doorbell went. Someone shouted, 'Mae, are you okay?' It sounded like Sophie Johnson. I hoped it might have been Kate.

She rang the doorbell again, and then everything went quiet for a while. She'd call for help, I thought. Surely, she would think it odd that our car was in the driveway. It seemed forever before the doorbell rang again, and this time, a strange voice called.

'Mae, I'm sergeant Wilkins, can you hear me? Is anyone at home?'

My heart raced. It was the police. The police were here.

'I'm here,' I called. 'Please help.'

But they couldn't hear me. My throat was dry, my voice hoarse and weak, and then I heard my mother's phone ringing.

Everything went quiet. Had they gone?

'No, come back.' I cried.

My skin felt clammy, and I was so thirsty. They must come soon. Someone must come soon. Finally, after what seemed an eternity, I heard movement downstairs. The same voice calling out. I cocked my ears. Then more voices.

Soon, they will find me. I waited. I was sweating copiously. There was the sound of sirens, distant at first and then much closer. I wrapped my arms around my body, and then I heard them at the door.

'This is DI Miller. We're coming in.'

The door burst open and the light blinded me. I had to blink several times to see who they were. Beth Harper saw me first. Her eyes widened in surprise, then shock, and finally, her face relaxed. She was relieved to see me.

'Blanche. Blanche Lethbridge?' she asked.
'I need the toilet,' I said.

*

'There was nothing I could do. Mum had locked the door, you see.'

'Did she always do that?' asked Beth. 'Or was that the first time she'd done it?'

'Mum always locked me in. She said it was for my safety.'

'Was she afraid of something?' Tom asked.

'I don't know. I don't think so.'

'Did you hear the person speak? Was it a man?'

Blanche shook her head.

'I didn't hear anybody talk. Just Mum screaming. I thought the screaming would never end.'

She started to tremble.

'I think that's enough,' said Rob. 'She's had a traumatic experience.'

'Just one more question,' said Tom. 'Do you know if your mum had any disagreements with anyone?'

Blanche looked nervously at her father.

'It's okay,' he said. 'They know about the birthday party argument.'

'I don't think so. Mum was friends with everyone.'

'Your mum had a suitcase of money,' said Beth. 'Did anyone know about that?'

'I don't think so. She wouldn't put money in the bank, said it was safer in the house ....'

She broke off and started to cry.

'Blanche, if you remember anything, please let us know,' said Beth. 'You can call me anytime.'

She gave Blanche a card and then nodded at Tom.

'We'll leave you in peace,' she said.

Beth waited until they were safely out of earshot before saying, 'Her mum was frightened of someone. Let's face it, You don't lock your daughter in her room every night if all the people in the village are your friends. Someone wasn't her friend, and she knew it.'

Chapter Sixty-Three

Matt, with a face like thunder, stormed into the station.

'Where's the Chief?' he asked.

'In his office.'

Matt threw a newspaper onto Beth's desk.

'Have you seen this?'

Beth looked at the news article. A photo of Tom Miller and his wife stared back at her. They were standing with another couple. A fundraising banner hung behind them. Tom was wearing a bow tie and his wife a long black evening dress. She looked at the headline and took a sharp breath.

Alcoholic detective leads local murder investigation.

Beth groaned. 'That bloody reporter.'

'There's a whole piece on him,' said Matt. 'There's no way he agreed to this.'

'It's out of order,' she said angrily. Any thoughts she'd had the past few days of opening up about Ben and Mark were quickly buried. There's always someone who would talk, especially if the money was good. No, it was better that it stayed a secret.

'You'd better show it to the chief,' she said. But the chief was already walking out of his office.

'I've seen it,' he said. 'I'm going over to their offices now. It's a bloody disgrace.

'It's a bloody disgrace him coming here,' mumbled Matt.

'Oh, do zip it,' said Beth, standing up.

'Pardon me for living,' Matt retorted.

*

Tom looked up as she walked in. She hesitated for a second and then placed the newspaper on his desk.

'I thought you should see this. The chief has gone to their offices. I don't want to do an 'I told you so,' but I did.'

Tom glanced at the headline and then handed it back.

'You don't want to do an 'I told you so,' but you're doing it anyway.'

'Look, you messed up. You left that witness alone ….'

'One mistake,' he interrupted. 'One mistake in twenty years ….'

'You can't afford to make even one mistake in this job.'

He met her eyes.

'We're human, Beth. We feel things too. Don't tell me you've never made a mistake.'

She turned away.

'What if you hadn't got back in time?' she asked.

'I did get back in time, the court case went ahead and the defendants were found guilty. I admit I went back to work too soon after Lorna. I wasn't ready. It was a mistake. I own it. I don't drink now. What was I supposed to do? Hide away like Lynch wanted me to do and never work again? What's my crime, putting away an evil paedophile? He was the criminal, not me. Am I supposed to pay the price for one mistake for the rest of my life? I left an important witness alone. It was a mistake. But I've done good things too.'

'People only remember the bad things,' said Beth quietly. 'Especially in a small village like this.'

'Their small minds are not my problem. I'm here to do a job.'

'You're not making friends.'

'I don't need friends.'

He got up from behind the desk, picked up his wallet and strode past her. We all need friends, thought Beth.

'We've got a crime to solve,' he said.

Beth picked up the newspaper and pushed it into her bag. Her hand brushed her phone as it vibrated. It was a call from the hospital.

'DS Harper,' she said, walking to the car.

'DS Harper, this is Doctor Werner. I wonder if you could spare some time to see me today.'

'Yes, of course. Is everything all right?'

'No, it isn't. I'd like to talk to you about Blanche Lethbridge.'

*

Doctor Werner's office was situated in a small modern building at the side of the main hospital. Beth and Tom waited patiently in reception while he finished his rounds.

'Didn't he give you any idea what this was about?' asked Tom.

'No, just that he wanted to talk about Blanche.'

The door opened, and Doctor Werner strolled in.

'Sorry to keep you waiting. Please come into my office.'

The office was large and airy. Doctor Werner gestured to two chairs and then sat opposite them. He removed his glasses and rubbed at his eyes.

'I've done many tests on Blanche Lethbridge, and I'm curious as to where her medication came from.'

Beth frowned.

'Came from?' she repeated. 'They were in the house. In Blanche's bedroom. Her mother kept them in a cabinet.'

'I'm sorry. I didn't explain myself very well. Where the medication was obtained is what I'm asking?'

Beth shook her head, puzzled.

'I don't understand. I presume from Blanche's doctor or her specialist.'

'Right,' said Doctor Werner, stroking his chin. 'That's a natural assumption. I made the same one, so I contacted her GP, and he confirmed that he'd prescribed the anti-seizure medication but that he didn't run any tests on Blanche. He took Mrs Lethbridge's word for it that her daughter had epilepsy. He didn't prescribe the other drugs you found. The medications that you handed in when Blanche came to us were for numerous conditions. I spoke to her father, who seemed very uncertain as to what those conditions were. He knew there had been fits and that there was a problem with her spine, and she also suffered from allergies, but he was unclear on what the spine issue was and more unclear on the allergies. He thought she had cancer but wasn't sure. Admittedly he hadn't seen his daughter for some time.'

'She's been very ill,' said Beth, realising she sounded vague. 'They did a lot for charity, and also the mother gave talks on living with a chronically ill child. Blanche is recovering from leukaemia.'

Doctor Werner raised his eyebrows.

'The drugs you gave us were sleeping pills, muscle relaxants and pain killers. There were also anti-epileptic drugs, anti-nausea medication and Rohypnol. Blanche does not have leukaemia or any other cancers.'

Beth stared at him.

'But her hair has fallen out from the chemotherapy.'

'Her head has been shaved. It didn't fall out. The hair is now growing back.'

'I don't understand,' said Beth, confused.

'What exactly are you telling us, doctor?' Tom asked.

'I have conducted numerous tests on this patient. She does not have epilepsy, is not asthmatic, doesn't have cancer, and all the allergy tests we have performed indicate she is not allergic to anything. Her body has taken a battering from the drugs she has been taking, but it should recover. Her spine is normal, so the body brace you gave us is puzzling. I should say that Miss Lethbridge still believes she needs it, and the only thing she admits she doesn't need is the wheelchair. She said her mother insisted her daughter use it.'

Beth struggled to comprehend what the doctor was telling her.

'Who shaved her head?' asked Beth, frowning.

'I'm none more the wiser than you.'

'Are you saying that Blanche is perfectly healthy?' asked Tom, surprised.

'That's precisely what I'm saying.'

'But she looked terrible,' said Beth, unable to believe what the doctor was telling them.

'So would you if you had that amount of drugs pumped into you over many years. I'd like to know where the mother obtained them. I'm presuming the painkillers were purchased online.'

'Does Blanche know she isn't ill?' asked Tom.

Doctor Werner shook his head.

'She believes that the drugs are controlling her illnesses. We've been giving her placebos. I'm not sure she is mentally strong enough yet to be told the truth.'

'Have you spoken to her father?' asked Beth.

'Not yet. I tried to speak to Mrs Lethbridge's previous doctor, Doctor Morris, but he has left the practice in Leeds. There are several referrals on her notes but no record of any hospital treatment, apart from A&E attendances, which were often. Some drugs were prescribed by her then GP. For example, the anti-nausea and anti-seizure drugs. I can only presume the doctor went by the information given by the mother. He told Mr Lethbridge that Mae was not a strong child.'

'But, why would Mae have told her daughter she was ill if she wasn't?' asked Beth.

'Attention,' said Doctor Werner simply. 'I think it most likely Mrs Lethbridge suffered from Munchausen Syndrome by Proxy. It seems she obtained certain drugs that would mimic the symptoms of the illnesses she claimed her daughter had. Several of those drugs were amongst the ones you gave us. I have to say this is a very extreme case. It's child abuse at its worst.'

'What's Munchausen by proxy?' asked Tom.

'A fabricated or induced illness is a rare form of child abuse. It happens when a parent or carer, usually the child's biological mother, exaggerates or deliberately causes symptoms of illness in the child to gain attention. Mae Lethbridge no doubt enjoyed the attention that a caring mother gave her.

'My God,' said Tom. 'She made money out of her daughter's illness?'

'It wouldn't be the first case where that has happened, Detective. I imagine if you look into her background, you'll find Mrs Lethbridge has a nursing history,' said Doctor Werner. 'I'll be speaking to the father. It's best if Blanche spends some time recuperating. It will be a shock when she finds out. She's become used to being the sick daughter.'

'I don't believe it,' said Beth.

'I'm transferring her to a rehabilitation centre. I'll continue to oversee her treatment.'

Beth left Doctor Werner's office in a daze.

'How can a mother do that to their child?' she asked Tom.

'It's an illness.'

'Supposing Rob Lethbridge knew this and saw the only way he could rescue his daughter was by killing his wife,' she said.

'Bit extreme,' said Tom. 'But we need to speak to him again and track down Mae's former doctor.'

'Mae could well have had many enemies,' said Beth, hurrying to keep up with him.

'Look, about earlier,' she said.

'Forget it,' he said sharply.

'Bloody hell, you're hard work,' she said, getting into the car.

'I'll drop you off at your place so you can pack a bag.'

'You what?'

'We're going to Leeds. I want to question Doctor Morris and see whether Mae Lethbridge had any enemies there.'

'We're staying overnight?'

'Think of it as a holiday,' he said with a smile.

Chapter Sixty-Four
Kate

Kate woke, her nightclothes soaked in sweat. She'd been dreaming of Mae. The dream didn't make sense, of course, but dreams never do. It had been so vivid. Mae had been wearing the red and white polka dot dress that she often wore on their summer picnics. Her hair had been shiny where she had just washed it, and she'd smelled of Body Shop White Musk perfume. In the dream, they'd eaten normal food for a change, and Kate kept trying to tell Mae that it might not be suitable for Blanche's allergies, but every time she opened her mouth to tell Mae, she'd end up saying something else instead. Suddenly Blanche had convulsed in front of them, gasping for breath.

'Why didn't you tell me about the cake?' Mae had demanded.

Kate had woken then, hot and feverish, the memory of Mae's murder hitting her all over again. She couldn't stop thinking about Dan's hammer. Where had it been all that time? Had it been in someone's house? Could it have been with one of the neighbours?

She planned to visit Blanche today. She phoned the hospital and was told that Blanche had been moved to Lindon House, a rehabilitation clinic close to Oxford. Kate was dreading it. She was worried she might see Rob Lethbridge. If he were there, she would have to speak to him, but what would she say? She had no idea what she would say to Blanche either. Mae's house looked bleak when she passed. It was still cordoned off. Kate could barely look at it without imagining Mae's horrified face as the hammer rained down on her body. Had I screamed, Kate wondered? Had he meant to murder me too? But why? She let the tears flow freely. She didn't care anymore if someone saw her. Mae had been a caring person, and she hadn't deserved this.

The memory of the day they had moved into the village was vivid in her mind. She'd taken them orange juice. It had been a hot day. Blanche had been unpacking her things from a box. She had been pale looking, even then. It was clear there was something wrong with her, but then, of course, no one knew what. Mae and Kate had become close very quickly. Within weeks they were having tea in each other's houses. Kate had helped Mae decorate her kitchen, and Blanche would often come and play at Kate's house. Kate had always been careful with food, not wanting to upset her diet. Who would watch her now? Would Rob tell the clinic about Blanche's special diet? Poor Blanche. What would happen to her without Mae caring for her?

Lindon House, a Victorian building with a long tree-lined driveway, was an imposing sight. Kate rang the doorbell and spoke to the receptionist through a crackly intercom. She desperately wanted to wake up from this terrible nightmare and see Dan smiling at her side, telling her it had all been a bad dream and that Mae was at home as usual. But Mae wasn't at home. She was in the morgue, and Kate would never see her again. After Blanche's birthday party, Kate had phoned her before going to bed.

'Are you okay, Mae?' she'd asked.

'Yes, Kate, thanks. With my ole mate at my side, I'll always be okay.'

Kate hadn't been at her 'ole mate's side when she had needed her the most. The least she could do now was make sure her daughter was all right.

The dream had triggered something, and on first waking, she couldn't fathom what it was, but now it was as clear as anything. The day Blanche took a muffin wasn't the first time. Kate now remembered that the first time had been a year ago. It had been a few days before Christmas. She and Blanche had made mince pies and chocolate cakes. Blanche was allergic to flour, so Kate always bought gluten-free ingredients for Blanche's cakes. They made some chocolate cakes for the boys and gluten-free mince pies for Mae and Blanche. The first time it happened, Kate had just presumed that one of the boys had taken it.

'There's no need to steal a cake', she'd told them. 'You only have to ask. I don't like you eating chocolate cake before dinner, though.'

They'd both fervently denied it. Kate thought of telling Mae but changed her mind. She couldn't be sure Blanche had taken the cake, and she seemed fine the next time she saw her, so she'd convinced herself it was one of the boys and then forgot all about it. She was conscious that the next few times she made cakes, none of them went missing, but when she and Blanche made cakes again, the same thing happened. Kate decided to let it go. Mae never mentioned Blanche being unwell after their baking sessions, so Kate figured there was no harm done, and from then on, she would expect one to go missing whenever they made cakes. She never mentioned it to Blanche. It was an unspoken secret.

She stepped into the foyer of Linden House and let out a small gasp. It was like walking into a five-star hotel. Soft music played in the background, and pretty vases filled with flowers fragranced the air. A young woman sat behind the reception desk. She smiled warmly at Kate.

'Hello, can I help you?'

'I've come to visit Blanche Lethbridge.'

'Certainly,' she said, glancing at her computer screen, 'Room 15 on the ground floor.'

Kate had only walked a short way down the carpeted corridor when she saw him. Rob Lethbridge looked weary and dishevelled. Kate looked for an escape route, but there wasn't one. She had no choice but to face him. A tremor ran down her spine. What if he was the person that had attacked her?

He looked up, and an awkward smile crossed his lips.

'Hello,' he said, stopping in front of her. His striking good looks were quite breathtaking.

'You were at Blanche's birthday party,' he said.

His eyes met hers. Kate wanted to ask him. Ask him outright. 'Was it you that attacked me?'

'Yes, I live close to Mae,' she said, watching his expression.

He didn't react but simply said, 'Blanche will be pleased to see you.'

'How is Blanche?' she asked.

'A lot better. She'll be pleased to see someone else. She must be sick of my face.' He smiled, but Kate could tell it was forced. She nodded and went to walk away. She didn't know how to make small talk with him. Fortunately, he didn't bother either and walked to the entrance. Kate exhaled, grateful that he'd left.

She didn't recognise Blanche at first. She'd expected to find her in bed. The woman sitting in the chair by the window couldn't be her.

'Blanche?' Kate questioned.

The woman turned from the window to face her, and Kate suppressed a gasp. Blanche looked completely different. Her cheeks were pink and glowing. Her eyes had a sparkle that Kate had never seen before. Even her face, which generally had some blemishes, was clear and translucent.

'Kate', she smiled. 'I'm so glad you came.'

Kate watched in amazement as Blanche got out of the chair and walked towards her. Before Kate could speak, Blanche had wrapped her arms around her.

'Oh Kate,' she said hoarsely.

'You're walking?' Kate said incredulously.

'I'm feeling so much better,' she said. 'I get tired easily, but otherwise, I do feel better.'

Kate sat in the chair by the bed. She couldn't speak for a few moments, the tears choking her.

'I'm so glad you came,' Blanche said, taking her hand and squeezing it.

'Oh Blanche,' Kate blubbered, feeling the tears wet on her cheeks. 'I miss her so much.'

Blanche looked into her eyes.

'Do you feel better?' she asked. 'Are you still having headaches?'

Kate felt like they were dancing around each other, knowing that sooner or later they would have to mention the murder and neither of them wanting to.

'I'm so sorry, Blanche,' she said finally. 'I'm so very sorry.'

Much to her shame, the tears came again, and Blanche comforted her. Kate felt ashamed. It should be her comforting Blanche.

'Dad said we might be able to have the funeral soon. You will come, won't you? I can't do it without you.'

Kate nodded.

'Blanche, do you know who did this? I understand if you're afraid, but you can tell me.'

'I don't know,' she said softly. 'Mum had locked me in my room like she always did. I didn't hear voices, just mum's screams. I was so afraid that whoever it was might come for me,' Blanche said, her voice trembling.

'The police will catch him,' Kate said, but there was no conviction in her voice. They hadn't found her attacker in the past six months, supposing they never find Mae's killer? Would she still be at risk?

'Dad said I could live with him when I'm better, You know, over the shock and ....'

Kate sighed. She didn't want Blanche to leave the village. She couldn't bear the thought of losing her too.

'Is that what you want? To move away from the village?'

'He said we'd live at Mill House, so I wouldn't have to move away.'

'Oh,' Kate said, surprised.

Blanche barely knew her father. What if he was violent with her like he had been with Mae, or if his new girlfriend found it hard to cope with Blanche?

'I brought some cake,' she said, changing the subject. 'It's Madeira. I made it yesterday.'

Blanche didn't ask what was in it. Instead, they ate two slices each, the sponge melting deliciously on their tongues. Blanche finished her second slice, wiped her mouth and sighed contentedly.

'Can we make sausage rolls when I get home?'

'If you like,'

Kate always wanted a daughter that she could teach how to bake. Now, she had one. She would help Blanche get better, and Mae would be able to rest. Her 'ole mate' would take care of her daughter.

Chapter Sixty-Five

Roger Waters was early for his appointment. There was no need to rush. He stopped at the red light and took the opportunity to fiddle with the radio. An annoying DJ was rabbiting on about a comedy show he'd watched the night before, and Roger wasn't in the least bit interested. He tuned into Radio 4, where a politician was talking about social housing. The traffic lights turned green. Roger put the car into gear and drove forward. He didn't see the oncoming Peugeot. He wouldn't have been expecting cars to come from the left where the traffic lights were red. The Peugeot was almost on top of him when he did see it. Roger pushed his foot hard down on the accelerator, but it was too late. The Peugeot crashed into the left side of him, sending his car careening across the road. Roger cried out as the airbag shot into his chest. He sat there in a daze, unaware of the people surrounding his car.

'Are you alright?'

Someone was knocking on his car window. He couldn't move because of the airbag.

'I think so,' he said shakily.

The door was pulled open, and after a few minutes, he was helped from the car.

'We've called the police,' said someone else.

'No need for that,' said another man, helping him out. He sounded angry.

'I saw it,' said a woman's voice. 'If you need a witness, I'd be happy to say what I saw.'

Roger was relieved to find that all his body parts still worked, although his head ached rather severely.

'I'm happy to pay for any damage,' the man was saying.

'You've been drinking,' said the woman, accusingly.

Roger looked up at the angry man. His wavy blonde hair was tousled where he'd run his hands through it. His cheeks were red and veiny. Roger could smell the alcohol on his breath.

'Why don't you keep out of this,' the man snapped.

'How dare ...' began the woman.

'Was it you that hit me?' asked Roger.

The sound of police sirens silenced them. The man turned to walk away.

'Hold on,' said Roger. 'You can't leave the scene of an accident.'

Several people formed a circle around them and the man had no choice but to stay where he was.

'I'll pay for any damage,' he said. 'No need to involve the police.'

'Drink driving is an offence,' said the woman as a policeman stepped into the circle.

'I'm Sergeant Wilkins. Is anyone hurt?'

'Just my head, I think,' said Roger, shakily.

'It was his fault,' said the woman, nodding at the other man. 'He's been drinking. He drove through a red light and straight into this man's car.'

Sergeant Carpenter glanced at the man. He could smell the alcohol on his breath.

'I'm going to have to breathalyse you, Sir,'

'I've only had a pint.'

'Can I see your driving licence?' asked Sergeant Wilkins.

'I've offered to pay for the damage.'

'Do you have your driving licence?' repeated Wilkins.

The man fumbled in his pocket and produced his licence.

Luke glanced at it and said, 'If you'd like to breathe into this, Mr Shaw.'

'I'll call an ambulance,' Wilkins said to Roger. 'Better to get checked over. We'll get your car towed to your local garage if you let us know where it is.'

Carpenter raised his eyebrows as Carl Shaw blew hard into the machine.

'You're three times over the limit, Mr Shaw. I'm afraid you'll have to come to the station with us.'

Carl Shaw sighed heavily.

'It was only a beer.'

'I think it was more than one beer,' said Carpenter, leading him to the police car.

'People like that should be locked up,' said the woman huffily.

Traffic was queuing up behind the crashed cars, and Wilkins phoned traffic police for backup. It's alright for some, he thought, thinking of Beth and Tom.

'Living it up in Leeds,' he muttered. 'Why do I get traffic control?'

'You what?' asked the woman.

'Nothing,' grunted Matt.

Chapter Sixty-Six

Leeds

Beth pulled a face when she saw the Travelodge.

'I take it you've booked?' she said.

'Actually, I haven't,' said Tom, unbuckling his seat belt.

'Where are we supposed to have dinner?' she asked, looking around.

The only places close by were a garage and a transport café, and that looked closed.

'Don't you ever stop thinking about your stomach?' asked Tom.

'It's nearly ten, and I'm starving. Of course, if we'd stopped on the way here ….'

'We wouldn't have arrived until the early hours,' he interrupted. 'Maybe they do some kind of room service,' he suggested.

'Some kind?' she questioned. 'I can see you don't often stay at a Travelodge.'

'Let's get the room, and then we'll find some food,' he said.

Beth grabbed her holdall from the back of the car. Tom was already at the entrance doors to the motel.

'Such a gentleman,' she muttered, hurrying after him.

'Good evening,' said the receptionist. 'A double, is it?'

'Two singles,' said Tom. 'Just the one night.'

'Certainly.'

'Is there anywhere to get food?' asked Beth, hearing her stomach rumble.

'There's a McDonalds about 10 minutes away. It's open until eleven.'

'Great,' smiled Beth.

It was better than nothing. If Tom had his way, she'd have to make do with a glass of water. Tom showed their ID and signed in for both of them. Beth wandered to her room.

'I'm number 23,' she said. 'See you in ten minutes for McDonald's.'

'If I must,' he muttered. 'I'm number 24.'

'I hope you don't snore,' she smiled. 'These walls are paper thin.'

'Ditto,' he said, unlocking the door.

Beth's room smelt of someone else's aftershave, and she wrinkled her nose. No doubt a one-night stand. She and Ben had done that once. In the early days of their relationship. She hadn't inherited the cottage then and was sharing a cramped flat in Cowley. Funny how she'd never noticed anything strange. He'd been the perfect lover. She shook the memory from her mind and shoved her ransack into the wardrobe. Pointless to unpack for one night. She could hear Tom moving around in the next room and found herself wondering what kind of lover he was.

'Bloody hell Beth,' she mumbled. 'Get a grip.'

Dinner was a Quarter Pounder and fries washed down with a vanilla milkshake. Tom reluctantly chose the chicken salad.

'So, what's the plan for tomorrow?' Beth asked.

'We visit Doctor Morris and take it from there.'

Beth chewed on her fries and finally asked, 'Heard from the chief about the newspaper article?'

'They're posting an apology tomorrow. But, of course, it doesn't undo what they've already written, and the apology will no doubt be so small you'll need a magnifying glass to see it.'

'Why didn't you just stop policing?' she asked curiously.

His lips tightened and Beth saw his jaw twitch.

'Because it's in my blood, and I figured I'd already lost enough. I considered it after Lorna died, but I knew she wouldn't have wanted that.'

'I'm so sorry. It must have been awful.'

He pushed his salad across the table.

'It was murder. We always kept the cars well maintained. Lorna was a careful driver, even more so during the pregnancy. The brakes had been tampered with.'

'I'm sorry. Benny Lynch shouldn't have got off.'

He let out a cynical laugh.

'Insufficient evidence. I should have stitched him up like he said. But I'm too honest a cop for that. I do things by the book.'

'I'm glad,' she said.

'I'm not,' he replied.

Beth didn't know what to say, so she drank her milkshake in silence.

Chapter Sixty-Seven

'Doctor Morris took early retirement in January,' said the receptionist.

'Yes, I know, but we need to talk to him about a patient,' said Tom. 'Do you have an address for him?'

'I'll have to check with the senior partner, but I think it will be alright to give it to you.'

They'd left the Travelodge around eight. Beth hadn't slept well at all. The mattress had been lumpy and the room too hot. They'd picked up a coffee from the garage and then driven to the surgery. Patients were already in the waiting room.

'Early start,' said Beth, glancing at her watch. It was only eight-thirty.

The receptionist came back smiling. She handed Tom a piece of paper.

'Grange Heights, it's just outside town,' she said. 'Buttercup Lane. Go left and continue until you reach a set of traffic lights. Turn right into Buttercup Lane and drive to the top of the hill. You'll find Grange Heights there.'

The directions were perfect, and they found Doctor Morris' house easily. An attractive, elderly woman opened the door. She held a package in her hand.

'Oh,' she said, surprised. 'I thought you were the delivery man.'

'Police,' said Tom, showing her his ID. 'Is Doctor Morris at home?'

She frowned.

'Is something wrong?'

'We'd like to talk to him about one of his patients.'

She looked confused.

'My husband doesn't practice anymore.'

'I'm aware of that,' Tom said. 'Is he home?'

'You'd better come in,' she said reluctantly. 'John, it's someone for you,' she called.

They stepped into the hallway. Beth glanced at the assortment of family photos on the wall. Smiling wedding photos, graduation pictures, christenings. A family that wanted for nothing, Beth thought. A man approached from a doorway at the far end of the hall.

'Hello,' he said. 'I'm Doctor Morris. How can I help you?'

'I'm DI Miller, and this is DS Harper from Oxford. We're here to ask you some questions about Mae Lethbridge,' said Tom.

The doctor nodded.

'I saw they named the victim,' he said. 'I'm very sad. Please come this way. Would you like some coffee?'

'That would be lovely,' said Beth, who hoped there might be biscuits included.

He took them into the living room, and they sat on soft velvet couches, surrounded by wall-to-wall bookcases.

'I'll make the coffee,' said Mrs Morris.

After she'd left the room, Beth asked.

'How long was Mae Lethbridge your patient?'

'The whole family were patients for several years. Mae also worked for me, of course.'

Beth sat forward.

'Really, doing what?'

'Phlebotomy and reception.'

'Phlebotomy?' queried Tom.

'Taking blood,' smiled Doctor Morris.

'Was she qualified?' asked Beth, jumping up to open the door for Mrs Morris, who carried a tray of coffee and biscuits.

'She was a fully trained nurse.'

Beth glanced at Tom. Just what Doctor Werner had said.

'So, she knew about drugs?' said Tom, accepting a cup and plate.

Beth noticed Doctor Morris looked uncomfortable.

'I'm not sure why you're asking these questions about her. She was murdered, wasn't she?'

'We're trying to establish why.' said Beth.

'Well, I can assure you we have no idea why. But, frankly, we were happy when we'd heard she'd left Leeds,' said Mrs Morris.

'Really?' said Beth, helping herself to a biscuit. 'Why?' They were ginger crisp. Beth had a penchant for ginger.

'She was always phoning here about Blanche and asking for advice. I was very patient at first and helped her a lot, but after a time, it got wearing,' explained Doctor Morris.

'Did she have access to drugs at the surgery?'

Doctor Morris looked even more uncomfortable.

'She did. For a time, she worked in the surgery's pharmacy. The patients would get their medications from there.'

'You said 'for a time' Did she stop working in the pharmacy?'

Doctor Morris sighed.

'I suspected her of stealing medication. I had no proof, of course, but the fact that drugs had never gone missing before it stood to reason it was her. It was a gradual thing. I questioned her, and she broke down, saying she didn't know why she took them. I asked her to return them, but she said she'd disposed of them out of guilt.'

'What drugs did she take?' asked Tom.

'Controlled drugs, mainly. Pain killers, morphine, sleeping pills.'

'Why didn't you prosecute?' asked Beth.

'I knew you would ask me that question.'

'Drink your tea, dear,' said his wife.

He smiled at her.

'My wife and I discussed it at length. Mae Lethbridge was something of a celebrity. She'd given talks and appeared on the radio talking about her sick daughter. Can you imagine the reaction from people if I'd reported her? I felt uncomfortable about it, and she begged me not to. She was scared for Blanche. So, I took her out of the pharmacy, and she never took anything again.'

Tom put his cup down.

'Would you like another?' asked Mrs Morris.

'No, thank you. Is it possible that Mae Lethbridge could have stolen prescription pads?' he asked.

Doctor Morris sighed.

'I hope not, but it's possible. But, quite honestly, I don't know.'

Tom stood up.

'Thank you for your time.'

'How is Blanche?' asked Mrs Morris.

'She's doing very well,' said Beth. 'According to the doctor at the hospital, there is nothing whatsoever wrong with her.'

Mrs Morris gasped. 'I knew it,' she said, sounding almost elated.

Doctor Morris looked stunned.

'But ...' he began. 'Her asthma...'

'I think Mae Lethbridge may have fooled a lot of doctors,' said Beth.

'When I treated her as a very young child, I can confirm she was unwell.'

'Perhaps then,' agreed Tom. 'Doctors at the hospital where she is being treated have assured us that she doesn't have any of the illnesses her mother claimed.'

'My God, why didn't I see it?'

'I wouldn't beat yourself up,' said Tom. 'I imagine Mae Lethbridge was very good at deceiving people.'

'Munchausen's by proxy?' he mumbled. 'Is that what they're saying?'

'Yes,' said Beth.

They left Mr and Mrs Morris to digest the news and made their way to Hammond Solutions to talk to Jo Grant.

Chapter Sixty-Eight
Oxford

'How is Blanche?' asked Doctor Werner.

'Looking great,' said Rob. 'She's doing well at Linden House. When can she leave? I'm keen to have her home. Obviously, we'll need all the information on her diet and medications. Mae always took care of that. If there is a nurse we could talk to ….'

'Mr Lethbridge, there's something you should know.'

Rob felt his stomach clench.

'What? I thought you said she was doing okay.'

'Mr Lethbridge, there is absolutely nothing wrong with Blanche. I've done extensive tests. The only thing I can find wrong with her is some muscle weakness which is most likely due to a lack of exercise. I'm confident with time that will improve.'

Rob stared at him.

'What? I don't understand what you're saying.'

'Your daughter is in perfect health. There's nothing wrong with her at all.'

'But … Have you got the right person? Blanche Lethbridge, that's my daughter,' said Rob, thinking the doctor must be mixing her up with someone else.

'Yes, I'm talking about Blanche, your daughter.'

'Of course there is stuff wrong with her. I don't understand. What about her fits?'

'Children can have seizures if they have a high temperature, but there is nothing to indicate that your daughter has epilepsy.'

Rob shook his head emphatically.

'No, you must be wrong. You must have seen her back brace and ….'

'There is nothing wrong with her spine. She does not have cancer. Her head has been shaved. It hasn't fallen out because of chemotherapy.'

Doctor Werner stood up and filled a cup from the water dispenser, and handed it to Rob.

'I appreciate this is something of a shock.'

'But, the asthma and allergies ....'

'Your daughter is in excellent health.'

Rob drank the water slowly, trying to take in what the doctor was saying.

'My daughter is very sick. She always has been. You need to do more tests. It was the Caesarean, Mae said.'

'Mr Lethbridge, I assure you that your daughter is no sicker than you or I. C sections are not unusual, and babies never suffer any ill effects normally.'

'She's mentally ill, is that what you're telling me? She's made her illnesses up?'

'Mr Lethbridge, have you ever heard of a condition called Munchausen by Proxy?'

Rob shook his head.

'Is that what Blanche has?'

'I believe that's what Blanche's mother had. Munchausen by Proxy is a mental health problem in which a caregiver makes up or causes an illness or injury in a person under his or her care, such as a child, in order to gain attention. Often, they will have medical skills or experience, seem devoted to his or her child and will look for sympathy and attention.'

Water spilt onto Rob's trousers. He realised he was shaking. He placed the cup of water onto Doctor Werner's desk.

'Mae was a nurse,' he said.

'I thought as much. Were you ever involved in your child's treatments?'

'Well ...I ...Mae made it impossible. She always took Blanche to the doctor, and why wouldn't I have believed her?'

'It's not unusual for the partner to be shut out. Your wife, I believe, created these illnesses and made Blanche believe in them too.'

'So, all these years ...' Rob stopped as his voice broke.

'I'm very sorry.'

Anger welled up inside Rob until he thought he would burst.

'They were given money, gifts and bloody holidays.'

'I can understand you're angry.'

'I struggled with the illnesses. It's what broke us up, and now you're telling me they didn't exist?'

'I'm afraid so.'

'Why didn't the doctors do something?'

'I'm afraid I can't answer that question.'

'They should have it.'

'I imagine your wife was very convincing.'

'I can't believe it,' said Rob. His mind was in a whirl. How could Mae have done this to her own daughter?

'Mr Lethbridge, I would suggest you go home now. Come back anytime and we can discuss it some more. I'm going to give you something to read. It might help you understand the condition better. At some point, Blanche has to be told. Right now, she thinks we are still medicating her, but I'm giving her placebos. I'm going to visit her tomorrow. I shall tell her the truth. You must remember that for her, sickness has become a way of life.'

'My God,' groaned Rob.

He finished the water and stood up. His legs felt wobbly beneath him.

'If ... If Mae hadn't been murdered, Blanche would still be under her spell.'

Doctor Werner didn't respond.

'Perhaps it's just as well she's dead,' Rob added before leaving the room.

Chapter Sixty-Nine

Leeds

Jo was not happy about them coming to her place of work and made it very clear.

'What did you tell my boss?' She asked crossly. 'I've got a good reputation here.'

'We explained that we were investigating a crime in Oxford and wondered if you could give some information,' explained Beth.

Jo looked slightly relieved.

'You'd better come into my office.'

Beth thought the two women couldn't be more different. Where Mae had been plain and conservative, Jo was exceptionally pretty and fashionable.

'Does Rob know you're here?' she asked.

Tom ignored the question and said bluntly, 'You were with Rob when he visited his ex-wife on his daughter's birthday ….'

'She wasn't his ex-wife,' she said with a sigh.

'What,' said Beth, surprised. 'I thought they were divorced.'

'No,' said Jo, tiredly. 'God knows I wanted him to be, but how can you divorce someone you can't find?'

*

'So, they were never divorced,' Beth said, biting into her burger.

'Which means he inherits the house and whatever was in her bank account,' said Tom.

'You think it was him that murdered her?'

'He had a motive. House, daughter, money and most importantly, revenge.'

Beth shook salt over her fries and offered them to Tom.

He took a handful and shook off the salt.

'Oh, for goodness sake', moaned Beth.

'Salt is bad for your blood pressure.'
'You're bad for my blood pressure.'
'I think we need to have another talk with Mr Lethbridge.'
Beth finished the last of her burger and stood up.
'Right, let's get back,' she said. 'I'm missing quiet old Oxford.'
Tom threw her the car keys.
'You're driving, remember.'
Beth grimaced.
'Right,' she said. 'Just don't fall asleep and snore.'

*

Kate made a cup of tea and went to the fridge to return the carton of milk when something flashed through her mind. The carton slipped from her hand and fell to the floor.

It was there, almost there. The voice, angry, upset. *'Kate, what do you think you're doing?'*

She spun around. No one there. Who was it? Who was it? Beth had told her there had been a spilt milk carton on the floor the day of the attack. Who was it? Who was it that startled her?

'Damn it, come on,' she cursed.

It was there, right on the edge of her memory. Finally, exasperated, she fell into the kitchen chair and started to cry.

*

'You're blooming today,' said Rob.

Blanche looked up from her book.

'I have some makeup on. Nurse Sarah gave it to me.'

'You look lovely.'.

Blanche turned her face from him and looked out of the window.

'Doctor Werner came,' she said.

'I know.'

She turned to face him.

'I'm not sick.' she said quietly. 'I'm not going to die.'

'Not for a long time,' smiled Rob. 'You're as healthy as any eighteen-year-old girl.'

Damn you to hell, Mae, he thought. It's the only place for you.

'I think your mother was unwell, Blanche.'

She nodded.

'I don't have cancer,' she smiled.

Rob's lips quivered as he smiled back.

'No. It's good news, isn't it?'

Chapter Seventy

Oxford

Luke Carpenter leant over Matt's shoulder.

'What the hell?' he said.

Matt quickly turned off his phone.

'Jesus,' exclaimed Matt. 'For a second, I thought you were the Chief.'

'You'll be out on your ear if he catches you looking at Tinder. You're supposed to be working.'

Matt opened his laptop with a groan.

'We're not exactly run off our feet, are we,' he said, lifting his feet onto the desk. 'Hey, do you fancy a game of squash later?'

'I'll have to check with Debs.'

Matt scoffed.

'You'll never get me answering to the old woman.'

'You'll never have an old woman, you clown. No one will put up with you. Have you written up your report yet?'

'What report?'

'The accident. The drunk driver.'

'It's in hand.'

Luke grabbed his ringing phone.

'Yeah,' he grunted.

Matt watched as Luke's expression changed to one of surprise.

'Are you sure about that?'

He glanced up at Matt.

'Send everything over asap.'

He put the phone down.

'I don't believe this,' he said. 'That guy, Carl Shaw, the drunk driver, he's got form. His saliva from the breathalyser showed a match to the blood found in Mae Lethbridge's suitcase.'

'What? but he's not even a suspect.'

'He is now.'

'Better let the chief know.'

*

'Here it is,' said Don. 'A partial match.'

'What about the hammer?' asked Tom.

'Yep, same. The blood in the suitcase and the blood on the hammer.'

Beth reread the report. They'd never heard of the guy. He hadn't even been on their radar. It made no sense.

'Who the hell is he?'

'Carl Shaw,' said Matt. 'Been arrested for a couple of burglaries. Houses were empty at the time. We breathalysed him after a traffic accident just outside the village. He was over the limit.'

'Where does he live?' asked Tom.

'On the Barton estate,' Said Luke.

'Right, get onto Oxford. We'll need armed police. If he's our man, then he could be dangerous.'

'How long will that take?' asked Beth.

'As long as it takes,' said Tom. 'We'll need to find out who else is in the house.'

'Crikey,' said Matt excitedly.

Beth glared at him.

'We don't know he's the killer,' she said.

It didn't make sense. The man's name had never come up in connection with either of the two women. Something didn't add up, but she couldn't work out what it was.

Chapter Seventy-One

Stonesend

Beth had never seen so many police officers in her life.

'Isn't this a bit much?' she asked.

Armed officers surrounded the ex-council house. Police cars were lined up outside. It reminded Beth of the TV series she'd been watching.

'We can't be sure he murdered Mae Lethbridge.' She said, watching more armed police climb from their vehicles.

'We can't be sure he didn't, and we can't be sure he isn't armed,' said Tom.

The area around the house had been cordoned off. No one was allowed into the street. A small crowd had already gathered and were being ushered back.

Beth glanced up at Shaw's bedroom window and thought she saw a curtain move. Carl Shaw lived alone. Beth felt she knew Carl better than he knew himself. It had been twenty-four hours since the DNA report had come in. Uncover officers had been watching the house while information had been gathered about him. Beth had read the report on him and attended, with Tom, the operational briefing. Carl Shaw was a loner. He worked at a local supermarket filling shelves and loading vans. Thursdays were his day off. He'd been arrested twice for burglary and once for grievous bodily harm after attacking an ex-girlfriend outside a pub in Oxford. There had been nothing to connect him to Mae Lethbridge or Kate Marshall. But there was no doubt that the blood found in Mae's suitcase matched Shaw's DNA.

Beth held her breath as a voice came over the radio.

'Ready, let's go.'

Armed police officers jumped from their vans and aimed their guns at the house. Beth thought she heard a woman scream.

'Carl Shaw, this is the police. You're under arrest. Leave the house with your hands in the air.'

Beth waited with bated breath for Carl Shaw to leave the house.

*

Carl was making himself a tuna sandwich. He fancied a McDonald's burger but couldn't be bothered to go out. He'd just spread a good layer of mayonnaise over the tuna when he heard a commotion outside. He could see two police cars from the living room window and a knot formed in his stomach. He rushed upstairs and pulled back the curtain.

'Jesus,' he muttered.

He let the curtain fall and stepped back. They couldn't be here for him. Could they? Not that many police. It was like an army.

'Carl Shaw, this is the police. You're under arrest. Leave the house with your hands in the air.'

Carl clutched his head in his hands and groaned.

'No, no,' he said quietly.

'Carl Shaw, come out with your hands above your head.'

Carl looked around the bedroom as though seeing it for the first time. He could see no way out. The cops would be round the back too. Carl began to shake. They had guns. He hurried to the bathroom and threw up. He stared in the mirror at his terrified face, wiped the sweat from his forehead, and walked slowly back into the bedroom. The window was stiff. He barely ever opened it. Cool air brushed his cheek and he looked down at the armed police, all there for him.

'Don't shoot,' he shouted. 'I'm coming down. Please don't shoot.'

*

His voice sounded so feeble and frightened that Beth found herself almost feeling sorry for him. He looked so small and harmless as he walked from the front door with his hands above his head.

'He doesn't look like a murderer,' she said.

'How do they look?' Tom asked sarcastically.

'Alright,' she snapped. 'I just can't believe he did it. What's the motive?'

'A burglary that went wrong.'

Beth wasn't so sure about that. She watched Carl Shaw being bundled into a police car. Soon she would question him.

'Search the property,' ordered Tom.

It didn't take long for the officers to find a bundle of money hidden in a box under the bed, along with some jewellery.

'We've got him,' said Tom.

*

Carl Shaw was taken to Oxford police station, where an interrogation room was made available for Tom and Beth.

'You guys want coffee?' one of the officers asked.

'Yes, thanks.'

Beth could tell the officers were fascinated to have Tom Miller at their station. Beth ignored their stares and followed Tom into the interrogation room, where Carl Shaw sat huddled in a chair. His face was white and scared. He didn't look in the least like a killer to Beth but, then again, Dennis Neilson didn't look like a murderer. You could never tell by looking at someone, just what they were capable of doing.

'Hello Carl,' said Tom, sitting opposite him. 'I'm Detective Inspector Miller, and this is Detective Sergeant Harper. We're going to ask you a few questions.'

He nodded to Beth, who turned on the recorder.

'I don't understand what's going on,' said Carl nervously.

'You know the procedure. You've been arrested before.'

'Not like this. I mean, bloody hell, guns, what's that about?'

'Do you know a Mae Lethbridge?' asked Beth.

His eyes widened.

'I want a solicitor,' he said.

'You know who I'm talking about, then?'

'I read about it in the papers. Everyone knows who she is. What's it got to do with me?'

'A lot, it seems,' said Tom, leaning forward. 'Your DNA was found at the crime scene and on the murder weapon.'

Carl pushed back his chair.

'I didn't kill her. You can't pin this on me.'

'You were in her house, though, weren't you?'

Carl shook his head manically.

'No, no, I wasn't.'

'Your DNA is all over a suitcase she owned,' said Beth.

'It can't be. I've never been to her house.'

Tom's cheek twitched. He sat back in his chair.

'How well do you know Kate Marshall?'

Carl shook his head.

'I don't know her.'

Beth sipped her coffee and then glanced at Carl.

'Was it a burglary? Did she disturb you? Was that why you grabbed the hammer? Did you panic?' She asked.

'You're not going to stitch me up like you did Lester Lynch.'

Tom grinned, stood up and left the room.

'Where's he gone?' Carl asked worriedly.

'No idea. He's probably got something up his sleeve, though.'

Carl bit his lip anxiously. Tom returned, carrying a box. Carl recognising it wrung his hands together.

'We found this in your bedroom. Do you want to tell us how you came by so much money?'

He lifted the lid of the box to reveal wads of fifty-pound notes piled neatly inside it.

'Thirty thousand quid,' said Tom.

'You're trying to stitch me up?'

'With your DNA all over the crime scene, I don't need to.'

'I've never been in her house, I'm telling you.'

'You're lying,' said Tom, his face close to Carl's. 'You know it, and I know it. Now stop pissing me about and tell me why you were in Mae Lethbridge's house? You took this money from her suitcase, didn't you?'

'I'm not answering any more questions without a solicitor.'

'Fine.'

Tom turned to Beth.

'Get one sorted.'

Beth nodded and left the interview room. If Tom was hoping for a confession, she thought, then he had a long wait.

Chapter Seventy-Two

Carl Shaw had no alibi. He said he was at home that evening watching television. Tom knew he could only keep him in custody for a short time. Otherwise, he'd have to charge him or let him go. Thirty minutes later, his solicitor arrived.

'James Read. I need fifteen minutes with my client.'

Beth showed him to the interview room.

'They're trying to stitch me up,' she heard Carl complain as she closed the door.

'Do you think he did it?' she asked Tom.

'His DNA is all over the murder scene. The suitcase was in the bedroom, and if that jewellery belonged to Mae Lethbridge, then that's proof enough. Get that jewellery over to Blanche Lethbridge and see if she recognises it.'

'Right, Sir,' said Beth with a salute.

She clicked into her ringing phone as she left the building.

'Beth, it's Miranda, don't hang up on me.'

Beth sighed.

'Are you charging Carl Shaw with the murder of Mae Lethbridge?'

'No comment, Miranda, and don't go publishing any names. Aren't you in enough trouble?'

'Don't the people of Stonesend have a right to know?'

'I'm on a case. Got to go.'

She clicked off the phone and hurried to her car. Her mind was full of Carl Shaw. If the jewellery belonged to Mae, then they indeed had their man.

*

Blanche was sitting in the garden. She turned as Beth approached and smiled.

'Isn't it a lovely day?' she said.

'It certainly is. How are you?'

Beth looked at the flower beds.

'I'm well. The doctor said there is nothing wrong with me.'

'That's wonderful, Blanche.'

'Did you know? asked Blanche.

Beth nodded.

'Doctor Werner told us. I'm so sorry.'

Blanche forced a smile.

'Thank you,' she said softly.

'Blanche, I need to ask you a few questions. Do you know a man named Carl Shaw?'

Blanche thought for a moment.

'No, I don't think so.'

Beth pulled an envelope from her bag and shook out the jewellery. Blanche took a sharp breath.

'Do you recognise these?' asked Beth.

'It's mum's brooch and bracelet.

'Are you sure Blanche?'

She nodded.

'Where did your mum keep them?'

'In her bedroom.'

'Are you sure about that?'

'Yes. Do you know who killed my mum? Is that why you're here?'

Her bright, cheerful expression had changed to one of anguish. Beth bowed her head.

'Not yet, but I think we're getting close.'

*

Kate nervously entered the station with Beth. Her body was trembling.

'This way,' said Beth gently, guiding her forward.

'He won't be able to see you, so don't worry.'

Kate nodded and followed Beth into a small room. Through a two way mirror, she could see the man sitting at a table. He seemed to be looking straight at her. She felt Beth's eyes on her. The tension from her was almost electric.

'Do you recognise him?'

Kate desperately wanted to say yes. She knew that was what Beth was waiting to hear. But the man was a stranger.

'No, I don't.'

'Did you feel anything when you saw him?'

Kate shook her head.

'Would it help to hear his voice?'

Kate turned to Beth.

'Yes, that might help. Beth, I'm so sorry.'

'You're doing just great,' Beth smiled, squeezing her shoulder. 'Wait here.'

Tom looked up expectantly.

'Well?' he asked.

'She doesn't recognise him. Maybe if he spoke.'

Tom sighed and walked into the interrogation room. Beth went back to Kate and waited. She watched Kate closely as Tom entered the interview room.

'I think we've kept you a long time,' said Tom. 'Can I get you a coffee, cold drink?'

Carl looked up, and Kate leant forward to get a closer look.

'Why are you nice to me all of a sudden?' asked Carl.

'Anything?' Beth asked Kate.

Tears formed in Kate's eyes.

'God, I'm so sorry, Beth. There's nothing familiar about him at all.'

Beth nodded.

'Okay, no worries. Let's get you home.'

Chapter Seventy-Three

Beth dropped Mae's jewellery onto the table between her and Carl.

'These belong to Mae Lethbridge. Her daughter confirmed they are hers. Now, do you want to tell me how they came to be in your possession?'

'I don't know anything about them.'

'They were found in your house,' said Beth.

She was tired and hungry. The combination was putting her in a bad mood, and it was beginning to show. Carl Shaw shrugged.

'Right,' she said crossly, standing up. 'I'm charging you with the murder of Mae Lethbridge and the attempted murder of Kate Marshall. Anything you say ….'

'Now hold on,' said the solicitor. 'You have no proof ….'

'I have enough to charge him,' Beth said. 'You do not have to say anything, but it may harm your defence if you do not mention when questioned something you later rely on in court. Anything you do say may be given in evidence."

'Wait a minute,' said Carl hurriedly, his face white and drawn.

'I've wasted too many bloody minutes with you,' she said, opening the door. She saw Tom eating a sandwich and looked on enviously.

'I didn't murder no one,' said Carl from behind her.

'Is that right?' she said, turning around. 'I don't believe you. You broke into Mae Lethbridge's house, didn't you? You went into her bedroom, and you took the jewellery. You found the suitcase in there, didn't you? That's where the money came from? But she woke up and saw you. You panicked. You hit her with the hammer you used on Kate Ma ….'

'No,' he yelled. 'I didn't go into the bedroom.'

There was a tense silence.

'So, you were in her house,' Beth said, finally.

Carl dropped his head onto the table.

'You're stitching me up. I didn't go into the bedroom. The suitcase was in the living room. The money and jewellery were in it ….'

Beth closed the door.

'Don't lie, Carl. We found the suitcase in the bedroom, along with her dead body.'

'Please,' he begged. 'I only robbed her, that's all. I didn't go into the bedroom.'

'Don't say anymore,' said James. 'Are you charging my client or not?'

Beth sat down opposite Carl and leaned across the table.

'You've got to start telling me the truth, Carl. You're in big trouble. Murder and attempted murder, that's a long sentence ….'

'I only burgled her,' he said, wiping the sweat from his forehead.

Beth noticed the fresh cut on the side of his right hand.

'I forced the back door. I swear everything was in the living room. I didn't even see the Lethbridge woman.'

Beth rubbed her eyes tiredly.

'The suitcase was in the bedroom, Carl.'

He shook his head frantically.

'It wasn't. I'm telling you it wasn't. It was in the living room, and that's where I left it.'

Beth looked him in the eyes.

'You'd better not be lying to me.'

'Look, you can check my laptop. I found out about the suitcase from someone in a chat room.'

Beth sat up straight.

'What chat room?'

'On the dark web. It's a site for ….'

'Low life like you?' she said, helping him.

'You don't have to …' began James.

'No, I want to. Can I have some water first?'

'Sure,' said Beth, walking over to the water dispenser.

She waited while Carl drank and tried to ignore the rumbling in her stomach.

'I met this guy online. He said he'd done some plumbing for this old girl and she had thousands stashed in a suitcase, so we get talking and he said he couldn't do it because he was just out of the nick, but if he told me the address, he said, I could do it and send him a quarter in bitcoins.'

'Did he tell you to murder her?'

'I didn't murder her. I swear. He must have set me up. Waited until I'd gone, and then he must have gone there and killed her. I tried to get hold of him about the money, but I couldn't trace him anywhere online. It was like he'd disappeared into thin air.'

'Did you get the wrong house, Carl? Was that when you attacked Kate Marshall?

'No, I never went to Kate Marshall's house. I don't even know where she lives.'

'You're lying, Carl. You fucked up the first time, didn't you? Got the wrong house.'

'No.'

'Then a few months later, when you thought things had calmed down, you tried again?'

He shook his head.

'You're trying to stitch me up.'

'What was this guy's handle online?'

'Mad Max. He said he would leave something for me to break open the case. He was doing some plumbing for them. It seemed a doddle.'

'A doddle?' questioned Beth. 'When did you cut yourself, Carl. Was it when you were bludgeoning Mae to death or ...?

'No!' he protested. 'The bastard had pushed a razor blade into the wood of the hammer. I cut myself, look,' He held up his hand to show them the cut. 'Don't you see, he stitched me up?'

'Everyone's stitching you up, aren't they, Carl?'

Beth pushed back her chair and stood up.

'Is my client free to go?' asked James.

'No,' she said bluntly and left the interview room.

'What do you think?' she asked Tom, who was now eating a custard tart.

'I think he's as guilty as hell. We'll check his laptop, but I doubt we'll find much on Mad Max. Plenty of porn in the house. It looked like he had a bonfire some time ago. It could have been the clothes he'd worn that night. We found some cocaine. He was most likely high that night. Probably doesn't even remember the murder.'

'What about the razor in the hammer story. Do you think he was stitched up?'

'I think he'd make up any kind of story to get himself out of this.'

Beth nodded.

'Where did you get the food from?'

'Café around the corner. They do a nice bacon sandwich.'

'Thanks for getting me one.'

'I don't know what you like.' He nodded towards the interview room.

'You're doing a good job. You want to carry on?'

She gave him a dirty look before walking back into the interview room.

'Are you charging my client or not?' said James, tiredly.

'When did you have the bonfire, Carl?'

Carl feigned surprise.

'What bonfire?'

'In your garden, what were you burning?'

'I don't know what you're talking about.'

'Were you high that night?'

Carl's face turned white.

'We found the cocaine? Were you high?'

'No comment.'

Beth's stomach grumbled.

'I didn't do it.' He said evenly. 'You're harassing me.'

He turned to his solicitor.

'Is she allowed to do this?'

'There's enough evidence to say you did do it. So why don't you two have a chat,' said Beth.

She left the room and walked past Tom.

'I'm getting a bacon sandwich before I eat my own bloody arm.'

Chapter Seventy-Four

'Why the hesitation?' Brian asked.

'I don't think he did it,' said Beth. 'I'm sure he would have cracked.'

'He was in the house. He took money from a suitcase that was in the bedroom, his DNA is all over the case and hammer ...' said Brian.

'I know,' Beth agreed. 'But I ...'

'Don't think he's the murdering type,' Tom finished for her.

Beth glared at him.

'And that's it?' asked Brian. 'That's your reason?'

'The hammer, why did he throw it in the garden?' Beth asked.

'I'm sure those questions will come up in court. Did you find the plumber?'

Beth lowered her head.

'The daughter said they never had a plumber at the house,' said Tom.

Beth didn't want to say what was really on her mind. Not in front of Tom. But maybe Matt was right. Benny Lynch had it in for Tom Miller. Perhaps he was screwing with his head. Maybe he was the Mad Max guy. But why kill Mae and attack Kate if it was Tom he was after? It didn't make sense.

'Charge him. That sodding Miranda is giving us bad press. Saying we're taking too long to crack the case,' said Brian irritably.

'With all due respect, Sir, I couldn't give a fig about Miranda.'

'Charge him. That's my final word. The courts will decide. We need to release the body for burial.'

Beth knew there was no point arguing any further.

'Yes, sir,' she said.

Beth waited until Brian was back in his office before turning on Tom.

'You didn't have to make me look stupid.'

'I only spoke the truth.'

She huffed and marched to her desk.

*

'Does this mean we can organise the funeral?' asked Rob. Beth noted the caravan was bare compared to the last time she visited.

'Are you moving out?' she asked.

'I'm moving into the cottage with Blanche.'

Beth raised her eyebrows.

'I see. It's all worked out well for you then, hasn't it?'

Rob looked at her.

'What does that mean? It wasn't an easy choice, you know. I've lived in Leeds for a long time. I now want to be with my daughter. She's at home here.'

'Does the name Mad Max mean anything to you?' she asked.

He shrugged.

'It's a movie, isn't it?'

'Do you own a copy of that movie?'

'No, I don't. Why are you asking me this?'

'So, you've never used that name on the dark web?'

He raised his eyebrows.

'The dark web? I wouldn't even know how to get onto the dark web.'

'Is that right?'

'I thought you had the bloke for these attacks. Why are you questioning me like this?'

'Just tying up loose ends.'

She turned to the door.

'I'll leave you to pack.'

*

'You've charged him?' said Kate.

Her voice was flat.

'Have you remembered anything since seeing him?'

'No,' said Kate, vaguely.

Beth laid a hand on her arm.

'What is it, Kate?'

'I felt sure it was someone I knew. Or at least someone that knew me. Maybe it wasn't the same person who attacked me, after all.'

'The same weapon was used, Kate.'

Kate sighed.

'I know, but he didn't take anything.'

'He got the wrong house. He was looking for Mae's suitcase. You must have interrupted him when you came home.'

Beth didn't mention Mad Max. There seemed little point.

'Kate,' said Beth hesitantly. 'I should tell you that the doctor treating Blanche has said there is absolutely nothing wrong with her.'

Kate looked puzzled.

'I don't know what you mean.'

'She's in perfect health. The doctor thinks that Mae suffered from Munchausen by proxy. It's a ….'

'I know what it is, but Mae never had that. She adored Blanche. Her only aim in life was to make her well, not make her ill. Did her ex-husband tell you that?'

'He's not her ex, Kate. They never got divorced.'

Kate's eyes widened.

'But I always thought ….'

'I think that was what Mae wanted everyone to believe. Blanche's doctor told us that Blanche doesn't have cancer or any other ailments her mother said she had. I'm telling you this because I know you were friends.'

Kate shook her head as if dismissing the idea.

'But Mae was so loving to Blanche. Being a mother meant everything to her.'

'I'm sorry, Kate.'

Kate shook her head.

'I don't believe it. Why would Mae do that?'

Beth sighed. 'It's an illness.'

She hugged Kate.

'I'm sorry to be the one to tell you.'

She left Kate to digest the news and walked through the village. Again, people waved and smiled as she passed, and she found herself wondering what Ben was doing, but this time there wasn't the sharp pain of loss that she usually felt and she smiled to herself. Maybe, at last, she was on the road to recovery.

The village would go back to its previous peaceful tranquillity, and in time, Mae's murder would be forgotten. There was just the funeral to get through. That reminded Beth of the small piece in the nationals this morning about Lester Lynch's remembrance service. She wondered if Tom had seen it. A judge had ruled that Lynch was not to have a standard funeral and that his ashes were to be thrown into the sea. Benny Lynch had given an interview to the Daily Mail and said that a private remembrance service would be held instead. Beth thought it was obscene and hoped it wouldn't attract a crowd.

Her phone beeped with a message. It was a text from Sandy.

'Dinner Friday night at 7. I'm making chilli.'

Beth texted back.

'Great. You're on.'

'Ray invited Tom Miller too, is that okay?'

Beth cursed and texted 'WTF?'.

'God, sorry, sis. Weren't me.'

Beth sent a tearful face.

'See you, then.' She typed.

'Bugger,' she muttered. 'Not another dinner with Tom bloody Miller.'

Chapter Seventy-Five
2019: Stratford, London

A strong police presence assembled outside the gates of St Mary's church in Stratford. A crowd had already gathered to watch the crème de la crème of the East End gangster world as they arrived for the remembrance service for Lester Lynch. Many held banners that screamed '*Paedophiles burn in hell.*'

Music by Lester Lynch's favourite composer could be heard playing in the church. Many thought it was in bad taste. Even the most hardened criminals couldn't find it within them to feel for Benny Lynch. His boy had been twisted and sick. No one condemned that kind of sick behaviour, but loyalty was loyalty, and Benny Lynch was not someone you crossed.

'A bit fucking sick playing that fucking music,' said Bad Dog Frazer, who had never liked Lester Lynch.

The young constables at the gate gave the mourners scathing looks. The last thing they wanted to be doing was protecting arseholes like these.

Benny arrived last; his arm draped protectively around his wife, Frances. Her eyes were red-rimmed and sore.

The vicar greeted them at the door. He was getting a nice donation for this. Finally, those jobs around the church that had waited for years, would get done.

Benny felt cheated. He wanted a fucking burial, for Christ's sake. A decent bloody funeral. What kind of ending was it, being thrown overboard? Fucking judge. What right did they have to decide how his son left this earth?

He'd pay. Oh, yes, he'd pay. Maybe not yet, but eventually. Benny would see his son off. Give him a decent goodbye, and then he'd tidy up loose ends. Who the fuck did they think they were, taking his boy's body and deciding what to do with it? That was their decision, his and Frances.

Soon it would be payback time, and he'd start with fucking Tom Miller. The thought of Miller gave him a sharp pain in his chest. He clutched it with his hand and took a deep breath.

'Benny, are you alright?' asked Frances anxiously.

'Of course, just a bit of indigestion.'

A drink was what he needed, a stiff whisky. Shouts and screams from the entrance of the church made him turn.

'Jesus,' he muttered.

Parents of the murdered boys were standing outside, screaming obscenities and holding up placards.

'Paedophiles don't have rights' 'Flush him down the bog' 'Murdering pigs'

'Oh, Benny,' Frances wept.

'Go inside,' said Benny.

Why didn't those fucking useless cops move them on? The screams made his chest hurt even more.

'Terrible times,' said Mad Dog Frazer.

'Sure are,' said Billy Mitchell, nodding.

'What the fuck do you know,' snarled Benny and walked behind Frances into the church.

Reverend Simon Greig looked down at his notes and cringed.

'We are here today to remember the life of Lester Lynch, a loving son who was taken from his family too soon.'

Benny leant his head back and listened to the sweet words about his boy. He knew they weren't true, but he could hear them through Frances' ears and enjoy them.

Chapter Seventy-Six

Stonesend

'I heard the funeral is going to be fairly soon,' said Sandy.

Ray followed her from the kitchen, carrying a steaming bowl of rice.

'I hope you're hungry,' he smiled.

'Looks good,' said Tom.

Beth made room on the table.

'Yes, apparently. I suppose you can't blame them,' she said.

She got up and went into the kitchen to help Sandy bring in the chilli and plates.

'He's nice, isn't he?' Sandy whispered.

'He's okay.'

'He's nice, Beth,' she said, looking at her slyly.

'Don't you start that,' said Beth. 'He's not my type.'

'Are you two coming with the rest of the food. Tom and I are starving,' called Ray.

'Sorry,' smiled Sandy.

They sat down and Ray dished up the rice.

'Are you going to the funeral?' asked Ray.

Beth nodded.

'We will, too,' said Sandy. 'We didn't know her that well, but it seems the thing to do after all that's happened.'

She shivered.

'What a terrible thing for Blanche,' said Ray.

'She seems to be doing okay,' said Beth. 'She's having counselling. Is it you?'

'You know I can't say,' smiled Sandy.

'It's you,' grinned Beth. 'I know that expression of yours.'

Tom looked on as the two sisters exchanged knowing looks. They were so different. Sandy was much more glamourous than Beth. Everything about her was perfect, from her painted nails to her well-styled hair. Beth, on the other hand, always looked nice but in a more relaxed kind of way. Her cheeks were rosy from the wine, and she looked pretty. She must have felt his eyes on her, for she looked up and smiled.

'How do you like Stonesend, aside from the murders?' asked Ray.

'Great chilli,' Tom said, tucking in. It was the first good meal he'd had since dinner at Brian's. He'd been living on tinned spaghetti on toast and microwave shepherd's pie. He'd never eaten so much junk food in his life. Lorna had always cooked such tasty meals. The kitchen had been full of cookbooks. She'd loved trying new things. She would be appalled if she could see what he was eating these days.

'It's quieter than London,' he said, pouring water into his glass.

'In the past, I would have said with less crime,' said Sandy.

'Beth tells me you're a counsellor.'

'We're both in the mental health business,' smiled Ray. 'I'm a psychiatrist, and Sandy is a psychologist.'

'So, you can counsel each other,' smiled Tom.

'We do, all the time,' laughed Ray.

'Have they counselled you?' Tom asked, turning to Beth.

Beth's heart skipped a beat. Oh God, he wasn't going to mention Ben, was he?

'We're family. It goes against the rules,' she said, draining her glass and reaching for the wine bottle.

'I think all police officers should have counselling,' said Sandy. 'It's a stressful job.'

'It can be,' said Tom.

'I thought that whole remembrance service they had for Lester Lynch was obscene,' said Ray, crossly.

'The whole family is obscene,' said Beth, topping up her glass. She ought to stop drinking. She always said things she regretted when she'd had one too many. For some reason, she got nervous socialising around Tom.

'Right, enough shop talk. Let's move onto dessert, and then we can play charades,' said Sandy.

Beth groaned.

'Sorry about this,' she apologised.

Tom grinned.

'Don't be. I'm enjoying it.'

*

Beth dug her hands into the pockets of her dress.

'I didn't think it would be so chilly walking back,' she said, shivering.

Tom pulled off his jacket and draped it around her shoulders. It smelt of him, warm and fragrant.

'I'm sorry for my nosy family.'

Tom laughed.

'It wasn't the ordeal you make it out to be.'

'Not for you.'

She missed her footing and he put out a hand to steady her.

'Okay?' he asked softly.

She nodded shyly. They were close to the cemetery.

'Fancy a coffee before you head home?' he asked.

'A coffee?' she said stupidly.

'Yes, that brown liquid that helps with sobering one up. I'll walk you home afterwards.'

Beth needed a coffee, and she suspected she needed walking home too if she wasn't going to end up in a ditch. I must drink less, she thought.

'I could do with a coffee,' she said. 'I don't normally drink this much. It's when I get nervous.'

'Nervous of what?'

'I don't do dinner parties very well, not even at my sister's.'

He opened the door to the cottage.

'Wow,' said Beth, stepping inside. 'You've had a clean-up.'

Tom laughed.

'I had a cleaner more like,'

'It looks great. Can I use your newly cleaned loo?'

'Upstairs, second door on the right.'

Beth climbed the narrow stairs carefully. She passed a small bedroom and peeked around the door and saw that Tom had turned it into a study. On the desk was paraphernalia of papers, a phone charger, keyboard and a laptop. Her eyes fell on another photograph of Tom, this time with a man and a woman slightly older. She stepped into the room to take a closer look when her eyes were drawn to the gun in an open drawer. She stared at it for a few seconds and then made her way to the loo.

Tom had brought the coffee into the living room and was sitting on the couch.

'You have a gun?' she asked.

He looked up.

'Sorry, I was nosy,' she apologised.

He'd loosened his tie, and the top button of his white shirt came undone. She could see some of his chest hairs. She sat on the opposite couch and pulled her eyes away.

'I don't think you should worry about it.'

'It's against regulations and the law,' she reminded him.

'I've had death threats. So I'm not going to be vulnerable.'

Beth picked up her coffee.

'I wasn't criticising.'

'I know.'

She sipped her coffee and said, 'My sister liked you. So did Ray. You played charades and did well. That always goes down well in Ray's book.'

Tom placed his cup onto the coffee table.

'I feel I've been a bit unapproachable. It wasn't deliberate. It's a self-protection thing. I'm sure you understand.'

She avoided his eyes.

'Sure, of course.'

'So, perhaps we could have dinner sometime.'

'Dinner with you?' she said, surprised.

'Unless you find the whole idea repulsive.'

She silently cursed.

'No, of course not.'

She finished her coffee and stood up.

'I'm knackered.'

'I'll walk you home.'

They walked in silence to her cottage. Beth was acutely aware of his body close to hers. It was only when they reached her front door that Beth turned to him and said, 'How far would Benny Lynch go to get back at you?'

Tom looked thoughtful.

'What's on your mind, Beth?'

'It just seems coincidental you coming here, and then we have a woman beaten up and another killed.'

'It's not personal enough. It's not Lynch's style.'

He leant towards her, and she found herself moving closer.

'Goodnight, Beth,' he said, softly kissing her on the cheek.

'Night,' she said, turning the key in the lock.

Shit, another beer and she'd have ripped that snowy white shirt off his back.

Chapter Seventy-Seven

Flowers had begun arriving shortly after nine. Many were from people that Blanche and Rob had never heard of. People who were mourning with them after reading about Mae's murder in the newspapers.

'People are so kind,' said Jo, who'd travelled from Leeds to support them.

Blanche was nervous. Her hands wouldn't stop shaking. Jo said it was only natural to feel that way on the day of your mother's funeral. Blanche liked Jo. She was modern in her outlook, and she and her dad got on very well. In time, Blanche was sure Jo would move to Oxford.

If only she didn't have to go to the funeral and see mum's coffin. She was dreading it. Someone said that reporters might be there. Blanche didn't want them taking photos of her.

A knock on her bedroom door made her jump.

'Blanche, can I come in?' called Rob.

She looked down at her black woollen dress and sighed.

'Yes.'

Rob was wearing a dark suit. Underneath the jacket, she could see a grey shirt.

'Is this dress alright?' she asked anxiously.

He looked at her proudly.

'It's perfect.'

She gave a nervous smile.

'Will there be reporters there?'

He nodded.

'I think so.'

He checked his watch.

'We have to go soon.'

Blanche could hear the clattering of dishes where Jo was preparing food for when people came back. Kate had brought homemade cakes and sliced up pie, and Sophie had made sandwiches and quiche. It's like a party, thought Blanche. She followed her father from the room and downstairs. Through the living room window, she could see the black funeral car. Her eyes refused to look at the hearse that sat at the front. Jo was going to walk to the church and meet them there. Rob had asked Kate and Dan to join them in the mourner's car.

'Blanche said you were like a sister to Mae,' Rob said.

'It's kind of you,' Kate had been touched by the gesture.

Blanche hugged her in the hallway and fought back the tears.

'How are you holding up?' Kate asked.

'I'm fine. How are you, Kate?'

Kate smiled.

'I'm fine.'

They followed Rob to the car, and Blanche tried not to look at the hearse.

'Lots of flowers,' said Kate, tearfully.

The drive to the church, although short, seemed endless to Blanche. Her eyes, while not wanting to look, seemed strangely glued to the hearse in front. She just wanted the whole thing to be over and to be back at the house. People were standing around outside the church. Beth and Detective Inspector Miller were there. To Blanche, it seemed like everyone from the village was there. They must have closed everything for the day, thought Blanche. All for my mum, a woman they never really knew. Several police officers stood at the gates. Beth had arranged that. Rob dad had said he didn't want reporters or photographers getting in. A few photographers were waiting, and they took photos as they drove by. Blanche put her head down. She didn't want her face in the paper. It was enough that she'd been in the local paper as the sick girl. She looked across to Kate, who was quietly weeping.

'Are you ready?' Rob asked.

Blanche nodded and laid a hand on Kate's knee as she climbed from the car.

'I'm so glad you're here,' she said.

Kate was too overcome to reply but just nodded. Blanche glanced briefly at the coffin and then entered the church.

*

Kate's legs were weak beneath her. She'd been dreading this day. A few weeks ago, she would have known the woman they were burying, but ever since Beth told her about Blanche, she hadn't known what to think. Had Mae been lying to her all along? Lying about Blanche and lying about her husband? Was that why Blanche had never fallen ill when eating her cakes? It was the money that bothered Kate. The airfare money for Disneyland, the money given for Blanche at their fundraisers. What had happened to that if it hadn't gone towards treatment for Blanche's cancer? Had she been friends with a fraud? Could all of it have anything to do with Kate's attack and Mae's murder? No, she told herself. You're letting your imagination run away with itself. The man who killed Mae went there for her money. They've arrested him. His DNA was found in the house. It was just a case of mistaken identity when he'd attacked Kate.

She felt a hand on her elbow.

'We should go in,' said Dan beside her.

She nodded, and they walked into the church.

*

Everyone turned to watch Blanche walk down the aisle with her father. There were whispers and gasps. Beth knew that in time the truth about Mae Lethbridge would come out, and she wondered if the Lethbridges would stay in the village when it did. The villagers wouldn't forget the money they'd forked out at her fundraisers or the money they'd spent on flowers for her funeral. Beth didn't feel it was her place to tell people the truth. She'd leave that to Blanche and Rob. She looked around at the faces, trying to gauge from their expressions what they were thinking. Her eyes searched out Rob. He looked nervous and uncertain. Blanche, beside him, was tearful, while Jo was impassive. The congregation fell silent when the vicar appeared. He spoke to Rob before walking to the pulpit. Beth sensed Tom tense beside her, and she suddenly realised how difficult this must be for him. She reached out a hand and placed it on top of his. He didn't move his hand away.

'I'm sorry,' she said.

He nodded.

*

Blanche fiddled with the piece of paper in her hand. She'd written the eulogy a few days ago, and still, she felt it wasn't right. Soon, when the vicar had finished talking, she would go up and talk about her mother, Mae Lethbridge. Her mother, the woman that had brought her into the world and the woman who had kept her sick. The woman who ...

She felt pressure on her arm and saw her dad's hand.

'You need to go up,' he whispered.

She lifted her eyes and saw the vicar looking at her. She stood. Her legs felt stiff and she wobbled on her heels. She wasn't used to high heeled shoes. Mum had never allowed her to wear them. Or makeup or perfume. She had both on now. Jo had helped her. It made her feel nice. She strolled to the podium and heard the whispers. She knew they were wondering how she could now walk. Her hands shook as she unfolded her notes. They were here for Mae Lethbridge. The woman who had helped with their coffee mornings. Who'd made mince pies for their Christmas Bazaar. The kind, caring, and loving mother to Blanche and the woman who had fed her daughter toxic medication for most of her life, for no reason, other than to get attention for herself. She wanted to shout into the microphone, 'Fuck Mae Lethbridge', But she had been her mother. No matter what else she had been, she would always be her mother, and nothing would change that.

'My mother would have been so happy if she could see all the people that came to say goodbye to her today. My Mum and I were very close. This terrible tragedy has robbed us of a good, caring woman ….'

Her voice broke, and she pulled a tissue from her sleeve to dab at her eyes. Around her, she heard tiny sobs and sniffles.

'Mum loved being a mother.'

It gave her control, control over me. It gave her attention and praise.

'It fulfilled her. She also loved this community. She felt at home here. That such a terrible atrocity should happen on her own doorstep is tragic. She had many friends who I know will miss her terribly. Kate,' she said, looking at her. 'You were such a support to us. Mum knew I'd be alright if you were here.'

Kate lowered her head to hide her tears.

'I know the person responsible for my mother's death will be brought to justice, thanks to the hard work of our police force.'

She looked at Beth, but Beth's eyes were on Rob Lethbridge.

*

Kate clutched the order of service and tried to fight back her tears. She looked at Blanche through misty eyes. Blanche standing, Blanche walking. It was too much. Everything she'd believed to be true, hadn't been at all. Nothing made sense.

A sudden, piercing pain jabbed between her eyes and she took a sharp intake of breath. Blanche's voice faded away, and from somewhere in the distance, she heard her name being called.

'Kate, what do you think you're doing?'

She turned, her mind reeling.

It felt as if her head would explode. It began to throb unbearably, and then like a tsunami, the memory of that afternoon flooded into her brain, like water rushing over the deck of a sinking ship. She heard those terrible screams again, saw the sparkle from the hammer as the sun hit it, and she had to fight the urge to cover her face. Nausea clawed at her throat until she thought she wouldn't be able to breathe.

'I have to go to the loo,' she mumbled, squeezing past Dan.

She stumbled to the corner of the church. She kept swallowing, and her throat kept clenching, but no matter what she did, it didn't stop the warm feeling rising through her chest. Then she tasted it at the back of her mouth. She reached the toilets just as she buckled over. A warm, clouded, cream coloured liquid spilt from her mouth and sizzled as it splashed over into the toilet bowl. She seemed to retch forever, but finally, it eased, and she was able to lean against the cold wall and wait for her heart to slow down. She sat there, unblinking, shaking her head in disbelief. Her brain was desperately scrambling to make sense of it all. Finally, she knew who her enemy was, and it broke her heart.

'Oh God,' she muttered.

'Kate, are you okay?'

It was Dan. He sounded worried.

'I'm okay. An upset stomach. I'll be out in a bit.'

'Are you sure?'

'Yes. I won't be long.'

She needed time to get her head straight. To think it all through before she decided what to do. It was an effort to pull herself up. She stared at her reflection in the mirror and then hurriedly applied some blusher to cover her paleness. Dan was waiting outside.

'I was starting to get worried,' he said.

'It must have been something I ate,' she said. 'Let's go back.'

The congregation were singing the final hymn as they returned to their seats. Blanche looked up anxiously as Kate and Dan made their way to a pew.

'Are you alright?' she asked, looking closely at Kate.

Kate kept her eyes on the coffin.

The Lies She Told

'I'm fine,' she said.

The pallbearers lifted the coffin, and to Andrea Bocelli's *Time to say Goodbye,* the congregation followed it out. Beth, having noticed Kate's sudden rush to the loo, made her way slowly towards her.

'Everything okay, Kate?' she asked.

'Can't a woman go to the bloody loo anymore?' Kate snapped.

Beth raised her eyebrows in surprise.

'Sorry, Beth,' said Kate quickly. 'I'm a bit edgy.'

'No worries,' smiled Beth.

'Just an upset tummy.'

Beth nodded.

'It's an upsetting day. I'll see you back at the house.'

Kate nodded and followed Dan to the waiting car.

'Do you mind if we walk back?' she said. 'I could do with the fresh air.'

He looked anxious.

'We don't have to go back to the house,' he said.

'It's fine. I'd just prefer to walk. The car might bring on the nausea again.'

'I'll let Blanche know.'

Kate watched Dan approach Blanche and Rob, who were talking to people at the entrance. He motioned to Kate, and Blanche looked over. She said a few words to her dad and then walked over to Kate. Their eyes met. Blanche licked her lips and then said softly, 'You've remembered,' It wasn't a question.

'Yes.'

Blanche swallowed as if she were swallowing down the words she could not yet say.

'Of all the days,' she said, finally.

Kate saw Dan approaching.

'We'll talk later,' Kate said.

'Ready?' Dan asked.

Kate nodded.

'We'll see you at the house,' said Dan.

Blanche watched them walk away and then re-joined her dad. She knew it had only been a matter of time.

'I'll make the teas when we get back,' said Jo, breaking into her thoughts.

Blanche nodded.

'It was a nice service,' said Rob.

You didn't even shed one tear, thought Blanche. Surely, she deserved that.

'Yes, it was lovely, wasn't it, Blanche?' agreed Jo.

Blanche only vaguely heard Jo. What would Kate do now, she wondered, now that she had remembered? It seemed strangely fitting to Blanche that it should have happened today.

'Is your friend all right?' asked Jo.

'My friend?'

'The one who came in the car with you?'

'Oh yes. Just a bit upset.'

Chapter Seventy-Eight

Kate's heart wouldn't stop racing.

'I'm just going to change,' she said when they reached their cottage. 'You go on. I'll be there in a bit.'

'If you're sure.' Said Dan, concerned.

'Honestly, I'm feeling much better. I just want to tidy up.'

She closed the front door and leaned against it. Everything was so clear now. She'd buried the memory for a reason. The truth had been too unbearable to face. The food mixer that she'd used earlier sat on the kitchen table. She could still smell the warm aroma of the chocolate muffins she'd baked. Mae had said they were her favourites.

She stared out of the window at the boy's football gear hanging on the line. She ought to bring them in, but she didn't move to do so. Instead, she wrapped her arms around her body and let out a sob.

'Oh Mae,' she groaned, falling onto a chair. She lifted her eyes to the ceiling and allowed the memory to flow until it seemed like only yesterday that it had happened and her life had then changed forever.

*

It had been unbearably hot that day. She'd had a mild headache and was keen to get home. Adam had held up his painting, his face beaming with excitement.

'For you,' he'd said proudly, holding it up. 'It's called 'Our Family.'

She'd smiled at the childish depiction of her and Dan.

'It's lovely, darling. I'll hang it in the kitchen. It will be there when you get home.'

She'd kissed them goodbye and headed to the cottage. It had been stifling in the kitchen, so she'd opened the back door and then had gone upstairs to shower. She had plenty of time to bang in a nail and hang the painting before Faith arrived for her lesson. She'd clicked on the kettle and had then wandered into the garage to get Dan's hammer. It had been cooler in the garage, so she'd taken her time. All the while, wondering what she should do. She'd finally decided to talk it over with Dan that evening. Hopefully, he would tell her she was stupid. Making a decision had put her mind to rest, and she'd hummed a hymn they'd sung in assembly that morning. The open carton of milk in the fridge had gone off, so she'd opened a new one. It was the sound of the gate latch that had stopped her in her tracks. She'd turned worriedly, thinking one of the boys had come home, but it had been Mae who walked into the kitchen, her hair wild and her face red. Kate had immediately known what was wrong. She'd sighed. She'd hoped to talk to Mae later that evening after discussing things with Dan.

'Kate, what do you think you're doing?' Mae had said without preamble, her tone hurt and angry.

'I was going to speak to you ...' Kate began.

'I thought you were my friend,' Mae had interrupted accusingly.

'I am your friend,' Kate had said softly. 'That's why ....'

'That doesn't give you the right to poke your nose into our business.'

'Let me make a cup of tea,' suggested Kate

'I don't want your fucking tea.'

Kate had reeled back at the obscenity. She'd never heard Mae swear before.

'I'm just concerned for Blanche.'

Mae's eyes blazed.

'Why are you concerned? She's my daughter, not yours.' She'd laughed cruelly. 'Just because you didn't have a daughter.'

Kate had felt tears burn her eyelids.

'I just changed her bed, Mae. You had a migraine.'

'You went through her medications.'

'I thought she might have needed something before bed.'

It had all seemed so innocent last night. Mae had phoned and asked if Blanche could have dinner with them as she felt a migraine coming. They'd had dinner, and later Kate had taken Blanche home. She'd never been in Blanche's bedroom before, but Blanche wanted to show her the book she was reading. Kate had been taken aback by Blanche's room. She had smelled the unwashed sheets and immediately stripped the bed. She found clean sheets in the airing cupboard.

'Do you need any medication before bed?' she'd asked Blanche.

'Mum left a pill out for me. The medicine cabinet is always locked, and I don't know where the key is.'

'Okay, I'll check.'

While Blanche was in the bathroom, Kate looked in the medicine cabinet in her room. It wasn't locked. Mae had obviously felt too unwell and had forgotten to lock it as usual. Kate went through the medication in case Blanche needed to take something before bed, but she could only find one bottle that was prescribed for Blanche. Everything else either had Mae's name on the label or nothing at all. It didn't make sense. She'd opened the bedside cabinet to see if Blanche's medication was in there and found a hair razor. She'd stared at it for ages. Mae had told everyone that Blanche's hair had fallen out, not shaved. Kate had left, confused.

'You went through things in her room. I know when anything gets moved.'

Kate had stepped back, creating a distance between them.

'This is an overreaction, Mae.'

Mae had moved closer. Their faces were just inches apart.

'How dare you?'

Kate had felt her own anger boil over.

'Why do the medications in Blanche's room have your name on them and not hers?'

Mae's anger had been evident in the way her nostrils flared.

'You had no right.'

Kate had clenched her fists.

'Is Blanche really sick, Mae, or are you making her sick?'

'What?'

'None of those medications in her room have her name on them. That doesn't make sense.'

Mae's cold, hard eyes had met hers. It was a different Mae to the one Kate knew.

'What's going on, Mae?' she'd asked.

'I'm not discussing this with you anymore.'

'She doesn't have allergies, does she?'

'Shut up, Kate.'

'She's eaten cakes I've made, and she's been fine. People gave money for Blanche, Mae. Some gave more than they could afford. You said she needed cancer treatment.'

Mae's eyes had pierced through Kate.

'I'm a good mother. Everyone says so.'

'Mae, let's have a cup of tea and talk about this.'

Mae had turned on her like an enraged panther.

'There's nothing to talk about. 'I'm only doing my best for Blanche.'

'It's wrong, Mae, when people find out … Why don't we discuss it with …'? But she never got to finish. Mae had lunged for the hammer, and her high-pitched scream had reverberated through Kate's brain. She'd spun around, a hand raised in defence, fear knotting her stomach. She saw the glint of the hammer's claw as the sun hit it and had heard Mae scream, 'I won't let you ruin everything.' She'd felt the pain as it shot through her body and, in horror, saw the second blow coming towards her. She'd been too dazed to fight it off. Something had exploded in her head, and the kitchen had become a kaleidoscope of colours.

'I'm a good mother. Do you fucking hear me?'

'Mae,' she'd gasped, lifting her hands to protect her face from the claw of the hammer. She'd felt the wetness of her blood as it trickled from her head into her eyes and mouth. Her body had turned cold with fear. She saw Mae's tortured face through her tears. She'd reached desperately for a chair, but Mae had quickly kicked it away.

'Someone help me,' Kate had cried, but there had been no one to hear her. The last thing she heard was the tinkling of the doorbell and Mae moaning, 'Aw Kate.'

Chapter Seventy-Nine

The village was quiet. There wasn't a soul to be seen. Benny Lynch pulled the car to a halt and climbed out. He crossed the road and walked into The Bell. The place was empty. Lee Warren stood behind the counter. He'd offered to help out for the day.

'Hello, are you here for the funeral?' he asked.

'Funeral?'

'Mae Lethbridge. That's where everyone is.'

Benny unbuttoned his jacket and pulled a stool up to the bar.

'I wondered why it was so quiet. No, I'm not here for that. I'll have a pint of whatever is your best. Why aren't you at the funeral?'

The lad laughed.

'I didn't know her that well. My uncle's the landlord, so I said I'd help out today.'

Benny nodded and then tried the beer.

'You know where Tom Miller lives? I'm looking for him. I want to surprise him. We haven't seen each other in a long time.'

The lad nodded.

'The police detective, do you mean?'

'That's him.'

'Yeah, he caught Mae's murderer.'

'He's good at that,' smiled Benny

'He'll be at the funeral.'

'Of course. Do you know where he lives? I can pop a note in his door.'

'In the cottage by the church. You can't miss it. End of the road, on the corner. You'll see the church and cemetery.'

'Great. I'll have a bag of crisps to go with this.'

He took his drink to a table by the window and looked out at the village green. He was looking forward to surprising Tom Miller.

*

Beth looked around the living room. It was messier than the last time she and Tom had visited. Space had been made for the buffet table, and Jo was hurrying back and forth with plates of sandwiches and cakes.

'Thanks for coming,' said Rob, approaching her. Beth forced a smile but found she had difficulty meeting his eyes.

'It was a lovely service,' said Tom, nudging her lightly in the ribs.

'Yes, it was nice to see so many people there,' Beth added while giving Tom a sideways glance.

'Well, we're glad you could make it,' smiled Rob. 'Do help yourself to food. There's plenty.'

Beth waited until he was out of earshot before turning angrily on Tom.

'What was that nudge for?'

'You were looking at him as a copper.'

'That's because I am one.'

'You're off duty.'

She looked at Rob, who was now talking to Sophie and Grant.

'There's something about him.'

'I'm getting a drink. Do you want anything?'

Beth feigned shock.

'Blimey, you remembered to ask me. I'll have an orange juice.'

She looked at Blanche, who was talking animatedly to Dan, and Beth wondered where Kate was. Blanche saw her looking and smiled. Beth walked over and kissed Dan on the cheek.

'Where's Kate? Is she okay?'

'She's just getting changed. She had a bit of an upset stomach.'

'Thank you for coming,' said Blanche.

'It was nice that so many people came,' said Beth, starting to feel like a parrot. 'You're looking well.'

'Isn't she?' smiled Dan.

'It must feel ….'

She broke off as her eyes landed on a row of DVDs on the bookshelf behind Blanche.

'Mad Max,' she said, more to herself than anyone else. Blanche turned to see what Beth was looking at.

'Are they yours?' Beth asked.

'The Mad Max DVDs? No, they were Mum's. She was a big fan.'

'I …'

Tom returned and handed her a glass of orange juice.

'I'll go and check on Kate, shall I?' Blanche asked Dan.

'She'll appreciate that, thanks, Blanche.'

Blanche walked confidently from the room.

'It's like a miracle,' said Dan.

'It's obscene if you ask me,' said Jack, joining them. 'All that bloody fundraising we did and for what? A kid who's as fit as the rest of us.'

'It's not Blanche's fault. She is just as much a victim as we are,' argued Dan.

'The mother pumped her full of toxic medication, Jack. It was a form of child abuse,' explained Beth.

'Yeah, well, I waived a lot of the food at those fundraisers. They took me for a bloody fool. I don't know what I'm doing here.'

He walked away, muttering to himself. Beth looked to Tom and nodded at the DVDs.

'What do you think? she whispered. 'A bit odd, eh?'

'I think a lot of people watch Mad Max videos.'

'You're so bloody unhelpful,' she snapped.

It was too much of a coincidence, but Beth couldn't understand what it meant.

*

Blanche hesitated at the front gate. She could see Kate watching her from the window. She hoped for a smile or a nod, but Kate gave her neither. She opened the gate and walked slowly to the front door, where she waited. A few minutes later, Kate opened it.

'I told Dan I'd check on you,' she said.

'You knew?' questioned Kate.

'Yes.'

'You lied to me,' Kate said stiffly.

'I know. I'm sorry. Can I come in?'

Kate hesitated.

'Give me one good reason why I shouldn't tell the police and the whole village, come to that?'

Blanche fought down the urge to touch Kate's arm. She knew Kate would recoil.

'Please let me explain.'

Kate stepped away from the door and went into the living room.

'Where are the boys?' Blanche asked, looking around.

'With Dan's mother.'

Blanche fiddled with her earring.

'I always knew I could walk,' she said finally, not meeting Kate's eyes. 'But Mum said it strained my back and that the wheelchair was better. Mum said I had cancer. That was why I let her shave my head. I didn't want to watch my hair fall out. I hated being sick. I really did. I wanted to be like Adam, to be normal. That's why I stole a cake. I thought even if I get really ill after eating it, I don't care, at least I'll be normal, but I wasn't sick, so I did it again and ….'

'You knew it was her, all along.'

Blanche nodded.

'She said you had betrayed her. That she was going to have it out with you, she was hysterical. I tried to stop her, but ….'

'Why didn't you tell me the truth?'

'Because I didn't know what the truth was, and I was scared. Mum lied so much, but she was all I had. I thought my dad didn't want me. I'd been dependent on her for so long. She made me believe I was sick ….'

'So, I was right.'

'For years, I thought I was very ill. Mum would lose her temper with me if I questioned anything.'

She lowered her eyes.

'She'd hit me, Kate,' she said, her lips trembling. 'One time, it was because I used her phone. I had a bruise on my cheek. She locked me in my room for three days and told everyone I was suffering from side effects from the cancer drug. Another time I threatened to walk to church and she hit my legs with my walking stick. There were other times too. I was afraid of her. She could be out of control. That time you asked about my bruised eye, that was Mum. I can't even remember what I did that time.'

'I have to tell the police,' said Kate, picking up her phone.

'Why, what's the point? Mum's dead. It will just blacken her name, and it will come back on me too. I was going to tell the police, but then you didn't remember anything, and Mum begged me not to. She was full of remorse and terrified you would remember. She was so afraid of going to prison. I was all she had. I'm not excusing her, but she was my mum and now she's gone. It was horrible. I can still picture that afternoon in my head.....' Her voice broke and she leaned against the living room door. 'She came in trembling from head to foot. Her dress had blood all over it, and her legs were covered in mud. 'I've killed Kate,' she said over and over again. I wanted to come and help you, but she said the doorbell had rung and she'd hurried out the back door and through the allotment. I thought it was all my fault. I was so afraid.'

'Blanche ...' began Kate, moving towards her. 'You could have talked to me.'

'I knew Faith came for her lesson that day. I always watched them arrive from our window. I prayed that they would get you to hospital in time to save you.'

'The hammer?'

'Mum took it. She hid it in the garage.'

Kate slumped onto the couch.

'She was my friend, Blanche.'

'She was full of remorse. She said you were going to the police because she hadn't been honest about the charity money, and she panicked.'

'I found out about you, Blanche. That it was her, making you ill. I said once people found out about that. That's when your mum lost it.'

'She was ill,' said Blanche simply, kneeling at her feet. 'I knew she hid money in the house. It was dangerous. Someone must have seen it and ….'

'I miss her,' said Kate.

'So do I,' said Blanche, sitting beside her.

Kate grasped her hand. Blanche, relieved, laid her head on Kate's shoulder and that was how Dan found them five minutes later

Chapter Eighty

'Amazing how many people turned up?' said Miranda. 'Considering a few know she was a con artist.'

Beth grimaced.

'She was sick.'

'Right,' smiled Miranda, downing the last of her wine. 'Look, I'm sorry about the article on Miller.'

'You should be telling him that, not me.'

'It got changed. It wasn't my original copy. You know what editors are like.'

'I don't, actually.'

'I'd like to put it right. Maybe an interview in his own words? What do you think?'

Beth sighed.

'Why are you asking me?'

'You're the only one he talks to, apparently.'

'Is that right?'

She saw Kate walk in and used it as her opportunity to escape. 'Excuse me, Miranda,' she said and approached Kate.

'Feeling better?' she asked.

Kate smiled, but Beth could see it was forced.

'Yes, thanks, Beth. Bad timing.'

Beth looked at her closely. She'd been crying. Blanche followed her in and it looked like she'd been crying too.

'I have to get back to the office,' Beth said to Blanche. 'Thank you for the tea and cake.'

She waved to Tom and mouthed, 'I'm going.'

She got into her car and drove to the prison where Carl Shaw was being held.

*

Tom took a slow walk home. The funeral had stirred up memories of Lorna's funeral. It had been a sunny day and had matched her personality. He'd chosen to carry their son's coffin while his father-in-law and brother-in-law had carried Lorna. He'd cried all through the service and hadn't taken his eyes off the beautiful photo of his wife. He stopped and leaned on the cemetery gates. He was glad Lester Lynch was dead. Now Benny would know what it felt like to lose someone you loved. He couldn't go in the house, not yet. The whisky would be too tempting.

'Reflecting,' said a voice.

Tom straightened to look at Reverend Scott.

'Not really. A nice service today, by the way.'

'That's praise indeed, from you,' smiled the vicar.

Tom gave a nod and continued to his cottage. He was thinking about what to have for dinner as he opened the door. He didn't recognise the music immediately, but when he did, his body froze.

'Welcome home,' said a voice from the kitchen.

Chapter Eighty-One

Carl Shaw looked surprised to see her.

'To what do I owe the pleasure?' he asked sarcastically.

Beth sat opposite him.

'Tell me about Mad Max. The guy you met online.'

Carl looked at her curiously.

'I already did.'

'So, tell me again.'

'Why are you interested now?' he asked. 'I thought you didn't believe me.'

'I don't. But I also don't like loose ends.'

'I didn't kill anyone. Why the fuck won't anyone believe me?'

Beth fidgeted in her seat.

'Tell me about Mad Max.'

'What's to tell? He was boastful. Saying how he'd done lots of houses, but he got caught and did some time. He'd done plumbing work for 'an old girl,' His words, not mine. He said there was a suitcase there with thirty grand in it. If I did the job ….'

'He told you the exact amount of money?'

'Yeah, and that the case would be locked.'

'If the case was locked, how did he know how much money was in there?'

Carl shrugged.

'How do I know? He was right, though. There was thirty grand, and the case was locked.'

'What was the name of the chat room?'

'I told the other copper that. It's called 'Little Monsters', but don't think you can just Google it. It's on the dark web. It's got an onion address. Here.'

Beth had no idea what an onion address was, but she was determined to find out. Carl scribbled a string of letters onto a scrap of paper and handed it to Beth.

'I hope you have better luck than I did.'

Beth scraped back her chair and stood up.

'By the way, the Lethbridges never had a plumber at their house.'

Carl shrugged.

'That's what he told me.'

'One thing that interests me, Carl. Why did you choose that night?'

Carl smiled.

'He told me to. He didn't say why. He just said the job had to be done that night, or he wouldn't give me the address. What did I care what day it was? He stitched me right up, didn't he?'

'He may well have done,' said Beth and signalled to a guard.

'You gonna get me out of here?' Carl called.

'Who knows,' she said.

*

Beth took the steaming spaghetti Bolognese from the microwave and sat at the kitchen table, where she had her laptop open. She was surprised at how easy it was to get onto the dark web. Between sips of wine, she entered the address that Carl had given her. As she'd expected, there was no Mad Max in the chatroom. She went through several rooms, trying to find him but with no luck. The spaghetti Bolognese was cold when she remembered it, and the bottle of wine half drunk. She was searching for Robert Lethbridge on Google when her mobile rang. She glanced at the screen and saw it was Miranda. She ignored it and carried on with her search when it rang again.

'For God's sake,' she cursed, switching it off.

She shoved the Bolognese into the microwave and sipped her wine while it heated up. She felt sure Carl was making up the Mad Max person, but supposing he wasn't? How the hell was she going to find out if it had been Rob Lethbridge? Some kind of sick joke of his, to use the name of the films Mae had been fond of. The microwave pinged, and she was about to take the bowl of sauce out when there was an urgent thudding on her front door.

'What now?' she mumbled, putting the sauce back.

She opened the door to a worried Miranda.

'I did phone, but … I've been to Tom Miller's cottage. Something is not right?'

'What are you talking about?' said Beth, struggling to hide her impatience.

'I went to his cottage to see if he would give me an interview. I rang the doorbell, but he didn't answer. I phoned his mobile but no reply. But I saw someone in the house. Not Tom, someone else. I could hear music and ….'

'Perhaps he's got a friend visiting,' said Beth.

'A big, burly, gangster looking type friend,' said Miranda. Beth felt a tremor go through her.

'Anyway, he doesn't strike me as the kind that would ignore a phone call or a knock at the door,' added Miranda.

Beth knew what she meant. He might be a pain in the arse, but he was also polite.

'How do you know it wasn't Tom you saw?' she asked.

'This guy was short but big and there's a silver Jaguar outside. I just sense something is wrong, Beth.'

It's nothing, Beth told herself, but she couldn't stop her stomach from churning. She punched in Tom's number. She waited for him to pick up, but after several rings, it went into voicemail. He had to be at home. Where else would he go?

'I'll drive over to his cottage.'

'I'll come with you,' said Miranda, and Beth heard the tremble in her voice.

She debated whether to phone the station. Tom would be annoyed if she panicked. This is silly, she told herself firmly. Everything is fine. He probably has the music too loud and Miranda, always looking for adventure, has it in her head that something terrible has happened.

Hoping for a juicy story, thought Beth.

They reached Tom's cottage, and sure enough, parked outside was a silver Jaguar.

'That was there when I arrived,' said Miranda. 'That's not Tom's car, is it?'

Her voice shook. Beth looked at the shiny, silver jaguar.

'That definitely isn't Tom's,' she said with a smile.

'Something is wrong, Beth. I know it.'

Beth peered at Tom's cottage. Lights were on and the curtains drawn.

'Let's try him again,' she said hopefully, but again her call went to voicemail.

'I'm going round the back,' said Beth.

'Shouldn't you call for backup?' suggested Miranda, nervously looking up at the cottage.

'He may just have the music too loud and can't hear us. We don't know, he could have a woman in there. We don't want to make fools of ourselves.'

'It didn't look like a woman to me,' said Miranda.

'He's entitled to have someone with him.'

He'll have her guts for garters if he ever finds out she'd spied on him.

'Beth ...' cautioned Miranda, but Beth was already walking to the cottage. She heard the music and stopped. There was something familiar about it, but she couldn't think what it was. Through the darkness, she could see the coarse, uneven pathway leading to the back of the cottage. Light from the kitchen shone onto the small back garden. God, she hoped she didn't find him in a compromising position with a woman. She stepped over a bucket and felt something crunch beneath her feet. She bent closer to see what it was, and as she did so, her eyes fastened on the broken pane of glass in the back door. She could hear the music more clearly now and realised what it was. The music Lester Lynch had played when he had ... Oh God, Miranda was right. Something was very wrong. She cautiously moved forward so she could glimpse into the kitchen without being seen. Her feet crunched on some more glass, and she winced. She lifted her eyes to the kitchen window and then widened them in shock at the scene in front of her. Her hand went quickly to her mouth to stifle her horrified gasp.

Chapter Eighty-Two

As soon as Tom recognised the voice from the kitchen, he turned back to the front door. But his hand didn't even reach the door handle before the electric charge from the taser gun ripped through his body. The Taser barbs felt like bees crawling through his skin. He crumpled to the floor and lay there looking up at Benny Lynch.

'I ain't forgot about you if that's what you've been thinking,' said Benny. He slid his hands beneath Tom's shoulders and, with difficulty, dragged him along the hall and into the living room, where he stopped to get his breath. Tom's brain failed to function. All he could do was listen to Benny's laboured breathing. He was dragged again to the kitchen, his body thumping against the hard floor. Pain shot through his spine and he fought back a groan. Benny lifted him roughly onto a chair and tied his hands with a piece of rope. He then stood back, struggling to get his breath.

'Jesus, you're heavy,' he panted.

Tom tried to speak, but his lips wouldn't move.

'You 'eard what they did to my boy? Slaughtered him, that's what they did,' wheezed Benny.

Tom continued to stare at him.

'It'll wear off soon,' Benny said. He pulled a chair out from under the table and placed it opposite Tom. He took a few deep breaths and then sat down heavily.

'I'm getting too old for this, you know. It's no joke. Fucking curse, that's what it is.'

He laid a hand on his chest and waited for his heart to slow down. Tom watched as Benny dragged a big black bag across the room. He pulled out a sawn-off shotgun and then relaxed, resting the gun on his lap.

'He was a good kid when he was young,' he continued. 'He wanted to be a vet, you know. He was good with animals.' Benny smiled at the memory.

The tingling had eased, and Tom stretched his legs. Benny's hand went to the gun.

'Wearing off, is it?' he asked.

The sound of the doorbell stopped Tom from answering. Benny lifted the shotgun and aimed it at Tom's head.

'Don't get any ideas. I have no qualms about shooting you.'

Tom knew that if Benny were going to shoot him, he would have done it by now. No, he had something much worse planned for him. Benny stood up and walked across the room. Through the window, he could see a woman standing at the gate. He ducked out of sight. A moment later, Tom's phone rang in his pocket.

'Fuck,' said Benny, ripping it out of Tom's trousers.

Tom was going over tactics in his head. There must be a way to overpower Benny, but his legs were still numb. He knew he wouldn't get far on them.

'Like I was saying, he was a good kid. He got led astray. It weren't him that did those boys ….' Continued Benny.

'It was him, Benny. He admitted to it. He enjoyed it.'

Benny stepped closer, his face contorted in anger.

'That ain't fucking true, and you know it. You stitched my boy up because you couldn't find the real killer.'

'He was the real killer. I saw what he did to those boys and ….'

'Shut it,' snarled Benny. 'Stand up,' he demanded.

Tom glanced at the shotgun.

'Don't even think about it,' smiled Benny. 'You wouldn't stand a chance.

From the black bag, Benny produced a rope.

'I'm too old for this malarky,' he grumbled. 'Do you think he suffered, my boy? They slaughtered him like an animal. On his birthday too. His mother has cried so much. She's got no tears left. Who's going to see justice done if I don't?'

He pointed at the beam above Tom's head.

'I know how depressed you've been since your wife died. Your depression has got much worse since they murdered my son. Guilt is a terrible thing. It makes you do crazy stuff.'

He threw the rope over the beam and then tied it expertly into a noose.

'I've done this before,' he smiled. 'I won't make any mistakes. I thought of all different ways, but I figured this would be the most enjoyable for me to watch.'

'No one will believe this was suicide,' said Tom, his mind racing. Was that Beth at the door? Would she realise something was wrong?

Benny reached into the bag again and, this time, pulled out a writing pad and a pen.

'We've got to write your suicide note first,' he said with a smile.

Chapter Eighty-Three

Beth pulled her eyes away from the noose that hung from the beam and focused on the sawn-off shotgun that rested on Benny Lynch's lap. He was stroking it gently as if it was a much-loved pet. Tom was writing something at the kitchen table. It had to be a suicide note, which meant she didn't have long.

She crept stealthily away from the back door and broke into a run as soon as she entered the side entrance.

'Oh God, what is it?' gasped Miranda, seeing the expression on Beth's face.

'I think it's Benny Lynch,' said Beth said breathlessly. 'We haven't got any time to waste.'

She yanked at the boot of her car and grabbed the jack that she kept there for emergencies.

'Shouldn't we phone for backup?' asked Miranda.

Beth hurried to the entrance of the cemetery with Miranda close behind. She looked around frantically until she saw what she was looking for resting against the church wall. She grabbed the shovel and thanked God for funerals.

'Grab those stones,' she said, pointing.

'But, they're on someone's grave,' protested Miranda.

'Trust me. They'll be glad to help.'

Miranda collected the stones and followed Beth back to the house.

'When I give the signal, I want you to smash the windscreen of the Jaguar with the jack. It should set off the alarm. Then go to your car and keep your hand on the horn. With your other hand call 999. Tell them a police officer's life is in danger.'

Before Miranda could speak, Beth took the stones from her and hurried to the front door of Tom's cottage. Her whole body was shaking. If she got this wrong and miscalculated one move, it would be over for her and Tom. She prayed Miranda wouldn't lose her nerve. She took a deep breath and nodded. Miranda shot into action and smashed the jack into the Jaguar's windscreen, triggering the alarm. The flashing light lit up the street. The screeching ripped through the quiet evening, just as she'd hoped. Miranda raced back towards Beth's car. Seconds later, she slipped and crashed to the ground. Beth's heart stopped. Get up, please get up, she prayed. As if she could hear her, Miranda pulled herself up and limped to the car. Beth let out a relieved breath and began to throw the stones at the cottage window before pushing her fist against the doorbell.

*

Benny read the note and smiled.

'Even I feel sorry for you. Admitting you made a mistake about Lester Lynch. The guilt and remorse had been too much for you. Then after losing your ….'

'Shut up,' growled Tom.

He looked up at the beam. One good swing was all he needed to knock the gun from Benny's hand. If he missed, it would all be over. He'd be shot at close range. He wouldn't stand a chance. Benny wouldn't think twice about shooting him, and Tom knew that. Benny tied Tom's hands together.

'A double knot this time just to sure,' he smiled.

There was a loud crash from outside. For a moment, Benny got sidetracked.

'What the fuck?' he muttered as a car alarm screeched. He pushed the nuzzle of the gun into Tom's stomach.

'Get up.'

He shoved Tom from behind. Tom's legs were still weak from being tasered, and he fell to the floor. In the living room, Benny could see the flashing of his car alarm. He glanced out of the window just as a stone cracked it.

'What the …'

The doorbell rang incessantly.

'Fucking hooligans,' he yelled, opening the door. 'What the hell are you doing?'

He pointed the shotgun.

*

Beth knew she didn't have a second to waste. She daren't hesitate. Once in the house, she knew she must not stop. Not even if Tom's body was hanging from the rafters. She needed to concentrate. To focus.

When the door finally swung open, she was ready. 'Fucking hooligans, what the hell are you doing?' yelled Lynch.

Beth swung the shovel. It connected with Benny's shoulder, sending him crashing to the floor. Beth didn't stop. She flew past him, knocking her knee on the door. Her injury now hindered her plan of racing upstairs.

'Fuck,' muttered Benny, confused.

Benny was angry now. The fuckers weren't going to get the better of him. He clambered to his feet and angrily kicked Tom several times in the face before lifting the shotgun and aiming it at Beth's back. She heard the shot, followed by a scream. She wasn't sure if the cry came from her. The crack of the shotgun reverberated through her brain. Had she been shot? She didn't feel anything. Oh God, had he shot Tom?

She heard footsteps on the stairs and laboured breathing. She limped into Tom's study and rummaged in the drawer for his gun. She should have closed the door. Fuck it. How could she have been so stupid? Her hands fumbled around in the drawer.

'Come on, come on,' she sobbed, but her hand only encountered papers, pens and other office paraphernalia. 'Where the fuck are you?'

If only her hands would stop shaking. Oh God, what if he'd moved it? She was a sitting duck. Behind her, she could hear Benny Lynch panting. He was close. Did she have the right drawer? Her brain was racing. She couldn't remember.

'Please,' she begged, the sobs catching in her throat until she thought she wouldn't be able to breathe at all.

Lynch was at the door, she could hear his wheezy panting. Then her hands felt the cold metal. Her legs almost gave way with the relief. What if it wasn't loaded. Oh, dear God, please let it be.

'Bitch,' she heard from behind her.

She spun around and, without hesitation, fired four shots into Benny Lynch's chest.

Chapter Eighty-Four

'I brought grapes,' said Beth, looking around for a place to put them.

'I can't eat them,' mumbled Tom.

Beth grimaced.

'Yeah, I kind of remembered that after I bought them.'

Matt handed him two paperbacks.

'I don't know if they're your kind of thing, but if not, no worries, they're second hand, so ….'

Tom raised his eyebrows.

'I bought the nationals,' said Luke, looking proud.

Tom's eyes lit up.

'Great, thanks.'

'So, how is it, the jaw?' asked Beth.

'Broken,' said Tom.

'It's not improved your temperament then?'

'Beth's a bit of a celebrity now,' said Matt.

'Ma'am to you,' Beth reminded him.

'She's got airs and graces now,' smiled Luke.

'She saved my life,' said Tom.

'At the cost of nearly losing my own,' said Beth. 'I must have been mad.'

Matt stood and gestured to Luke.

'We ought to get back, Sir. Good to see you looking well.'

Beth hung back, and when they had closed the front door, said,

'It was Miranda that really saved you. She sensed something was wrong.'

'You could have been killed.'

'I wasn't, though.'

'It was stupid what you did.'

Beth sighed.

'Don't be too grateful.'

He tried to smile, but it hurt too much.

'Has your sister recommended a good counsellor?'

Beth rolled her eyes.

'Don't you start.'

'You killed someone.'

Like she would ever forget. The ringing in her ears had seemed to go on forever. She'd dropped the gun as if it had burnt her. Benny Lynch had laid still on the floor of Tom's study. It had seemed to Beth that blood had seeped from every pore in his body. Tom had screamed her name. The sound had broken through the ringing in her ears, and she'd calmly stepped over the body and made her way downstairs.

'I'm alright,' she'd called. 'I shot him. I shot Benny Lynch.'

The words had sounded strange to her ears. She'd shot Benny Lynch. She hadn't heard the police sirens or Miranda's shouts.

'Are you okay?' she'd asked Tom, surprised to hear the steadiness in her voice. She'd not been able to remember much after that. She must have gone into shock.

'I've been thinking. It's probably best if I leave Stonesend,' said Tom, breaking into her reverie.

'What, why? You can't leave. We've got the trial and ….'

'You could have been killed, and it would have been because of me. I've spoken to the chief and ….'

Beth stood up.

'This is ridiculous. We need you here. Besides, you still haven't taken me to dinner.'

How ironic, she thought. One minute, all I wanted was to see the back of him and now ….

Tom smiled.

'What did the chief say?' she asked.

'He wants me to stay.'

'There, that's two of us. We can't both be wrong.'

'You might live to regret it.'

Beth laughed.

'You're probably right.'

She walked to the door.

'I'll see you later,' she smiled.

Beth closed the door of Tom's hospital room and let out a long breath. The night of Benny Lynch's murder had made her realise just how vital police work was to her. Getting the bad guys was what it was all about. She wanted to get the bad guy who had killed Mae Lethbridge and almost killed Kate. She felt sure that person wasn't

Carl, but how could she prove it? That night had also brought home to her how she felt about Tom. He was the only copper with whom she wanted to solve this crime. She had three months before the trial of Carl Shaw to find the murderer, and she had no idea where to start.

*

Kate had thought long and hard about telling Beth the truth. She finally decided not to. After all, Mae's killer had been caught. There was enough evidence to show it was him. It wasn't as if she was shielding a killer. They'd found the hammer. Just a coincidence that he used it too. His prints were everywhere, Detective Miller had said. They found Mae's money and her jewellery at his house. She was safe now. She'd begun to pity Mae. It hadn't been her fault. She'd been mentally unstable. Perhaps, if she'd gotten help, but Kate wouldn't let herself dwell on what-ifs. Life would soon go back to normal in the village, and that was all Kate wanted.

Chapter Eighty-Five

Life did return to normal in the village sooner than anyone could have imagined. Beth spent most of her time trawling through old cases, trying to find some link to Mad Max. A feeling that they had not found the real killer hung over her like a black cloud. Carl's trial was just a few weeks away and it worried her that they would be convicting an innocent man. He was no angel, she knew that, but she felt sure he wasn't a killer. Tom had insisted on returning to work as soon as possible. In the evenings, they would sometimes have dinner, discuss the trial, and prepare for their part in it. Beth had visited Carl twice more in an attempt to get some more information from him that would lead her to Mad Max, but she always reached a dead end. Mae Lethbridge never had a plumber to the house, so she couldn't even follow that lead. Once a week, she visited the counsellor that Sandy had recommended. It helped a lot, especially when Frances Lynch hung herself. It was the end of an era and many Londoners were relieved. But Beth felt she had murdered two people.

'I'm glad the counselling is helping,' Tom said.

They were having dinner in the French restaurant she and Ben used to frequent. She never imagined she would eat there again and certainly not with someone else. She sipped her glass of wine. It was a good one, rich and fruity.

'I still see his eyes when the bullets hit him.'

'His heart gave out, don't forget that. It was only a matter of time before he had a massive heart attack. He would have killed us both. You did the only thing you could. You had no choice.

She nodded and pushed Benny Lynch from her mind.

'I'm getting nowhere trying to trace this Mad Max.'

'Have you ever considered that perhaps he doesn't exist?' Tom asked, cutting into his steak.

Beth sighed.

'There's nothing to prove that Carl Shaw was in that bedroom. That's going to be the defence angle. His DNA wasn't on the body, the bed, any of the furniture.'

'If it wasn't him, then we still have a murderer on the loose but don't forget, the same weapon and with his DNA on it, and he admitted to being in the house.'

Tom nodded at her plate.

'Aren't you going to eat that?'

She smiled. He looked exceptionally handsome this evening, Beth thought, or maybe he had always looked incredibly handsome and she just hadn't noticed before.

'It's not like you to forget to eat,' he joked.

The night Benny Lynch was killed had changed their lives. Beth had realised how fragile life was and how she needed to get on with it. Tom had learnt that life was for living and to put the past behind him and move on.

Kate had gone back to teaching, and Blanche had applied to go to university. Everyone was pleased for her. No one had a kind word for Mae anymore. Rob had settled into village life, but Beth couldn't help her dislike of him showing whenever they bumped into each other in the village. If only she had a lead. She knew she had to be careful if she didn't want Rob Lethbridge accusing her of harassment.

She glanced at Tom to see him looking at her. The attraction was mutual. She felt sure of that, but supposing she was wrong. If she made the first move and he rejected her, she wasn't sure her fractured heart would cope. No, she decided. Best to let him make the first move.

*

The day of Carl's trial arrived and Beth couldn't meet his eyes in court. She'd promised to do her best to find the killer, but she'd failed miserably.

'You're banging your head against a brick wall,' Matt told her. 'He's as guilty as hell.'

'Why is everyone so sure?' she asked.

'Why are you so convinced it isn't him?' asked Luke.

But she couldn't answer that question with facts. It was just a gut feeling. She took a week off work so she could attend the trial every day. Tom never said a word. Maybe he felt she needed to get it out of her system.

The defence team were excellent, she thought. There was no concrete evidence that Carl Shaw was in Mae Lethbridge's bedroom and they were determined to prove it, but the prosecution was just as good and it was hard for anyone to predict the verdict. Beth gave her evidence. It wasn't as hard as she'd expected. Still, she didn't meet Carl's eyes. Then it was Don's turn. He looked smart, Beth thought. The times' Beth had seen him, he'd been wearing the same brown jumper and brown corduroys. She'd begun to wonder if it was all he owned. But today, he wore a suit.

'Did you find any forensic evidence that would confirm that Carl Shaw had been in Mae Lethbridge's bedroom?' asked the defence.

'No, none.'

'Nothing at all?'

'That's correct.'

'But you did find his DNA in other parts of the house?'

'In the living room, yes, and on the murder weapon.'

'Would you say, in your experience, that it is unusual not finding any DNA of the murderer at the scene of the murder?'

'One would expect to find some, yes, but as I said, there was matching DNA in the house.'

'But that just proves he was in the house, doesn't it?'

'Yes.'

'Mr Shaw has never denied he burgled Mrs Lethbridge.'

'I'm sorry, is that a question?' asked Don.

'You would agree it's a bit odd that no matching DNA was found at the murder scene?'

'I would have expected something.'

'That's all, thank you.'

Beth finally met Carl's eyes, and he'd smiled.

'Surely they will find him guilty,' Sandy said over coffee one afternoon.

They'd met in town. Beth had been attending the trial, and Sandy had gone shopping.

Beth sighed.

'But what if he didn't do it?'

'Then the murderer is still out there and we're not safe.'

Beth lowered her head and looked into her cappuccino. She stirred it and watched the chocolate swirl in the milk.

'Do you really believe he is innocent?' asked Sandy, surprised.

Beth exhaled and bit her lip.

'I don't know anymore.'

'You've done your best, Beth.'

Beth glanced out of the window, then took a deep breath.

'Sandy, I need to tell you something about Ben.'
Sandy nodded.
'He didn't leave me for another woman.'
Sandy cocked her head to one side.
'He left me for a man. His name is Mark.'
Sandy placed a hand over hers.
'I knew there was more to it. Why didn't you tell us?'
'I felt humiliated. I know I needn't have, now. But back then ….'
'Tell your counsellor. I promise you it will help.'
Beth nodded and checked the time on her phone.
'I should get back to court.'

*

The trial lasted ten days. Beth felt Blanche gave the most heart-breaking evidence. Beth didn't think she would ever forget it. Blanche's lip had trembled and her voice had shaken as she answered the questions. Rob Lethbridge had sat stony-faced watching the drama play out.

Beth didn't go to the summing up but waited nervously for the verdict. She was edgy and tense. The thought of seeing Carl's face when the guilty verdict was returned was too much for her, so she waited at home, her eyes fixed on her phone. This is ridiculous, she told herself. It could be days before the jury came to a decision. But it wasn't days. It took just six hours. Her phone bleeped with a Breaking News message. *'Verdict in for Stonesend Murder'* With her breath held, she clicked into the news. The words screamed at her. CARL SHAW HAS BEEN FOUND NOT GUILTY OF THE MURDER OF CARING MOTHER, MAE LETHBRIDGE.

Carl Shaw was a free man.

Chapter Eighty-Six

There was a sense of unease in the village. Mae's murderer and Kate's attacker had got away with it. No one, except Beth, believed he was innocent.

'It's a disgrace,' Kate said. 'He clearly did it.'

Beth had gone round to see Kate and found her and Blanche trying on dresses.

'I'm sorry, Blanche,' Beth said. 'You must be so upset about the verdict.'

Blanche lowered the dress she was holding.

'It's not your fault. What happens now?'

Beth couldn't say that she would like to continue looking for the murderer. As far as everyone was concerned, they had the murderer and he had got off.

'There isn't much more we can do. Carl Shaw had a fair trial, and they found him not guilty,' she said.

'So much for law and order,' muttered Kate.

'So,' Beth said, attempting to change the subject. 'What's the new dress for?'

Blanche's face lit up.

'We're having a party to celebrate me getting into Uni.'

'Oh,' said Beth.

Beth thought it somewhat premature to have a celebration so soon after Mae's death.

'You'll come, won't you?' Blanche asked.

'I guess I should get a new dress too, then. I can't remember the last time I bought something new.'

Blanche clapped her hands.

'These are from Alice Heart. She's on Facebook. You can try them at home.'

She handed Beth a card.

'Have a look later.'

'Thanks.'

Beth discovered from Sophie that the party had been Jo and Rob's idea. Why didn't that surprise her? Sophie said that Jo had felt it would be a good way for her to meet the villagers and for Blanche to celebrate her place at university. They'd been worried she'd be turned down, but after considering her case and based on her submitted work, they had accepted her. Blanche was over the moon. Kate agreed to help with the hall decorating and rallied around some of the villagers to make food for the party. Some were hesitant, still feeling they had been made fools of by the Lethbridge's.

'None of it was Blanche's fault,' Kate would tell them.

Beth had no idea what to wear for the party, and that evening she went onto Facebook to look at Alice Heart designs. The dresses on her Facebook page were lovely but far too frilly and feminine for Beth. She was about to close her laptop when curiosity got the better of her, and she typed the name, Rob Lethbridge, into the search box. She recognised his picture right away and clicked into it. His new profile pic was of him and Blanche together. She typed into the search box again and found herself on Blanche's Facebook page. She scrolled down. There weren't many posts. The latest one was about her being offered a place at uni. She clicked a few more times, and there it was. As clear as day. If she'd believed in God, she would have claimed he sent it to her as a sign. How could she not have realised? Of course. It made perfect sense.

*

Beth had never been inside the newspaper offices before and was surprised by its busyness.

'I'm looking for Miranda ….'

The man who'd been passing her in the corridor pointed ahead of them.

'Third door on the right.'

Beth thanked him and made her way along the corridor. Miranda was tapping frantically at her keyboard. Beth knocked lightly on the open door.

'Okay to come in?' she asked.

Miranda looked up, pleasure lighting up her face.

'I never thought I'd see you here,' she smiled.

'I think you can help me,' said Beth.

'Happy to.'

Miranda lifted her eyebrows, and Beth told her what she needed.

Chapter Eighty-Seven

The doorbell rang, and Beth grabbed the handcuffs from the bed and slid them into her handbag. She opened the door to Sandy and Ray.

'Nice dress,' said Sandy, looking at her appraisingly.

'You don't think it's a bit too bright?' Beth asked, looking at herself critically in the hall mirror.

'No, it looks perfect on you.'

Beth took one last look in the mirror. If only she were prettier or more glamourous or ….

'Oh sod it,' she said. 'Let's go.'

Tom was already in the hall. He waved on seeing them, and annoyingly she felt herself blush.

'Hey,' said Sandy. 'How are you feeling?'

'I'm fine, pretty much back to normal.'

'He's talking again,' said Beth. 'Usually a load of rubbish, though.'

'Full of compliments is your sister,' Tom smiled.

'It means she likes you,' smiled Sandy.

Beth rolled her eyes.

There were more people here than Beth had imagined there would be. Even Jack was helping behind a makeshift bar. It seemed the Lethbridges had finally been forgiven. None so fickle as village folk, she thought.

'That's a nice dress,' Tom said.

Beth felt her face grow hot. Shit, why couldn't she control that?

'Thanks. That's a nice suit.'

Ray and Sandy went to the makeshift bar to get a drink.

'Kate wasn't happy about the verdict,' she told Tom.

'The whole village isn't happy,' he agreed.

'He didn't do it,' she said quietly.

'According to the jury.'

She was about to speak when a hand touched her shoulder.

'I'm so pleased you came. The dress looks amazing. I told you Alice Heart was incredible.'

Beth turned around. Blanche was wearing a similar style dress but in white. She looked like an angel. Beth didn't like to say she hadn't bought her dress from Alice Heart.

'Hi,' said Beth. 'It's a nice party.'

'There's a lot of food,' smiled Blanche. Beth looked over to the buffet table and nodded.

'It looks good.'

'Congratulations,' said Tom. 'You must be very excited.'

'I am. I never thought I would go to Uni.'

'What are you going to study?'

Beth walked away from them and made her way to the buffet table.

'Isn't it wonderful to see Blanche looking so healthy,' said Dan, joining her?

'Yes,' said Beth, leaving the buffet table and walking to the bar.

'A large white wine,' she said.

'On the house, or should I say, on the Lethbridges,' Jack smiled.

Rob Lethbridge was watching her. She could feel his eyes burning through her skin. She met his eyes for a moment and then turned away. Within minutes he was at her side.

'Good of you to come,' he said.

'It's a good turnout. Blanche seems very excited.'

He looked over at his daughter.

'Yes, she is. It's a good University.'

Beth sipped her wine.

'What can I get you?' Jack asked.

'I'll have a beer, Jack, thanks.'

'Getting on with the locals, I see,' said Beth.

'We don't blame you that Carl Shaw got off,' he said bluntly.

'He didn't do it,' she said.

He stared at her.

'You sound very sure about that.'

'I am,' she said before excusing herself and taking her drink outside to the well-tended garden. She turned to look at him through the open doors. He had walked to the buffet and was filling a plate with food.

She moved her gaze away from him. She could just see the church spire from here. She sipped her drink slowly, her mind busy. She should speak to Tom, but what if she was wrong?

It was chilly. She should have brought a cardigan. She could feel goosebumps on her arms.

'It's chilly this evening', said a voice behind her.

Blanche was holding a plate of food.

'I brought you this.'

'Thanks,' said Beth, taking the plate and sitting it on the wall. She wasn't really hungry but nibbled on a sausage roll.

'You're looking well,' she said, taking in Blanche's smooth skin and bright eyes.

Blanche smiled.

'I have makeup on,' she said in a confidential whisper. 'It makes such a difference.'

Beth went to sip her wine and realised it had all gone. Blanche touched her arm gently.

'You did everything you could to find mum's killer.'

'Did we?' Beth questioned.

'Yes, you brought him to trial and ….'

Beth wished she could get another glass of wine.

'He didn't do it,' she said firmly.

'What?' said Blanche, her brows knitted in confusion.

'Carl Shaw didn't kill your mother.'

'How do you know?' asked Blanche, surprised.

'Because I know who did.'

*

She'd discovered the truth when she hadn't even been looking for it. Rob's Facebook hadn't given much away. There had been photos of him and Jo. Old pictures of him with his wife and daughter. Always, Beth noted, Mae was holding Blanche. Rob had seemed like an interloper in all of them. Then there had been the last photo of him with his daughter taken recently. This time, of course, there had been no Mae in the picture. He'd tagged Blanche, and she'd commented below. *I love you, Dad. X*

Beth had clicked into Blanche's profile and been disappointed. There were just a few posts. They were a few years old. The latest had been about Uni. Beth had then clicked into 'Blanche's about info.'

She'd stared at the screen, her mind reeling. Finally, she'd closed the laptop and left the cottage and driven to Miranda's offices.

'There were only two articles. I did them both,' said Miranda clicking into a file. Beth had sat in front of the laptop reading until, finally, bingo. She had what she needed.

'Thanks, Miranda. See you later at the party.'

'But aren't you going to tell me what this is about?'

'Later.'

*

Now here she was. Much later. Blanche reeled back at her words.

'You know who killed my mother?'

Beth nodded and licked her lips, wishing again for a glass of wine.

'Who was it?' Blanche asked breathlessly.

'It was you,' Beth said.

Chapter Eighty-Eight

Blanche didn't so much as flinch.
'Are you going to deny it?' Beth asked. Her heart was racing. She'd been dreading this moment. What if she was wrong?
Blanche looked at the floor and then back to meet Beth's eyes.
'I didn't want her dead,' she said quietly. 'I just wanted to be free.'

*

Blanche
I don't remember when I decided to kill my mother, but I'm sure the idea was cemented after the day mum nearly killed Kate. I'd been so scared. What if Kate had died? Kate had looked terrible for months, and the guilt of knowing the truth nearly killed me. I discovered so much about my mother that day. Kate had left our house the night before, looking worried. I knew it had to be connected to my medication because she had been fine before that.

'Your Mum forgot to lock the cabinet,' she told me. 'But I can't find anything that you need to take before bed.'

Her worried look had concerned me, and as soon as she left, I took the opportunity to look through the medications myself. Mother always locked the cabinet, and the pill bottles always placed so that I couldn't see the labels. Now, the labels were on show. Kate had not put them back the usual way. How was Kate to know? I stared at the labels in disbelief. I was confused. Why were the medications in my mum's name? Only one had my name on it. I couldn't understand it. I quickly wrote down the names of the medicines on a scrap of paper and shoved it into my pocket. I decided I would check them on Google in the morning. Mum always took my tablet away at night. She liked to keep a check on what I'd been browsing.

On the morning of Kate's attack, Mum had been grumpy. She had the hangover from the migraine, and she was techy.

'What the hell did Kate think she was doing, nosing through our things. I won't have it,' she yelled.

'She didn't,' I said.

'I know when things have been moved,' Mum said, pacing the room. 'She had no right. I'm going to have it out with her.'

As the day wore on, she became more and more agitated. By five that afternoon, she was brimming over with uncontrolled rage.

'I'm going to see Kate,' she said. 'She'll be home now.'

'Please don't,' I begged. 'She didn't mean to upset you.'

'Stay here.'

She'd hurried round to Kate's cottage and I'd sat anxiously at the kitchen table waiting for her to come back. It seemed like she was there forever when she suddenly came crashing into the kitchen. She was in such a terrible state. Her dress was covered in blood and her legs splashed with mud. A hammer, with fresh blood still on it, in her hand. I stared at it, horrified. It was like being in a nightmare. She was hysterical. Pacing the floor like a lioness.

'Mum?' I said, terrified. 'What's happened?'

'Oh God,' she sobbed. 'I didn't mean it, you know. I just …'

'Mum, what have you done?' I gasped.

She ran water from the kitchen tap and splashed it over her face.

'Oh God,' she groaned.

'Mum,' I pleaded. 'Tell me.'

'I ran through the allotment,' she sobbed. 'I don't think anyone saw me.'

'What did you do?' I asked again, urgently.

'I killed Kate. I just … I didn't mean to kill her. I just lost it. She pushed me too far. How dare she get involved. I'm your mother. I'm a good mother.'

I felt like someone had punched me in the stomach. Nausea rose in my gut.

'Killed?' I stuttered.

'I didn't mean … she shouldn't have ….'

'Oh God,' I groaned, heading for the door.

'No!' she screamed. 'Someone rang the doorbell. They'll see you.'

'Alice,' I said. 'She has her lesson. Oh, what have you done?'

Mother hung onto me like a life raft.

'I just lost it,' she said.

She'd just lost it. Like she had many times with me. The Mae Lethbridge I lived with wasn't the same Mae Lethbridge that everyone else saw. Mum often lost it. Like the time she'd lashed out at me when she saw me walking. I had a black eye for days. She told everyone I was sick from my chemotherapy. Or the time she lashed out with my walking stick, bashing it forcefully against my legs, so I crumpled to the ground, all because I'd threatened to walk to church. Mum made sure I never made that threat again. Of course, I know now that I never had cancer or any of the other illnesses she said I had suffered from, but how could she have done that to me? She said she loved me.

If I ever asked questions before we visited the doctor, she would threaten to lock me in my room without food or drink. I never doubted she would do it. I kept my mouth shut throughout the consultations.

That day I'd watched as she hid the hammer under some dust sheets in the garage. The next thing we heard was the ambulance sirens and I prayed that Kate would be alright. Days later, Mum made me sit beside her on the bed and with my hand on the bible, we prayed that Kate would never remember.

I looked up the medications on my tablet. None of them was for treating cancer or any of the other illness I had, apart from the epilepsy drug. The pill Mum gave me at night was a sleeping pill and not a cancer tablet at all. I felt sick and angry. She'd been controlling my life. I hated the charity functions and everyone feeling sorry for me. I just wanted an ordinary life, as Kate's kids had. After the business with Kate, I felt lost. I stopped taking the night-time tablet and hid them in a jar under the bed. I felt less sleepy after that, and my head was clearer than it had been for years.

'You must never tell anyone what happened, do you understand?' Mum had said. 'Kate doesn't remember and isn't likely to now.'

'But ...'

'No buts. Do you want me to go to prison? Who'll look after you then? Who'll give you your medication? I don't think your father will be bothered. Kate is alright, isn't she? We just have to keep praying that her memory doesn't return. It's just the two of us, Blanche, and we must not let anyone come between us.'

But what if Kate's memory did return? What would Mum do then? I couldn't let her hurt Kate, not a second time.

I was tired of charity events and everyone asking me how I was. I was becoming a freak show, and I hated her for it. Mum used me to get the donations, and she kept the money. I wanted to run away but mum was with me all day, and at night she would lock me in my bedroom. I wanted to ask the doctor about my medications but couldn't work out a way to do it. I would lay awake in bed and fantasise what it would be like to live with Kate or my dad. That's all it was at first, a fantasy. I only went into the chat rooms out of curiosity. It was easy to get on to the dark web once you knew what to do.

To begin with, It was just an imaginary game. I pretended to be a man, a plumber. It was more exciting like that. I don't remember when it crossed the line from fantasy to reality. It was exciting planning everything and fantasising about my perfect life afterwards.

I discovered the diary by accident. Mum had a migraine. At least she said she had one. After a while, I realised that Mum often had migraines when she wanted attention. She'd often ask Kate to take care of me, and Kate would be sympathetic and caring. This time, I think it must have been an actual migraine because she didn't want Kate or anyone, come to that.

'Just get my pills from the drawer and then go to bed,' she ordered.

I couldn't find the pills at first and had to move Mum's undies around. That's when I saw the diary. I pushed it under me in the wheelchair and gave mum her pills.

That night I read about grandma, the grandma I had never met because my mother had killed her before I was born. The diary was full of hate for my father and the doctors who argued with her. Mum was concerned about the money she'd taken and her fears that someone would ask for the accounts. I started to worry about Mum. I became anxious. I didn't know what she was capable of, and she seemed to be more erratic since the argument with Kate. I realised with a heavy heart that I would never have a normal adult life. I would never meet a man and fall in love. Mum wanted it to be just the two of us forever. I didn't sleep at all that night. I tried to visualise a future, but I couldn't, not if Mum was around. The discussions in the chat room became more serious then, and my plan began to take shape. I just had to make sure Mad Hatter, who I now know was Carl Shaw, left some evidence on the hammer. I timed everything.

I pushed the razor blade into the handle of the hammer, and I wore my knitted gloves so I wouldn't leave prints anywhere. I told myself that Mad Hatter wouldn't come and that I would never have to do it. Mum made her usual gin and tonic nightcap, which she always had to help her sleep. While she watched a drama on TV, I spiked it with some of my pills. My hands were shaking when I emptied the powder from the sleeping capsules. I'm surprised the powder didn't go everywhere. I kept telling myself nothing was going to happen. It was just a fantasy. But after reading the diary and seeing how much Kate was suffering, I had come to hate my mother.

It was easy to lock myself in my room. Mum kept a spare key in the kitchen drawer.

Mum was asleep in no time and didn't even stir when I moved the suitcase from under her bed. I put the bottle of sleeping pills and the bedroom key on her bedside table. Deep down, I didn't think Mad Hatter would come. It was just fantasy. Still, I couldn't stop shaking and almost cut myself with the razor. If he did come, it still didn't mean I had to go through with it.

I sat trembling and sweating, and when I heard the back door being forced, I almost screamed. I was tempted to see what he looked like, but I couldn't move. I should have stayed there, but I didn't. It was nearly an hour after he'd left when I pulled myself from the bed and put on my gloves. I needed to put the suitcase back in Mum's room. If she so much as guessed what I had done, she would beat the hell out of me. I looked around my room and my eyes landed on the oxygen cylinder and the back brace. Just a few days ago, Mum had said she thought my eyesight was suffering. I didn't want someone touching my eyes. Without even being aware of what I was doing, I carefully removed the razor from the hammer and flushed it down the loo. It took two tries, but eventually, it disappeared. I looked at my face in the mirror. I looked awful. There were dark circles around my eyes. I was the living dead.

I'd stormed into her room, throwing the empty case onto the floor, the hammer gripped in my other hand.

'Why are you doing this?' I asked. 'Why? It's my body, isn't it? Why can't we have normal lives like everyone else?

Of course, she didn't answer. She was drugged, just like I had been for most of my teenage life.

'You killed grandma,' I said, crying. 'Now, you're going to kill me. I can't stand this. Do you understand? I can't stand this! You drove Dad away with your hatefulness. I can't stand it anymore.'

She lay there, looking innocent, peaceful, the perfect mother.

I must have hit her lots of times because there was blood everywhere. I heard my name being called, but I couldn't stop my arm from coming down on her over and over again. My face felt wet, and sweat ran down my back. I'd been oppressed for so long and controlled beyond my limits. At that moment, I hated her with all my being.

'I can't stand it. I can't stand it,' I'd yelled.

She'd woken up and screamed my name. She may have begged me. I can't remember. I know her eyes were wide with horror. She'd lifted her arm to grab mine, her fingers connecting with my fingers. I dropped the hammer, then. When I looked at her *awaegain*, she was dead.

'No, no,' I sobbed. I shook her limp body. 'Mum, Mum, wake up.'

What had I done? I lifted her lifeless body into my arms and hugged her close to me. I could smell her musky perfume. I inhaled it into me. I wanted it to stay with me forever. How would I live without her? She'd been part of me all my life.

'I'm sorry. I'm sorry,' I sobbed. 'I love you. Please forgive me.'

I don't know how long I held her. It seemed like forever. Finally, I let her fall back onto the bed.

'I love you, Mum, but I can't live like this anymore.'

It was better this way. If anyone discovered the truth, my mum would have gone to prison or a hospital for the mentally insane. It would have broken her completely.

I pulled off my blood-stained nightie along with my slippers until I stood completely naked. I then washed the blood from my face and changed into a clean nightgown. I put the clothes into a carrier bag and hid them under my mattress. I felt sure the police wouldn't search my room. Why would they? As far as they'd be concerned, I'd been locked in there all night. I'd get rid of them later. I threw the hammer in the garden, the whole time refusing to allow myself to think. For the first time in my life, I felt energetic, like I could climb a mountain. I locked myself in my room with the spare key and waited. I didn't dwell on what I'd done, although I could feel the tears raining down my face.

'I had to be free,' I whispered.

*

'Free?' said Beth, her voice husky. Her throat felt so dry.

'You have no idea what it was like. I felt like a caged animal with no way out.'

'Does Kate know that Mae attacked her,' Beth said, breathlessly

'Yes, she remembered at the funeral. I just wanted a normal life, Beth.'

'So, you had to murder your mother?'

Blanche shrugged.

'You wouldn't understand.'

'I'm trying to.'

'What gave me away?'

'The about page on your Facebook profile.'

Blanche looked puzzled.

'Under likes were Mad Max movies. Your first post referred to a Mad Max film. You lied when I asked you about Mad Max, didn't you?'

Blanche tried not to look impressed.

'I opened that Facebook account a year ago. Kate let me set it up on her computer. I'd forgotten about 'the about' page.'

'It wasn't enough to confront you. So, I looked at the interviews you and your mother gave to the local rag. A reader offered to send you the Mad Max movie collection because you were a fan. You remember that?'

Blanche nodded.

'That's what I saw on the shelf, wasn't it? You used the name Mad Max to arrange your alibi.'

Blanche sighed. She never imagined being caught, thought Beth.

'What did you do with the bedroom door key, Blanche?'

'I hid it in my pocket and later dropped it into one of the hospital bins.'

'You deliberately framed Carl Shaw.'

'I didn't think he would get caught.'

Tears filled Blanche's eyes.

'I wasn't afraid of being discovered. I was the sick kid. No one was going to suspect me.'

Someone stepped from the house, and Blanche hurriedly wiped away her tears.

'You two okay?' asked Rob, approaching them.

'Yes, we're fine,' said Blanche, turning with a wide smile. 'Just having a girlie chat.'

'Oh, right,' he grinned. 'I'll leave you to it, then.'

They waited until the door closed.

'Does he know?' asked Beth.

'Dad?' said Blanche, surprised. 'No.'

'Why didn't you speak to me? I could have helped.'

Blanche laughed cynically.

'She was an angel in everyone's eyes and, no doubt, yours included. She was a good mother, the perfect mother, doing all she could for her desperately ill child. She was sick. I know that now. What was I to do? I couldn't contact my dad. She told me he didn't want anything to do with us. I believed I was sick. I was afraid of the illnesses but more afraid of her in the end. The iPad that Kate bought me was a lifesaver. I just wanted to be free of her. I was afraid, even more so after Kate's attack. What if Kate had remembered? What would Mum have done? They would have put her in prison, Beth. She would have gone mad in there.'

She looked Beth in the eyes.

'I truly believed it was her or me. She would have killed me in the end. One way or another, she would have killed me. What choice did I have? Kate has recovered. Carl Shaw was found not guilty.'

Beth sighed.

'Are you going to arrest me? I can't bring my mother back. I'm not a danger to anyone. I finally have my life. She would have kept me sick, Beth. What kind of mother is that? I'd never have gone to Uni. Never would have had a boyfriend ....'

She broke off, and Beth, visibly upset, fumbled in her dress pocket for a tissue. She wiped her eyes and turned to look over at the church spire.

'An innocent man stood trial for murder. He could have been convicted. It will always hang over him. You know what people are like, no smoke without fire.'

'He was a criminal,' said Blanche.

'He wasn't a murderer,' said Beth, turning around.

'Neither am I?' protested Blanche. 'What's to be achieved by arresting me?'

Beth thought of Tom and how he'd messed up. She'd been hard on him. Virtuous even. She, Beth Harper, had always believed she would never mess up, but cops were human too, weren't they? Carl Shaw was a free man. Kate had recovered. What was there to gain?

'I never thought I'd have a chance to go to university,' said Blanche.

Beth looked back at the church spire and then closed her eyes. She turned, reached into her handbag and pulled out the handcuffs.

'Blanche Lethbridge, I'm arresting you on suspicion of murdering Mae Lethbridge. You have the right to remain silent. You have the right to a solicitor, and if you cannot afford one, then one will be appointed for you. If you waive these rights and talk to us, anything you say may be used against you in court.'

Blanche gasped.

'No,' she whispered. 'You don't have to do this.'

Beth pulled the handcuffs from her bag and turned Blanche, so her back was facing her.

'Beth, please.'

'I became a police officer to uphold law and order, and that's what I'm going to do. You killed your mother, Blanche ….'

'I was dying,' cried Blanche. 'Besides, you'll never prove anything. They won't convict me because I watched Mad Max movies.'

Beth shook her head sadly.

'I recorded our conversation, Blanche.'

'I was dying, and she would have killed me in the end.'

'We're all dying,' replied Beth and led her through the now hushed hall.

Tom looked questioningly into Beth's eyes.

'Blanche has just confessed to killing her mother.'

Kate's tortured cry of 'No,' broke the silence.

Blanche looked at her, tears glistening in her eyes.

'I'm sorry,' she mouthed.

Rob stared, his eyes full of horror, his legs immobile until Blanche called out to him.

'Dad.'

He rushed over and glared at Beth.

'You're making a big mistake,' he said.

'I'm not,' said Beth softly.

Tom took Blanche by the arm.

'Let's go,' he said.

Beth followed them and didn't look back. She passed Miranda, who tapped her gently on the arm.

'You did the right thing,' she said, reading Beth's mind.

Beth nodded and closed the hall doors behind them.

Chapter Eighty-Nine

'She denies it,' said Tom.

Beth sat outside the incident room with a cold mug of coffee in her hand.

'I nearly didn't arrest her. I came close to letting her go.'

'But you didn't, he assured her.

Beth dabbed at her eyes.

'Her mother almost destroyed her life, and now I've finished it off.'

He sat beside her.

'You did your job. She'll most likely plead manslaughter. Chances are she'll get 12 years, and with good behaviour, she'll be out much sooner.'

Beth looked down at the cold cup of coffee in her hand.

'It was Mae that attacked Kate,' she said.

Tom raised his eyebrows.

'Why?'

'She discovered the truth about Mae. Kate's attacker was under our noses all the time.'

Tom nodded.

'We need to give Carl Shaw a public apology.'

'I'll go and see him,' she said, standing up.

'Tomorrow,' he said, laying a hand on her arm. 'Right now, let me take you dinner. No shop talk allowed.'

Beth smiled.

'I'd like that.'

His hand was warm and she wanted it to stay there as long as possible.

'I shouldn't have judged you so harshly,' she said.

'I forgive you,' he smiled. 'Now, let's go. I owe you my life, remember. No expense spared.'

He held out his hand. She slid hers into it and allowed him to lead her out of the station.

Epilogue

Six Months Later: The Visit

Beth looked around, her eyes taking in the other visitors. A woman cradling a baby in her arms smiled.
'Is it your first time?' she asked.
Beth shook her head.
'Not really,' she said.
'It gets easier.'
Beth was about to reply when the door opened and the prisoners walked in. Beth's heart began to beat faster. She almost didn't recognise Blanche. Her hair had grown and she'd gained weight. Her skin was glowing, and Beth thought how pretty she was. She sat opposite Beth. Her eyes took in the other visitors before turning back to her.
'Thanks for coming,' she said.
Beth licked her dry lips.
'How are you?' she asked.
'I'm okay. I get visitors.'
'You're looking well.'
'That's what Dad says.'
'Does he come often?' asked Beth.
'It's a long way from Leeds. He and Jo come when they can. Kate visits regularly.'
Beth nodded.
'I see the house is on the market.'
'It's for the best,' said Blanche. 'I don't want to go back to Stonesend.'
Beth took a deep breath and said, 'I was torn about arresting you. I really was. My heart was breaking when I took out those handcuffs. I understand the pain you've felt, but you had plenty of opportunities to get help. You could have done it any time that you were online. There were other choices. You didn't have to frame an

innocent man. I gave you my card. You could have phoned me anytime.'

'You'll never understand,' said Blanche, glancing down at her nails. 'You have no idea what it was like living with mum. Supposing I had phoned you and said I'm a prisoner here. Would you have taken me seriously? What if Mum had found out? I wouldn't have been allowed out of the house for days. I am sorry about Carl Shaw, though. I really am.'

'You know he got a public apology?'

'Kate told me.'

Beth struggled to think of something to say.

'I'm studying for my degree,' said Blanche, with a smile.

Beth felt a huge sense of relief. She hadn't taken Blanche's education away after all.

'I'm pleased.'

'Dad said I should be out in five years.'

Beth nodded. Blanche chewed her nail.

'I loved her, you know. It was self-preservation.'

'I know.'

The ringing of the bell silenced the room for a second, followed by urgent chatting.

Beth stood up, relieved to be going.

'Will you come again?' Blanche asked.

'If you like.'

'Yes.'

Beth nodded and walked from the hall, conscious of Blanche's eyes on her. The judge had said he didn't believe Blanche was a danger to society. He was most probably right, thought Beth. Mae had been a compulsive liar. All those lies thought Beth, and everyone had believed her. All Blanche had ever wanted was to be normal, just like everyone else. Beth turned back, but Blanche had gone. At last, here in prison, Blanche was free, free from her mother and free from the lies she told.

Printed in Great Britain
by Amazon